CAVERNUM

OUTER WALL

FLATS

RANGE

GUARD TOWER

STABLE

PLAZA

CORE

RING

PALACE MAP

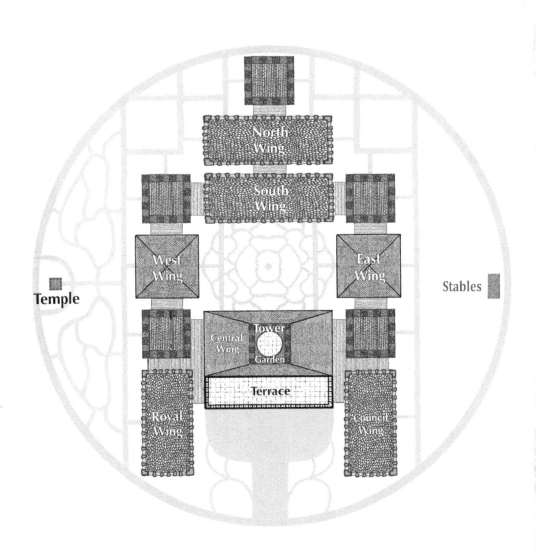

THE SURVIVING

The Adamic Trilogy Book 2

Devin Downing

Published by Devil Down Books, 2021

This is a work of fiction. Similarities to real people, places, or
events are entirely coincidental.

THE SURVIVING

First edition. Jan 12, 2021.

First edition

Cover design by Ricardo Montaño Castro

Library of Congress Control Number:
2020925872

This book is also dedicated to all of my unborn children. Seriously, you guys better read this thing.

Acknowledgements

First, I'd like to acknowledge my Instagram followers. Thank you guys so much for all of the support and encouragement. You guys pulled me from the depths of obscurity when I needed it most. You'll always hold a special place in my heart.

Another shoutout to any soul that has ever left me a review (assuming it was a positive review). You guys are the bee's knees. Virtual fist bump to each and every one of you.

Lastly, I was going to try to make this personal, but I've changed my mind. It's 3:00 am on release night, and I'm too tired to write anything else, so how about this: Mel, Derek, Mom, and Dad. If you guys are reading this, remind me to thank you in-person for all of your help. I won't bore everyone else with your contributions.

Table of Contents

Prologue

18 years earlier...

Zezric paced along the outer wall, his hand perched on the hilt of his Adamic blade. For the second time that night, he leaned over the ledge, careful not to slip on the slick stone. The rain was relentless, pelting him through the thin seams of his cloak.

"Waaah... wahhahhh," came the supple sob of a newborn baby.

Zezric leaned out further. *No! That can't be possible. It's a trap. It must be.*

"Waaaaah… waaaahhaa!"

The longer Zezric listened, the more unsettled he became. The cries sounded like Rose, sweet newborn Rose. She was only a day old. She wouldn't last in the rain. He needed to run to her. He had to save her!

No, Zezric. It's a trap! he thought to himself. Feeders were known to manipulate sounds. They were trying to lure him away from the wall, yet with each wail, Zezric began to doubt.

The weeping infant wasn't far away. He could be out and back in a matter of seconds. He trotted down the steps and tentatively traversed the threshold into the beyond.

It was dark in the beyond, blindingly so. With each footstep, the cries grew louder, and the sanctuary grew farther away. Then, Zezric spotted it. A bundle of cloth on the floor. The fabric wiggled with each fussy kick of the infant.

Rose!

Zezric ran to his daughter, scooping her into his arms. Once he was sure she was safe and warm, he looked around. "How did you get out here? Where's your mother?"

It doesn't make any sense.

Zezric took a step toward the sanctuary and froze. A feeder stood in the path, watching Zezric silently. "I'm a guardian," Zezric called. "Leave now, and I'll spare you."

But the feeder wasn't alone. Another figure darted in the corner of his eye. Then another, a flash of movement among the trees. Zezric turned around, finding himself surrounded by a dozen shadowy forms, each with its hollow eyes watching Rose.

The first feeder took a step closer. "Give me your daughter, and we'll let you live."

Zezric tightened his grip on Rose. He knew what they were capable of. He'd seen their victims, everything from infants to the elderly. The feeders spared no one.

"I can kill most of you," Zezric called out for all to hear. "This isn't a fight you want."

The feeder smiled, lips revealing razor-sharp incisors. "That's where you're wrong."

All at once, the feeders charged. Zezric reached for his amulet, but it was no longer around his neck. He did the next best thing. He unsheathed his Adamic blade and thrust into the nearest feeder's chest.

The feeder gagged and gasped, clutching at the dagger still embedded up to the hilt. Yet, something was off. The gasp was the gasp of a woman.

Slowly, the dream dissolved. The feeder's face, with every blink, morphed into his wife, her flawless features contorted in agony. She clutched at the knife in her chest, failing to form a single word.

It was a dream!

"No!" Zezric stumbled back in the bed, blood already staining the sheets. "No! Violet, no! Hold on! We can fix this. Don't take out the knife. Oh, God! Oh, God!"

"MEDIC!!!" he screamed! "HEALER! I NEED A HEALER!"

Servants burst into the room, lighting lamps and gaping at the blood. They hovered several feet from the bed, unsure how to intervene. A maidservant finally picked up Rose from her crib, but the newborn only screamed louder.

"I'm sorry, Violet. I love you! I didn't mean to!" Zezric gasped, the extent of her injuries becoming apparent.

Violet was dying.

She didn't speak. She was already unconscious.

"I'll fix this," he whispered. "I promise, on God's name, I won't let you die. I'll do whatever it takes."

Chapter 1

Matt

The moon is almost full, outlining my surroundings as I tiptoe through the outskirts of District 14. My amulet is tucked inside my uniform. The weight of my Kevlar vest ensures constant skin contact. Four of my men follow close behind, their black uniforms blending with the shadows. There aren't many torches this deep in the ring, but for once, I'm grateful. This raid is supposed to be a surprise.

Normally, the night shift is quiet. I've been working for nearly a week, and still, I haven't had to flog a single soul. However, all that might change tonight.

Togum stops, pointing to a small alley on the right-hand side of the road. He has dark scruff, burnt almond skin, and his top lip is oddly larger than the bottom. "That's the alley, third door on the right. Whenever you're ready, Lieutenant," he whispers.

I'm still not used to the title. It feels fake, like a make-believe game of soldier. Technically, I have six men under my command, but I only asked three to accompany me. Togum is the most veteran with 22 years in the guard. Keizer and Kork are only a few years older than me, but they're more than capable. In all honesty, I'm the weak link of the group. My dominion may be strongest, but I have no idea what I'm doing.

I take a deep breath and crouch walk into the alley. I have eyes on the apartment now. It has no windows in the front, and I can't see any light around the doorframe.

Their neighbors reported that the father is hiding firearms. He has a wife and three children—two little girls and a teenage son. I wish we had more to go off of, but it's only hearsay. We're raiding a house based on a rumor—no warrant, no nothing.

Suddenly, I see a flicker of a candle in the upper story window. I raise a fist in the air—the signal to hold position. After a few moments, when the light recedes from the window, I give two flat handed chops.

Advance.

I tiptoe the last few yards with Togum on my heels. His hand is raised, ready to illuminate the home the moment we breach. When I reach the warped wooden door, I stop.

I'm sorry.

I take a deep breath and kick the door with the heel of my boot, sending it bursting open. The second I step inside, Togum turns himself into a human spotlight, illuminating the interior. We're standing in a small living space—half living room, half kitchen. At the back of the room, a hallway extends into the darkness.

Keizer and Kork are already moving into one of the rooms, followed by the terrified shrieks of children. Kork drags out both girls by their arms, each in a matching cotton nightgown. Keizer follows behind with his rifle raised and ready.

"Nooo! Don't hurt them!" A woman comes barreling down the hallway without an ounce of hesitation. "Don't you dare hurt them!"

Keizer points his weapon at her, but I step between them.

Thicken!

I command the air molecules to condense around her body. She stops in her tracks, as air resists her every move. Her arms wave

2

sluggishly through the gelatin air. She's trapped, but she doesn't stop struggling. Her words sound like they're underwater. "If you harm a hair on their head, I'll...

I step closer and hold out my empty hands. "It's okay. Your family is safe. We won't hurt them. We're just here doing a search. You have my word."

The woman stiffens at the word 'search,' but she stops clawing at the air. Satisfied, I release the air around her, and she rushes silently to her daughters, who already sit on the living room floor.

Once the wife is seated, Kork moves to the back room and waves for me to follow. I touch my amulet and hurry after him. He's already nearing the end of the hall.

Kork grins. "Get ready for a fight." He kicks open the back room, revealing what appears to be a workspace of some kind. There's already a candle burning in the center of the room. I see animal hides and wood piled against the walls. Newly constructed sofas sit in the middle of the room.

My eyes immediately focus on the two figures in the corner— the father and his son. They stand with their hands raised high above their head. Unlike the other children, they look like they're dressed for work, from their dirty overalls to their leather boots.

"Don't shoot! Please, don't shoot. We are not resisting!" The father frantically chants.

I motion at the door we just entered. "Come to the front room, please. We're just going to do a quick search. As long as you comply, everything will be fine."

The father nods at his son. "Do as the man says, Brayden. I'll be right behind you."

The son starts walking down the hall, holding his hands above his head the entire trip. He doesn't lower them until he's seated next to his mother. The father joins them a moment later.

Togum finishes lighting a lantern, which now casts a sickly glow across the packed dirt floor. It's not as bright as dominion light, but it allows Togum to take on another task.

"Alright boys, let's get crack'n," Togum says, rubbing his hands together.

How can he enjoy this?

Kork swings his rifle behind his back, letting it dangle by the strap. While I watch the family, they start in the kitchen, tearing through cupboards like a class 5 tornado. A plate falls and shatters. Then another. The mother winces at every crash.

"Careful!" I call out, but it lacks conviction.

Keizer waves his hand without turning around. "You got it, boss." But the chaos continues unhindered. I may be Lieutenant, but they call the shots.

Next, they move to the bedrooms. Togum stays behind, rapping on the walls with his knuckles, checking for any hollow cavities.

Finally, from down the hall, I hear the tearing of fabric and the crunching of wood. I can't see the back room, but I know what's happening. They're breaking open the furniture like a piñata, hoping that firearms fall out.

The mother, trying to offer the slightest sense of security, wraps one arm around each of her daughters. The whole situation makes me sick. We don't have a warrant. We don't have any reason to be here other than a neighbor's report, which could have been made up for all I know.

I hold my breath as they watch their home get destroyed. The father briefly makes eye contact, but quickly looks away. All I can do is hope they return empty-handed.

"I'm sorry, guys," I whisper so that the other soldiers don't hear. "We'll try to wrap this up quick."

Suddenly, Kork whoops from the hall. "We found 'em. Make the arrest!"

Togum doesn't hesitate. He grabs the father's wrist, and the blue sparks of electricity crackle between them. The man goes rigid before collapsing onto the packed-earth floor. Togum handcuffs the man and rolls him onto his side. He's already bleeding from his eyebrow.

Togum circles the father like a shark. Eventually, he squats down next to his shoulder. "So, where did you get those weapons? You don't strike me as a blacksmith. If you didn't make them, who did?"

The man squeezes his eyes shut. "I don't know. They're just delivered to my door. I d—"

Tzzzzz.

With a touch to the shoulder, the man convulses, letting out a guttural cry. When the electricity finally stops, the man is gasping for air. "You're hurting me," he cries. "Please. I'm not resisting."

"Then tell us who made the weapons."

Tzzzzz.

Togum electrifies him once more, this time for twice as long. The father clenches his jaw, every muscle in his neck bulging.

"Stop," I quietly command. "Just leave him. We have what we came for."

"Not until he gives the supplier," Togum refuses. "We hang him tonight, and he'll be replaced by tomorrow. We have to stop it at its source."

Slowly, Togum extends his hand. "Last chance. Where did you get the guns?"

"I don't kn—"

Tzzzzzz!

The man clenches, and I hear his teeth snap together. Every few seconds, I think it's going to stop, but the buzzing continues.

Tzzzzz!

"Stop!" I clench my teeth.

Tzzzzz!

"Togum, stop! You're gonna kill him."

Tzzzzz!

Togum's eyebrows are knitted together. He stares at me, his chest inflated full of defiance. "He'll be hung tomorrow. So what if he dies tonight?"

Tzzzzz!

5

I bite my tongue. I don't know what to do. It's been 20 seconds. Maybe 30. The man is going to die. I need to act now.

With each second, the family gets more frantic. The daughters are screaming. "Stop it! You're killing him. You're killing daddy!"

I can't think with all the noise. It's all too much! I can't take it anymore.

Silence!

The room grows quiet as I neutralize the sound waves from the screaming girls. Their mouths move, but I don't hear a thing.

Then, I see it. In the silence, the son reaches into his belt and pulls out a revolver. He points it at Togum's head and squeezes the trigger.

I don't have time to make a shield, not a reliable one anyway. Instead, I focus on the boy's hand.

Push!

BANG!

I wince at the intensity of the gunshot. My ears ring as I struggle to make sense of what just happened. Togum touches his hand to the side of his head, where the blood is beginning to stream down his neck. At first, I fear the wound is fatal, but then I notice his ear. The upper half of the cartilage is torn off, but the rest of Togum's head is unscathed.

It only struck his ear.

Terrified, the boy drops the revolver and stumbles back. He's not afraid to kill; he fears retaliation.

At the sound of the gunshot, Keizer and Kork burst into the room. "Demons! What just happened?" Keizer gasps.

I intervene before they have a chance too. I kick the revolver to Kork and approach the boy. "Brayden, right? Do you have any other weapons on you?"

The boy shakes his head.

"Kork, pat them down," I command. He obeys, quickly giving them a thorough search.

I look at the mother, who gapes at her son with horror-stricken eyes. She knows the terrible truth: her son attempted murder. Her son is now as dead as his father.

I won't let that happen!

I snap my fingers in front of the mother's face. "Hey, do you have someone you can stay with tonight? Friends or family?"

"What?" The mother finally looks at me, turning her head suddenly."

"Do you have someone you can stay with tonight?" I say it loud and slow. "Do they live close?"

"Y-yes. My sister lives down the street."

"Take your kids, and go there, now! Don't come back here."

The mom hesitates, glancing hopefully at her son, who Kork is now putting in handcuffs. "You mean?"

"Yes, take them all and go! Now."

I point at the boy. "Kork, let him go."

"But, boss, he—"

"I said let him go."

Kork twists the key, releasing the cuffs. The boy rushes to his mother. After one last look at her husband, she ushers her children to the door.

"Oh, no you don't." Togum lunges forward, grabbing the boy by the throat. He's finally come to his senses, fear replaced with wrath. Togum unholsters his own pistol and holds it to the boy's ear, parallel to his head. "I'll show you how it feels, then you can hang with your father."

"Togum, let him go."

"Or what? I may not be lieutenant, but I've been running this district for decades. No refugee is going to come in here and change that. The boy hangs."

I instinctively place my hand on my chest, ensuring the contact of my amulet underneath. "Togum... Let. Him. Go."

Togum shakes his head. "Here's what's gonna happen. I'm gonna kill the boy, right here, right now. Then, we're all going to agree that he shot me first. I'll do some paperwork, and that'll be that. And you—" He smiles right at me. "—aren't gonna do a damn thing about it."

"Noooo!" The mother reaches for her son, but Togum shoves her into the wall. She slumps to the floor and sobs.

I lock eyes with Togum, letting my mind drift toward him. As I approach his conscious, I stop, barely close enough to dip a toe in his pool of emotions.

Togum isn't bluffing. His murderous rage taints the air around him. I feel it seeping into my soul, urging me to violence. Togum looks down at the boy, and then I hear it.

Time to die, picker!

Before Togum can pull the trigger, I command the polymer grip of his pistol.

Heat!

Instantly, Togum screams, tossing the gun from his hand. A melted layer of plastic coats his palm. He scratches at the plastic goo, but only squeals louder as it burns his other hand. Thin strands of plastic stretch between his hands like cheese on a freshly baked pizza.

I don't wait for him to retaliate, and I don't hold back. I focus on the flesh underneath his chin.

Squeeze!

Togum gurgles as I apply pressure to his throat. I don't lift him up, but I push until his back is against the wall.

I can still feel his anger and pride. I embrace them, knowing I have to be cruel to save the family. Togum has to fear me. It's the only way he'll obey.

I walk until our faces are inches apart. "You do as I say, or defying me will be the last thing you ever do." I know it's not like me, but Togum's rage still lingers in my mind. "I own you. Is that clear?"

Fi—

Togum tried to use dominion, but I squeeze harder, severing the thought before it can harm me. Then, I loosen my grip enough to let him gurgle in some air. I can feel his hatred still limping through my veins. I turn his prejudice against him.

"Next time, I shoot you and say the pickers did it. You're lucky I'm feeling merciful."

I release my hold on his neck, and Togum sucks in a breath. "You won't get away with this!" he chokes.

"Who's going to stop me? The commander?" Our commander is Antai Elsborne, but he's been out of action since the massacre. "Tell me who," I demand. "The guardians? General Zane brought me here. You really think he'll side with you?"

Togum bites his cheek and looks away. He's submitted. For once, I'm in charge.

I look at the mother. "Go! Get out of here! Don't come back!" I want to send the father too, but I know I can't. I have to report these guns, and someone needs to be held responsible. As much as I hate it, the father has to die.

I look down at the man on the floor, and all I see is another Enrique, another man fighting for his family. I've been putting it off, but it's time I reach out.

It's time I pay Diego a visit.

I hold the seven gold chips in my hand. They're thin like coins, but they're rectangular with rounded edges. Each gold piece is worth 100 bars. 700 bars for a single week as a lieutenant. The pay is generous, but I don't deserve it. It belongs with Diego.

I raise my hand to knock, but I can't bring my fist to make contact. *What will he think of me?* We haven't spoken since the massacre—since he was expelled from the guard. One part of me wants to explain everything. If I had known, I would've never taken the shot. I would've let Enrique get away.

The other part of me knows I'm guilty. Judy would agree. I can almost hear her lecture in the back of my head. *You knew the consequences, Matthew. You knew when you pulled the trigger that you were taking a life. If it wasn't Diego's dad, it would have been someone else's.*

The thought only makes me feel worse. A part of me wants to dump the money on the doorstep. I could knock and bolt. Mary will get her antibiotics, and I won't have to face Diego. It's the perfect solution, but I know it's too risky. If no one answered, the money would get stolen in a heartbeat. I won't leave Mary's life up to chance.

I'm still debating my options when the door swings open. Abuela gapes at my uniform from the doorway, a dirty pot sandwiched in the crook of her armpit.

The pot clatters to the floor as she charges. Her arms are barely long enough to reach my face, but that doesn't stop her from trying. She screams as she swings.

"You guard swine! You satanic scumbag! Tell your king he's gonna rot in hell for what he did to my son!"

I don't try to deflect her blows. They pelt my neck and occasionally my face, but I don't mind. I killed her son. I deserve every one and more.

"God will make you suffer!" Abuela wheezes. "You guards will burn in hell for what you did! Every one of you! You're no different!"

Isabela comes running from down the hall. "Abuela! Stop it. He's a lieutenant now. Show some respect."

"How's this for respect?"

I turn my head as Abuela clears her throat. Then, she spits. The mass of phlegm slaps me on the side of the neck. I try to wipe it away, but it clings to the sleeve of my uniform.

"What are you going to do? Hang me too?" She hisses. "You might as well! I have nothing left to live for!" Then, Abuela sees the gold. Her mouth hangs open, and the insults fall silent.

"I uhhh… I wanted you guys to have these." I hand the bars to Abuela, who clings to them with her gnarled fingers.

After a second, her surprise hardens back into hatred. She holds the money up at me. "What? This is the worth of my son?" She quickly counts in her head. "700 bars? That's supposed to make up for his death?"

I force myself to look her in the eyes. "In another week, I'll make 700 more. I'll need 50 for myself, but you can have the rest."

"We don't need your charity," Abuela snarls, coming back the coins to hurl at Matt.

"Abuela! Are you crazy?" Isabela snatches one of the gold chips. "We can buy antibiotics with this."

Between words, a finicky cry pierces the stone walls. "Abuela, I'm thirsty." The voice is weak and strained.

"Coming, María!" Abuela gives me one last glare as she hands the coins to Isabela. Then, she retreats into the side room.

Relieved, I turn to leave.

"Wait!" Isabela calls. "You gave us your paycheck, at least let me get you some coffee. We have some extra."

"No thanks. I actually work nights. I'm going to go home and go to bed for the day."

Isabela grins. "Well then, I should tell you it's not actual coffee. It's just a barley blend. Tastes similar, but we can't afford the real stuff." She smiles to herself. "Don't tell Javier. He swears it's the only thing to get him up in the morning."

I laugh to avoid an awkward silence. "I don't know. I should probably get going."

"It won't take long," Isabela says. "Please. It's the least I could do." She holds up the stack of coins.

"Alright, just for a minute." I finally say. I don't feel comfortable hanging around, but I want to offend her even less.

"Great." Isabela turns and marches down the hall. "I would ask you if you want any sugar, but we just ran out."

"That's fine. I don't mind." I take a seat at the table as Isabela pours me a cup. I take a sip. It tastes earthy and bitter—nothing like the coffee I've had—but ultimately, it's not bad.

11

Isabela sets the gold coins on the table and pours her own cup. She sips as she stares at the moneybag.

"I want to thank you for everything you've done for Diego. He's always had good things to say about you since you both arrived. I can tell you mean a lot to him."

I feel like I just got punched in the stomach. I want to put up my arms, but I can't defend myself from the guilt.

"He was a better friend than I was," I say. "I wish I could've done more."

"Well, you did what you could." Isabela takes another sip of coffee. "He told me about the bully you punched for him. And when you waited with him for the convoy. I just wanted to say thank you."

I look at the table. "You don't have to thank me. I didn't do anything he wouldn't have done for me." *Stop thanking me. I killed your father.*

Isabela looks at the coins on the table. "I uh… I know why you're giving us your money, Matt. It's because you feel guilty."

I stiffen in my seat. "What do you mean?"

"Diego told me what happened… all of it. About the man who took our mother. About the vault and the carriage, how you went along to help him. He didn't know it was our dad when you took the shot, and I assume you didn't either."

I can't bring myself to look her in the eyes. "I should've checked first. I should've been more careful. I could've avoided it."

"It's fine, Matt. You didn't know. It's not your fault. My father knew the risks when he joined the equalists. If it hadn't been you, someone else would've shot him. He killed himself." There's a hint of anger in her voice. A subtle touch of betrayal. "I don't hold anything against you."

"Thank you." It's an understatement, but it's all I can think to say. Already I feel a thousand pounds lighter.

"Don't get me wrong," Isabela slowly turns her cup on the table. "I'll never forgive Cavernum. I'll never forgive the king for his laws, but I don't blame you. Heaven knows you don't need to blame yourself. Diego feels responsible, and it's tearing him apart."

"How's he doing? I haven't seen him since…" I don't have to say it.

"He's surviving, I guess," Isabela sighs. "We all are. Diego is taking things the hardest. He won't talk to me about it. I know he wants to leave the sanctuary, but he feels like he has to provide now that Dad is gone."

"Has he found another job?"

"He's in the fields with Jorge and Javier, but I worry he's going to get himself in trouble. He got in a fight the other day and got five lashings."

"What?" I nearly spit out my coffee. "Is he okay?"

"He's fine, but I wonder how long until he does it again." Isabela glances down the hall to make sure Abuela isn't listening. "Twice now, I've caught him sneaking out at night.

"Sneaking where?"

"He leaves at midnight, Matt. I can only think of one reason. I think he's joined the equalists."

"But…" *Why? After his father just died?* Deep down, I know that's precisely the reason. Because his father just died. Because Cavernum killed him.

Isabela sits up in her chair and takes a deep breath. "Matt, I didn't just invite you in to forgive you. I need to ask you a favor. I need to keep Diego safe. You're the only one who can help him now."

Chapter 2

Rose

I watch as his chest goes up and down. His breath is steady and strong. His hands are warm and soft, just like the hands that used to hold mine. Every part of him looks flawless, healthy, and whole. He looks like he'll wake up at any minute, but he hasn't. It's been 10 days, and he hasn't moved a muscle.

Don't lose hope, Rose. He'll wake up. He has to.

I watch as the nurse adjusts the feeding tube. The plastic tube runs into his nose and down to his stomach. Without it, he'd already be dead. She replaces the empty bag with a pouch full of brown goop—Antai's breakfast. Then, she gives me a pitiful smile and leaves.

Once she's gone, I crawl into Antai's bed and cuddle next to him. I'd never been in Antai's bed before this week. I'd day-dreamed about it once or twice, but I'd never imagined it like this.

I position my head so that I'm speaking into his ear. "I don't know if you can hear me, Antai, but I have an update for you. Remember how I told you about how Grandpa interrogated my assassin? He learned that the Holy One is living beneath Cavernum.

14

In the next week, he wants to raid the sewers and kill the Holy One. The plan is almost final."

I laugh to myself, but it sounds more like I'm blowing my nose. "I'm sure you'd love to be a part of that raid. Maybe it's good you're still asleep. At least you're safe here. I don't know what I'd do if—"

Tap. Tap. Tap.

I already know who it is. A healer comes every morning to do a check-up. "Come in," I call.

A blonde girl steps into the room, leaving the door ajar. She wears the traditional healer's dress, and her meticulous makeup makes me self-conscious. After the week I've just had, I must look homeless.

I scoot out of the bed and try to straighten my hair. "Where's Madame Xantone?" I ask.

The girl curtsies. "Hello, Princess. I've been requested by the king." She looks around. "He wanted me to perform the evaluation today. He said to meet him here."

The girl is young and looks oddly familiar. Then it dawns on me. "I know you. You were at the party. You're a first-year."

The healer nods. "I'm Kendra, and I just want to say I saw what you did at the party. How you fought those feeders and killed the… well, the demon. It was pretty amazing. You're amazing."

I smile. "Thank you." My thoughts turn to Velma, and I suddenly feel worse.

"I'm sorry," Kendra gushes. "I didn't mean to remind you of anything. I…"

"It's fine. No need to apologize."

We both turn to the door as the hollow tapping of a cane echoes down the hallway. A moment later, Grandpa shuffles inside. "Ahhh good, you two have already met. Rose, I requested that Kendra evaluate Antai today. From what I've heard, she has a special knack for interacting with the soul. On top of that, she is specializing in healing the mind, two skills I think Antai could benefit from."

Kendra takes a step toward the bed. She lifts one knee onto the mattress, then lowers it again. "Princess, do you mind if I climb up?"

15

"Go ahead," I say, forcing a smile. I motion to Antai. "He's all yours."

She climbs onto the bed and kneels at Antai's side. Next, she drapes an amplifier over his head and tucks it under his shirt. "To amplify his soul." She says quickly as she glances my way. Finally, she rests her palm on his forehead and closes her eyes.

I don't know where to watch, so I focus my eyes on Antai, secretly hoping his eyes will flutter open and he'll gasp in a breath.

Kendra's eyelids wrinkle with focus. After a few seconds, She adjusts her grip, placing both hands on the back of Antai's skull. "Hmmm."

I shift uncomfortably on my seat, and my face feels warm with jealousy. This girl—a random healer—is connecting more to Antai than I have in days. I can't help but wonder what she feels deep inside his soul.

Kendra shifts her hands to his temples, then to his chest. "Hmmm." After what feels like an eternity, she retrieves the amplifier and climbs quietly out of the bed. She purses her lips and looks back at Antai. Her hesitation can only mean one thing: bad news.

"What has Madame Xantone told you so far?" Kendra finally asks.

"Absolutely nothing," I groan. "All she says is that it's too soon to tell."

Kendra glances nervously between us. "Well, I'm afraid I have some terrible news for you both. I'll say it how it is. I can't sense his soul. Not even a remnant of it. Antai's body remains fully functioning, but his soul is gone. Without a soul, the brain remains dormant."

I'm speechless. Antai can't be gone. He can't be. *There has to be a mistake.*

Grandpa looks equally grieved. He leans on his cane as he grimaces at the news.

"What are the odds you're wrong?" I say. "What are the odds he still wakes up?" I'm desperate. I'm desperate for any inkling of hope. I need Antai. I can't go on without him.

"I… I suppose it's possible." Kendra reluctantly offers. "In many ways, the soul is its own entity. It grows and lives independently from the body. As the brain develops, so does the soul." She points to my amulet. "And when you strain the soul with dominion, it can heal and recover over time."

"What does that have to do with Antai?" I mutter, earning a glare from Grandpa.

"Well, we hoped that when Antai was resurrected, a small, undetectable portion of his soul remained. We hoped that, despite not being able to sense it, that his soul would grow and heal over time. Unfortunately, after ten days, there's nothing detectable. While it's possible he will recover, the odds seem slim. To be clear, we've never dealt with resurrection before. This is uncharted territory. We have no idea what will happen. All we can do is wait."

"So what? He's just gone? He's braindead?" I feel the rage rising within me, suffocating all sensibility.

"Personally, I think we should give it another week or two, just to be sure. There's still a chance his soul could present itself. However, if it doesn't happen in the next few weeks, we might want to look into alternative options."

"Thank you, Kendra," Grandpa says weakly. "You are dismissed."

Kendra bows one last time before hurrying eagerly out of the room, escaping the death and despair.

Once she's gone, I let go of the last of my strength. I think of our future and the tears start flowing. This year, he was supposed to take me to the fall festival. I'll never see him become a guardian. I'll never know how he would've proposed. I'll never be his queen. Everything I ever hoped for is gone all over again. I've lost Antai twice.

"What am I supposed to do now, Grandpa?" I whimper. "It wasn't supposed to happen this way."

Grandpa pulls me into a hug, which hardly helps. "Don't let hope die just yet. It may die soon, but don't be the one to kill it." His own voice wavers. "In the meantime, be the very best Rose you can be. Antai wouldn't want you mourning like this, spending every hour at his side. Be the princess he'd want you to be. Cavernum needs you." Grandpa steps back and silently wipes the tears from my face. "Focus on the future."

"What future?" I know I'm being pessimistic, but I can't think of one thing to look forward to. I'm definitely not excited to fail as princess. "Everything is falling to pieces, Grandpa. I don't even know where to start."

"Sometimes it feels that way," Grandpa agrees. "So start with something small."

I look at Antai and wipe my eyes once more. Perhaps, Grandpa is right. I've hardly left his side in 10 days, and it's taking a toll on me. It's time I take action. *Be the princess he'd want you to be, Rose!*

When Antai finally wakes up, I want to have news of some kind—something to fill him in on. I want to make a difference. Suddenly, I have an idea. "Be right back, Grandpa."

I rush out of the room and run down the hall, I'm hardly dressed to leave my quarters, but I don't mind. This isn't about me anymore.

I catch up to Kendra as she nears the exit of the Royal Wing. "Kendra, Wait up!"

"Princess, What is it? What's wrong?"

I stop and take a few deep breaths to recover. "Nothing. I just want to ask a favor of you. Would you mind accompanying me on a special assignment?"

"Of course!"

I smile. "Good, there's a girl in the ring who needs our help."

The carriage slows as we pass under the palace wall. Kendra sits across from me, looking eagerly out the window. "So, who are we going to heal?"

"There's a girl who is sick. Her name is Mary. To be honest, I don't know what she has, but I think it's bad, maybe typhoid."

"And she's a laborer?" Kendra asks.

"She's ring-born. She's only 12."

The corner of Kendra's lip twitches at a smile. "Just to be clear, I might not be able to heal her in one session."

I nod. "Come back as many times as you need to. Just make sure she recovers, please. I really need her to recover."

Kendra, now grinning openly, nods her head. "Of course, princess. I'll make sure of it."

She opens her mouth to say more but instead turns her head at the sound of shouting. I follow her gaze out the window where a small crowd of commoners has gathered on the sidewalk. Each of them is looking toward the same doorway, whose wood has been painted bright crimson. As the carriage approaches, I notice the paint is fresh. It glistens in the morning sun.

Kendra leans her head out the window. "Is that… blood?"

"Slow the carriage," I call to the driver.

At the edge of the crowd, a man is standing on a wooden crate, shouting to the masses. "People of Cavernum, the Holy One is among us. He has been sent to judge our people and to strike down the wicked. This home has been sealed with the mark of death—the blood of the field beast. Once marked, none can be saved from the Holy One. God's wrath cannot be stopped!"

"Carry on," I shout, and the driver obeys. As the carriage pulls forward, the preacher points his fingers at the crowd. "Death will find all who merit God's wrath. You cannot hide fro—" his voice trails off as the crowd grows smaller behind us.

The color drains from Kendra's face. "How can they say this is of God? When is killing ever of God?"

"It's not," I seethe. "The Holy One sent my assassin. He planned the massacre. Whoever he is, he isn't of God."

Kendra leans back and falls quiet. I do the same. The mood is too dark for small talk.

After a few last turns, the carriage stops in front of Diego's alley. "We're here," I sit up, pointing down the alley. "The apartment is in the basement of this building here. Go down the alley, and it's the first door on your left."

"You're not coming?"

"Not today. I have another matter to attend to." *I can't face them. Not yet.*

Kendra looks uncertain as she hops down from the carriage. "What should I tell them?"

"Tell them Lynn sent you… and tell them she's sorry."

Kendra nods, taking hold of her amulet. "Best of luck to you princess. I'll see you tomorrow, I presume." She starts down the alley as the horses tug the carriage onward.

After a few minutes, we stop along a busy road near the outskirts of the ring. The nearest apartment is clearly rundown, but I expected nothing less.

I'm wearing a simple beige sundress—nothing too flashy. As I step out of the carriage, a few bystanders take notice, but I slip into the doorway before they have a chance to recognize me.

The stairwell smells of mold, and the corner of each step has crumbled into a rounded edge. I take them slowly, running through a fake conversation in my head. I stop at the third floor and knock quietly on the door.

Tap. Tap. Tap.

"Eric, the door!" a female voice yells.

"I'm busy!"

"Would someone please get it?"

The door swings open slowly, and a small child waddles in the threshold, wearing only an oversized t-shirt. She looks like a miniature version of Velma—no older than five—complete with black bangs and sassy eyebrows.

"Who are you?" she squeaks.

Suddenly, her mother appears, sweeping her out of the doorway. She carries a squirmy toddler in her arms. "Hello, miss. How can I help you?"

"Hello, you must be Mrs. Venderson. I'm Roselyn, a friend of Velma's. Do you mind if I come in?"

The woman reels back and nearly drops the toddler. She offers a quick bow. "P-princess. Forgive me, I didn't... I hadn't realized... come in! Please, come in!"

Mrs. Venderson rushes to the living room and begins kicking wooden blocks out of the way. "Eric, we have company. The princess is here."

"Princess? What princess?" Velma's dad is stirring a pot of oatmeal, dividing it into different bowls. When he sees me, his eyes bulge. "Princess, h-hello! My goodness! What are you doing here?" He looks at his wife. "What is she doing here?"

"Eric!" the wife hisses. She motions me toward the kitchen table. They don't have stools. Instead, a series of logs are placed around the table. I sit on one as Velma's parents sit across from me.

Before I can properly introduce myself, Velma's mom is already rambling. "My name's Aliyah, and this is my husband, Eric. I hope there isn't a problem, your highness. We are loyal servants to the royal family. We are in full support of the king, I assure you."

I laugh, which elicits confused faces. "Don't worry," I say. "You can both speak freely. I'm not here to judge, and I won't take offense." I shift on my stool and clasp my hands together. "As you may have guessed, I've come regarding Velma."

Mrs. Venderson grows still and looks at the floor. Eric pushes his jaw forward and nods his head slowly. Their pain is unmistakable.

"She was a great friend of mine," I explain. "I was with her in the beyond when she died. She actually saved my life." I pause and swallow down my rising emotions. *Be strong, Rose... for Velma.*

I focus my attention on Velma's mom. "She had many wonderful things to say about you, about your tale of the moon." It feels silly, but I invert my wrist, revealing the tattoo above my palm.

"I wanted to tell you in person how grateful I am for everything you've taught her. She showed me so much about Cavernum… so much I didn't want to see."

"Well, that was our Velma. She didn't take no for an answer." Mrs. Venderson doesn't cry, but her jaw is taught and strained.

"Your daughter sacrificed herself to save me. I know I can't bring her back, but if there is anything I can do for your family… anything at all…"

Mrs. Venderson looks at Mr. Venderson, who shakes his head. "We appreciate your concern, princess, but we are doing just fine. We must decline."

"Are you sure?" I doubt. "If you need help financially…"

Eric rolls his eyes. "Please, do not insult us."

Mrs. Venderson slaps him on the thigh. "Eric!"

"What? It's true." Mr. Venderson looks at me as if I were a feeder. "You take all of our money. You take the food we grow. You take it all, and then when you give the slightest bit back, you feel like a savior. You think you're God's great gift to humanity. Let me tell you, you're no savior, princess. You're a plague."

"Eric!" Mrs. Venderson gives him another good whack on the thigh.

"It's the truth," he asserts.

So that's where Velma got it. He's as bull-headed as she was, if not more so. I take a deep breath. "I'm sorry if I have insulted you. I assure you, I was only trying to help."

"That's the problem with you people. You always assume we're in need. Let me tell you what. I have one wife and four kids. For as long as I have lived, I have kept them alive. I have fed them and clothed them, all without your help. And yet, the moment Velma joins your guard, she dies? You want to know why, princess? Because we live in a world where you are more valuable than my daughter. We live in a world where soldiers are taught to sacrifice themselves to save the likes of you. Don't you see? You should be dead, princess, not her. Unless you can give her back, we want nothing to do with you."

Part of me is furious. How dare he say that? How dare he? Yet another part is engulfed in guilt.

He's right. If it weren't for me, she wouldn't be dead. I bite my tongue and squeeze my eyes shut until the frustration recedes.

Now, Mrs. Venderson is speechless. Genuine fear consumes her semblance. "Forgive him, princess. He doesn't mean—"

"I do mean," Mr. Venderson insists. "You said to speak my mind, so I'll tell you how it is. There's only one person who's going to fix the way things are, and it sure as hell won't be you."

The Holy One. That's who he's referring to. He thinks the Holy One will right all wrongs. I want to argue, but I know it will only make things worse.

Remember why you're here, Rose.

I take a deep breath and choke down my pride. "Very well. I thank you both for your time. Before I leave, is it alright if I have a word with your daughter, Wendy."

Mrs. Venderson purses her lips. "I'm sorry, but she's not here. She's currently in the palace."

"The palace?"

Mrs. Venderson nods. "She's working as a kitchen maid."

"Oh."

I shouldn't be surprised; it's a fairly common practice among laborers. Anyone can forfeit their right to be divided by accepting a lower class job. Many ring-born children join the workforce in their teens. As for Wendy, I suppose she's now a kitchen maid, and she will be for life.

The mother sees my concern and elaborates. "This wasn't our doing. It was her choice. I don't know if you're aware of her... current condition. You see, she's pregnant. If she can prove she's self-sufficient before the baby is born, the courts may let her keep it."

I feel sick to my stomach—sick and ashamed to be a part of such a system.

I have to fix this.

I stand. "Thank you both for your time. I'm... I'm sorry for everything you've been through." *I'm sorry I couldn't save her.*

They follow me to the door, and Mrs. Venderson bids me farewell. Mr. Venderson doesn't say a word. He glares until I'm into the carriage and out of sight.

As we ride back to the castle. I can't stop thinking about what Mr. Vernderson said. *You're a plague. Everyone is taught they must sacrifice themselves for you.* How many have died for me. Velma, Tick, Antai, Nevela? It seems I kill everyone around me.

Suddenly, the carriage jerks to a stop, interrupting my self-pity. I peer out the window at a small gathering in the road. We're back at the house with the blood-smothered door. This time, the feeling in the street is different. More chaotic. More fearful. Several people are pointing into the air!

That's when I see the body—an older gentleman by the looks of it. He's laying face down on the sidewalk in a pile of his own blood. My eyes trail up the building, and I find a shattered window on the second floor. It doesn't take much imagination to piece together what happened; he was thrown from the window, but the fall wouldn't have been enough to kill him. He must've been dead before he made the descent.

Several guardsmen are already at the scene, holding back the crowd. The people are restless. They chatter amongst themselves and push to get a glimpse of the body.

"Come all and witness the swift justice of God!" The same preacher is standing on his wooden crate. He points at the body! "The Holy One has judged this man to be wicked. He couldn't outrun his own condemnation. He is dead, never to transgress again."

He swings his arm threateningly at the crowd. "The time to repent has passed! Judgment is upon us! The Holy One will purge us of all iniquity! We must all ask ourselves, am I righteous in the eyes of the Holy One?"

A shiver runs down my spine.

Something tells me that I'm not.

I've never been in the kitchens, and frankly, I feel like a fish out of water. The place is in total chaos. Servants run in all directions, dumping potatoes into massive pots, chopping celery, buttering bread. Amid the disorder, no one notices me. The chefs are engrossed in their work, and the servants don't say a word.

Already, I'm beginning to sweat, and not just from nervousness. A dozen ovens line the front wall, turning the kitchen into a sauna. Bubbling pots of soup only add to the humidity.

I move to the back of the kitchen and into a separate room—the scullery. Several large basins, easily the size of bathtubs, are filled with soapy grey water. Two dozen servants girls encircle the basins like vultures, rhythmically scrubbing dish after dish. Their fingers are swollen and pruned, and their feet are soaked with splashing water.

I stand in the corner with my back pressed against the wall. When I'm sure I'm not in the way, I begin searching for Wendy. It doesn't take long to find her. She's standing along the far basin, her enlarged belly pressed against the rim.

She looks different than Velma, but just as gorgeous. Her black hair is much curlier, almost frizzy, and her nose is slightly hooked. Her limbs are thin, and her frame, petite. I can tell her waist would be tiny, but it's already well-stretched from the growing baby.

I try not to stare.

Of all the girls, she seems to struggle the most. Her protruding belly prevents her from leaning over the basin. Instead, she dips the dishes in the water and scrubs them over the rim.

Before I can approach her, a series of whispers sweep across the room. "—The warden is coming. The warden is coming.—" At the word 'warden,' their steady pace becomes fearful and frantic. The basin water churns as they scrub.

"This is what I like to see, hard-working women." A honeyed voice announces. The warden struts into the scullery, swinging a switch in her right hand.

I know the woman. Her name is Lola, but she only responds to 'warden.' She's big for a lady, with broad shoulders and meaty hands. Antai used to joke that she should have joined the guard.

Squinting with one eye, she walks around the basin and studies the pile of clean dishes. "Hmmm." Her face darkens and she plucks a plate off the top.

"Who washed this dish?"

No one says a word.

"It didn't wash itself. It was stacked right here on top. Who washed it? Answer me!" She slaps her switch against the edge of the basin with a resounding crack.

"I… I think maybe I did," an older woman confesses. Her hair is grey, and her eyes are clouded with cataracts.

"What's your name?" The warden demands.

"Penelope," the woman utters, already shaking in anticipation.

"Penelope, perhaps you can tell me what this is?" The warden lifts the plate in the air. At first, I don't see much, but as she adjusts the angle, I spot a small yellow smear along the rim. "Go on. What is it?" She shoves the plate in the old maid's face and shakes it. "Take the plate. Tell me what you see."

The woman squints, holding the plate inches from her opaque pupils. "I-it looks like egg yolk."

The warden shakes her head, walking circles around the workers and snapping the switch against her palm. "Tell me, ladies. I pay you to take dirty dishes and make them clean, do I not?"

"Yes, warden," the maids echo in unison. Something tells me they've had this lecture before.

"And ladies, does this dish look clean to you?"

"No, warden."

"So, would you say that this maid has done her job?"

"No, warden."

The warden smiles. "And should I pay her for not doing her job?"

"No, warden," they reluctantly reply.

"Very well, then it's decided. Penelope will forfeit today's pay. Everyone, back to work!"

The warden retreats to the doorway, only pausing when she spots me. "Princess? What a pleasant surprise. What brings you to the scullery?"

"Actually, I've come to speak with one of the kitchen maids, Wendy Venderson."

At her name, Wendy's head snaps up. Then, at the warden's gaze, it drops back to the basin. She continues scrubbing before the warden can scold her.

The warden points at Wendy to confirm. "That one?"

"Yes, that's her."

"Very well," the warden says. "She is my staff, you may address me about the matter."

"Actually, it's sort of personal. I was hoping I could speak with her alone."

"No." The warden replies flatly. "If it is personal, you can speak to her on her personal time. Once lunch is served, she has a ten-minute break. You can find her then."

"But…"

"But what, princess? I am the warden. When her work is not done, I am held accountable. Contrary to what you may believe, you are not entitled to every servant in this palace."

"Well… fine," I stew. When I can't think of a rebuttal, I resign. "I'll be back after lunch."

I'm halfway way out the door when the sound of shattering glass stops me in my tracks.

T'Shhhhhh!

I slowly turn around. *Please don't be her.*

Sure enough, every single maiden is staring at Wendy. Large chunks of broken porcelain litter the floor around her feet, growing more sparse the further from the point of impact.

The warden doesn't miss a beat. She marches over to Wendy, complete indifference on her face. "Was it a bowl or a plate?"

Wendy is already wincing. "A plate, ma'am." Her voice is a distant songbird. I have to listen intently or it goes unheard.

"Very well, you know the drill. The punishment is three. Now pick it up."

Wendy bends over, but before she can reach the porcelain, the warden swings her hand.

SLAP!

Wendy's head whips to the side, and a whimper escapes her lips. Then, she clenches her jaw, breathing out the pain in deep, heavy breaths.

"We do NOT break plates." The warden shouts, unleashing a burst of rage. "Do you hear me, Wendy?"

Just like that, the anger is repressed and the warden's face grows solemn.

When the warden steps back, Wendy scrambles to pick up the glass. She moves quickly, but she doesn't fumble, collecting the pieces in the fold of her dress.

The warden waits until she's finished. "Now, stand."

The second Wendy lifts her chin, the warden swings.

SLAP!

Her slender frame shudders under the blow. I can barely watch as the porcelain tumbles from her dress, breaking into even smaller pieces. Without a word, Wendy retrieves them.

Everyone, say it with me. "We do not break plates!"

No one is scrubbing anymore. They watch Wendy with quiet sympathy. Judging from the looks on their faces, they've been in Wendy's shoes. This isn't an anomaly.

Wendy picks up the last of the large chunks, dropping it into the dress pouch she has created.

"Now, stand," the warden commands.

Wendy hesitates, staring at the floor. Her frizzy hair shields her face from view. She sniffles.

"I said STAND!"

Wendy lifts her head as the warden lifts her arm.

"STOP!" The words erupt before I can stop them. "Stop already!"

The warden lowers her hand, slowly turning to face me. "Excuse me?"

Don't back down, Rose.

"I said stop. So what if she dropped a plate? She's only human. You don't have to hit her."

Every head turns to me. No one moves a muscle.

"You think you can tell me what to do?" The warden hisses. "How to treat my own employees? Watch closely, princess." She raises her hand, aiming her body at Wendy.

"I'll have you fired!" I scream, my heart racing. "If you hit her one more time, I'll have you fired."

The warden shakes her head. "You can't fire me. You can't do a damn thing. I answer to the council, the council of whom *you* are not a member." She grins at me, challenging me to retaliate. I can't do anything now.

Maybe it's Wendy's pregnant belly, or possibly her Velma-like features, but something in me snaps.

"If you hit her... I swear to God, you'll live to regret it. The moment I become queen, I'll demote you a common maid, and then you'll know what it's like to be treated as they are."

The warden sneers. "The moment you become queen, you'll realize that Cavernum is led by a council—a council who doesn't bend to your every wish and whim." She steps closer to me, and for a second, I fear she might hit me. "Listen very carefully, princess. I do not fear your threats. I know what they say about you. That you defend the laborers, that you'll elevate their class. Well, consider this a wake up call. The council likes my methods. They like the results I bring, and until you convince the council, you have no pow—"

She stops mid-sentence, noticing something behind me. Then, she drops to one knee, bowing her head.

"You're highness. I..."

Grandpa stands in the doorway behind me. His face is a mixture of disappointment and disdain. "Lola, let the girl speak with the princess in private. I'm certain the council will support me on this. They will forgive any mealtime delays."

"Yes, your highness." She turns to Wendy. "Get going, girl. You heard the king."

I expect grandpa to say more, but he turns and hobbles briskly out of the kitchen.

That's it? He didn't defend me. He hardly said a word.

I don't have time to dwell on it. Wendy has already tossed the porcelain in a trash bin and is standing at my side. I lead her into the hallway of the Central Wing, being sure we're out of earshot of any kitchen staff.

Before I say anything, I look Wendy over. I can see some redness in her chestnut-colored cheeks. They're moist, but whatever tears were there have already been wiped away.

"Are you okay?" I ask.

"I'm okay," Wendy says softly. "They say the first time is the worst. She wants to teach me a lesson. Next time shouldn't be as bad."

"It shouldn't happen at all if you ask me."

Wendy shrugs. "With all due respect, princess, can we make this fast? I don't want to make the warden any madder than she already is."

I smile. "Actually, Wendy. If you'd like, you never have to go back in there again. I'd like to offer you a new job; I'm in need of a lady-in-waiting." I try my best to avoid the word maid. "The pay would be higher because you'll be on call day and night, and the workload is much lighter. You'll be given a room next to mine. I assure you, it's a much better position."

Wendy considers it. "What would the work include?"

"Helping me with my makeup, assisting with my wardrobe, running personal errands…"

To my surprise, Wendy frowns. "Thank you for the offer, but… I have to decline."

"What? A-are you sure?"

Wendy nods. "I don't think I can do that kind of work. I'm not a seamstress. I know nothing about makeup. I'm not very good at reading or writing. I'm telling you, princess, I wouldn't make a good maid. I can't accept. I'll manage just fine in the kitchen."

"Please," I beg. "I can have you trained in no time. I'm choosing you for a reason."

"Because my sister saved you?" Wendy says. "It's okay, princess. You don't owe me anything."

Yes, but...

When I don't say anything, Wendy starts getting anxious. "I'm sorry, princess. Can I please go back now? I don't want to lose today's pay."

"Wait!" I beg.

She doesn't need me, but I need her.

"The truth is, it's not a free handout. It sounds pathetic, but more than a maid, I need a friend. I need someone to talk to, someone who knows what it's like outside the palace. If you're anything like your sister, I think we could be great friends. Please. If you won't do it for yourself, do it for me."

Wendy sucks in through clenched teeth. Her foot taps as she's considered what I've said.

I jump on her indecision. "Is there anything else I can offer to help you say yes?"

"Hmmm. You said I'll be living in the palace?" Wendy asks. "Assuming I keep my baby, does that mean she would live here with me?"

"Of course," I say. "Your child would share your chambers with you. They'll go to the royal academy. They'll have all the opportunities of any other high-born."

Wendy scrunches her lips to the side, gradually forming a subtle smile. In the end, it wasn't about what I could offer her; it was about what she could offer her baby.

"Okay," she announces. "I accept. I'll be your servant."

"Really?" I struggle to contain my excitement. "Okay. I'll prepare your room. You can begin tomorrow. You won't regret it. I promise."

"Until tomorrow, princess."

I leave Wendy in the hallway and hurry to arrange her chambers.

Now, when Antai awakens, I'll have at least one thing to tell him.

If he ever wakes at all.

Chapter 3

Matt

My room is starting to grow on me. It's not that big, but it's beautifully furnished. I have a desk, a wardrobe, and a little nook by the
window that looks great for reading. The bed is as comfy as my
mattress back home, and a plush, black rug covers the marble floor.

Tonight is my first night off-duty. Normally, I'd be out patrolling the beyond at this hour, and my body knows it. Sleep evades
me like the plague.

The cascade of raindrops is muffled by the stone, the lulling
sound of liquid drums. I've always loved to fall asleep to the sound
of rain, but I don't expect it to come anytime soon. I lay my head
back on my pillow and close my eyes.

My mind goes in circles. I think of Enrique and his hanging. I
think of Diego in the fields. I think of the boy, Brayden was his
name, and his father, doomed to die in the gallows. My mind is a
merry-go-round, oscillating between death and tragedy.

I look at the cup on my desk. The servant called it a sleeping
tonic. I told him I didn't want it, but the later it gets, the more
appealing the drink becomes.

Finally, I groan and roll out of bed. I tip the cup back and swallow the contents in two gulps. It's not as bad as a thought. It tastes like wood, with a mild hint of something sour.

I lay back in bed and focus on slowing my breathing. I may not be asleep, but I might as well relax. I let my muscles sink deeper into the bed. After a few minutes, my limbs start to feel heavy.

I lay like that for who knows how long. Eventually, the sound of rain fades into the background of my brain. My mind wanders, thinking of Judy and of Lynn. Next thing I know, everything is silent.

The rain has stopped.

I open my eyes, but I don't see anything. The world is black. The gentle glow of the moon has vanished. Then, I realize it. My bed has vanished as well. There's nothing around me, I extend my arms and my legs, but I feel nothing. I hear nothing. It's as if I'm floating in an empty void.

Help! I try to yell, but nothing happens

I'm panicking, but my heart isn't racing. In fact, I can't feel my own heartbeat. I don't feel myself breathing either.

My body is gone! I'm dead!

I can still think, so I must be alive in some way. Or maybe I'm trapped in some bleak, black afterlife. None of it makes sense.

The tonic!

Am I hallucinating? Did someone spike my drink? Is this some kind of twisted dream?

Then, I feel it—or rather, I sense them. Atoms swirl in the void around me. It's the same sensation when I use dominion. I don't feel them with my body, but with my soul. I sense the air and the bed beneath my back. I try to take a step, and I feel things move. The bed drops away behind me.

I can move!

I'm not walking, but drifting through the air. I pick a direction and will myself forward, perceiving the stone passing underneath. I don't go far when, suddenly, I sense wood in front of me. *My desk.* I will myself to the left. I can only sense the world directly around me as if I'm surrounded by a spiritual fog. I move like a blind man, feeling my way along the stone wall. Eventually, a wooden wall appears before me. *My door.*

I reach for the handle, but nothing happens. *Turn!* I try to command the elements, but if they hear me, they don't obey.

I can't use dominion.

Instead, I will myself toward the wood. For a split second, the wood surrounds me in all directions. Then, the wood is behind me, and I'm in the open space of the hallway.

So what... I'm a ghost?

It seems like the only explanation.

I move down the hall, debating what to do next. I only have two options: explore the palace or return to my body. I'm still undecided when a guard walks directly through me. I sense their flesh, followed by a flash of their emotions—boredom and fatigue. And then they're gone, moving outside the range of my soul.

I decide to turn back, willing my soul down the hall the way I came. I'm almost to my room when I feel it. Another soul brushes past me, but this time, I don't sense a body. The soul is bare... naked, just like mine.

Another ghost?

Intrigued, I move closer, letting the emotions engulf me. Focus. Determination. The desire for justice. The soul feels familiar, and I find myself pushing deeper. I see memories. Shoving amulets into a wooden trunk. A carriage flipping on its side, my body tumbling inside. I know this soul. I've possessed it once before.

Iris?

As soon as I think it, the soul lurches away and disappears into the darkness. I don't try to chase her. I don't even know what I'd do if I caught up. Instead, I will myself back through my door and to my bedside.

I sense my body, like a corpse, lying still under the sheets. I urge my soul into it, as deep as I can force it.

"Guhhh," I gasp a breath as my eyes flutter open. My body is half asleep, and my mind is groggy, but there's no mistaking what just happened.

I think of Iris, the pixie cut demon. The first time I possessed her, I saw a memory of Zane. He was teaching her about possession. He knew her personally. If there's anyone who will have answers, it's him.

I put on my shoes and grab a hoodie from my coat rack.

Zane lives across the palace in the Council Wing, but I'm not waiting till morning.

I need answers now.

I wait in the eerie silence for his door to open. I've already knocked twice, and I don't want to risk a third. I'm not even sure I'm at the right door, and the last thing I want is an upset council member.

I raise my hand and swallow.

Tap. Tap. Tap.

I jump back as the door swings open. Zane is wrapped in a black cloak. He holds up a candlestick and squints at me. "Go away." He barks before slamming his door shut.

"Zane?" I whisper into the seam of the door. "I need to talk to you. It's about Iris I think she might be in the pal—"

The door flies open. Before I can react, Zane grabs me by the hood and yanks me inside, closing the door immediately behind me.

"Sit." He pushes me toward a desk chair and stands with his arms crossed. The only light is the candle he still holds in his hand. It illuminates his face like a camper telling ghost stories.

"You think Iris is in the palace? Tell me why."

"Well, I didn't really see much of anything." I begin. "I wasn't there. Not in person. I went to bed, and the next thing I knew, it's like I left my body. I couldn't see or feel anything, but I could move around and go through walls. I went into the hallway, and that's when I felt her. It was Iris. The same demon that tried to steal the palace amulets."

Zane rests his elbows on his knees. "You're sure it was her? You're certain?"

I nod. "I felt her, but it wasn't her. I mean, it was her, but there was no body to possess. It was just her soul? It felt like we were both outside of our bodies? Is that even possible?"

Zane thinks for a moment before sitting on the edge of his bed. He rests the candlestick on his knee. "It's possible." He rubs his beard, collecting his thoughts. "It's called soul-travel. In the beyond, they call it astral projection. It's rare... very rare. According to the legends, spiritual gurus trained their whole lives to achieve it. The ability to detach your soul from your body. They called it enlightenment, and very few succeeded."

"But... wouldn't that strain the soul?"

"It doesn't work that way," Zane grumbles. "You're not stretching your soul like when you use dominion, you're detaching it. You could travel for miles without any strain, even without an amplifier."

"So... how does my body stay alive?" I ask.

Zane shrugs. "I ain't got the slightest clue how it works. They say that even during soul-travel, there's some kind of bond between body and soul. The living body prevents the soul from passing on to the afterlife. If your body dies during soul travel, the soul passes on.

Powerful demons used to use it to possess people permanently. They would bury their bodies in coffins to protect them in case they ever wanted to return."

"Let me get this straight. You're saying I can possess someone indefinitely, with or without an amulet?" It sounds too good to be true.

Zane frowns. "It's not that simple, Matt. What you're referring to is known as true possession, and it has consequences. When you possess someone at close range, your soul stretches, but it remains anchored to your body at all times. However, to possess someone during soul-travel, your soul must anchor to their body. It doesn't just possess it, it binds to it. If the host body dies while you possess it, you'll die along with them."

"Oh." Suddenly, soul-travel is less appealing. I think a moment longer. "So, if soul travel is so rare, how did I just do it by accident."

Zane smiles through his bush of a beard. "Because, Matt, you're a mystic."

"I'm a what?"

"A mystic—someone with an affinity for soul-travel. It comes easy to them, sometimes without even trying. Throughout history, your people were seen as spiritual leaders. They could see things that others could not. Some were even said to speak with the dead. Your father was a mystic like you. As was his father."

"Did... did you just say my father?" I rise to my feet. "You're telling me you knew my father after all this time?"

Zane touches his soul anchor as my voice rises, no doubt to prevent any eavesdropping. "Listen, Matt. There's a lot I haven't told you. I knew if I did, I'd have to tell you everything, and I wasn't ready to face the facts. But it's time you heard the truth, so sit back down and don't interrupt."

I swallow my frustration and nod my head.

"Good." Zane leans back, scratching the side of his neck as collects his thoughts. "Remember that friend I told you about? Kildron, the demon who taught me to use dominion? Well, Kildron was your father. He—"

"Kildron was my dad?" The question bursts from my lungs, unrestrained.

Zane flashes a smile. "Yes. Kildron was your dad. He came from a long line of powerful mystics. This made them powerful demons as well."

Zane continues, denying me the chance to comment. "I never lied about your father. He was my best friend. We grew up together. I watched him fall in love with your mother, Jenevrah. She was Hogrum royalty."

"No way?" It sounds too good to be true—the orphan peasant discovers he's a prince.

Zane smiles at my excitement. "Her uncle was the king. She was never considered for the throne, but she had a knack for Adamic. King Valerium saw her talent and decided to teach her."

When Kildron and Jenevrah got married, I was his best man, and he was mine at my wedding. My wife and I had a girl, and so did your parents."

My head spins. "I had a sister?"

This time, Zane doesn't smile. "*Have...* you have a sister, Matt. Her name is Iris."

"Iris is my sister?" The words explode from my mouth. "Iris? Pixie-cut girl? The girl tried to rob the palace? The one who nearly killed me? She's my sister?"

Zane grunts an "mmhmm."

"Why didn't you tell me about her? Does she know about me?"

"Let me finish, and I'll get to that," Zane growls.

I sit back in my chair and bite down on my tongue. My mind is already in overdrive.

"Anyways," Zane says. "When your sister was two, she started going unconscious, sometimes for days at a time. One time it lasted a week. Your parents couldn't wake her no matter what they did. Your mother worried it was soul-travel, that Iris might get lost and never make it back to her body, so your mother made your sister a soul-anchor to prevent it. After that, the problem went away. When you were born, they didn't take any chances, your mother made you a soul-anchor too."

"You're saying this whole time, my soul anchor was to protect me from soul-travel."

"That's what I'm saying." Zane nods, his brown beard swaying. "Now, around the time that you were born, the real trouble started. The demons became powerful in Hogrum. Kildron was among them, but he had a good heart. He always talked about leaving the cult, so I suggested he spy for me instead. I was already a guardian, and I was tasked with destroying the demons. Your father agreed.

That's when everything fell apart. There was a demon. While the other demons called him Master, he preferred the term Holy One."

My eyelids jump at his name. "You mean…?"

Zane nods. "The very same. He was after the Book of Life—a book that teaches how to speak Adamic. He wanted to find it and master the language."

"For what?" I wonder. "World domination?"

"He claimed he would perfect the world… that he would bring true justice. He said he would end death and suffering. That the earth would be a paradise once more, like the Garden of Eden."

"Well, that doesn't sound so bad," I admit.

Zane flares his nostrils, and his breathing grows louder. "Sometimes evil is unintentional. His plans as he described them could never work. A perfect society is impossible. The only way to ensure perfection is to limit freedom. The Holy One would be all-powerful. He would be able to decide everything, who lives and who dies. What is right and what is wrong. He would be the judge, jury, and executioner. He would be God… do you understand, Matt? No man can have that kind of power without corruption."

"Yeah, I guess...." Already I'm running through scenarios, fantasizing about a perfect world, a world where my parents are back alive and Judy is well.

"I know what you're thinking, Matt, but it could never work. Say the Holy One brought back your parents. Well, what if your parents wanted to bring back your grandparents, and they wanted to bring back your great grandparents. The cycle would continue forever. Death would cease to exist, and who knows what the consequences would be. The dead are meant to stay dead. That means your family, and that means my family as well."

"Okay. I see what you mean." As nice as it sounds, he's right. No one should have that kind of power. "Then, what happened?"

"In an attempt to get the book, the Holy One destroyed the sanctuary, letting in hundreds of feeders." Zane looks down, his voice growing raspy. "I tried to save my family, but I was overwhelmed. They all died. I would've died too, but your father showed up and saved me. He had your sister with him, and we managed to save a few others on our way out, Roselyn and Antai. He gave me the children before going back to kill the Holy One. That's when I fled. I never saw him again. Or your mother. They died protecting us all. I had always assumed you died with them, that is, until this summer."

I wait for Zane to continue the story, but he just looks at me sadly. "That's all I know. I wish I had more to tell you. They were heroes, Matt."

"What happened to Iris?"

Zane sighs. "Iris is my fault. I tried to help her the best I could. I got her adopted by a family in the core. It was a good family, but they were equalist supporters. They had a lot of influence on Iris. With a little convincing, I trained her and persuaded her to join the guard. She got recruited—top of her class. She would've climbed the ranks, but she fell in love. This boy, Jazon, he was her everything. One day, he got killed for being out past curfew. The report said he was reaching for a weapon, and they fired in self-defense, but Iris never accepted it. She quit the guard and joined the equalists. From what I've heard, she serves the Holy One now. I never told you because I was afraid you'd join her. He can be persuasive, but the Holy One is not to be trusted, Matt. The Holy One is no savior."

I sit in silence as I try to digest the knowledge I've devoured. My dead dad was Zane's best friend. My mother was an adalit. My sister serves the Holy One. And then, there's me. I still don't know where I fit in the grand scheme of things.

Zane stands and stretches his back. "I'm sure you have questions, but it's late. We can discuss this more another time."

I'm ready to leave, but I have one more question first. "My family, what was our last name?"

"Kaimor. Your parents were Kildron and Jenevrah Kaimor." Zane smiles bigger with each syllable. "It's a name to be proud of."

"And what name did they give me?"

Zane grins, a flash of white in a mess of brown hair. "Ezra. Your birth name is Ezra."

Chapter 4

Rose

I walk slowly so that Wendy doesn't fall behind. Her eyes flutter wildly from one palace adornment to the next.

"This is the courtyard garden." I gesture in a circle. We're standing in the middle of the palace, surrounded by towering stone walls. There's a small stone path through the grass and a bubbling fountain in the center.

"Feel free to relax here amid your free time. It's open to all palace occupants." I point to the wall on the far side of the courtyard. "The entrance to the Royal Wing is right over there. I'll show you the royal library, and then I'll show you to our quarters. Your room is right next to mine."

As we walk, a servant hurries past with today's lunch—a platter topped with yellow melon, ham, and a steaming bowl of soup. Wendy's eyes follow the food like a dog begging at the dinner table.

"I should probably know this," I say, "but did they let you eat the food in the kitchen?"

Wendy shakes her head. "We'd eat the scraps that came back, but the good stuff was always gone."

I try not to gag at the thought of it. "Well, now that you're a permanent resident, I'll make sure you get your own meals. That's how it worked for my old maid. Once you bring me my meals, you'll be permitted to return to the kitchen for your own."

For the first time today, I see Wendy smile. She looks around, taking in the beauty of the courtyard. "What do I do if I get lost?"

"I'll have Lady Dana assist you the first few days. She should have a map for you. It's pretty easy once you get the hang of it."

Wendy nods and we continue through the garden. She's so different from Velma. Level-headed. Thoughtful. Not quite timid yet far from outspoken.

We're passing the fountain when Crasilda's voice pierces the silence. "Who brought the picker whore to the palace?"

Wendy stiffens, and I stop in my tracks. *Not now. Not on her first day.*

I spin around as Crasilda struts toward us. She's wearing a teal maxi dress with white flower print. Her amber hair is wrapped into two separate buns like bug antennae.

"Aren't you a commoner now?" I shoot back. "Shouldn't you be in the core and not here, harassing my maid?"

Crasilda shrugs. "It's my day off and my father invited me to lunch." She smirks at Wendy. "But you never answered my question. Who invited this mutt?"

I speak loud and proud. "I did. She's my maid now, and you will treat her with respect."

Crasilda shrugs, casually twirling her dress around her waist. She grins at Wendy as would a hunter who spots their prey. "You know, I've heard rumors that the Holy One is killing sinners. I'd be careful if I were you. Sex before marriage is a heinous sin. You might just find your door covered in blood one of these days." She smirks, challenging me to respond.

"Wendy is not a sinner. She's done nothing wrong, and you will show her respect."

"I don't know," Crasilda twirls a loose strand of hair. "I've heard the pickers have uncontrollable appetites. How do you know she didn't want it?" Crasilda smiles and points at Wendy's belly.

I'm already reaching for my amulet when Wendy takes off across the courtyard. I let Crasilda see my hatred before chasing after her.

"Wendy! Wendy, please stop. Let's talk about this. Wendy!"

She finally stops in the middle of the hallway, on the verge of tears. "I don't belong here. I want to go home," she cries.

"Wendy, please listen to me. That girl is a snake. She's God's trash of a human. She'll put down anyone she can. She even bullied your sister. You don't need to listen to a word she says."

"Why is she against me?" Wendy clutches her stomach. "She's a woman too. Shouldn't she understand?"

"I…" I have to think for a second, and then it hits me. "I think she's scared. I think she's scared of what happened to you. She puts you down because she wants to create distance. She wants to think that she's better. That way, in her mind, she's safe from what happened."

"Is she safe?" Wendy asks. "Am I safe here?"

I think of Vyle and the way he tortured me. The way he watched me slowly suffocate. He could've done whatever he wanted. "As long as you're with me, you're safe," I lie. "I won't let anything happen to you, okay?"

She nods.

"Let's go back to our quarters. You can relax in your room for a bit."

"Okay. Thank you, princess."

We're halfway there before I muster the courage. "Wendy, your sister told me a little about what happened to you. About how the baby wasn't... wanted."

Wendy says nothing. She doesn't acknowledge my words.

"Well, I just want you to know that you have options in the palace. We have healers that can remove the pregnancy. I want you to know you have a choice."

"No." Her voice is stern. "I'm not killing the baby. She's as much a victim as I am." She wraps her arms around herself. "She's all I have to look forward to."

She? Wendy speaks as though she already knows the gender. I would ask, but I don't want to make her any more uncomfortable.

"Of course," I soothe. "That's your choice to make."

She stares straight ahead and the muscles in her throat quiver. "I want to go to my room now, please."

"Of course," I wave to a passing servant. "Excuse me, are you currently on an errand?"

The man stops. "I am, but it isn't urgent. How can I be of service?"

"Can you escort my maid to her quarters? It's her first day. Royal Wing, room 12. The door should be unlocked."

"Of course, m'lady."

Wendy frowns. "Where are you going?"

"I want to have a little chat with Crasilda. I'll only be a minute."

The walk to the Northern Wing is long, and it gives me time to rehearse my lecture. I won't let her get away with what she said. Crasilda will learn her place.

When I finally turn the corner to the Northern Wing, I gasp. Crasilda is kneeling before her father's door, snot seeping from her nose as she sobs. The door is painted bright red. Small drops of coagulated blood bubble across the surface.

"He's marked," Crasilda sobs. "I can't lose him. He can't die."

My mind struggles to comprehend what my eyes are seeing. Judge Lumb's door isn't the only one with blood.

Two, three four, five, SIX! Six doors are marked with death.

The Holy One has reached the palace.

Judgment is upon us.

Grandpa's study is open when I arrive. He's sitting at the head of the table, reading a leather-bound text. When he sees me, he claps the books shut. "Rose, just the granddaughter I wanted to see."

I shut the door behind me and sit on the spare chair. Already, the metal foil and chisel are laid before me.

"Excellent. It's time we get back to your studies. Adamic won't teach itself." He cracks a smile.

He talks so casually as if the palace wasn't breached this very morning. "Grandpa, the Holy One marked six elites for death. Aren't we going to talk about this?"

Grandpa leans forward, his long grey braids swinging inches above the table. "Rose, the Holy One is going to take the offensive. People will die. I do not wish to make light of it, but I will not let it sour my time with you. I take comfort knowing your room is safeguarded."

It's true. After my graduation from guard training, Grandpa applied an Adamic lock to my room. My door is impenetrable.

"It's not myself I'm worried about, it's everybody else in Cavernum." *Wendy and her family. Diego and his family.*

"Leave that to the guardians," Grandpa dismisses as he slides the gold foil closer to me. "If you want to protect Cavernum, the best thing you can do is master Adamic. When I'm gone, you'll be Cavernum's only adalit. This must be your number one priority."

I don't like imagining a future without Grandpa, but I know he's right. He won't live forever. I pick up the chisel.

"Do you remember the order for the Adamic lantern?" Grandpa asks.

"I think so." Adamic spells are complicated. They must be written in a specific order and pattern. Every movement must be precise. I pick up the chisel and begin dragging the tip into the foil, leaving a slight indent. I start with the looping symbols, then finish with the center circle. It only takes a few minutes before I'm staring at the complete symbol.

The symbol is perfect in appearance, but it doesn't glow.

"Not quite," Grandpa says cheerily. "Try keeping the outer circles tighter. And maintain an even speed on the inner circle. Everything must be one motion, continuous."

"Yes, Grandpa."

I grab a new piece of gold foil and focus on my Grandpa's instructions.

Antai, when you wake up, I'm going to be an adalit.

I work quickly, arcing the tool in one motion. I've attempted this spell so many times, my hand moves on autopilot. Finally, I finish with the squiggles of the sun symbol and gasp. A faint glow illuminates from gold foil.

"It worked," I laugh. "I can't believe it worked."

"Well done, Rose. Well done." Grandpa relaxes his shoulders, obviously relieved. "For the rest of your life, you'll be able to bring light wherever you go. Every spell you learn makes you that much more capable as a queen. A little more practice, and you'll have the spell mastered." He slides a fresh piece of gold foil in front of me."

"Actually, I was hoping I could learn a new spell."

"Very well," Grandpa grins. "I presume you have a specific spell in mind."

"I want to learn the armor-piercing spell. I keep thinking about that night in the beyond. The feeder had Adamic armor. If it weren't for Antai's Adamic blade, I wouldn't have made it."

"An Adamic blade has its risks," Grandpa warns. "It can be taken and used against you, empowering your enemies." He looks down at the glowing foil and smiles. "How about this. When you can make your own Adamic blade, I'll let you carry one. It'll be yours to keep."

"Really?"

Grandpa nods. "Don't be fooled, Rose. The armor-piercing spell is very complex. It was specifically designed to debilitate another spell. It'll take some time to master... but yes. When you learn it, you can keep your own blade. I trust you with the power you wield as an adalit. Someday, you will be able to create soul-anchors, and you must have the wisdom to keep them from the wrong hands."

"I've actually wondered about that. Only Adamic can defeat Adamic, right? Well if they're both Adamic, what makes one spell more powerful than the other."

Grandpa tilts his head to the side. "An excellent question. I have only theories if you'd like to hear them."

"Yes, please."

"Very well. You are correct that some spells take precedence over others. The armor-piercing spell trumps the Adamic armor spell. Likewise, the spell that marks Cavernum's walls is the most powerful spell we know of. It trumps the armor-piercing spell and every other spell in my arsenal. Some see this and assume that a longer spell is always more powerful, but that is not necessarily true."

Grandpa fishes through his dresser, and finding an Adamic blade, he sets it on the table so that the spell in in clear view

Then he lifts his crown from his head. He places it on the table next to the dagger and points to the spell on the inner band.

"Here, we see that the crown relic has a protection spell of six characters, yet the armor-piercing spell is still dominant with its four. An Adamic blade would pierce directly through my protection. You see, Rose, I don't believe it is the length that determines strength, but the words themselves. As with English, it is sometimes the shortest phrases that carry the most power."

"So, when do I learn the spell?"

Grandpa leans back in his chair. "Come back tomorrow, and I'll teach you everything I know about the armor-piercing spell. The sun is setting, and you need your rest."

"I won't be able to sleep for hours. Please, can you show me the spell?"

"Not tonight, Rose. I have some matters I must attend to."

So that's the real reason. "What kind of matters?" I persist.

"Oh, It's nothing to concern yourself with, my dear. It's a discussion for another time, believe me."

I can't hide the suspicion. My eyes narrow on their own accord.

Grandpa notices. He folds his hands in his lap. "You don't believe me, do you?"

"Grandpa, I understand that you have secrets, but I don't see why you don't trust me with them. How am I supposed to trust you when you don't trust me?"

Grandpa sighs. "Very well, Rose. The truth is, I'm going to use the Demon Amulet on my father, Titan. He spoke Adamic. He must know the location of the lost library. With the demon amulet, I hope to extract the knowledge from his mind, forcefully if necessary."

"Is this the first time you've done this?"

"No, it is my third attempt."

"Have you learned anything yet?"

Grandpa shakes his head. "It's as if the memories are damaged. Or they don't exist at all. He has scattered knowledge of the language in his mind, but I can't find a source. It's as though the memories have disappeared."

"Oh… Alright." I already feel at ease.

"What other questions do you have? Now is the time to ask. I want you to trust me, Rose. If we are to survive what comes, you must trust my judgment."

"Well, first off, how did the equalists have a key to the vault? Only you had a copy, right? How did they have it unless you gave it to them? To be honest, Grandpa, logically, it seems like you gave them the key."

Grandpa nods. "I've thought about this a great deal myself. The only conclusion I've come up with is that Hogrum's vault is identical. Hogrum and Cavernum are sister cities. They're almost exact replicas. If it's true, then the Holy One could have obtained a key from his attack on Hogrum 18 years ago. I imagine that's where he found the morph mask as well."

I find myself nodding along to his reasoning. "Okay, and what about what my assassin said after you possessed him? He said you knew what the spell meant, the one that was hidden in the inheritance box. What reason would he have to lie about that?"

Grandpa's face is as blank as the marble floor. "I don't know, Rose. I wish I knew."

He's lying.

Grandpa never says 'I don't know.' He always has some kind of theory, no matter how absurd. *To get in your head, Rose. To sow distrust.* Any of these answers I would've accepted, but not ignorance. Not 'I don't know.'

Grandpa's hiding something. I've never been more sure.

"And what about the relic?" I ask. "The assassin showed me a relic. It had two stones, almost like glasses. He told me you could talk to me through it. That's how he tricked me into removing my amulet. I guess my question is how did he know about it? Why did he know, and I didn't?"

"That... is a valid concern." Grandpa frowns. "I should've shared this with you. I'll try to be more transparent from now on." He stands and opens up one of the drawers, removing the very relic I had just mentioned—two crystal orbs embedded in a thick silver band. There's a small indent between the two plum-sized lenses where a nose could fit. Grandpa lifts it over his head and puts it on like a pair of goggles. The Adamic symbols are visible on the outer surface of the band.

"Titan called it his seerglass. They aren't used for communication. That was a lie. They are used to see."

"See what?"

Grandpa lifts a finger. "Not what, whom. This relic is a spyglass. It can locate any individual anywhere in the world. All you have to do is describe them to the relic."

"Can we use this to spy on the Holy One?"

Grandpa grins, amused at the notion. "If only we could. Unfortunately, the relic can only find someone we know well. Someone we understand. Seeing someone's face isn't enough to find them. You have to know them personally. You have to describe them, both body and soul. Only then will the seerglass find them."

Grandpa hands me the goggles, and I rest the metal frame on my ears. The lenses are misty white, like staring into a cloud. I blink, imagining Antai. I think of his face, his dark eyebrows and his luscious lips. His olive skin and his muscular frame. Colors swirl before me, but I don't see Antai. "It's not working."

Grandpa smiles. "The more you describe, the easier the relic can find them. Passions, personality, fears, desire."

I think of Antai's stubbornness. His unbending character. I think of his passion for the guard—for keeping me safe. His sarcasm and his charisma. With each new thought, the image swirls before me, but Antai doesn't appear.

"It's still not working." I squint harder into the white orbs. "Am I doing something wrong?"

The corners of grandpa's lips sag. "Rose, I must ask. Are you trying to see Antai?"

"Yes, why… oh... I see." My heart sinks like a stone, splashing into my stomach.

Grandpa confirms my worst fears. "The relic tracks using both body and soul. If his soul is no longer present, I fear the relic will be unsuccessful. I suggest you try with someone else. I'm sure you'll get it." He says the last sentence quickly, hoping I won't dwell on Antai.

I think of Diego, banished from the guard. I imagine his round face and stocky build. I remember his love for his family, his pain when Velma died. His once-positive attitude and his playful humor.

Within seconds, the crystal morphs into a crisp image. I see Diego wearing a tattered tan shirt and jeans. I can't see his surroundings, but I know where he is. He holds a scythe and swings it side to side. He's taking part in the wheat harvest. He's in the fields.

I'm sorry, Diego.

Next, my mind wanders to Matt. I haven't seen him since his promotion. I think of his wavy blonde hair and his shy smile. I think of his adoptive mother and his mysterious past. I remember the way he danced in the beyond and the way he saved me from the feeder."

Matt materializes before my eyes. He's dressed in a black uniform and walks briskly. I can't hear anything, but his lips are pursed as he whistles. He looks carefree, happy. Blotches of sunlight drift over his head creating a pattern of shade I've only seen from leaves. He must be in the forest—in the beyond.

Nevela!

How could I have forgotten? My thoughts are rushed as I envision my short little maid. Her high pitched voice and her cheerful demeanor. Her long, golden hair, and her love for sewing.

I gasp at the seerglass. "No!" The girl before me is almost unrecognizable. She's curled in a ball, head tucked to her chest. Her hair is blackened with smut. Her arms, thin as a twig, are wrapped tight around her, and her dress has strings of frayed fabric dangling in all directions.

I can't look any longer. I tear off the glasses, meeting Grandpa's concerned glance.

"What did you see?"

"I saw Nevela. She's… she's some kind of prisoner. She looks terrible. She looks utterly terrible, Grandpa."

Grandpa sighs. "I'm sorry, Rose. I know that must've been hard to see." He puts a shaky hand on my shoulder. "If the Holy One has her, it's only a matter of time before she's liberated. We invade the tunnels this week. Don't lose hope."

I grit my teeth, trying my best to cling to the future. *Hang in there Nevela. We're coming for you. Hang in there just a few more days.*

I hand the seerglass to Grandpa, who sets them down on the table.

"Grandpa?"

"Yes, Rose?"

53

"Remember when you told me how my mother died? You said that you never found her body. That you think she was cremated."

"That's correct."

I hesitate. "Have you... have you ever tried to find her with the seerglass?"

Grandpa bows his head. "I have... many times. I'm afraid I see nothing each time. I'm sorry, Rose. I wish I could say otherwise."

Grandpa stands suddenly. "Come, Rose, you have a big day tomorrow. You need your rest."

Tomorrow is Vyle's disciplinary hearing. Normally, it would be held in one of the minor courts, but because a crime against the princess is punishable by death, the High Council will be passing judgment.

"Grandpa, are you sure you can't represent me? I heard Vyle's dad is representing him."

"I'm sorry, dear, but General Kanes is not king. I must remain impartial. I assure you, your lawyer is one of the best. I'll be there the entire time. You have nothing to worry about. Trust me."

But I don't trust him. I don't trust anyone. The only person I trust is brain dead.

Still, I push that aside. I force all my worries to the back of my mind. Right now, all that matters is Vyle.

He will pay for his crimes. I'll make sure of it.

My hands are already sweating as Vyle enters the High Council Room. His dad walks at his side. As all guardians must, General Kaynes has studied years of law. He's more than qualified to represent his son.

My lawyer, Mr. Grandel, is a balding man with circular glasses and disheveled brown hair. He's everything I'd expect to see in a lawyer, complete with a clipboard full of notes and a stiff grey robe.

Grandpa stands. "Welcome, everyone, to the disciplinary hearing of Vyle Kaynes. As tradition dictates, the prosecutor will present the crimes. At their conclusion, the defendant will have their chance to refute. The time is now yours, Rose."

My lawyer steps forward and flips through his papers with one finger. "The case today is a simple one. In the next few minutes, I will prove that Vyle Kaynes is a dangerous man who not only abused his power as a guardsman but who tortured another recruit, ultimately threatening the life of the princess."

He motions at me. "Princess, will you please give your account of the incident."

I step forward and clear my throat. "As Princess, I kept an amulet for my own safety. This wasn't my decision, but the request of the king. However, I removed my amulet to compete in the final assessment. I was in my room when Vyle entered with two other recruits, Zander Otalmer and Croyd Gazabee. All three of them were armed with amplifiers."

Grandel interjects. "And these two other men, who were they in relation to you?"

"Strangers, really, but they appeared to be Vyle's friends. They spent a lot of time together."

"And then what happened?" Grandel asks as if he genuinely doesn't know.

"Well, Vyle told his friends to hold me down with dominion, then Vyle began to search my clothes for my amulet. When he didn't find it, he suffocated me with dominion."

Grandel looks out at the High Council. "To those of you less familiar with dominion, this is achieved by removing all the air from around a victim's head, essentially creating a vacuum." He turns back to me. "And, princess, how long did this suffocation take place?"

"It lasted for as long as he thought I could survive, maybe a minute or so. He did it three times. The last time, I passed out and woke up on the floor."

I hear Chancellor Gwenevere gasp, which makes me feel a little validated.

I hold my head high. "He only stopped when I revealed that I was the princess. Then, he left."

Grandel lowers his clipboard. "Did you hear that, members of the council? Three times, Vyle repeated this torture on the princess. He only stopped, when he realized that the victim had the power to enact justice. Only when he could be held accountable for his actions, did he treat the princess as a human being. I don't know about all of you, but this is not the kind of person I want as a guardsman. Not only did he disrespect the process of our law, but he needlessly threatened a human life. In response, my client is willing to be merciful. She proposes that Vyle Kaynes be expelled from the guard without any further legal action."

When we make eye contact, Zane gives me a supportive nod, but grandpa's face is utterly expressionless. "Thank you," Grandpa says. "The defense may now give their remarks."

General Kaynes steps forward. "Today, I will explain how a young guardsman took a risk to keep Cavernum safe. I'm not suggesting he made the right decision, but I'm here to prove his intentions were noble. This incident was not the result of a violent, reckless guardsman, but the result of the king's own irresponsibility."

At that, Grandpa raises an eyebrow. The other members of the council grumble their surprise.

General Kaynes smiles at the reactions. "You see, my son was suspicious of the princess from the first day of training. She was divided under the false name 'Lynn.' My son noticed flaws in her story, and became cautious. He watched her closely and soon saw evidence that she was harboring an illegal amulet, not an amplifier but a dangerous soul-anchor—a suspicion that turned out to be true."

General Kaynes holds up one finger. "But that's not all. Vyle followed protocol. He spoke to his supervisor, Proticus Tyre, about his suspicions, and do you know what Mr. Tyre said?" Kaynes pauses, looking slowly over the council. "He said not to worry. He suggested my son forget all about it. Rather than tell my son the truth, he perpetuated a lie."

General Kaynes paces in front of the map wall as he speaks. "Now, we must look at this from Vyle's perspective. He knew that a student was harboring an amulet. He also knew that equalists had stolen amulets in the past. Finally, he knew that his superior was ignoring the situation. What choice did he have but to confront her? Of course, this had risks, but Vyle was willing to accept those risks in order to keep Cavernum safe. This is what he had always dreamed of doing as a guardsman."

General Kaynes takes a sip from a glass of water and sets it back on the table. "Now, the princess insisted that Vyle wished her harm. That he desired to inflict pain, but logic tells us otherwise." General Kaynes looks at me and grins. "Princess, may I ask you a few questions?"

I straighten my shoulders and try to look confident. "Of course."

"Why did you lie about your amulet? Why use a false name?"

"For my own protection. The fewer people who knew who I was, the safer I was."

General Kaynes nods. "Perhaps true, but you knew Vyle personally. Did you have any reason to suspect he was an equalist?"

"Well, no but... I had seen him hurt others in the past. He used an amulet on two other recruits, Matthew MacArthur and Diego Ortega."

General Kaynes nods confidently. "True, but Vyle was acting in self-defense. Matthew MacArthur attacked first, did he not? He punched my son in the jaw."

"Well... yes, but..." I'm at a loss for words. I know he wished me harm, but I can't prove it.

General Kaynes smiles wider. "And princess, why did you finally reveal your identity to Vyle?"

"To save myself!" I gasp! "He was going to kill me!"

"So you knew that telling the truth would pacify my son? Correct?"

"I… yes, I figured it would, but only because he would feel accountable. He feared that I could punish him for his crimes."

General Kaynes holds up two fingers at the council. "Two things. First off, if you knew telling the truth would terminate this entire encounter? Why wait so long? Why not tell the truth the first time Vyle confronted you?"

"I…" My brain is whirling, but words won't form. "I don't know."

"Second, you mentioned that Vyle only stopped because he feared repercussions, but logic will tell us otherwise. Princess, what happened when you were paired with Vyle at the final evaluation?"

"He forfeited."

"He forfeited!" General Kaynes sweeps his hands through the air. "Vyle could've killed you in the arena without any legal repercussions, yet he feared for your safety. He relinquished any chance he had of ranking first in his class in order to keep you safe. And princess, what happened when the feeders attacked in the beyond? When a feeder stole your amulet, who saved you?"

As much as I hate it, I won't lie in court. "Vyle did."

"And then he saved you a second time when your own supervisor was possessed, did he not?"

I speak through clenched teeth. "Yes."

General Kaynes gives the council a 'see' look. "Vyle could've sat idly by as the feeders attacked. He could've let the princess die, and this entire scandal would've died with her. If he was truly afraid of repercussions as the princess claims, he would've done exactly that. He would've let her die. But Vyle wasn't afraid of punishment; he feared for the safety of the princess. He put her life before his own. Yes, he made a mistake. He used force when he should have trusted his advisor, but he only did so in Cavernum's best interest. It was the confusion of unnecessary secrecy that led Vyle to act so desperately."

General Kaynes sweeps his arms dramatically into the air. "In conclusion, my dear council members, I propose that Vyle's punishment be a week of unpaid suspension for his bold behavior, but I exhort you to dispel these notions of expulsion. To expel Vyle from the guard would be a great loss to Cavernum. If it was not for my son, the princess would be dead. How many more will he save in a lifetime of service?"

Grandpa sits up on his throne. "Council, any questions before we vote?"

Gwenevere presses her glasses higher on her beak-like nose. "General Kaynes, you suggested that the princess should have revealed her identity to your son, but wasn't that the whole point of her alias? So that none of her fellow recruits knew who she was? Why, when someone is threatening her with an amulet, would she think she could trust them? If you ask me, the princess was right to lie, and Vyle had no excuse to torture her. He was acting out of place."

Chancellor Bolo slaps the table. "The girl was suspicious! What choice did he have? He thought the amulet was stolen."

Gwenevere rolls her eyes. "There's always a choice."

The room falls silent. After several seconds, General Kayne's bows. "Thank you, council. I conclude my time."

"If there are no further questions, we'll proceed with a vote." Grandpa looks around the room. "All those in favor of expelling Vyle from the guard, please indicate by raising your right hand."

Zane raises his hand. Then, to my delight, Gwenevere does as well. Grandpa hesitates, then slowly lifts his hand in the air. I'm already furious. Not only did we lose, but Grandpa hardly seems convinced. It's as though he's defending me out of obligation, simply because he's my kin.

"Any opposed?" The remaining five diplomats raise their hands. Grandpa taps his cane on the ground. "Very well. The defendant's proposal will stand. Vyle will receive one week of unpaid suspension. If there isn't anything else, the council will adjourn."

I don't want to see Vyle smile, or to see his father gloating with his ugly grin. I want out of the council room. *There is no justice in Cavernum. If I want justice, I'll have to find it myself.*

I'm about to stand when General Kaynes speaks. "Your highness. If I may, I would like to bring one more matter before the council."

"Proceed."

"It has been established that the princess has been bonded with a soul-anchor. I imagine this isn't a surprise to the council, but it begs the question: does the council approve of this? I don't remember voting on the matter, and the law states that only a guardian can wear a soul-anchor. So who made an exception? Or is the princess above the law?"

"Is this not the tradition?" Grandpa asks. "My father, Titan, was not a guardian, yet he holds a soul-anchor. As did his father before him."

"But tradition is not law, your highness." General Kaynes insists.

"Then it should be law," Grandpa snaps. "If it weren't for Rose's soul-anchor, Cavernum would be without an heir. I did it for the good of Cavernum."

"What gives you the right to decide what's best for Cavernum?" Kaynes raises an eyebrow. "Last I checked, Cavernum isn't a monarchy. You may preside over the council, but it is the council that creates the laws, is it not? To act against the council would be treason."

Grandpa maintains his composure. He doesn't babble or beg. He lets the silence fill the room until he's ready to speak. "I was under the impression that the council was in agreement. Otherwise, why would you not have voiced a complaint sooner? Rose has had the amulet since she was an infant. It was her father who made the decision, not I. However, if the council wishes, we can revisit the matter."

General Kaynes looks at me hungrily—hungry to avenge his son. Or perhaps it's not his son he cares about, but his family's reputation. "Yes. I propose we revisit the matter. Please tell us, your highness, why should we make an exception for the princess?"

Grandpa shifts in his seat. "The princess has been targeted three times in the last month. She has been possessed by a demon and nearly kidnapped. Without her soul-anchor, she would not have survived. I understand your concern, but my granddaughter needs a soul-anchor for her own safety."

"Interesting." General Kaynes strokes his chin for dramatic effect. He's putting on a show for the other council members. "You say the princess only survived because she had a soul-anchor. This may be true, but what about Proticus Tyre? Would he have survived if he had a soul-anchor? Or Antai Elsborne? Or any other guardsmen for that matter? Odds are, they would all be alive if they had been given soul-anchors. So I beg the question, why don't we give soul-anchors to everyone, your majesty?"

Grandpa looks slowly around the room before responding. His voice is flat, defeated. "Because soul-anchors are dangerous. In the wrong hands, they can cause great destruction."

General Kaynes grins. "So what you're saying is, the risks outweigh the reward. Only those who have proven themselves—the guardians—can be trusted with a soul-anchor."

Grandpa sighs, "Yes, that is correct."

"Then, do we all agree that the princess has not yet proven herself? She has not met the standards we have established. So I ask the question again: is the princess above the law?"

"No!" Chancellor Bolo hisses. "She is not!"

A few heads bob their agreement. Somehow, in a matter of seconds, Vyle has gone free, and I've been placed on trial.

Zane slaps his hand on the table. "How many of you have had an assassin sent after you? How many of you have been possessed?" he growls. "Clearly the princess is a target, even beyond the High Council. She's already bonded, and so far, she's only used the amulet in her own defense. Why not let her keep it? What does it harm?"

Chancellor Quine raises his trembling voice. "That raises another question. Are we not safe in the palace? If the princess needs a soul-anchor simply to stay alive, is my own family safe? Because if they aren't, I suggest we need some drastic changes, and immediately."

"You are safe," Grandpa insists. "You are all safe."

Chancellor Quine throws his hands in the air. "Then the princess is, too. I say she lose the amulet. Titan as well. Why should they deserve special treatment?"

"I believe it's time for a vote," General Kaynes smirks.

Grandpa looks wearily around the room. "It is proposed that my granddaughter be stripped of her soul-anchor. All—"

"Titan as well." Chancellor Quine reminds.

Grandpa sighs. "Titan as well. All in favor, please manifest."

I count as the hands drift into the air. Bolo, Quine, Gwenevere, and Kaynes, and Moriander.

It's a majority.

"It's decided then," General Kaynes sings. "Rose, please remove your amulet. The king will return it to the vault, and I will be a witness that he does so."

At first, my arms don't move. I look to Grandpa and he gives me a defeated nod. *I have no choice.*

The entire council watches as I reach into my blouse and remove my amulet. Then, I lift it over my head and toss it into the center of the table. Just like that, my only gift from my father is gone. Once again, I'm defenseless.

I feel the prick of fear. It starts small, like a venomous sting, but it quickly spreads, making my muscles shake and my heart rate spike. I try to keep my knees still, but all I can think about are the last two times I removed my amulet. The first time, Vyle assaulted me. The second time, I was possessed, nearly killing Antai in the process.

I can't survive without my amulet. I'm vulnerable. I won't survive.

Then, the thought of Velma scolds me. I know what she would say. *Now, you know what it's like to be vulnerable. Now, you have a little taste of what I felt, of what Wendy feels every day. Nothing is safe for the rest of us. Why should you be any different?*

I remember Wendy's question. *Are we safe here? Are we safe in the palace?*

Now, I know the answer.

None of us are safe. None of us ever were.

Chapter 5

Matt

After the chaotic night I just had, I'm stoked for some daylight. Normally, my amulet would be locked in a guard tower, but I received special permission from Zane to visit the beyond. Guard policy states I can't leave the walls unarmed, and I don't mind the extra protections.

The bulletproof vest is hotter than I'm used to. I wear one on my midnight shifts, but never in the sunshine. The kevlar doesn't breathe, and my back is sweating up a storm. The black uniform only makes things worse.

I pat my pistol and then my back pocket to double-check my phone. It's almost dead, but there's a phone charger at the bunker, and Klinton promised to give me a tour.

It feels good to be outside the walls. I whistle as I walk, moving parallel to the road, enjoying the shade of the overgrowth. I savor every sensation. The subtle sinking of the soil beneath my feet. The calming crinkle of the leaves above my head. There's a crisp breeze that cools my sweaty back. It's deliciously nostalgic, and I do my best to soak in the moment. I spot a patch of lilies, and my heart throbs. If I were in Colorado, I'd pick them for Judy. I pat my phone once more.

Hang in there, Judy. I just need a little more time.

I bend down to grab hold of a lily.

SHLINK.

A knife whizzes past my ear and embeds itself in the soil. As I'm standing, something dense thuds against the back of my Kevlar vest.

I catch myself with my hands and try to stand as a log lands on top of me, crushing me with the weight of a solid pine. I cry out as something pops in my ribcage. The side of my face is pressed against the soil, and I struggle to draw a breath.

It all happens in less than a second. Then, I hear the feeder running up behind me.

Shield!

A turtle shell of an energy shield warps the air around me. I throw my whole soul into the command, making an impenetrable barrier of force. I wait for an attack, but the feeder doesn't try to break my defenses. It doesn't want to waste the energy.

It knows it's already won.

I try to inhale, but the weight of the log compresses my lungs and pinches my spine. I can't attack without releasing my shield. I can't move the tree without releasing my shield. I'm stuck.

I'm going to die!

A leaf crunches somewhere by my feet. I can hear the thing breathing, reviving memories of being bitten in Hogrum. The ambush attack. The approach from behind. It's all too familiar. Next, it'll grab me by my hair and feast until it's full. This time, I won't have a soul-anchor to save me.

I'm shaking uncontrollably, either from agony or terror. Maybe both. *Please, God. Don't let me die.* And then I remember.

It's the only way. I close my eyes and thrust my soul in the direction I last heard the feeder. As soon as my shield dissolves, I sense him closing in. He moves quickly, but I intercept him, latching onto his body and burrowing inside. In an instant, I'm inhaling his emotions. Hunger. Desperation. The excitement of a fresh kill.

I see memories too—fresh, newly formed. I'm watching a dance party from the darkness of the forest. I'm holding down a guardsman and latching into his throat. Recruits are running every which way.

When I open my eyes, my hand—his hand—is reaching for my neck.

No!

I wrench his hand away, controlling his muscles from the inside. Then, I force his body to take a step back. I feel the power just beneath his skin. The strength of a hundred souls. It's my power now, and it's begging to be released.

For the first time, I survey the scene. I spin around, searching for other enemies, but I'm possessing the only feeder in sight. We're alone, and I'm in control.

I look down at my body, half-buried under the log. The tree trunk isn't that big—maybe a foot in diameter—but it's long and heavy. It rests on my lower back, preventing my body from taking a breath.

Move!

With a simple command, I send the log flying.

That's when I see it. A knife is lodged in the upper left corner of my Kevlar vest. I stare for a moment. Without my vest, I'd likely be feeder food already.

I reach down and pry the knife from my vest. The feeder squirms beneath my skin, but I refuse to relinquish my hold on his arm. I take a deep breath and raise the knife to his neck. I'll feel this too, but I don't have a choice. I can't risk leaving him alive. Not after what he's done. He's killed guardsmen. He tried to kill me. *He deserves to die.*

I press the knife into the soft flesh of his throat. I feel the prick of the blade, but I can't stop now. I push deeper.

Forgive me, master! You were dressed as the enemy. Have mercy, I beg of you. I was confused.

His thoughts take me by surprise. They're not bloodthirsty or sinister. I actually sense remorse in his words. He no longer wishes me harm.

Master? I don't mean to think it, but the feeder senses my confusion.

Yes, you are of the order. Satan has bestowed you with dominion over man. Let me live, and I will serve you with my life. I am loyal to the Demon King.

I don't want to believe him, but his words feel genuine. The feeder sees me as superior. He won't attack me again. He actually fears me.

I am your humble servant. Please, master. Let me live to serve you?

I should kill him. I should slit his throat before he does the same to someone else. But I can't. Even as a feeder, he feels too human.

Very well. I say in my head. *But I have a few questions for you.*

I feel relief course through me—his relief. *Yes, master. Thank you, master.*

I retract my soul and wake up on the forest floor. The sudden loss of power only emphasizes my pain. Part of me wants to go back, to feel the sum of a hundred souls coursing through me, but I shove the urge to the back of my mind. Groaning, I push myself to my feet.

The feeder has a moment to strike. He could kill me with a quick blow to the head, but he doesn't. He waits patiently as I turn to face him.

His skin is the first thing I notice. It looks grey and colorless, like a human corpse before burial. His face is gaunt, and his teeth, razor-sharp. Everything about him looks dead, but then he smiles.

"You're surprised, master?" His voice is nothing but air scraping on throat, as if all but one of his vocal cords have been snipped.

"I, uhhh, how old are you?"

"I was born in 1812. Does this please you, master?"

1812? I try to hide my surprise. "You must have... lots of experience?"

The feeder nods as it approaches me, eyeing me up and down. "You're powerful for a young demon. The Demon King must have a special task for you?"

"Yes." The word leaves my mouth before I have a chance to think them through. I look down at my uniform. "I'm undercover. The Demon King wants me to become a guardian."

"Ahhh, yesss. This is why you do not feed. The Demon King has others in the palace. You will make a great addition."

"Others? I didn't know there were others?" I pretend the idea intrigues me. "The Demon King never told me about the others."

The feeder smiles. "Oh, his influence is getting stronger by the day. It won't be long before we rule Cavernum."

"What can you tell me about the Demon King?"

The feeder's eyes double in size. "Master, why do you question my loyalty? I am thy servant, but I serve the Demon King above all. I have taken the oath of secrecy. I will not betray him."

I nod my head as if I'd expect nothing less. "Very good. You will make a great servant." Once again, I must pretend to be pleased. "Do you have a name?"

"Aramaias, Master."

"Well, Aramaias, I have a job for you. I need you to stay away from Cavernum until I send for you. I'll be traveling through here often, and I can't be seen with you, understood. Go far away from here."

"Yes, master."

"Well, what are you waiting for? Go!"

Aramaias reaches down and picks up his two knives. "Be cautious, master. The archangel hunts. Even now he may not be far."

"The archangel?"

"Yesss. He is a demon, but he is an enemy to the Demon King. He serves the Creator. He has killed many of our kind. Be cautious, young demon. I fear your gifts may not protect you from the Archangel. He is God's last attack on our kind. May the devil bless you."

Before I can ask more, Aramaias takes off into the woods. I watch until he disappears behind the tree trunks. Then, pick up my rifle and continue my march. My ribs are sore, my back aches, and I've befriended a feeder. If only I could tell Judy about all of this.

Judy!

I dig into my pocket and grab my phone. The screen is cracked, and pieces of glass are crumbling inside the case.

Please work! I don't have Judy's number memorized. It changed a few years back, and I never had the need. It was always saved in my contacts. *Pleeease don't be broken!*

I hold down the power button, and the low battery symbol flashes on the screen.

Thank God.

I stuff it in my pocket and hurry along the road, trying in vain not to flex my core. With each step, a searing pain courses up my side, like a scalpel in my lungs. I try not to count the steps, but the journey feels like it takes forever.

Klinton calls out to me as I approach the meadow. "What took you so long?" When he sees my limp, his face drops. "You're limping. What happened?"

I wait until I don't have to yell. Talking loud hurts my ribs. "I, uhhh, I got attacked by a feeder."

"What? You're joking?"

"No, it just happened on my way here, but I scared him off. It's not a big deal."

"Hurry inside. My friend can take a look at it. He has medic training." Klinton swings open the hatch and motions for me to go first. "Demons! I can't believe that. In broad daylight…"

"It's fine." I insist. As I take my first step on the ladder, I groan, wincing with each rung. "I'll swing by the healing loft on my way home." I force a smile. "But first, how about that tour you promised."

The ladder drops me in a small circular hallway, like a bear cave made of metal. Somewhere in the bunker, a bird squawks.

Klinton points at a closed door as we pass. "That's the dorm- itory, where we sleep. My brother's taking a nap right now."

"How long are your shifts?" I ask.

"24 hours, 3 days a week. But three of us work at a time. So one person is free to sleep whenever they need to."

Klinton points in each of the following rooms as we pass. "That's the bird room where we house the messenger hawks. This is the kitchen." At the end of the hallway is a wide room complete with several small computers and a giant screen.

"And this…" He gestures at the giant screen, "is the commun- ications center." The computers are Macs, the latest model by the looks of it. Wires run across the floor in every direction and feed into various holes in the wall. There's only one man in the room. He's typing away furiously at one of the computers. He looks up as we approach and smiles at Klinton. "You just couldn't stay away, could you?"

Klinton waves back to the other guardsman. "Matt, meet Ronald. He was divided two years ago. Ronald, this is Matt."

"You must be little miss survived a feeder." Ronald leans in closer. "So, let's see the scar I've heard so much about?"

"You told him about my scar?" I laugh.

Klinton gestures at the steel walls around him. "We live in a metal box. We run out of things to talk about."

Ronald pouts. "Oh, come on. Your scar is legendary. Embrace it."

"Fine, but just a peek." I pull down my collar to reveal the raised pink scar tissue.

Ronald grimaces. "Oh wowzers, he took a big ole bite. Poor thing must've been starving."

Klinton slaps him on the shoulder. "Don't sympathize with the feeder, you sicko!"

"How would you feel, taking a bite of food, and then your meal runs away. That would be tragic." Ronald laughs as he turns to me. "I'm just playing, Matt. I'm glad you're okay." He turns and gestures at an unoccupied swivel chair. "Here, take a seat. Feel free to relax."

I take a seat in the chair and look at the computers. One monitor in particular displays a map of the US. Random yellow markers dot the map.

"What do these yellow dots mean?" I point at New York City, where the dots are so dense they overlap.

Klinton's face lights up. "That's my current assignment. Those dots mark areas of recent feeder activity," he says. "Our computers automatically search through news and police reports for feeder activity. Captain Renshu created the algorithm himself. If we find any sign of a feeder attack, we mark it on this screen. That way we can direct the convoy to make a rescue."

I raise an eyebrow. "Sounds fun... you know. If you like sitting in dark bunkers all day," I tease.

Klinton shrugs. "Hey, if you prefer whipping children, be my guest."

"Ooooh." Ronald smiles. "Got'em!"

I let myself laugh too. "Okay, fair enough. Working in the bunker wouldn't be so bad."

"The days go by quickly," Klinton says. "Between monitoring and messaging the convoy and sleeping and cooking, the days practically fly by."

"Uno is a godsend, that's for sure. We can play a few rounds if you want."

"That sounds fun, but do you guys mind if I charge my phone first? I want to make a phone call."

"iPhone, right?" Klinton digs around in a drawer of wires while Ronald smirks at me. "You came all the way out here for a phone call? Must be some girl?"

"It's his mom," Klinton says, pulling out a charger cable.

"Oh, your 'mom.'" Ronald flashes two exaggerated winks. "Gotcha."

Klinton shakes his head, grinning. "Ignore him. There's an outlet in the kitchen. Feel free to call from there."

"Thanks, guys. Be right back." As soon as I'm out of the room, I hear Ronald whisper something, and Klinton bursts into laughter. I've never seen Klinton like this with anyone. So comfortable. So confident.

I flip the switch and a fluorescent lightbulb buzzes to life after several short flickers. The kitchen is small, with a stainless steel sink to match the steel walls. I plug in my phone and wait the excruciating minute for my phone to resurrect. Then, I tap Judy's name.

If I wasn't restricted by the charger cable. I'm sure I'd be nervously pacing. There's a long pause before it starts ringing.

"Hello?"

The voice isn't Judy's, but an unfamiliar woman. Instantly, my heart starts racing.

"Hi, this is Matthew MacArthur. I'm trying to reach my mom. Is... is she there?"

"Hello, Matthew. I'm Rachel, your mother's hospice nurse. Your mother has had a bit of a rough day. She's resting now. Do you think you can call later today?"

"Is everything all right with her?"

The nurse pauses. "You're aware of her current condition, I presume."

"Yes, I'm aware."

"Well, she's in a lot of pain recently and hasn't had much of an appetite. We're trying to make her as comfortable as possible, but there's only so much we can do."

"I understand. When she wakes up, can you tell her I called, and tell her that I've been promoted to research supervisor? And... tell her that I miss her and that I'll try to call again soon."

"Is that all?" the nurse asks.

"Yeah, that's all. Thanks."

"Have a nice day."

"You too." I hang up the phone. When I stand from the chair, a piercing pain erupts in my side. "Aahhh!"

I hear the metal thumping as Klinton and Ronald come running down the hall. "What's wrong?"

I clench my jaw and force myself to stand, groaning through the pain. "It's nothing. My side is just a little sore from when the feeder attacked me."

"What did he do to you?" Klinton asks.

I crack a small smile. "He may or may not have hit me in the back with a log."

"Pull up your shirt," Ronald says. "Let's check it out."

I untuck my uniform and raise the fabric up to my chest. Ronald covers his mouth and gasps. "Oh my God. You need to see a healer. That looks bad. You must have quite the adrenaline rush to be walking around like you are."

From the corner of my eye, I can see purple blotches. It stretches from the top of my hip up to my rib cage.

"Yeah, I think I'll head back to the palace now. It's starting to hurt worse."

"I'll walk you back," Klinton offers. "Safety in numbers."

Ronald sticks out his lower lip. "Okay, yeah, you guys go on a leisurely stroll. Don't mind lil ole Ronald. I'll just be here holding down the fort."

"Oh, shush. I'll be back in no time."

"Don't forget this." Ronald hands Klinton a walkie-talkie. "Drop him off and come right back. If anything happens to you, your brother will kill me."

"Nothing's going to happen," Klinton insists as he climbs the ladder. "I'm bloodless, remember? I'm the culinary equivalent of unbuttered toast."

Ronald points a finger at Klinton. "Don't you act like a toast expert. You wouldn't even know about toast if it weren't for me."

"It's just twice-baked bread," Klinton says. "It's not that special."

Ronald grows serious. "Just be careful! I'll see you in a bit."

I wince as I take the ladder one rung at a time. Halfway to the top, I loop my elbow around one of the bars and take a breather. As I approach the hatch, Klinton gives me a hand and pulls me to the surface. Without a word, we begin the short walk to the outer wall.

Out of the corner of his eye. Klinton watches as I clutch my side. "Are you sure you're going to make it to the palace? I could call a carriage to come get you."

The truth is, a carriage sounds nice, but I wave him off. "I'll be fine. It's just a little bruising." *And maybe a broken rib.*

Klinton looks down at the road. "So... what did you think of Ronald? He's pretty cool, right?"

"Yeah," I raise an eyebrow at Klinton. "The real question is, what do you think of him?"

Klinton gapes at me. "W-what do you mean?" His face turns bright red.

I shrug, trying not to make him uncomfortable. "I could be wrong. It just seemed like you two were pretty fond of each other."

Klinton looks down at his feet and thinks for a moment. "Is it that obvious?"

"All I know is, you laughed more today than our entire training. That's gotta mean something."

Klinton smiles. "You think he likes me back?"

"I'm no romance expert," I admit, "but it seemed to me like he was into you."

Klinton is about to say more when the radio suddenly crackles to life. Ronald's voice pierces through the static. "Klinton, do you copy? We have an emergency!"

Klinton snatches the walkie-talkie from his belt and presses a button on the side. "I'm here. What is it?"

"We have movement on the main road. Whatever it is, it's big and it's moving fast! It's not one of ours. Get out of there! Now!"

Then, I hear it. The mechanical whining of a car engine. A black van appears behind us, moving dangerously fast over the gravel. The windshield reflects the canopy. In a matter of seconds, the van will be on top of us.

Klinton is already holding his pistol in hand. "What do we do?"

I'm tempted to run, escaping into the forest, but my side hurts more than ever, and if the feeders give chase, they'll catch me in no time. The guard might never find my body. On the bright side, I'm wearing my amulet. My odds are better if I face them head-on.

I unholster my pistol and face the oncoming van. "I can't run. I say we fight."

Klinton kneels on the road and aims his pistol at the Van. It's several hundred yards away, but that doesn't discourage him.

BANG! Klinton fires a single shot, readjusts, and fires again.

BANG!

With every blink, the van is closer.

200 yards.

BANG!

150 yards.

BANG!

100 yards.

BANG!

I remember the feeder and the way he trapped me with a tree. I spot a pine tree located directly next to the road. It's wide, tall, and mostly bare of branches. At the last second, I push with my mind, commanding the tree to topple, begging every particle with my mind.

CREAAAAK!

A splintering of wood drowns out all noise, followed by a deafening crash. The pine tree collides with the road a few yards in front of us, sending a blast of gravel, like shrapnel, in all directions. It settles perfectly parallel to the road, creating a four-foot wall of tree trunk between us and the oncoming van.

Metal squeals as the driver hits the brakes. The car slides in the gravel, but it doesn't stop fast enough.

CRUNCH!

The front bumper crumples against the trunk of the pine tree. Klinton doesn't waste a second. He unleashes the rest of his magazine as fast as he can pull the trigger.

BANG! BANG! BANG! BANG! BANG!

The air ripples around the van, deflecting each bullet into the dirt. Someone inside the car is creating an energy shield. *The feeders are still alive!*

Klinton releases the magazine and shoves a fresh one into the base of his pistol. I keep my finger on the trigger, but neither of us shoots. We don't want to waste our ammo.

Smoke billows from the smashed engine, clouding my view of the windshield. I hunch my shoulders and reach out with my mind. I'm ready to ignite the wreckage at the slightest threat.

I expect them to retaliate, but nothing happens. For several tense moments, all I can hear is ringing in my ears.

Then, I hear shuffling within the van. With a screech, the side door slides open. An empty hand peeks out and waves in the air. "We're guardsmen. Don't shoot! I'm coming out!" The man has a thick French accent. "Don't shoot. We seek refuge in Cavernum."

He holds his hands in the air and steps slowly out of the van. The first thing I notice is his eyes. They're fearful and tentative, not the bloodthirsty eyes of a feeder.

The man has a dark complexion with a bald, shiny scalp and long, lanky arms. His nose is bulbous and his eyebrows are barely visible. Despite his bald head, he doesn't look older than 40. Two gold pendants dangle from his neck. One is small and simple—an amplifier. The other is large and beautifully crafted. The symbols glitter in the shadows of the forest.

I stare in disbelief at the soul-anchor. My hand slowly lowers to my side. "You're a guardian?"

"I'm not." The man looks down at the soul-anchor and touches it gingerly. "It was my brother's, but he is dead. I am not bonded to it. It is useless to me. I wish to give it to your king. But first, we seek refuge. We are tired from a long journey."

Two more men slither out of the wreckage and climb to their feet. They wear blue uniforms with a white circle on the shoulder. They're definitely guard uniforms, but they're not Cavernic.

Klinton is stunned. He still hasn't moved an inch. "Where are you from?" he calls.

"Lycon," the man says. "We're the only survivors."

Chapter 6

Rose

Everyone stares as I move through the palace. They normally stare, but not like this. This is different. Perhaps it's a pity stare. It's common knowledge that Antai is in a coma. If people didn't know how we felt about each other, they definitely do now.

Or maybe it's a stare of unfamiliarity. I'm wearing my royal guard uniform, spotless and tantalizingly white. Few women attain the position of palace guard, and even fewer at my age. Their eyes move from my face to my uniform and back to my face again.

I don't let the stares discourage me. It's my first day as a royal guardsman. I would've started last week, but no one rushed me after what happened. I wasn't in the right mindset to protect anyone, but today, I think I'm finally ready.

Octavian is waiting for me in the palace courtyard. Gardeners and servants move through the pathways carrying trays and clipping hedges, but Octavian doesn't pay them any heed. He rubs his hands together as I approach. "Alright, princess, a few ground rules if I'm going to be your trainer. First, you will do as I say. When you are off-duty, you are my superior, but as long as you wear that uniform, you will obey me? Yes?"

"Yes, sir."

"Now, did you read the manual I gave you?"

"Yes, sir."

Octavian nods. "Good. Let's see how much you remember. How many guards must be stationed at the palace wall?"

"A minimum of ten patrolling the wall walk, and four stationed at the gate."

Octavian nods. "Very good. And what reason would a guard have to leave his post?"

I speak slowly, giving myself time to remember. "A guard must never leave their post unless they are replaced, their supervisor gives permission, or someone is in imminent danger... or to sound the alarm," I quickly add.

"Very good." Octavian smiles. "What do you do if you suspect a servant is an imposter?"

"Ask to see their papers?"

Octavian purses his lips. "And if they say they forgot?"

"Temporarily detain them."

"How many entrances does the palace have?"

"18, sir. The central hall has 6 entrances, and the Eastern, Western, and Royal Wings each have 4."

"How long is each shift for a royal guard?"

"A typical guard's shift is twelve hours, but royal guards must be extra aware. Our shifts are only 8 hours.

Octavian stops pacing. "Very good, princess. You read the manual well, I'm pleased. Now, this is how things will work for the next few weeks. The first hour of every shift will be spent training here in the courtyard. The remainder will be spent patrolling the palace. Yes?"

"Yes, sir."

"Good, let's move on. Here's your final test. Let's say you're stationed at the entrance of the Eastern Wing. Show me how you would stand?"

I place my feet shoulder-width apart and place my arms flat at my sides. "Like this."

Octavian frowns, puts his hand on the top of my head, and tilts it back until my chin is level. "Good." He proceeds to sit down in the grass. "Now, hold that position until the top of the hour."

"What? You've got to be kidding me?"

"I wish I was, but this is how you will be spending every day until you are promoted, possibly the rest of your career. Standing, watching, and being silent while you do it. When danger comes, you must be ready, but until then, you will stand at your post. Now, do as you're told."

I slap my hands to my sides and face forward. The position isn't particularly uncomfortable, but unbearably monotonous and mind-numbing.

"Your chin is drooping," Octavian barks. "Lift it up."

"This is ridiculous," I gripe. "Am I supposed to be guarding myself? God knows my grandpa doesn't need protecting."

Octavian pushes himself to his feet, stepping uncomfortably close. "You think you're the only thing worth protecting in the palace?"

I say nothing, realizing the implications of my complaint.

"Do you, princess? Don't you think the other civilians are valuable? Don't you think my son is worth protecting? Or my wife?"

"Of course! What I meant was—"

"And not just the people, what about the amulets? Don't you think the palace vault needs defending?" He sighs and rubs his head. "Hell, it almost got robbed only a week ago. And don't you think there are other secrets that need protection. I've been around long enough to know your Grandpa has quite the collection of secrets. If you don't defend those, who will?"

I think of the tiny slip of paper. My assassin killed Antai for that simple Adamic phrase. *Faza Le Bakanzah.* I can still remember it. Whatever it is, it needs protection, as does Antai. Anyone could walk in and end his life without a fight.

"I'm sorry, Octavian. I spoke without thinking."

He collapses back to the grass. "I've watched you grow up, princess. I've defended you with my life. I'm happy to say I've seen you grow into a fine young lady, but you have much to learn, starting with humility. Now, stand at attention!"

Once he's satisfied with my posture, Octavian lays back in the grass. He interlocks his fingers and places his makeshift pillow hands behind his head. "Let me tell you a little story about your grandfather. My first day as a royal guard, I made the mistake of locking my knees. Before the first hour, I fainted like a startled goat. When I woke up, someone was wiping my face with a cool washcloth. Not a servant, not a fellow guard, but your grandfather... the king himself! He used to say, 'A king is a servant to all.' You can't keep looking for ways to benefit as a princess; you need to start looking for how you can serve others."

I nod and straighten my back. A minute goes by, and then a few more. Just when my mind is beginning to wander, a young boy servant approaches.

"Are you the princess?" he squeaks.

"I am."

He bows. "The High Council requests your presence."

"What for?" I demand. *They already took my amulet. What else can they want?*

The boy glances timidly toward Octavian, as if no one else should hear.

"It's okay. You can tell us."

The boy steps closer and whispers. "Survivors have arrived. Survivors from Lycon."

As soon as everyone is seated, Grandpa stands. "If you haven't yet heard, several survivors have arrived in Cavernum. I wanted you all to be present as they give their report." He nods at one of the guards by the door. "Bring them in!"

The guards haul open the door, and a man enters. His bald head looks like polished leather. His face is narrow, adorned with a knobby nose. The man stops a few feet shy of Grandpa's throne and kneels, touching his forehead to the floor. "Commander Gideon Bousche of the Lycon guard, at your service." His words are flowery, with a soft nasal tone—French, if I'm not mistaken.

Grandpa stands up and shuffles forward extending both arms. "Gideon, my friend. I presumed you dead!" They embrace, clapping each other rhythmically on the back.

"Where are the others?" Grandpa asks.

"My comrades do not speak English. If it is permitted, I will be speaking for all three of us."

"Very well." Grandpa looks at him with tight lips and a strained smile. His eyes are creased with regret. "As King of Cavernum, and on behalf of the council, I welcome you and offer my deepest condolences."

Gideon bows again. "Thank you, my king." He steps timidly forward and falls to one knee. From his uniform, He pulls out the soul-anchor—a silver cube with one symbol on each of the center-most sides.

Next, Gideon removes a short Adamic blade from his belt. He lifts them on the flat of his palms, like a platter before the king. "These were recovered from my brother. They are a gift to you, my king."

Grandpa lifts the amulet by its chain. He inspects the Adamic bond on the back. "A well-crafted soul-anchor. The bonding spell seems simple enough." He sets the amulet on his lap next to the dagger. "I accept your gift. Thank you, Gideon. You may rise."

Grandpa takes a deep breath, setting the soul-anchor down on the table. "Gideon, would you share with us everything you remember about that night? I know this won't be pleasant for you, but your memories could prevent another tragedy."

Gideon bows a third time. "Of course, my king." He stands still for a moment as he organizes his thoughts. Finally, he clears his throat. "I was in the palace when it began. It was sometime before sunrise. I heard a loud explosion. It was very powerful. Unlike any dominion I've ever seen. I knew right away something terrible had happened. I ran to find my brother, but he was already waiting for me outside my chambers. That is when I heard the second explosion. I got to a window, and I could see the flames at the outer wall. They nearly reached the clouds."

Chancellor Gwenevere wrinkles her forehead. "What do you mean by explosion?"

"I felt the shockwave from the palace. It shook the ground like an earthquake. Then, came the noise. It was deafening. I wish I could explain more, but words cannot do it justice. The power was unearthly."

Gwenevere rolls her eyes. "Sooo, like a bomb?"

Grandpa doesn't even give Gwenevere the respect of eye contact. "The children of Cain have powerful technologies. They have bombs that can flatten cities, but even these devices should be useless against the binding properties of Adamic."

"Or maybe you're wrong," Gwenevere says. "At least, it would appear that way."

"Let the man finish," Zane grumbles.

Gideon continues. "We had just left the palace when there was another explosion. This one was very close. It happened on the other side of the palace. I could see the wall crumble. Stone was launched into the palace. The guards near the wall were all killed. That's when we decided to evacuate. We grabbed the horses from the stables and rode. A few other guards came with us."

Gideon takes a deep breath and releases it slowly. "The feeders were already at the inner wall when we got there. Dozens of them. Many of them had Adamic armor tattooed from head to toe. I killed as many as I could, but before long, we had to retreat."

General Kaynes cocks his head to the side. "Did I hear you right? You killed feeders... with Adamic armor?"

Gideon nods. "I am an archer. King Soltaire bestowed me with Adamic arrows. With them, I was able to kill many feeders, but as my arrows dwindled, we retreated to the outer wall. That is where I used my final arrow. We tried to flee, but a feeder gave chase. He, too, was armored."

Gideon waits for a reaction, but grandpa only nods. "Then, what happened?"

"Lucky for us, my brother had an Adamic blade, and he killed the feeder. We escaped, but my brother's injuries were grave. He died that night."

"And how did you make it to Cavernum?" Chancellor Quine asks.

"We rode on horseback a few days until we reached a city. Then, I drove us to the airport in Chambéry and we flew to America. I visited Cavernum years ago with King Saltaire. It took us longer than expected, but I managed to find the way."

Grandpa nods as if he remembers the visit. "I have a question for you. How much time passed between each explosion?"

Gideon doesn't have to give it much thought. "Only a few seconds, my King, maybe a minute at most. I hardly had time to leave the palace."

General Kaynes raises his eyebrows at Grandpa. "What are you thinking, your majesty?"

Grandpa scoots to the edge of his throne and sighs. "It's no secret that there's an adalit fighting against us. The only thing capable of overcoming an Adamic spell is Adamic itself. I'm wondering if one adalit had time to create each explosion, or if it was three separate individuals. I fear we might have multiple adalits working together—perhaps a master and his students." Grandpa turns his attention to Zane. "Does it sound the same as what you experienced in Hogrum?"

Zane frowns. "Exactly the same. Three separate explosions and a flood of feeders. There's no way to be certain, but I'd say we're dealing with the same guy."

Chancellor Bolo rubs his hands over his hairless head. The underarms of his robes are dark with sweat. "What are they after? Why would an adalit destroy a sanctuary? And why wait 18 years to do it again?"

At first, I think Grandpa is going to play dumb, but instead, he takes a deep breath. "I have no evidence, but I will share my theories with the council. The adalit believes there is a record hidden in Cavernum—The Book of Life. According to legend, this record would allow him to speak Adamic in its entirety. It would be the source of infinite power.

This adalit, I believe, also has influence among the equalists. He calls himself the Holy One. The laborers view him as a kind of savior. However, I believe he is much more sinister. His followers call him the Devil's Champion, the Lord of the Dead… the Demon King."

"This is blasphemy!" Gwenevere sneers. "The Holy One is nothing but a rumor—folklore to strike fear in our hearts. This self-proclaimed prophet is nothing but equalist propaganda."

Grandpa shakes his head. "I fear these threats are not unmerited. Demons overwhelmed Lycon just days before it's downfall. And barely two weeks ago, demons led the charge on this very palace. We captured one, and he acknowledged his loyalty to the Holy One. His followers say he's preparing for an attack. I fear it won't be long before history repeats itself."

"This is madness!" Chancellor Quine cries. "I won't believe this. I refuse to believe this."

"It's true," Zane growls. "Before Hogrum fell, I was charged with exterminating a demon uprising. They tried to infiltrate the High Council. Only after their plans failed were the walls destroyed. I'm afraid I agree with the king. The threat against Cavernum is urgent. The Holy One will attack; the only question is when. If the council has any sense, they'll take action before it's too late."

"And what type of action is recommended?" Gwenevere asks.

"We want to mobilize the guard," Grandpa declares. "We've managed to collect a rough sketch of the sewers from one of our spies. We know where they are hiding. If we take the offensive, we can overcome the equalists when they least expect it. Ideally, the Holy One as well."

"If we know where they are, why don't we just collapse the tunnel on the little bastards?" Chancellor Bolo blunders.

General Katu responds. "The caverns are large, Chancellor. Doing so would deface the surface of our city. Entire city blocks could sink into the holes we'd create. It is a risk we are not willing to take."

Gwenevere raps her knuckles on the table. "So... what's the plan?"

Grandpa looks to Zane. "General, you crafted much of the plan; would you mind elaborating?"

"Sure," Zane grunts. He stands and walks to the city map on the wall, pointing at various streets. "We have sewer entrances at each of these points. Each Commander and each captain will be thoroughly briefed on their specific tunnel route. According to our spies, their headquarters are located in a massive cavern. It's nearly the size of the dueling cavern beneath the royal plaza. It has half a dozen entrances and its own water source. We want to arrive simultaneously from each entrance and attack in unison. We suspect there will be demons and other threats, but the king will lead the charge. We anticipate a swift victory."

Chancellor Quine furrows his brow. "And when will this attack take place?"

"In two days' time," Grandpa says. "We are already in the process of briefing our commanders."

"Two days?" Gwenevere scoffs. "That will not be enough time to train the soldiers. The caverns are labyrinths, are they not? Our men will be lucky to make it out alive."

General Kaynes narrows his eyes at Chancellor Gwenevere. "You may be unaware, chancellor, but we are very concerned about traitors among the guard. The Holy One has ears all around Cavernum. One was even disguised as the princess's maid."

Eyes turn to me, and I look at the table. The thought of my assassin still makes me queasy.

"Now," Kaynes continues. "We are taking many precautions. Once briefed, the commanders will not be permitted to leave the palace until the attack commences. All other officers will be kept in the dark until the moment of the attack. They will be briefed by their commanders en route. If a spy is among their ranks, there won't be sufficient time to warn the Holy One. We will be victorious."

Grandpa nods, "Any last questions before we adjourn?"

I raise my hand. "You mentioned that commanders and captains would lead each district, but Antai is... still out of action. Who's going to lead his district?"

General Kaynes smiles. "My son, Quill has accepted the role of commander in Antai's temporary absence." He emphasizes the word temporary in a way that boils my blood.

I look at Grandpa in disbelief, but he only nods his head. "Captain Quill is more than qualified to lead in Antai's stead."

Zane gives me a sympathetic frown, but my frustration is insatiable. I remember the old woman he whipped in the flats. The way he would've killed her if I hadn't intervened. *Quill is nothing but a bully. He could never replace Antai!*

General Katu slowly raises his arm.

"Yes, General?" Grandpa asks.

General Katu motions at the Lycon survivor, who I had forgotten was still in the room. "Our friend Gideon has brought us another soul anchor. We have not discussed what we will do with it."

"Toss it in the vault," Bolo says. "Problem solved."

Zane shakes his head. "I wouldn't do that if I were you. The guard is well aware of the soul anchor. Rumors of the survivors are spreading among the ranks. They are waiting to hear what we do with the amulet. Every guardsman dreams of becoming a guardian. If they learn we've hidden it in the vault, they will not forgive us. Even more important, another guardian will protect Cavernum. Soul-anchors are our only defense against possession."

General Katu nods. "I couldn't agree more. Protection must be our first priority."

"And how do we choose this guardian?" Gwenevere asks.

"Forgive my boldness," General Kaynes says. "But I'd like to volunteer my son. He is, I believe, the only reasonable candidate. As my apprentice, he's already finished his law studies, and he has mastered nearly all aspects of dominion. General Zane has not yet selected an apprentice, and General Katu's apprentice is still in training. With Commander Elsborne out of commission, I believe Quill is our only reasonable choice."

Grandpa's face wrinkles in disagreement, but he says nothing. Zane looks like he's about to punch someone.

Gwenevere holds up her palm. "Let's slow down. Say we elect your son as guardian. I imagine you will then take another apprentice. At your death, you'll have directly elected two people to the council. Meanwhile, each of us will have only appointed one." She looks around. "I'm sorry, but does anyone else find that concerning?"

General Kaynes eases his lips into a smile. "Perhaps we can compromise. If my son is accepted as a guardian, my next apprentice could be a collective decision of the council. That way, each of us has equal representation."

Chancellor Quine furrows his brow. "We'll never agree on a single candidate. We may as well draw straws."

"What if we each pick a candidate and have them duel like in the old days?" Chancellor Bolo asks.

Zane shakes his head. "There's more to guardianship than dueling. If a new guardian is going to join the council, they need to be a leader and a thinker."

Grandpa suddenly smiles and sits up straight. "Perhaps we could do both. Anciently, each council member selected a single champion, who then dueled to the death. The lone survivor was accepted as the next guardian. They called it The Surviving, a competition of merit alone. It's a tad barbaric, but The Surviving was my father's inspiration for The Dividing. Perhaps, instead of a duel to the death, we could send our champions on a task of our own design. These tasks will reflect the duties of a guardsman, and thus, we will have a preview of their performance in the council. Failure to complete the tasks will result in disqualification. The tasks will continue until only a single champion remains."

Zane doesn't smile, but I can see he's pleased. "I approve. This way, the champions will be fighting for a purpose—killing feeders rather than each other."

"What kind of tasks will they perform?" General Katu asks.

Grandpa fiddles with his cane and closes his eyes for a moment. "We need to see how they act in real situations. How they solve problems. How they respond to danger. The specific tasks can be determined later—whatever the council needs completing. What matters is that we are in agreement. We will each choose one champion for The Surviving. The winner will become General Kaynes' apprentice."

When no one argues, Grandpa taps his cane on the floor. "All in favor?"

Eight hands rise in unison.

"Excellent. In one week, I will bond Quill Kaynes to his new soul anchor, and he will join us on the council. You will have until then to choose a champion."

Grandpa gives me a proud smile across the table. "If the council doesn't mind, I will be the first to announce my champion. I choose my granddaughter, Roselyn Malik."

Chapter 7

Matt

I groan as I climb the final step to the healing loft. I walk through the familiar curtain of beads and collapse onto one of the knee-high beds.

A healer girl is loitering by the wall. She takes one look at my uniform and moves to assist me. "Hello, lieutenant, how may I be of ser—"

"Don't worry, Amira, He's one of my regulars. I'll take it from here." Kendra strolls out of the side room and shoos away the other healer. "What is it this time? Another feeder bite?"

I smile. "I didn't let him bite me this time, but he did hit me with a tree trunk."

Her jaw falls open and her eyes widen with concern. "Wait, you're serious?"

I force a smile. "I told the feeder there was this girl I wanted to see, and all I needed was a quick trip to the healing loft. He was happy to oblige."

Kendra laughs, and if I'm not mistaken, the tips of her ears turn pink. "Funny. But seriously, Matt, what happened?"

I try to leave out as much detail as possible. "Well, I was visiting the communications bunker when I got attacked from behind. He really did hit me with a tree. When I fought back, he ran off. It only lasted a second. I'm fine except for some bruising."

"How big was the tree?" Kendra holds up her hands, suggesting sample sizes.

"It was about this big around." I make a circle with my hands about the size of a basketball.

Kendra winces. "And where did it hit you?"

"On the lower back. It pinned me to the ground for a bit, but like I said, it only lasted a few seconds. Any walking or bending hurts, but when I'm laying down on my stomach, it isn't too bad."

Kendra takes hold of her amulet. "How about you take off your shirt and lay on your stomach. Then, I'll assess the injury."

My heart starts racing. *My tattoos.* I'm already cringing inside for what I have to say. "Actually, is it alright if I keep my shirt on? I just don't feel comfortable without it."

"Bwuahh!" Familiar laughter erupts in the corner. Commander Noyen is lounging on one of the beds in the corner. This time, there isn't a healer attending to him. Either they just finished, or he's waiting to be treated.

Commander Noyen slaps his hand on his thigh. "A beautiful healer asks you to remove your shirt, and you refuse? Boy, what's wrong with you? You're a lieutenant now. No need to be shy."

Kendra clears her throat and raises her voice. "Commander Noyen, if you'll please leave us be, I'd like to focus on my patient undisturbed."

Commander Noyen laughs and climbs to his feet. "Very well." He gives me one last look. "Be a man and ask her out already." Before Kendra can scold him, he chuckles and disappears through the curtain of beads.

Kendra groans. "I'm sorry about that, Matt. Commander Noyen just loves to push my buttons."

I'm still watching the swaying beads that he left through. "What's wrong with him? I didn't see any injuries."

"It's internal," Kendra says. "But I'm not supposed to talk about the other patients. If you ask him, I'm sure he'd be happy to tell you."

"He has kidney failure," another healer interjects.

"Amira, we're not supposed to talk about other patients."

Amira shrugs her shoulders. "Like everyone doesn't know? Besides, that man is in everyone's business. He doesn't deserve confidentiality."

Kendra sighs. "It's true. He has lupus. His immune system is attacking his kidneys, and he has to come in every other day for dialysis."

"He's lucky he has you guys," I say as I lower myself onto my stomach.

Kendra nods, already distracted by the task at hand. "Are you already wearing an amplifier?" Kendra asks.

"Yeah, it's tucked in my uniform."

"Perfect. If you could close your eyes and think about allowing me access to your body, I can begin."

I close my eyes as Kendra's hands drift across my back like a feather duster, sending chills down my spine. I peek a glimpse and see her jaw tighten. Her neck is long, and the tendons bulge with strain. I follow the tendons to her collarbone before I manage to avert my eyes.

"Suddenly, she lifts her hands. "Well, I'm afraid I have bad news. We're going to have to amputate from the waist down."

"Wow, that bad?" I hold a straight face.

Kendra's cheeks puff, and then she laughs, her golden hair falling in her face. "Fine. You have two broken ribs, and some internal bruising, but I'll have you fixed up in no time."

I let myself sigh. "You had me for a second. I was about to run for it."

Kendra smiles, a friendly flash of white. She puts both hands on my side. "Just relax. You might feel some discomfort. I need to hold the bones together while I repair them."

"Ugh!" I groan as she leans on my side without warning. Then, she closes her eyes. I feel a tingling sensation that borders discomfort, like a hundred tiny needles poking me in the side.

"How does it work?" I ask. "I'd love to learn what you're doing."

Kendra keeps her eyes closed, speaking slowly. "As a healer, I don't repair the bone myself. I merely help your body do what it's made to do. You have specialized cells called osteoblasts. They're responsible for building bone. All I'm doing is directing these cells to the location of the injury. I want the concentration of those cells to be a hundred times the normal level. Then, I'm increasing the rate of reaction."

The tingling intensified until it's almost ticklish. My breathing grows ragged as I try not to squirm.

"Almost done," Kendra says. The weight of her hands is no longer painful. Slowly, the tingling fades. My ribs are left with nothing but a soothing warmth. Once again, I'm in awe.

Kendra stands. "Stay laying down for the next hour, healer's order. Your cells will continue to heal at an accelerated rate until the blastocysts diffuse throughout the bone."

She turns to leave but stops. "Can I ask you a question, Matt?"

"Sure. Ask away."

She squats next to me so that our faces are at eye-level. "Do you have nightmares? About feeders specifically?"

"Ummm..." The question takes me by surprise. I shift on the bed. "Yeah, sometimes. Why?"

"Well, I'm specializing in healing the mind. Guardsmen often have nightmares after a trauma like you've experienced."

"PTSD," I say.

Kendra nods. "I'm developing a method to treat it. If you'd like. I can try it on you. There's very little risk, and the results have been very promising."

"Okay. How does it work?"

Kendra's face brightens as she explains. "In the brain, there is a region for memories and a region for emotions. Normally, these two regions have a weak connection. Thinking of something sad in your childhood might make you a little sad, but you won't be bawling like you were as a child. However, with traumatic memories, the connection is strong. The memory of the trauma can bring back all the fear, as powerfully as you first experienced them. All I'm going to do is weaken this connection. You'll still have the memory, but you won't feel the same panic."

I'm about to say yes when I remember the feeder I possessed. *She can't find out!*

"To do this, will you need to see my memories?" I ask.

Kendra holds up her palms like a scale and tips them side to side. "Yes, but just that specific memory. You have complete privacy of your own mind. As a healer, I can only view memories you specifically give me access to. The rest of your memories will remain private."

I breathe in through my teeth. "It's not that I don't trust you, Kendra. It's just that I'm not ready to share those memories. I'd prefer if we didn't for now."

"Of course," Kendra rambles. "I completely understand. That's entirely your choice. Don't worry about it."

"Out of curiosity," I say. "Could you alter memories if you wanted to? Take them out or put them in?"

Kendra frowns, disturbed by the thought. "Memories are complicated. They invoke a network of different connections in the brain. But with enough practice, I suppose it's possible." She looks at me, her suspicious eyes nothing but a sliver of green. "Why do you ask?"

"Oh, no reason, I just find the concept interesting."

Kendra relaxes. "It's certainly interesting. Is there anything else I can do for you, Matt?"

I look around the room. No one is looking my way. No one seems to be listening. I prop myself on my elbows so that my head is a bit higher. Then, I muster my courage and ask. "Kendra, will you teach me to heal?"

Kendra looks around the room as well. After a brief pause, she leans in close. "I'll consider it, on one condition. If you teach me to fight. I want to learn elemental dominion."

I smile. "Deal!"

Kendra stands. "Excellent. Well, I wish you the best, Matt. Rest up, and you should be ready for your mission tomorrow night."

"My what?"

"Oh, they haven't told you yet?"

I shake my head. "Told me what?"

"Madame Xantone told every healer that we need to be on call tomorrow night. She said the guard will be launching an attack. It must be dangerous if she needs every healer standing by. I figured they would've told you already."

I shake my head. "No, I haven't heard anything."

"Hmmm." Kendra glances around the room once more. "Well, maybe I shouldn't have mentioned it." She flashes a nervous smile.

I pretend to be disinterested. "Whatever it is, I'm sure they'll tell me soon."

Kendra nods, backing away as she speaks. "Well, rest up, and I look forward to hearing from you. Stay safe."

"Thanks, I'll see you soon," I call as she disappears into the back room.

But I can only think of one thing.

Diego! I have to warn Diego.

The clock above my doorway reads 10:07 pm. The sun set nearly two hours ago, but I can't sleep. I pace back and forth in my guard uniform. My plan is more of a suicide mission. I'm not on duty. I have no amulet—no way to read minds—but I have to try. If I don't, Diego will die.

I could try to warn him tomorrow, but he'll be in the fields all day. I could leave a message with Isabela, but there's a possibility she won't be home either. I definitely wouldn't trust Abuela with a message. The only way to be sure is to go at night.

I take a deep breath and turn the handle slowly. Once in the hallway, I avoid the urge to creep. I walk as if I belong, head held high and hands in my pockets. Small torches hang from the wall every ten paces, like fiery nightlights.

I turn the corner and nearly run into a boy. He's dressed in a long white nightgown. His hair is as red as the torches, and his eyes a pale blue. He looks no older than 12.

"Pardon me, sir. I'm on nightly errands for my master." He scuttled around me, carrying a platter with a glass of water, and tiptoes down the hall.

I smile. *This just might work.*

As I exit the Central Staircase, a guard holds up his hand. "Halt. Name and business."

"Lieutenant Matthew MacArthur. I sent my servant for a glass of water ten minutes ago." I lace my voice with disdain. "The little bastard isn't in the Eastern Wing. I'm going to check the central kitchen and demand what's keeping him."

The guard sighs. "Very well, but be swift. And wait till morning to punish him. I don't want any of the residents awoken."

"Yes, sir. This shouldn't take long." I barrel onward toward the kitchens. I don't look back until I'm out of view. The next guard I pass doesn't say a word. He looks like he's on the verge of sleep.

Once in the palace kitchen, I unlock a side door to the courtyard and slip into the night. Once again, I try to walk proudly. The courtyard is dark, as are the surrounding garden, but should I be spotted, I must look as though I belong.

I'm almost to the palace gate. This will be the hardest part. I count four guards at the archway. One is leaning against the wall. The other three are rolling dice on the ground and laughing. I spot a bottle on the floor and hope it's ale. I'll need their judgment to be as impaired as possible.

I rehearse my plan one more time before approaching the gate with an eager smile.

The man against the wall sees me first. He moves to block my path, hand in his holster. "Who goes there?"

"Matthew MacAuther, sir."

"And what is your business at the wall?" The man has an elongated nose, and a disproportionately large forehead, like a live-action version of Squidward.

"I uhhh…" I bite my lip and look at the floor. "You see… I…"

"Spit it out," Squidward demands. "What's your business?"

"Well, my girlfriend lives in the core. Today, she said if I could come over tonight, that we could… you know… we could spend some alone time together." I look to the gambling group of guards and bounce my eyebrows twice.

"Spend time how?" Squidward asks. Like the real Squidward, his voice is devoid of amusement.

"He wants to bed her!" One of the gambling men roars, gyrating his hips.

"That's as noble a cause as any," another guard laughs. "I say let the boy pass."

Squidward narrows his eyes at me. "If you wanted to bed this girl, why not stay at her house before sundown? Why sneak out in the middle of the night?"

"Her mother hates me, sir. I'm not afraid of feeders, but this woman would kill me if she knew. I have to be out of the house before sunrise. Please, sir. If I don't meet her tonight, she might change her mind. I promise I won't take too long. She lives right over there past the plaza."

Squidward purses his lips and frowns.

"Oh, come on!" the gambling guard calls. "He's a guardsman. We've got to look out for each other. Let the boy have his fun. Tonight, he becomes a man!"

"Aye!" The other men cheer.

"Fine," Squidward says. "Just don't dilly dally. I don't want to be waiting long. If you're not back within two hours, I'll have no choice but to report you."

"You got it, sir. No cuddling for me, sir. I'll be back before you know it."

"Aye!" the other guards cheer. "Bed her well!"

I take off into the plaza, running as if I just can't wait. As soon as my back is to the guards, my smile disappears. *I can't believe that worked!* Now, I just have to make it to the ring.

The core is quiet as usual. The only movement I see is mice chirping in the gutters. A stray cat crosses the street, pausing to watch me wander past. A few guards see me, but they don't question my motives. In the ring, my uniform matches theirs. For all they know, I'm on duty.

Finally, I cross through the inner wall and into the ring. I'm not far now. Left. Right. Left. Right. I jog down one last alley and stop at the top of the steps—Diego's steps.

I can't see any light through the cracks of the front door. They've likely been asleep for hours. If they're smart, they won't answer the door at night, but I need them to. I have to warn Diego.

I cringe as my knuckles thud against the door. Tunk, tunk, tunk. Chains jingle as the door sways loosely in its frame, but no one comes to answer.

Please, answer the door. Please!

I knock again and hold my breath, listening to the silence of the night. I don't hear any movement on the other side of the door. I don't see the spark of a match or the glow of a candle. If they can hear me knocking, they're choosing to ignore me.

"Diego," I whisper into the door. "It's me, Matt. Open up. I have to tell you something important."

Silence. I knock one last time. Then, I pull out the note. It's my backup plan—a simple letter without a signature. It only says a few words.

There will be an attack on the equalists. Soon.
Stay at home if you want to live.
Sincerely,
A friend

I slip the note through the door and let it fall. Then, I turn to leave.

Clink, cachink.

The rustle of chains tickles my ear. I spin around as the door swings inward. Diego lurks in the doorway, just out of reach of the moonlight. "Leave." He throws the folded note at my feet. "I don't want your stupid paper." He starts to close the door.

"Wait, Diego!" I scoop up the letter and hold it out to him. "I have to tell you something important. Just read the lett—"

"I said leave!" His voice is a low hiss, nothing but hatred. The same voice he used to question his mother's kidnapper. "Leave and don't come back. I don't want to hear another word." He glanced at the upper apartments in the alley, no doubt wondering who is listening to the conversation.

"Diego, You don't understand. I'm trying to s—"

"LEAVE!"

The air ripples in front of me, and the next thing I know, my back collides with the concrete steps. My head strikes the corner of a step, and all I see is a strobe light of white and black.

When my vision clears, I see Diego tearing the note into tiny pieces. "If I see you again, I'll kill you. On my father's grave, I swear I'll kill you."

Then, the door slams shut.

My mind is spinning. *Diego used dominion on me! Diego has an amplifier!* I don't know how he got it, but I know he didn't get it from the guard.

By the time I stand, I hear voices. The soft glimmer of candles seeps through a second-floor window. The voice of a boy penetrates the glass. "Dad, there's a man."

"Shhh. Quiet," a deeper voice responds.

I climb to my feet and run. There's nothing I can do for him now.

Diego is on his own.

The clock reads 12:22 am. I'm safe in my bed, but I only feel worse. Diego didn't listen. When the guard attacks tomorrow night, Diego will die. He'll be shot on the battlefield or hung at the gallows.

Diego will die!

And then there was his threat. *I'll kill you.* What if he actually does? What if I'm dead before he is? The more I think about it, the worse I feel.

What would Judy say? I have only guesses. *You tried your very best, Matthew. Now, get your sleep. You need a clear head tomorrow if you wish to save your friend.*

I squeeze my eyes shut, hoping my brain will take the hint. My heart thuds in my chest like a war drum. Dum dum, dum dum.

Finally, I can't take it. I kick off my blanket and grab the cup off my desk. I down the sleeping tonic in a few quick gulps and hop back in bed. I cocoon myself in my blankets once more and wait.

Dum-dum... Dum-dum.

I focus on my heartbeat and try to slow my breathing. Time ticks on. One minute. Five minutes.

Dum-dum... Dum-dum.

The room is peaceful, and I don't hear a sound other than the blood rushing through my ears. It's almost as if time is frozen, and I'm the only one aware at this obscure hour of the night. The isolation is almost soothing. No one can reach me and no one else matters. Finally, I can relax.

My heartbeat!

It's gone. I can no longer feel the drum in my chest. Just as last night, the physical world has vanished from my senses. I can only sense things on a spiritual level.

Amazing!

I'm asleep, yet I'm awake. I don't know what to do, so I urge my soul onward. I can only sense the space of my wingspan—about six feet across—but it's enough to find my way around. I may as well explore.

My soul drifts through the palace, taking careful notes of how to return to my body. Now that I know what's happening, I no longer feel afraid of soul-travel. I drift through a library and into another hallway, this one unfamiliar.

The Royal Wing?

It's the only part of the palace that I'm forbidden to enter. I urge my soul onward. Drifting from room to room. I sense people sleeping, mostly servants from what I can tell. Their rooms are small—even smaller than mine.

Then, I emerge in a wide-open space. For a moment, all I sense is air, and then I find a massive wooden frame—a bed. I can sense a body on the bed, tossing and turning in their sleep. The soul inside it is familiar. I've only sensed it once, during my final duel.

Lynn!

I'm about to turn away, but something catches my attention. The emotions are raw and unfiltered. Fear. Urgency. Desperation. I find myself being drawn closer. If the princess is in danger, I need to help her.

I let my soul drift towards the source of the emotions, directly inside her head.

Chapter 8

Rose

I linger by my mirror, searching for a reason not to retire to bed. I've already gone to the restroom, written in my journal, and changed my pajamas twice. I'm out of excuses.

"Shall I put out the candles, m'lady?" Wendy asks.

"Yes, thank you, Wendy. All but one, please. I like to leave a candle burning."

Wendy doesn't question it. Her own sister had a fear of the dark. She licks her index finger and pinches the candle wick with her thumb.

"Doesn't that burn? Why not just blow?"

Wendy looks at the floor. "It's how I was taught, m'lady. It doesn't burn, and it preserves the wick longer. Less smoke too."

"Oh, I didn't know that. How clever."

Wendy says nothing. There's an awkward pause that seems to drag on forever.

"Do you think he deserves it?" She finally asks.

"Who?"

"Judge Lumb?" Wendy says. "When he decided to take away my baby, I prayed he would die. I thought he deserved it, but now I'm not so sure. He has a daughter. Why would God kill him?"

I clench my fist. "Whoever the Holy One is, they aren't God. They claim to be God's servant, but all they do is kill. The Holy One destroyed Lycon. They killed thousands of people. God would never do that."

Wendy falls silent, hugging her belly. I can see her concern.

"But don't worry. We're safe here," I add. "We have the safest room in the whole sanctuary." I motion towards the door, a small gold lock is embedded in the oak. An inscription gleams in the candlelight.

"Our quarters are sealed with an Adamic spell. Your door is as well. Nothing can get in here without the key, and my grandpa and I are the only ones with copies."

Wendy relaxes her shoulders. "Thank you, M'lady. That is comforting to know."

"Of course. I'll keep the maid's door unlocked during the night, so if I call for you, you can come in or vice versa. Don't be afraid to ask if you need anything."

As my maid, Wendy's room is the one directly next to mine. There's a small maid's door which connects our two rooms. This way, Wendy has access without passing through the main hall.

Wendy bows. "That's very kind of you. Thank you, M'lady."

"You don't have to call me that. My last maid called me princess. Rose is fine too."

"But the maid's keep said—"

I hold up my hand. "Rose or princess, please. You're my maid, so my word is final."

"Yes, princess."

I smile. "Thank you, Wendy. Feel free to retire to your chambers. I'm not in need of anything, and I don't want to keep you up."

Wendy hesitates. "M'la—" she stops mid-word. "Princess," she corrects, "Do you pray before bed?"

"Pray?"

"Pardon me, princess." Wendy looks to the floor. "My mother prayed nightly with us. I thought perhaps you did the same."

"I don't usually pray, but if you'd like to, I'd be happy to join you."

"Okay. I would like that, princess." She lowers herself to her knees next to my bed and waits for me to do the same. Then, she presses her palms together and closes her eyes. When she speaks, the volume of her voice startles me.

"Hello, God. It's me and the princess speaking to you from the palace. I would like to give my thanks for her, and her kind invitation. Please put a blessing on her to protect her in the night. May her dreams be pure and peaceful. And please bless the Commander Elsborne that he may wake up. Amen."

"Amen." As we sit back on the bed, I look over at Wendy, trying to hide my newfound fondness. "How do you know about my dreams? I've never mentioned them to anybody?"

Wendy looks away. "Last night, you were screaming, princess, for nearly half the night. I didn't know what to do."

"Oh…I didn't know… I'm sorry, Wendy." It's my turn to look down in embarrassment. "If I'm ever keeping you up, please wake me. I don't wish to disturb you."

"I don't mind, princess." Wendy's voice grows almost inaudible. She clutches her belly. "After what happened, I had nightmares for a long time." She looks away. "Ever since Velma died, they've come back. I always felt safe when she was around." She smiles weakly, pinching the fibers of my rug with her bare feet. "Anyway, a prayer always helped me. I hope they help you too." She stands. "Goodnight, princess. I'll let you sleep now."

"Thank you, Wendy, and goodnight." I climb into bed as she closes the maid's door behind her. Then, I lie still, waiting for sleep to come. *Please, don't let it be a sleepless night.*

I feel like bait, waiting in my trap of a bed for my monster of a dream to devour me alive. Each minute feels like a small eternity. When sleep finally finds me, it catches me by surprise.

Suddenly, I'm in the hallway outside my grandfather's study with no recollection of how I got here. Nevela is running in front of me. She's almost to my grandpa's study now. In my mind, the facts are already clear. She's trying to steal from the inheritance box.

"Stop!" I scream. There's a gun in my hand, and I aim it at Nevela's chest. "I know who you are," I stammer. "You're not Nevela. You're wearing the morph mask. Your name is Jack!"

Nevela stops in her tracks and raises both hands in the air. "Rose, I swear it's me. Just trust me. You can trust me. I know you'd never do anything to hurt me." She takes a step toward me.

"Don't make me kill you, Jack. Take another step, and I shoot." My hand is now trembling. If she wasn't so close, I wouldn't trust my aim.

Nevela smiles wider. "You won't hurt me, Rose. You could never hurt me." She's almost to me now. Another step, and she'll be able to reach my gun. I act before she can. I close my eyes and pull the trigger.

BANG!

Nevela collapses at my feet. "Rose...why?" Her mouth is stained red with the blood of her lungs. "I trusted you," she cries. Then, her head slumps.

Ever so slowly, I reach down and feel along the edge of her jaw. I'm hoping to feel the edge of a mask—the cool metal surface to confirm my suspicions, but it isn't there. I find nothing but Nevela's soft skin.

"No!" I feel again, up and down her jaw. I scrape with my nails, but they sink into nothing but flesh. "Nevela! No! No! HELP!" I scream, but no servants rush to my aid. "Nevela! I didn't mean to. I thought you were someone else. Please don't die!"

"You can't save her." A rich Australian accent whispers in my ear, sending icy spiders crawling down my spine. I don't have to see him to know it's my assassin.

105

I turn around, my finger tightening on the trigger. "You'll die for that!" I hiss.

Jack raises his hands, a subtle smirk telling me he isn't scared. "Now, Rose, don't go doing something you'll regret. I'm not your enemy. Believe me."

Only I don't believe him. I hate him! Because of him, I've shot my two best friends. *He deserves to die.*

Bang!

The gun lurches in my hand as Jack staggers back. "Rose, it's me." He falls to the floor, his right hand reaching for his face. Then, he falls still.

It's me?

Why would Jack say that? Why would those be his dying words?

Uncertainty eats me from the inside as I creep closer. When I'm sure he can't attack me, I kneel next to his ear. I reach under his chin and feel for a ridge of any kind.

To my horror, I find one.

As I lift the morph mask, I catch a glimpse of Antai's complexion.

No!

Adrenaline courses through me as I toss the mask onto the tile, applying pressure to his wound. "HELP! SOMEONE HELP US!" I maintain pressure as I hold my breath.

No one comes to help us.

"It's alright, Antai. We'll get you to a healer. It's not lethal. I'll be right back with a healer. Hang in there."

I'm about to make a dash for it when his eyes flutter open. "Rose!"

"It's me, Antai! It's Rose." I lean over his head so he can look into my eyes. "I'm here. You're going to be okay."

"Rose, promise me you'll do what I ask."

"Of course. Anything."

"Kill me!"

For a moment, the words don't register. I must've misheard. "W-what?"

"Kill me," Antai pleads. Despite the bullet in his chest, his words are strong and unmistakable. "Shoot me. End it. I want to die."

"No! No, I won't! You're going to live."

"Please!" Antai flares his nostrils. "I can't take it any longer. I'm going insane. Kill me. Please!"

Going insane? "I... I don't understand."

Suddenly, Antai's eyes roll back in his head. His head lolls to the side, but his chest continues to rise to the rhythm of life.

That's when I feel it. Like a window is being opened in the back of my skull and I can feel the draft blowing through. When I think it can't get worse, a person crawls through, making their way deeper inside my mind. The closer they get, the more of them I can sense.

Antai?

I'm sorry, Rose.

My body goes rigid as Antai takes control. Already, my arm is moving, pointing the pistol at Antai's face.

"Antai! What are you doing?" He's possessed me, and he's trying to kill himself. It makes no sense, but I don't have time for rationality.

This is what I want. It'll only take a second.

Antai presses my finger against the trigger. I can't stop it. All I can do is scream!

"Nooooooo!—"

"Lynn!"

Like the rumble of thunder, the name reverberates through my entire being and shakes me to the core.

"Matt?"

I blink and he's there, dressed in full uniform. He looks around wildly, confused by the scene. Intentional or not, he's blocking my shot at Antai's body.

Once he's assessed the scene, Matt holds up his hands and takes a step closer. "It's okay, Lynn. Just put down the gun." His body emanates emotion—gentleness and concern.

I try to spread my fingers, but Antai still has control. The gun now aims at Matt's heart.

I feel the tears building on my lashes, spilling over as I blink. "I can't. I'm sorry, Matt. I can't stop it."

I pull the trigger.

BANG!

I expect Matt to scream—to fall to the floor as he bleeds out— but instead, he only smiles. He holds out his fist and unfurls his fingers. A mangled wad of lead sits motionless in his palm.

The bullet!

"But… how did you? You're not even wearing an amulet?" I look at Antai's body, still breathing on the floor. Bewildered, I look back at Matt. "You're… you're okay?"

"I'm fine. Everything's going to be fine. It's all in your head." Matt takes a step closer and touches my hand. A wave of warmth washes over me, expelling Antai's hold. The fear that clouds my mind begins to dissipate. Then, Matt pulls me into a hug. The feeling is unlike any I've felt before. My skin swells with serenity. I feel weightless and calm. An overwhelming sense of safety slows my thoughts.

I killed Nevela! I shot Antai! I don't say it, but Matt understands.

"No. It's just a dream. Everyone will be okay. It's not real. Everything is going to be fine." He waits until my mind is calm before taking a step back. "I shouldn't stay, but you'll be alright." He smiles, regretfully. "Have a good night, princess."

Just like that, he's gone. The air around me grows darker until all I see is black.

My eyes flutter open, and I find myself tangled in my silk sheets. The feeling of peace still lingers. *It was just a dream. Thank God, it was just a dream.*

"Are you alright, princess?"

I jerk upright in my bed. "Oh, God. Wendy, you scared me." She stands like a scarecrow at the foot of my bed, her blanket draped around her like a cloak.

"You were screaming, princess. I was going to wake you, but... then you stopped." Her voice is mild, almost completely unaffected.

"I'm sorry, Wendy. I was having a nightmare, but it passed." I think of Antai trying to kill himself and Matt's sudden arrival. I remember the overwhelming sense of security. *What a strange dream indeed.*

Wendy sits on the edge of my bed. "Was it about Antai again?"

I sit up. "Yes, but this time it felt different. More vivid. I don't know how to describe it." *It almost felt real.*

"Who's Nevela?"

"What?"

"Nevela," Wendy repeats. "You said her name a few times."

I nod, replaying the dream in my head. "In my dream, I'm often killing someone I love. Usually it's Antai, but this time it was her as well."

"Can I ask what happened to her, why she's no longer your maid?"

"She was kidnapped." The words leave my lips with surprising ease. I wait for Wendy to gasp but if she's surprised, she hides it well. She simply nods, waiting for me to elaborate.

"I wouldn't want to bore you with the details. It's a complicated situation."

Wendy lifts her legs onto my bed and wraps her blanket around them. "I have all night."

I sigh. "She was kidnapped. Supposedly, the equalists have her." I feel my heart rate beginning to rise. "Tomorrow night, there is supposed to be a tunnel raid on the equalist headquarters, but I'm going to be stuck in the palace. I should be out looking for her. I was supposed to keep her safe. There's so much that could go wrong. What if one of the soldiers thinks she's an equalist? What if they kill her by mistake? She's only there because of me. I feel like I have to do something."

Never does Wendy break eye contact as I ramble. She watches intently, her gentle brown eyes soothing my worried soul. "Is there someone you can trust to watch out for her? Someone who will be on the mission?"

"I would trust Antai, but that's off the table. My trainer, Octavian, maybe." *Matt.* I think, but I haven't spoken to him in nearly a week.

"And what about the king? He'll be there won't he?"

I bite my lip. "He will but... he'll be distracted with the Holy One. Besides, he's been keeping secrets from me lately. He has motives I don't yet understand. I—" I catch myself. "I'm sorry, Wendy. I don't want to burden you with my anxieties."

Wendy responds with a twitch of a grin. "In all honesty, princess, I don't mind at all." She smiles wider, glancing down at my bed. "Hearing that the princess has problems makes me feel better about my own."

"Is that so?" I laugh. "Very well then. I fear the king is keeping secrets from me, which some might say is to be expected, but how am I expected to be queen if I can't know the secrets of the throne?"

"I'm sorry, that must be tough," Wendy says.

I nod, but in truth, it's not that tough at all, not compared to what Nevela must be going through. I think of her battered body lying on the cold, hard floor of a dark, cruel prison, wondering if each day will be her last. She deserves better. Cavernum deserves better.

I'm not so sure if it's guilt or love that is guiding me. "She was taken because of me," I say. "I won't leave her to die. I owe her that much."

Wendy purses her lip, and I think I see admiration in her cinnamon-brown eyes.

"I'm going," I say the words aloud before I can back out.

Wendy's eyes expand. "But... what if you get caught? You'll be whipped!"

That's the thing, I wouldn't be whipped. I'd get a slap on the wrist, maybe a week's suspension. Even if I got expelled, I could probably convince the orchestra to take me. Life would go on. My social standing is almost immune to misconduct, but I can't admit that to Wendy.

"I'll be fine," I say. "It'll be dark and we'll be underground. Maybe they won't recognize me. I got away with it last time, didn't I?"

Wendy frowns. "All due respect, princess, but won't someone recognize you? I don't want to see you get in trouble."

I sigh. As much as I hate to admit it, Wendy is right. This isn't like The Dividing. These will be commanders and guardians. God knows, Grandpa will spot me from a mile away. And if by some miracle he doesn't, Zane or someone else will.

"What if I do something drastic?" I say. "I can cut off all my hair. I can dye it too. I'd look like a totally different person.

That's it! How did I not think of it earlier? It was staring me in the face.

Before Wendy can respond, I jump to my feet. "Wendy, I have a plan, and I need your help."

"Of course, princess. Whatever you need."

I smile. "We're going to steal something from the king."

My hand shakes as I start the final symbol. I press my graver into my medium, a crude plank of gold no larger than my forearm. To resemble a knife, it's been flattened and shaped to a point.

I begin at the center of the symbol and drag my pick in the half spiral. While the Adamic lantern spell demanded careful coordination and seamless movements, this spell is much more complex in nature. Each step must be in the correct order and fashion, like an elaborate game of connecting the dots.

An elegant Adamic long sword, which nearly spans the entire length of the table, is my reference. I glance at the symbols between every stroke.

⚡⚔🜚◉

I finish the spell and angle the knife so that it catches the light from the window.

"How'd I do, Grandpa?"

He leans over and inspects the marking. He points at the first symbol. "The piercing spell needs to be straighter. The spaces between each point should run parallel." He slides his finger to the third symbol. "Also, you need to start at the tip of the scythe and work backwards. The center cross is the last element for that symbol. Remember that."

"So, you don't think it'll work."

Grandpa slides a piece of paper forward. It has the impenetrable spell zigzagging across it.

"Go ahead," he says. "Give a try."

I take the golden knife in my fist and swing it down at the paper. Upon impact, my fingers almost slip from the handle, and the force jars my shoulder joint. When I hold up the knife, the first two inches of the golden tip are bent at an odd angle. Yet miraculously, the gold foil is utterly undented.

"That's a great start. Much better than I did my first time. Perhaps you're ready to learn the method."

"The method?"

Adamic blades are created with a special method. You see, most amulets are made with soft metals: gold, silver, brass. These metals can be etched by hand. However, Adamic blades, to truly be worthy of battle, are smithed from hardened steel. To etch this steel by hand,

and to do so accurately, is nearly impossible. My father taught me a different method using acid."

"Acid?" I echo.

Grandpa nods. "Acid has the power to dissolve steel, slowly granted, but enough to leave an indent. The key is to limit the acid's effect to only the Adamic symbols."

"Sounds complicated," I say.

"It's a fair amount of prep work, yes, but I've already done it." Grandpa bends over and reaches underneath the table. With a grunt, he hoists a small plastic tub of a thick orange substance. "Bee's wax," Grandpa laughs at my puzzled complexion. "It protects the steel from the acid." He scoops an apple-sized glob of the orange goop and slathers it up and down the blade. Then, he lays out several wooden tools resembling chopsticks of various widths. On the tips, they come to a flattened point, resembling a chisel.

Grandpa holds one in the air so I can see. "They're wood because they only need to work the wax. The wax provides a barrier from the acid. Your job is to scale away the wax where the symbols will be. Once the symbols are etched into the wax, you only need to dip the blade in the acid. As the acid transfers the symbols to the metal, the spell is transferred as well."

"That's incredible."

Grandpa begins working away at the waxy blade. His hands, normally shaky, are perfectly meticulous. In a matter of minutes, the silver characters are visible, brightly contrasting the surrounding orange seal.

"The acid takes about a quarter-hour to run its course. Do you have any questions for me?"

"I have a question. I've been thinking a lot about the spells Titan spoke... the verbal ones. The spell he used to burn my assassin, it was short. I think I still remember it."

Havaknah Ra.

Grandpa suddenly sits up straight, his voice like the sharpening of steel. "Listen to me very carefully, Rose. The spoken language is not to be trifled with. We do not know the intricacies of controlling such spells. Titan clearly has some experience, but we do not know what other elements are involved in a spoken spell. Should you attempt it, you might accidentally burn your own body to ashes. Do you see how that would worry me?"

"I just... It could be a powerful weapon is all. I tried to speak the spell that was hidden in our inheritance box, and nothing happened."

Grandpa raises an unkempt eyebrow at me. "You spoke the spell out loud? Interesting."

"I probably just pronounced it wrong."

"Perhaps. Or perhaps the spell was inapplicable. Say the spell was designed to wake someone from slumber. If you use the spell when no one is sleeping, it becomes inept. It's very possible you said the spell perfectly. I suppose we'll never kn—"

Tap. Tap. Tap.

"Hmmm, who could that be." Grandpa shuffles to the door and lifts the deadbolt. Wendy is apologizing before the door is fully open.

"I'm sorry to bother you, your highness, but I was walking down the hallway and a man stopped me, and he wanted me to send you a message that he needs to speak with you immediately, and he says he'll be waiting at the base of the tower."

"Slow down, my dear. Slow down. Who was the one who sent this message?"

"I..." Wendy starts. "I think he said his name, but I don't remember. He had a brown beard and he wore a black cloak."

Grandpa frowns. "You realize you described half the palace." He takes a deep breath to compose himself. "No matter. I'll find out soon enough. At which tower did he say he'd be waiting?"

Wendy's mouth falls open. "I uhh... I'm not sure. I didn't know there were multiple towers. I'm sorry, my king. I'm no good at this."

I can't help but smile. She delivered every line perfectly, and I know Grandpa will have pity on her. How could he not? She appears to be nothing but a nervous, rambling child.

"Fear not, my dear." Grandpa touches her lightly on the shoulder. "Come, we'll get to the bottom of this together." He turns his head like an owl until he's almost looking back at me. "I'll be back in a moment, Rose, practice carving in the wax."

"Yes, Grandpa."

I wait until I can no longer hear their footsteps, and then I leap to action. I don't know how long it'll be until they return. I head straight for the inheritance box perched upon grandpa's bookshelf. At my touch, the box radiates heat, a telltale signal that it's now unlocked. I swing open the lid, and sure enough, a brilliant silver mask is nuzzled inside.

I take it in my hands. This part, I've thought a great deal about. The easiest way to sneak it out, I've decided, is to wear it myself. I press the mask to my face, cringing at the gooey sensation of the mask adhering to my skin.

Roselyn Malik.

I picture my own face and feel a tingling sensation wash over my face. When I trace my finger along my cheeks, I feel only the smooth skin of my flesh.

It worked. I'll be wearing the mask as I exit, and grandpa will be none the wiser.

I'm coming, Nevela. Hang in there.

I hastily close the inheritance box and set to work on my next attempt at a spell. Tonight, I raid the sewers in disguise.

Tonight, I save Nevela, or I die trying.

Chapter 9

Matt

The palace is rumbling with the news. Every officer must report to the terrace at midnight for a mandatory training exercise. Whoever doesn't arrive risks expulsion. From what I've heard, a training of this scale is more than unusual; it's unprecedented.

I was supposed to report to the ring hours ago, but the palace gates have been locked. No one is to leave until the training begins. The middle-class guardsmen will be on their own tonight.

I think of what Kendra told me. *Why would they need healers for a training exercise?* Whatever is going on, they're keeping us in the dark. Of that I'm sure.

I'm armed for war, with several spare magazines, a rifle, and an amplifier. My Kevlar vest tugs on my shoulders in a way that makes my neck ache, but I'm grateful for it. Something tells me I'll be needing it.

It's nearly midnight when the king arrives. He's hunched over his cane with a simple brown robe. The only evidence of his king-ship is the gold crown perched on his head. He smiles at us, the wrinkles in his face deep enough to cast shadows. In all honesty, he looks harmless, but I have no doubt he's the deadliest man here.

Zane stands by his side, along with Commander Noyen and some other guards I don't recognize. They wait in silence until the guards have grown still.

Zane steps forward. He's wearing jeans with a baggy long sleeve shirt. A silver zigzag pattern glimmers like chain mail in the moonlight.

I've never seen Zane wear Adamic armor. Whatever is about to happen, it's enough to make Zane fear for his life. The thought quickens my pulse.

"Welcome, soldiers," Zane calls out. "I'm afraid we've lied to you. We told you this is an exercise, but let me assure you, it's not. For the past few weeks, our spies have been collecting information, mapping out the tunnels. Finally, we know where the equalists are hiding."

"Aye!" The men roar, beating their fists on their Kevlar vests.

"More than that, we suspect the Holy One is with them. This is the same 'Holy One—'" He bends his fingers in air quotes. "—who tried to kill the princess. The same Holy One who marks our doors with blood. This is the same Holy One who killed my wife and daughters. Who killed our friends in Hogrum and in Lycon. Tonight, the Holy One will face what he deserves." He draws his short sword from its scabbard. "Tonight, we send him to hell!"

"To hell!" the crowd calls in unison.

Zane steps back, and King Dralton lifts his hunched head to the crowd. "My dear brethren, tonight, we hope to end the unrest in our city, but victory won't come easy. It is imperative that each of you follows the instruction of your commanders. They know what must be done. Officers of the eastern quadrant, you will follow Commander Quill Kaynes. He will be leading in Commander Elsborne's stead."

Commander Quill? He's the one who got his butt whooped by Tick in the fields. He was a level-10 douche. Without a doubt, he's one of the last people I want to follow into battle.

The king smiles. "Now, go! When we gather again, it will be to celebrate our victory. Godspeed!"

I reluctantly make my way over to Commander Quill with a dozen other men. His lion's mane of a head has only grown bushier. He holds a piece of paper in his hand as if it were calculus, squinting and tilting his head.

"Alright, boys, let's go find ourselves some sewer people. Whoever kills the most pickers, I'll personally cover their tab tomorrow."

Another man whoops. "All the gin I can drink? I don't know if you can afford me, Quill!"

The other men laugh, and Quill sneers. "Hold on now, Pluggot. There's a catch. If you can't keep it down, I don't pay a single bar."

The Pluggot laughs, and Quill leads us off the terrace and out of the palace. As we enter the plaza, we're surrounded by the other squadrons, but they quickly disperse the farther we travel from the palace.

I walk at the back of our squad, praying that Diego won't be there. Quill continues to tell jokes, laughing with the other lieutenants.

We turn down a small alley and stop at a square metal grate. Already, I can smell the sewage permeating from below.

Using dominion, Quill lifts the grate and tosses it further down the alley. "Alright, boys. Light your torches. Also, I suggest you bring a bubble of fresh air along with you. It's about to get nasty."

He starts climbing down the iron rungs into the tunnel below. The men follow one at a time. I'm the last to descend, holding my torch in one hand, and climbing with the other. My rifle sways by the strap, clanking into the concrete walls.

The tunnel is narrow but taller than I imagined—tall enough that I can walk standing up. The floor slopes into the middle like a V, and we walk with wide feet to avoid getting our boots wet. Every 50 feet or so, we pass a tunnel that juts off to the side. I've lost count by the time we finally turn right. We turn twice more before the tunnel gets wider. The sewage is replaced with a sandy earth floor, some kind of volcanic stone. When my arm gets tired from holding the torch, I switch hands.

Finally, we come to another fork in the tunnel, and Quill consults his map. "Alright, boys. We're getting close now. Everyone be alert. Whoever's last can carry a torch, but the rest of you put them out. I want two hands on your weapons."

Being the last man, I watch as the others plunge their torches headfirst into the rocky floor, twisting them until the flames sputter out. Once everyone is battle-ready, Quill leads us deeper and deeper underground. With every fork in the tunnel, he squints at the map for much longer than necessary.

A flickering glow emanates from my torch, lighting the jagged lava rock for all to see. The tunnels are large and oblong. Every few minutes, the tunnel diverges. It's eerie, but I can see why the equalists hide down here. Not only is it remote, but the temperature is stable, and it's safe from the elements.

Suddenly, a dead-end materializes in the darkness, jet black stone towers from floor to ceiling. Only it isn't a dead end. A narrow crack splits the rock wall in two. The crevice continues into the darkness, barely shoulder-width apart.

Quill takes a look at his map and holds up his hand. "This is where we wait," he declares.

Pluggot snorts. "We came to fight pickers, not the earth's ass-crack."

Quill isn't amused. "Our instructions are to block off this cavern. The king will confront them as they sleep. Our job is to detain any who flee through this tunnel." He grins. "If they resist, we fight to kill."

"That's it?" another man asks.

"I didn't make the plan," Quill snaps. He shrugs as if he suddenly doesn't care. "I guess the king wants the glory for himself."

Another man laughs. "Old geezer will be lucky to make it out of these tunnels alive. He can barely climb the palace steps."

Men laugh around the tunnel. A man with a gold tooth snorts. "Pretty soon he'll be as crazy as Titan. Poor bastard just won't die. Heaven doesn't want him, and neither does Hell."

That elicits even more laughter. Over the noise, I almost don't hear it. The soft bubbling of a stream. I look down and find a thin layer of water flowing through the narrow crevice. Once it surpasses the mouth of the crack, it spreads out until it's hardly flowing it all.

"Huh? What's with the water, Commander?"

Quill leans down and touches it with his fingers. "It's... blood." He flicks his fingers, splashing the guard in the face.

The other guards laugh.

Quill revels in their reaction. "It's water, you dimwits. Quit your worrying. Like I said, we're only here as backu—"

KA-BOOM!!!

The tunnel shakes, sprinkling my hair with the earth above us. My heart takes off like a sprinter, racing with no end in sight.

"What the hell was that?" a soldier grumbles.

Quill shakes out his mane. "That was the signal. The attack has begun. Everyone on your toes. No one gets through this tunnel."

From the back of the pack, I can hardly see down the narrow crevice, so I wait. I hold the torch high, making sure it illuminates the opening.

Everyone is on edge. The Holy One could come running down this tunnel any second. So could Diego. What if he showed up now? What would I do? *He said he'd kill me.*

One of the soldiers closest to the crevice suddenly stumbles back. "Did you hear that?"

"What?" Quill demands. "What did you hear?"

"It sounded like footsteps." He points his hand toward the crack and illuminates it with a flash of blinding light. The crevice is empty. "Huh, I guess—"

Suddenly, his arms go rigged and he blinks rapidly.

"Prestwix, you okay, man?" Another guard asks, putting a hand on his shoulder.

His body relaxes, and he unsheathes a dagger from his belt. "Yeah, I'm fine. I just—" In one quick motion, he swings the blade across his buddy's throat. Then, he grabs his amulet.

SCREEEECH!!!

The cavern goes dark as my comrades crouch in agony. I drop the torch, slapping my hands over my ears, but I don't panic. I've seen this attack before. I project my soul onto the space around my head. *Silence! Light!*

The cavern glows, but I'm too late. Three of the guards are already face-down. A guard with a long black beard points his gun at Prestwix. "I don't want to kill y—"

Before he can pull the trigger, the air ripples with a twang, launching the guard into the wall. His head cracks against the stone before he slumps to the ground.

Finally, Quill acts, dousing the tunnel in bright orange flames. They engulf Prestwix, but he doesn't scream. It's as if he feels no pain at all.

BANG! BANG!

Quill puts two in rounds in Prestwix's head and holsters his weapon. Then, he quivers. It's brief, but I'm already convinced.

"He's possessed!" I yell as loud as I can.

The second the words leave my tongue, Quill swings his Adamic blade, catching the nearest guard in the neck. Before the body hits the floor, Quill is lunging at the next guard in line. The knife plunges straight through his Kevlar. He's unbelievably swift, moving towards his next victim the instant the blade makes contact. I hear a guttural cry, and then a thud. Another scream and then a thud. I can't see much in the dimness, but the bodies are dropping in a rhythm, nearly a thump a second. I barely have time to think, much less retaliate. The guards in front of me are no different. Some manage an energy shield, but the Adamic blade slices clean through. He's almost to me now. Quill slices through another energy shield and spears the next guard in the gut.

There are only three of us left. The guard to my left fires his weapon.

BANG! BANG! BANG!

Quill uses the dead guard like a shield, holding him up by the knife in his gut. The bullets catch in his vest, shaking his body with each blow. Then, Quill dumps the body and stands tall.

"Go ahead, kill your commander to save yourselves. I can see inside his mind. He wouldn't hesitate in your shoes. Go on... kill him. He deserves to die."

This time, the guard hesitates. I push my mind forward until I feel her mind.

Iris

It's her, as calculating as ever. She doesn't delight in these deaths, but she views them as necessary.

Where is she? In order to be possessing them, she has to be nearby.

She sets her eyes at the level of my neck. I can sense what she's thinking. We're standing side by side. We're all the same height. Our necks are easily aligned.

She raises Quill's arm and sweeps it like a machete.

Slice!

I duck as a gust of air sweeps above me. I hear two distinct thuds, one to my left and one to my right. Then, their headless bodies crumple.

I'm the only one left.

"Stay back," I scream. "Leave his body or I collapse this tunnel on all of us. If your body is anywhere close, you'll be crushed too!"

Quill smirks, somewhat amused by the notions "Fine." In the blink of an eye, she tosses his head against the tunnel wall. His body crumples, sprawling across the floor. His chest moves. At the very least he's alive.

Before I can run, Iris materializes by the mouth of the crevice. One second, she's nowhere to be seen. The next, she's just there. She casually ambles closer, fiddling with a ring on her finger. It's hard to tell in the torchlight, but I think I can see Adamic symbols on the silver surface of the ring.

She was invisible!

"So, have you decided to join us yet?" she asks calmly, as if we aren't surrounded by freshly slain bodies. She's wearing skintight jeans and a white t-shirt. Her pixie cut hair is exactly as I remember it.

"I…" I don't know what to say. I don't want to join her, but I can't tell her that. It's the only thing keeping me alive.

"Don't waste my time, Matt. I'm giving you another chance. If you're not with us, you're against us."

"You just killed all these people, and you expect me to take your side?"

"It can be undone," she hisses. "All this can be undone. Don't you see? I'm on the good side." her eyes are desperate and wild. She wants me to believe. "The Holy One can fix everything. He can finally make the world fair."

"Then why did our parents fight against him?"

Iris rears back and blinks. "What did you say?" She looks me over and frowns. "Did you say *our* parents?"

She doesn't know about me!

I take a step forward, growing in confidence. I can't outfight her, but maybe I can outtalk her. "Isn't it obvious? I'm a demon after all. And a mystic as well."

Iris shakes her head. "N-no. That's impossible. My brother is dead."

"No, I'm not. I'm Ezra Kaimor." I take a step closer. "Zane told me himself."

"Zane is a liar!" Iris screams, waving her hands wildly through the air. "Zane killed our parents! They fought for the Holy One, and he killed them for it."

Now I'm the one in denial. *Zane wouldn't do that. Zane loved them.* I could sense it in his mind.

Then, I remember. "I have the tattoos to prove it. Our bonding spell is the same." I wrestle with my sleeve until my entire shoulder is exposed. "Our mother gave me these tattoos. You can't deny it."

Iris squints in the torchlight, then her face grows taut. I can see the tension in her neck. Her hand instinctively reaches to her shoulder, then it pulls away. "It doesn't matter who you are, it only matters which side you're on. With the Holy One, we can bring them all back. If you're really my brother, you'll trust me on this."

What if she's right? I let myself play with the notion. Maybe the Holy One could bring them back. What if I could see my parents again, Judy again.

After a moment, I shake my head. "Why don't we talk with Zane and get everything figured out?"

Iris steps closer. "I don't have time for this. Are you going to join us, or do I need to kill you?"

"You won't kill me. I'm your brother, Iris."

"I'll do whatever it takes, and when we find the Book of Life, I'll bring you back." Her face hardens. "I won't let anyone get in my way, not even family."

"Then you're as crazy as the Holy One," I hiss.

"Ugh!" Iris throws her hands down. "For being blood, you sure are dense. We're the good side. We're fighting for a better world." Suddenly, she glances at the crevice behind her as if she's just had an Idea. "Matt… that's what you call yourself, right? What if you could bring back Enrique? What if you could save Velma? Wouldn't that be worth it? To help a friend? To fix your mistakes?"

I clench my teeth. "How do you know about them?"

"Oh, I heard it from the source." Iris glances behind her once more. "Diego, why don't you come out now?"

Diego squeezes through the crevice and into the light of the torches. He says nothing. He only stares, his gaze dripping with disgust.

"Diego?" He was listening the whole time, and he did nothing to help me.

124

Iris faces me once more. "Answer my question!" She scolds. "Would that make it worth it? Would you serve the Holy One to save them? To right your own wrongs?"

I look to Diego. Already, my heart aches from what I'm about to say. "I want to save them. I really do." I echo Zane's words. "But I can't do it; no person should have that power. I won't."

Diego takes a sudden step closer. "You don't understand, Matt. You can keep living your life without Velma and my dad, but I can't. What happens when you lose someone you can't live without? You really don't think the world would be a better place without death? Without suffering?"

"It's not that simple," I say. "Diego, just hear me out."

"No!" His voice is a steel block. I watch as titanium spreads across his face. "We can fix this, Matt. There's nothing to argue. Tell me you'll help us."

I squeeze my hands out of frustration. "I'm sorry. I can't."

Iris frowns, genuinely disappointed. "Shame. Diego, now's your chance to prove yourself." She tosses him Quill's Adamic blade. "Kill him."

Diego wastes no time. He kicks at the ground, and a slab of rock erupts from the cavern floor barely inside my energy shield. The stone collides with my knee and my leg gives out.

"Ahhh!" I hit the ground and roll as another rock erupts where I was just laying.

Shield!

This time, I wrap my shield underneath my feet and around my back.

Iris watches like a referee. "Don't even think about possessing him, Ezra. The second you leave your body, I take off your head."

I squeeze my amulet, running through my option. "I don't want to fight you, Diego. You don't have to do this."

Diego charges and kicks at my energy shield. The force is enough to push me back.

"Then join us!" he cries. "Join us and this ends!" He looks like he's on the verge of tears. He doesn't want to kill me, but he's not backing down either.

Force wave!

I send the energy at Diego, but he slices right through it. Then, he charges.

I focus on the air around him.

Condense.

Diego slows, fighting with the air like a fly in a spider's web. Then, he stops struggling. He doesn't look at me, but at the earth above my head. I sense the thought a moment too late.

Crumble!

I scream at the air above me as the ceiling gives way.

Shield!

The earth piles onto my shield, but it's a losing battle. For the first two seconds, my command holds, but I won't last long. My soul is aching with strain. My brain feels like it's splitting down the center.

"Ahhh!" I angle my shield like an upside down V and let the stone fall to either side, piling up beside me. Before the rock has settled, Diego dives at me. He tackles me on top of the rubble, jagged stone cutting into my back.

With his titanium skin, the weight is unbearable. "Ahhh!" I grit my teeth and imagine a tremendous force launching him back. Before I can command it, Diego rips my amulet from my neck. I watch as his fingers dig into the amulet like Play-Doh.

He raises his other fist to his ear and hesitates.

"Kill him," Iris says. "Kill him or you'll never see Velma again."

My breathing comes quicker as I try to wrestle out from under him. One punch from Diego would be a hammer blow to the head —certain death.

Diego takes a deep breath and scrunches his eyes. "I'm sorry." His metal muscles flex as he prepares for the swing.

"Matt!" A voice echoes through the crevice, loud and desperate. It's Zane, and he's not far down the tunnel. "Matt!" His voice bellows again, this time closer.

Iris fiddles with her ring, and suddenly I'm staring at the wall behind her. Her voice whispers from the darkness. "End this, and let's go! Kill him now!"

"Diego." I stare into his muddy eyes, the only color left in his silver body. A single tear dangles on his metal lashes. I watch it stream down his cheek.

"Goodbye, Matt." He closes his eyes and swings for my head.

I know the consequences—dominion without an amulet can be deadly—but I have no choice. I stretch my soul into the space above my face. The pain is instantaneous, like a hot knife sawing through my skull, but I don't stop.

Shield!

The air ripples above me. Then, blackness. The transition is immediate. The pain is gone, my body is gone, the world is gone.

I didn't just strain my soul, I tore it to pieces.

I feel myself dying. My soul is like a pebble, sinking deeper and deeper into the ocean of the afterlife. With every passing second, the murky water blocks my view of what's above. Then, I see a light far in the distance. In my gut, I know I want to go there. In the black void, there's only one thing between me and the light. It looks like a panel of glass, extending for all eternity in every direction. I slow as I approach the glass, almost coming to a stop. The glass directly in front of me is perfectly transparent, but as my eyes wander to the periphery, the glass darkens. I keep my eyes trained straight ahead, straining to see the light on the horizon. It's distant, but the light is pure. I see my parents in the light. I see laughter and peace. I step forward and stretch my hand toward the glass.

"Are you sure you want to do that?"

The voice catches me by surprise. Then a figure moves on the other side of the glass. It's the last person I expect to see.

It's Antai Elsborne.

Chapter 10

Rose

I follow a dozen steps behind Grandpa, trying my best to breathe steadily. Every time I look down, I have a minor heart attack. My hands are veiny and my knuckles enlarged. I don't even want to think about the hair on my chest and all the other elements of manhood. I choke down the bile rising in my throat and press my hand to my amplifier. It sits uncomfortably flat on my chest.

I step over a large crevice, careful not to fall in the river. We're walking on a narrow path along the bank of a babbling underground river.

Grandpa shuffles slowly at the lead. Commander Hunt follows close behind, along with the officers of the Northern Quadrant, myself included.

Grandpa stops a few paces before the trail dips right, diverging from the river. It descends at a sharp angle.

"This is where I wait," Grandpa declares, stepping off the trail to allow the others to pass.

Commander Hunt nods. "We'll await your signal, your highness." She continues down the trail, lighting the way with dominion.

I follow the others, careful not to make eye contact with Grandpa. I can't do anything that will give myself away. I'm about to pass him when he looks up at me.

"I'm glad you're feeling better, Captain Wex. Are you sure you're still up to assist me?" Grandpa looks at me expectantly.

The truth is, Wex isn't feeling better. That's why I chose to steal his face. He's laying in the healing loft, retching up his dinner. However, no one will realize this until after the mission, and by then, Nevela will be safe.

"Of course, your highness." I try my best not to cringe at my ragged smoker voice. "It's an honor to be in your service." Of all the soldiers, what are the odds that Captain Wex would be his personal assistant?

Grandpa waits until the other soldiers disappear down the tunnel. Then, he adjusts his grip on his cane. "Now, captain, tell me what you remember of our plan."

I suck in a breath. "Yes, of course. Well, you see..." I try to take a step closer, but the toe of my enlarged boot catches on the stone. I shriek, managing to catch myself before I barrel into Grandpa.

He chuckles and shakes his head. "I know it's you, Rose. There's no need to pretend."

"But... what gave me away? Could you sense me?"

The king chuckles. "Oh, no. Relics are immaculate in their design. I can sense many things, but your disguise wasn't one of them. I can, however, see, and you've touched your face five times in the last minute."

"Are you upset?"

Grandpa shrugs. "I would've expected nothing less. I do wish you consulted me first, but we can't change the past." He peers at the gurgling river. "I must admit. I am pleased to have your company. Are you ready?"

"For what?"

"To get wet," Grandpa grins. He steps off the trail, sinking up to his knobby knees in the river. The current is swift, but not swift enough to sweep him off his feet. "We don't have far to go."

I step into the water, cringing as ice water saturates my socks. The bottom of the river is jagged, and I have to lift my feet high to ensure I don't trip. Grandpa's light illuminates the way, but it only reaches a few feet ahead. He's restricting the light so that our enemies won't see us approaching.

"Grandpa, are you sure you can-"

"I'm fine." He insists. "I can manage myself."

We continue for another few minutes when Grandpa's light suddenly extinguishes.

"Hey," I whisper. I look up and my heart starts pounding. I can see a yellow light at the end of the tunnel. With every step, the light grows gradually more brilliant. I can already recognize the hue as Adamic lanterns. As we approach, we step more carefully, keeping the noise at a minimum.

I don't see much until I'm almost in the opening of the tunnel. The river drops away into a brilliant waterfall. The cavern before us is gorgeous—almost twice the size of the trench. Adamic symbols are spaced along the walls of the cave, drenching the space in the essence of gold. Several streams crisscross the space below, collecting onto one central river. The jagged stalagmites hang from the ceiling like chandeliers, moisture dripping like little beads of liquid gold. On the far side of the cavern, the river drains into a gaping black abyss the size of a carriage.

And then, there are the equalists. They sleep, padded with blankets and animal hides, along the walls of the cavern. The edges of the cavern offer the only level ground, the rest of the rock sloping down towards the central river like a natural drain.

There aren't as many equalists as I expected, maybe 50 at most. Most of them are men, but I spot a few women as well. They have erected tables beside the river. I see a cooking station and a make-shift restroom. The location is perfect. Not only is it hidden, but they have unlimited light and running water. They can drink and wash and cook, all beneath our noses.

Where are you, Nevela?

I scan the sleeping bodies, but I see only strangers. They're all either too tall, too dark, or a combination of the two. There are several watchmen as well. They pace back and forth, struggling to stay awake. I see amulets around their necks.

Grandpa watches me from the corner of his eyes. He leans over and whispers in my ear. "Don't lose hope, Rose. We'll find her."

I nod, but I don't believe him. He said the same about Antai, yet nothing's changed.

Grandpa shuffled toward the edge of the falls and peers down below.

"So what's the plan?" I whisper, my voice immersed in the roar of the falls.

"By now, everyone should be in position. I'll give the signal, and our forces will converge."

"Do you really think you can take them all?"

"I don't have to take them all, only the ones with Adamic blades. My crown will defend against everything else."

The thought puts me at ease. Grandpa's crown is no ordinary emblem; it is a relic of protection.

"And what should I do?" I ask.

"When the fighting commences, you are to stay put and keep on the mask. The Holy One cannot know you're here."

I want to argue, but I'm already breaking rules to be here. I should quit while I'm ahead. "Yes, Grandpa."

"Good, now watch carefully." He grins playfully. "Maybe you'll learn something."

Grandpa shuffles to the edge of the falls and takes a step into oblivion. I expect his frail body to drop, but like a feather in the wind, he drifts slowly to the cavern floor.

He's halfway down when someone takes notice. "Intruder." The watchman chokes on the word, barely audible above the rushing river. His eyes double in size as he scrambles for his gun. "Intruder! Everyone, wake up!"

The equalists are quick to their feet, flinging off blankets and grabbing their weapons. A woman shrieks as she awakes, hastily smacking her sleeping friend. I search the faces, one by one. *Not Nevela. Not Nevela.*

Diego?

He's changed. His waist is smaller, and his face more defined, but there's no denying it. He's one of the first on his feet. He grabs his gun and stares wide-eyed at Grandpa. After a few seconds, he runs. I watch as he darts along the cavern wall and disappears down a slender side tunnel. It's barely the size of a palace door.

Coward! I don't want to, but I can't help but feel resentment. Equalist or not, how could he abandon his men before a fight?

I don't have time to think much of it. As grandpa descends on the central river, he slows to a stop, his feet hovering mere inches above the current. He says nothing, waiting for the equalist to assemble. They form a line on each opposing riverbank. To my surprise, nearly every single equalist is armed with an amulet, most with pistols as well. The air ripples around them as they envelop themselves with force shields.

It's subtle, but I notice something else, the river below Grandpa has nearly slowed to a standstill. The water spirals around grandpa's feet like a small eddy. Grandpa is the moon, and the water gravitates around him.

Finally, grandpa speaks. "Beloved citizens of Cavernum, I am King Dralton, I—"

BANG! BANG! BANG!

Each bullet deflects into the water without a tiny splash. On the riverbank, an equalist holds a rifle as the muzzle spews smoke. He looks genuinely disappointed that the king survived.

Grandpa frowns. "I wish to make you an offer." His voice projects to the edge of the cavern and back again, creating a slight echo. "I wish to inform you that we have you surrounded. If you try to flee, you will find certain death. If you try to fight, you will find certain death. However, it has been brought to my attention that there may be some of you here against your will. Whoever would like to surrender now will be given safe passage and fair trial; you have my word. If this describes you, please relinquish your weapons and exit now."

Three women, after a slight hesitation, dash into one of the side tunnels. Another boy follows soon after. He looks no older than 12.

Grandpa grins, obviously pleased with himself. He waits a moment longer. "No one else?"

I look down at the water and see that the river is rising up each opposing bank. It's no longer draining, held in place by the king's gravity. With each foot the water ascends, the river grows wider, looking more like a pond every second.

A man steps forward. He's massive, at least 7-feet tall, with a silky baritone bass of a voice. "How do we know you're not bluff-ing?" he rumbles. "How do we know you're not here alone?"

Grandpa's face is unreadable. Not angry, not excited. "If I wanted you dead," he calls out, "I would've slain you in your sleep. I would've filled this cave with poison, but I did not. I am here for the Holy One. If he is here, I ask him to make himself known."

Silence. Still, the water climbs higher. Some equalists take a step back as the water soaks their bedding. Blankets now float, swirling with the currents.

The king cocks his head and listens a moment longer. "No? Pity." He straightens his back, still hovering above the water. "This is your last chance. Surrender now, and you'll have a fair trial."

Another soldier drops his gun and flees into a side tunnel. The rest hold their ground. The water is up to their ankles now. They have nowhere left to go, so they wade in it.

The 7-foot equalist turns to his comrades, an amulet clenched in his hand. "The king is here alone. He thinks that he, a single man, can face an army. He is a fool king. He has walked into his own doom."

The water is now knee-deep. It surpasses the edge of the bank and drains into several side tunnels.

The 7-foot equalist puffs out his chest and yells. "We will strike him where he stands. Today, the king falls." He raises an Adamic sword above his head and points his meaty finger directly at the king. "Give me equality, or give me d—"

KA-CRACK!!!

A blinding flash of white erupts from Grandpa's fingers and surges into the water below. A horrid ensemble of screams erupts around the cavern. It only lasts a second, but the effects are devastating. Men seize where they stand. Then, in unison, they collapse into the water. A cacophony of splashes, each indiscernible from the next.

In one fell swoop, Grandpa has incapacitated half the equalist army.

The thunder shudders through the earth, no doubt heard by every guardsman around. *The signal.*

Those who are conscious abandon any notion of a fight. In a frenzy, they rush to pull their drowning comrades from the water. Blindly, they thrust their hands beneath the golden glazed water.

Grandpa doesn't attack. He lets them salvage their soldiers. Still, the water doesn't drain. It swirls in sweeping circles around Grandpa.

Those who can try desperately to separate themselves from the water. Some freeze the surface and ascend above. Others use their force shields to keep the water at bay.

Then, comes the roar. It isn't a roar of thunder, but of blood-thirsty soldiers. Guardsmen burst from the side tunnels, amulets at the ready. They leap on the nearest equalists and open-fire on any who resist.

The 7-foot equalist lumbers forward, running atop the water. Each step sends tendrils of ice plunging into the water like roots. He carries with him a steel blade. The Adamic symbols gleam gold.

In a matter of seconds, he crosses the flooded cavern. "Die, King!" He raises the blade above his head and leaps.

With a flick of Grandpa's wrist, a wave intercepts the behemoth of a man. Then, with a crash, the wave retracts back into the swirling mass of water. The man doesn't resurface. The stillness of the water is almost eerie.

By now, the equalists have regrouped. A barrage of attacks converges on the king. Flames spiral around the king. Boulders are launched from the cave's edge, shattering into shards against his crown's spell. The king doesn't bother with defense. He basks in his own imperviousness.

Grandpa smiles and waves his hand. The water consumes any who raise a hand against the king while swirling harmlessly past the guardsmen. Of the dozen who are dragged down, none return. The battle only lasts a minute. Before long, the few who still live raise their arms in surrender. They'll be hung, but this way they'll get to give their final words to their families.

As the bodies are retrieved, the water begins to recede. Grandpa forbade it, but I deem it safe to descend. I don't have time to waste. What if Nevela was captured in the side tunnels? *I need to find her.*

I step off the waterfall and command the air to support me. I descend quicker than I'd like, but nothing my knees can't handle. I drop to a crouch and move along the edge of the cavern, scanning the bodies for her long, golden hair.

Then, it dawns on me. To Nevela, I look like some stranger. If she's here, my best bet is to remove my mask. The battles over anyway.

Rose!

I imagine my own face, shuddering as my body returns to normal. Hair erupts from my head, and I feel my spine compressing.

Zane stands motionless up ahead. He's scanning the battlefield just as I am, searching for someone among the fallen. When he sees me, he does a double-take. "Rose? What are you doing here?"

"I—"

"It doesn't matter," he interjects "Have you seen Diego?"

I point to the skinny tunnel. "He went through there before the battle began."

135

Zane follows my gaze, his eyes snapping open. "Matt." He breathes the word a second before taking off for the tunnel. Something about his urgency jolts me to action. *Matt!* He saved me at the graduation party. If he's in danger, I have to help.

Before I can overthink it, I take off after Zane. I run blindly into the narrow tunnel, refusing to slow down despite the darkness. I hear Zane's heavy footsteps ahead of me, and I use them as my guide.

The tunnel only grows narrower, and I only fall farther behind.

"Matt!" Zane bellows as he runs. "Matt!"

The walls drift closer and closer together, and soon I have to angle my shoulders to squeeze through. Just when I think I've lost him, I collide with the bulky muscles of Zane's backside. His hips are like a blow to the stomach.

I gasp as I take in the scene. We're standing in a much wider tunnel. Matt is lying limp on a pile of rubble. Diego, whose skin is a lustrous silver, is kneeling next to him. A collage of dead guardsmen is strewn between them and us.

"What happened?" Zane marches over the bodies without a second glance.

Diego says nothing. He stares at Matt in disbelief.

"What HAPPENED?" Zane's voice is grizzly and untamed. He grabs Diego by the metal face and shakes him. "YOU TELL ME NOW!" For a second, I wonder if Zane will kill him.

"Sh-she made me fight him. I took his amulet. He made a shield anyway."

Zane roars and swings his fist into the wall. The entire cave rumbles. "Where is she?"

Diego shrugs. "I don't know. She left."

Zane falls to his knees, pressing two fingers to Matt's throat. He holds his breath. When he looks at me, his eyes seem to quiver. "Go get the king. He has no pulse."

No pulse. I can't think of anything beyond those words. *Not, Matt. Not him too.*

Diego is already on his feet. "I'll go. I'll get the king." He takes off down through the narrow tunnel.

I watch Zane place his hands on Matt's chest and pump.

Thump. Thump. Thump.

After what feels like an eternity, he pinches Matt's nose and blows into his lungs.

"C'mon, Matt, stay with me. You can come back from this. Wake up, Matt."

He pumps his chest several dozen times and gives him another two breaths.

He pauses, pressing his fingers along Matt's throat once more. "Dammit. C'mon!"

"Let me try something." In my studies, Grandpa once taught me about the breath of life. It's been years, and I've never so much as tried it. Regardless, I refuse to do nothing.

I drop to my knees on the stone and lean over Matt's face. I approach slowly, as if he might protest at any moment. When our lips are about to meet, I close my eyes.

The first thing I notice is the dust on his lips, which stretch against my mouth like a limp rubber band. *He's dead.* The thought makes me want to recoil, but instead, I blow. As the air leaves my lips, I push my soul along with it. I move a part of me into his body, which is quiet and desolate. If Matt is here, I don't feel him.

Then, comes the hard part. Like chopping off a hand, I sever a piece of my soul. My body shudders as I do, but I keep my lips against his. I fear it's a bandaid on a bullet wound, but with the last of my strength, I breathe my soul into Matt.

When I finally sit up, I meet Zane's fear-gripped gaze. His fingers, noticeably trembling, are placed across Matt's wrist. He says the words I fear most.

"Still no pulse."

His hands leap for Matt's chest once more. Thump. Thump. Thump. The compressions resume, this time harder than the last. Zane thrusts with enough force to lift Matt's head from the cavern floor. I slip my finger underneath his skull. It's all I can think to do. I failed… and now, Matt will die.

"Come on!" Zane abandons the compressions and holds out his hand. Electricity leaps between his fingers, jolting Matt's entire body. "Wake up, Matt." He lowers his hand to Matt's chest, and shocks him again, sending his back arching into the air. Still, Matt doesn't breathe.

"You're not done. You hear me, Matt." He drops his hand again, and Matt jolts. His head lolls to the side with each electric shock.

Zane lifts his fist until his elbow is at his ear. "WAKE UP!" He throws his hand down, and Matt's body lurches with electricity.

"Ptuhhhhh" Matt sucks in a breath, and his chest swells.

"Oh, thank God!" Zane wraps his arms around Matt's chest and pulls him into his lap.

Matt has come back from the dead!

It's been nearly a day, and still, Matt hasn't stirred. I stare at his motionless body, hoping he'll rise with the morning sun. I can't shake the inkling that he'll become another Antai—that his spirit will pass on, and his body will endure as a constant reminder. Perhaps it's a punishment from God for a crime I wasn't aware I've committed.

Why else would so many die?

Of all the people I've ever called friends, nearly half are dead, and the other half are on the verge. Velma, Proticus, Antai, Nevela, Matt. Who's next, Grandpa? Wendy? Diego? *Who else do I have?*

I watch him sleep from across the healing loft. Sleep is a generous term. In reality, I watch him fight for his life. He's breathing, but he's no further from death than he was in the tunnels.

Grandpa stands at my side, watching Matt with meticulous concentration. At first, I thought he was only here to support me, but as I've left for meals, Grandpa has stayed behind. Whatever the reason, he's deeply invested in Matt's survival.

A flash of white fabric catches my eyes. Kendra glides around Matt's cot, dress rustling with the breeze. She pauses at his wrist to check his vitals. Then, she moves back to his head. I know what's coming next; I've seen her do it twice already. She uses two fingers to tilt back his head by his chin. Then, she kisses him.

Her lips seal securely over his mouth, and I watch his chest rise as she gently exhales. It isn't like my attempt, a quick and violent breath. Kendra lingers, allowing her soul to slowly diffuse into Matt. Before their lips break, her knees buckle and she grabs the bed for support. The breath of life is costly, and Kendra is paying in full.

"Is that really going to save him?" I ask Grandpa under my breath.

He nods, never taking his eyes off of Matt. "It's certainly his best hope. His soul has been severed, unlikely to heal on its own. The breath of life is like a grafting of the soul. Matt will be able to absorb her soul and apply it wherever he is most damaged."

I don't know why, but the thought irritates me, like a jealous itch I just can't scratch. It's not that I want to be with Matt, I simply want what Kendra has. I wish I could give a piece of myself to Antai— that I could make my soul a permanent part of him. I wish I could save the one I love.

"Will he remember it?" I wonder.

The king smiles. "If he survives, he most certainly will. Her soul will be a part of him forever." He looks at me from the corner of his eye. "You'll be a part of him as well. The soul carries everything that you are. Memories, emotions, desires. Some of you is now in him."

For some reason, the thought makes me smile. Knowing that I played some role, no matter how small, in Matt's survival makes everything worth it. It means I made the right decision to steal the morph mask, to jeopardize my own life. I've made lots of mistakes, but the raid wasn't one of them.

"I must be going, Rose." Grandpa wraps his robes tighter around himself. "The council is meeting to discuss the results of the raid. If you like, I'll excuse you from attending?"

"What is there to discuss? The Holy One wasn't there. The whole attack was a waste of time."

Grandpa's head droops. "Very well. I'll tell them you are recovering." He starts to turn away but pauses. "I know it hurts, but don't lose hope quite yet."

I don't bother responding as he shuffles away. Instead, I watch Matt. The healers have left him alone now, and he lies prostrate on the leather bed. They haven't managed to change his clothes yet. His uniform is speckled with reflective drops of dried blood. I watch his chest rise, wondering what I'd do if it suddenly stopped. Surely, I would call for Kendra, as I'm hopeless to do much else.

I don't cry. If I cry about Matt, then it only makes sense that I cry about Velma and Antai and Nevela as well, and I simply don't have the energy.

"He might just make it," Kendra says from beside me.

I flinch. "Oh, I didn't see you there." Had I seen her coming, I may have walked out.

"Forgive me, I should've announced myself." She bows briefly before directing her gaze at Matt. "I know you two were friends. I saw you dancing at the graduation party. I thought I'd give you the update."

I nod and she continues. "We thought we might lose him, but he's starting to pull through. We think he's going to be okay. Thank you for what you did princess." Before I can stop her, she leans over and gives me a hug.

At first, I resist, only to let my arms fall around her. I forgot the comfort of a simple hug. I embrace it, like a salve to my broken heart.

Her arms relax, signifying the end of the embrace. "You're so strong, princess. We all see it. I wanted you to know that."

I nod my head, suspicious of the noise my voice will make should I try to speak.

"Well, I should get back to Matt. But he would appreciate your presence here. Thanks again for keeping him alive."

"Wait," I call out as she turns to leave. "Do you really think he'll wake up? You're not saying that to comfort me?"

Kendra purses her lips until I can hardly see her pink lipstick. "I do. Right now, it looks hopeful, but I can't make any promises. There's much we still don't understand about the soul. The rest is up to God."

The rest is up to God. Suddenly, I have an idea.

"Thank you, Kendra. Thank you." I give her another quick hug before rushing out of the loft.

I stop at my room, collecting all of my favorite novels. With a stack up to my chin, I hurry to the ground floor, the books balanced precariously against my chest.

The palace temple sits on the west side of the palace courtyard. It's a small glass building with white opaque windows and silver beams. It looks as though someone poured liquid silver over a greenhouse. Through the windows, I see the glow of the sacrificial fire, yet the misty glass makes it impossible to see much else.

I stop at the door. A small quiver of arrows is leaning against the adjacent window. It's customary to leave your weapons outside the temple, but a quiver of arrows is an unusual sight.

My books make it difficult to open the temple door. Still, I try to be as reverent as possible. I catch the latch with my pinky and slowly tug it open, shuffling inside.

The temple interior is both simple and elegant. It's a single room with a rostrum on the far side. A fire pit is set in the ground a few feet from the podium. The rest of the building is filled with pews, but only enough to hold 50 elites. Around the room, several Adamic symbols are embedded in the stained glass. Not spells, according to Grandpa, but ancient scripture.

The temple is empty except for a single man in the front pew. I recognize his bald head and slender limbs. It's the survivor from Lycon.

He rises as I enter and moves to assist. "Welcome, Madame. Allow me." Without waiting for permission, he scoops the top half of my stack into his own arms. "And where are we going with these books?" His voice flourishes with a lofty French accent.

"To the fire," I say. "They're my sacrifice."

"All of them?"

"I need a special blessing," I say. "This is my payment."

The Lycon survivor looks down at the pile of pages and proffers a smile. "You know, I don't think God has much use for your books."

I laugh, mostly to be courteous. "I know, but it's all I have to sacrifice." I toss the first few books into the fire, *The Book Thief.* Then, I drop *Pride and Prejudice* and *The Fault in Our Stars.* One after the next, each book is consumed by the flames.

"And why such an odd sacrifice, may I ask?"

There's something about his demeanor, innocent and caring, that draws out my story. "Growing up, these books were my only glimpse at the outside world. The palace libraries don't have an extra copy. They're gifts from my father. It's the only sacrifice that I can't easily replace."

"Very well then." The man tips his pile, letting them slide off one by one. One by one, each of the Harry Potter books tumbles into the blaze. He watches as they burn, then suddenly turns to me. "Pardon me, madame, I did not introduce myself." The man bows curtly. "My name is Gideon. And you are the dauphine, are you not?"

"Dauphine?" It's a word I don't recognize. A word from the beyond.

"Forgive me. It is French for future ruler. I say it with the utmost respect."

"Oh. Then, yes. I guess I am."

He eyes the fire without turning his head. "If you'd like, I can leave the temple. I've been here most of the day, and I imagine the princess would like to pray?"

"No, I insist you stay. My prayer is short, and I don't plan to be here long. I'll say it in my head if you don't mind."

"Please," Gideon says.

I close my eyes and bow my head.

God, if you can hear me, please don't let my friends die. I'll do whatever it takes. I'll be whatever princess you need me to be, just please don't let them die. Wake up Antai. Matt too. Keep Nevela safe from the Holy One. Help me find her. Don't let them die! Please!

"Amen."

I lean back against the pew and look up, hoping to see a sign among the glass panels above me. All I find is misty white glass and the evidence of bird droppings on a silver beam.

"So," I say to Gideon, "you said you've been here all day?"

The nods, his cheery expression saddened by some memory. "I'm afraid I'm in search of peace. My brother was killed in Lycon, as were my parents. I'm seeking consolation, something to get me through the day."

"I'm so sorry," I gasp. I've already forgotten that other people have it worse. At least my sanctuary is still standing. "I can't imagine what you must be going through," I whisper.

Somehow, Gideon smiles. "It is no competition. Pain is pain, and I'm sure you carry enough of your own." He looks toward the sacrificial fire. "As for myself, I am lucky to be alive. God is great, my dear dauphine. I have many blessings to be counted."

Something in me is vexed by his comment. "I don't mean to be rude, but how? How can you say God is great after everything that happened?"

Gideon frowns. "You question the goodness of God? And why is that, may I ask?"

I swallow and try to keep my voice like water, neither sour nor bitter. "Well, for starters, why did he let Lycon fall? If God is so great, why didn't he save Lycon? Or warn them? Or do anything for that matter?"

Gideon drags his thumb along his eyebrow and rests his chin on his knuckles. "You, my dear dauphine, pose a very important question. Before I answer it, I have a question for you first. Why are we here? What is God's great goal of our creation?"

I feel as though I have an answer, but I'm suddenly self-conscious of my response. "The scriptures say we are here to be tested, but my grandpa says we are here to experience joy. Either way, I don't understand why this suffering is necessary?"

Gideon smiles. "Both true, but I believe the answer is even more simple. We are here for one task: to learn how to love."

I frown. "And I can't learn to love without my friends dying?"

"I understand your pain, princess, but that is part of the challenge. Learning to love the righteous is easy, it is in our nature. True learning comes when we must love our enemies—those who commit atrocities. That is when we become godlike."

"Well, God asks too much of us in my opinion," I say.

Gideon sighs. "Indeed, dauphine, sometimes it feels too much, but I believe it serves a purpose. Before the attack, my father had Alzheimer's, a terrible affliction that stole his memory. I had to care for him, and most days he didn't know my name. I'll tell you, princess, I learned to love him in a way I could never love in a perfect world. Our sympathies and our mercies are dependent on tragedy. There is no other way to experience such love."

As much as it hurts, his reasoning resonates with me. It's an answer Grandpa would give. "Perhaps you're right," I sigh. "Thank you for your wisdom, Gideon." I look into his soulful mahogany eyes. "Forgive me, but can I ask… do you love your enemies? Do you love the feeders that ravaged Lycon?"

To my surprise, Gideon shakes his head. "Don't let me fool you, princess. I'm no saint. I'd skin them alive if I could. Each and every one. But perhaps that isn't so wrong of me. We must learn to love, but it is my belief we must also learn to hate. In some scenarios, this too is godlike."

Hate… godlike? "You really think so?"

"Oh, yes, dauphine. Without a doubt. Hate and violence have their place. To truly love, we must protect. We must fight, and at times, we must kill. Is God not our perfect example of wrath? How many nations has he struck down?"

"But that's what bothers me." I insist. "He doesn't protect us. He doesn't kill the feeders. He doesn't do anything. Isn't Lycon evidence of that?"

"You're not wrong. God rarely does something for us that we can do ourselves, protection included. He has made us to be warriors as much as he has made us to worship. As you said yourself, God will not come down. He will not strike our enemies, but he will guide us in our own salvation. The only reason my men survived was because I had trained with the bow. I had 30 Adamic arrows when the feeders attacked. When we made it out, I had none. I don't believe that was a coincidence. God gave me exactly what I needed."

What about your brother? What about your father? I don't have the heart to ask. I try a different approach instead. "Did your king make your arrows?"

Gideon nods. "I have asked Dralton to do the same, but he has refused me. He is a cautious man, your grandfather. Arrows, unlike daggers, are easily left behind to scavengers. He's not willing to take that risk."

"Actually, I'm learning that very spell." I bite my lip, hoping my next words aren't a mistake. "If you'd be willing to teach me archery, perhaps I could make you some Adamic arrows in the future?"

"Oh, yes. That would be exceptional! Oh, yes. We can begin today if you'd like. I believe I have found my consolation in your offer."

I smile, a hint of sadness in my eyes. "I'd love to, but there's something I must do first. Your words have given me an idea. I have a friend in danger, and I think there might be a way I can help her."

"Very well, dauphine. Sometime in the future no doubt."

"Thanks again, Gideon. Next time you see me, let's arrange a time to shoot."

"Of course. I will do just that."

I rise and move toward the door. *You have to take matters into your own hands, Rose.* I didn't find Nevela in the sewers, but there's someone who might just know where she is.

It's time I have a talk with my assassin.

Chapter 11

Matt

"Commander Elsborne?" He stands on the other side of the glass as if he were my reflection. He appears fully tangible. He's in uniform, and his hair is neatly combed, but there's something else. A thin strand of light coils in the air above his shoulder. Like a stream of luminescent spider silk, it trails from behind Antai, passes directly through the glass, and continues toward the oblivion where I came from.

I move to take a step toward the glass, but the commander holds up his hands.

"Careful, MacArthur, the veil is a one-way ticket. Once you step through, you can't get back." To prove a point, he slams his fist against the glass. The barrier warps almost like an energy shield, but it doesn't budge.

"I don't understand."

"We're dead, MacArthur. You're just a spirit. A ghost. An entity. And so am I."

I crease my brow and squint. "You're sure?" I look down at my body. When I soul-travel, I feel like a soul. I'm blind, and I can pass through walls. I can only sense the world around me with my mind. Yet right now, hovering before a panel of endless glass, I feel as physical as any living body. "We both look pretty alive to me,"

"That's because this is the spirit world," Elsborne says, "or at least the border of it. Spirits interact with the spirit world the same way physical objects interact with the physical world." He turns around, pointing at the glorious array of light in the distance. "That's heaven, I imagine. All I have to do is get there."

He turns around and gazes at the light, but I'm distracted by something else. The strand of shimmering thread leads directly into the commander's back, meshing seamlessly with his uniform. He looks like an astronaut bound to the physical world by a glowing cable.

"What's that?" I point at the trail of light connecting to his back.

When Antai sees what I'm asking about, his face darkens. "I call it my lifeline. It connects my soul to my body. When I died, the thing was severed, and then, after I had already passed through the veil, it reappeared out of nowhere. Now, the damn thing is a prison." He grabs onto the glowing cord and begins to walk away from the glass, toward the distant light. He only takes a few steps before the line grows taut. Antai pulls, like a game of tug-of-war, but the celestial twine doesn't budge. Defeated, he sulks back to the glass. "I've even tried to chew through it, but the damn thing is invincible. As long as my lifeline is intact, I'm anchored to my body, and I can't pass on. Even worse, I can't go back because of the veil. I'm stuck."

"Your body is alive," I say. "They say you're in a coma. That must be why your lifeline still exists."

Elsborne sighs. "Pity. It would be better if I just died. I'll never get back. I've tried a thousand times. The veil is impenetrable. I just want to move on." He stares into the distant light. "My parents are out there. I can hear them calling to me. It's where I belong."

"I'm sorry. I wish I could help you."

I follow his gaze into the heavenly light. Once again, I hear the familiar laughter, a woman's voice. It calls to me. Something ancient inside me beckons me forward. *Paradise.* It's just a little further. All I have to do is cross the veil.

I take a step forward and reach out. My fingertips are inches from the glass when I feel it. It feels like a rush of wind, warm and gentle. It blows in my mouth and fills me like a summer's breeze. Once inside me, the wind takes substance, clinging to my lungs and filling my blood vessels. I feel myself grow stronger, gaining mass.

Matt, wake up! The wind is sentient, and it speaks to me. I can feel it thinking. *C'mon, Matt, Please!* It fills me with desperation and with hope. Then, I recognize the voice.

Lynn?

Her soul molds into mine until the two are indistinguishable. Then, come the memories. I'm giving my Remembrance Day speech in the royal plaza. A moment later, I'm horseback riding with Matt—with myself—through the pasture. Then, the memories take a dark turn. I'm running behind Antai somewhere underground. I'm in a room I've never seen, yet somehow I know it's the king's study. A man is there. He makes me open a small wooden chest. He pressed a mask to my face. Finally, I see Antai standing in a hallway. I raise a gun, compelled by a demon, and pull the trigger.

When I open my eyes, I'm back in front of the endless glass wall, still as dead as I was before. I turn around and look back at the physical world. That's when I see my lifeline. A glistening silklike stream extends from my spine and stretches toward the physical world. Antai notices too.

"Congrats. You get to go back." He starts to turn away when his eyes erupt. "You get to go back! You can save me. You can end this!" He's grinning now, and for the first time since my arrival, I can sense his hope. "All you have to do is kill me, and I'll be free. Just kill me, Matt. I want you to do it. Do you hear me? I beg you to do it!"

"I can't kill y—"

"KILL ME!" he screams. "Please! Please, kill me. I can't go on like this."

I'm about to refuse when I feel something tug on my lifeline, dragging me several feet back.

"I believe in you, MacArthur. You can save me."

Another jerk drags me back, and then another. The tugs are constant. Thwump. Thwump. Thwump on the line, dragging me back to the world I left behind. Suddenly, I can sense the elements once more—the savory stone of the underground. There are people too. Zane, Diego, and… Lynn? I sense them with my soul. They're mourning, mourning my death.

Then, I reach my body, and all I feel is pain.

I'm not awake, but the agony transcends through my dreams. The pain is constant—my head more than anything. It throbs in my temples and aches above my eyes. My brain feels like a cup of jello after being dumped on the floor. My thoughts are scattered, and no matter how hard I try, I can't scoop them into a collective whole.

My brain is broken. The thought is hardly a whisper and quickly forgotten. My mind is an ocean, but it's quickly draining. Memories are swiftly sucked into the abyss. Once again, I feel my soul slipping from my body, passing silently into the great beyond. The lifeline that anchors me grows more and more slack.

And then I feel the lips. They press, soft and warm, against my soul and exhale life. I can feel it. The air inflates my head and spreads through my veins. It's a woman, and just as before, her soul blends with mine. Her every thought is quiet and soothing. Comfort and love. The more entwined we become, the more I begin to recognize her.

Kendra?

Once again, the memories come flooding all at once, threatening to wash away my own identity. I see her parents and a younger brother, all gathered around the dinner table. I see her stooped over Mary's body as Diego stands in the corner, anxiously chewing his nails. Finally, I see myself lying lifeless on one of the cots in the healing loft as Kendra brushes my hair out of my face.

The next thing I know, the healing is underway. The pain doesn't diminish, but I feel each thought growing more pronounced. My internal voice returns, and then come the memories. A dark tunnel. Diego swinging his fist. Someone calling my name... it was Zane. Zane was calling my name.

My eyes snap open.

"Matt! Oh, thank God," Kendra gasps. "I thought we had lost you." She's holding one of my hands but quickly lets go.

"Diego! I need to find Diego." I push against the leather bed, but Kendra holds me down. I try to muscle past her before quickly giving up. I can hardly lift my head.

"Matt, listen to me. You strained your soul worse than I've ever seen. You need to rest. You'll recover, but you really need sleep. Do it for me, please."

I meet her eyes and relax back into the bed. Her smile is hypnotic, and I find my eyes drawn to her pointed incisors, her flushed cheeks. Her hair is curled like usual and bounces above her shoulder.

"You... you kissed me?"

Kendra's ears burn pink, and she glances down. "I gave you the breath of life. It was the only way to save you."

"It was nice," I say. "Thank you."

She smiles, her cheeks nearly as red as her lips.

I look down at my body. Rather than a guard uniform, I'm dressed in a baggy t-shirt and grey sweats.

My tattoos!

"Did you dress me?" I stammer.

"No," Kendra says. "Zane did. He insisted he do it himself."

Thank God.

I let my head fall back against the pillow. "How long have I been out?" I manage to ask.

"Three days."

"Three days?" It sounds insane, but I believe her. "Three days," I breathe. "What happened to the raid? Did we catch the equalists?"

"Most were hung. A few were kept for questioning."

I groan as I try to stand once more. "I need to find Diego!"

"No, Matt." She scolds, holding me down with one hand. "You need to rest." She grows serious, once again resuming the role of caregiver. "If you'll let me, I can help you fall asleep. There's a region in the brain called the thalamus. One of its functions is to inhibit all sensory information while we sleep. Sounds still reach our ears, but the thalamus prevents us from hearing it in our sleep." She leans closer. "If you'll let me, I can use healing to make you sleep. All you have to do is give me permission."

I only agree because of the pain. A dagger of agony is embedded in the back of my skull. "Okay, I'll let you."

Kendra closes her eyes. This time, I feel her mind moving through me. It inches beneath my scalp and she politely moves to the center of my brain. It feels like possession, but more gentle. She can't access my memories, only the ones I willingly share.

Suddenly, the world goes dark. I'm still awake, but I'm blind. Little by little, I can feel her inhibiting all of my sensory input. A second later, my body goes numb. The last thing I hear is Kendra's voice.

"Goodnight, Matt. Sweet dreams."

Then, silence.

My eyes flutter open, and I suck in a gasp. One second Kendra is next to me, and the next she's gone. It's early morning and for once, I feel normal—or as normal as I can remember feeling. My head hardly aches, and my veins don't feel pumped full of lead.

Diego! Kendra said the hanging already occurred. If Diego is alive, there's only one place he could be.

I sit up with ease, feeling an amulet swing from my neck. The healers must've given it to me to assist in the healing and help stabilize my soul. I look around the healing loft and see several other guards sleeping. One looks like he's missing a leg. Another has his

152

torso wrapped in bandages. From the side room, I hear a few healers chatting.

They talk unrestrained in the back room. "—And then he said, you can heal it, right? And I said, boy, I can't heal ugly." The women laugh in unison.

I stand, still wearing sweats and a t-shirt. During the next bout of laughter, I tiptoe to the exit and push my way through the bead curtain. I let my weight carry me as I run down the stairs.

He tried to kill me! I shake the thought from my head. He didn't have a choice. Iris would've killed him. *He didn't have a choice!* I have to believe it's true.

The servants stare as I pass, heads swiveling like sprinklers. I rush on. I know the staircase that leads to the pit. It's unguarded. They're not worried about people breaking in, only breaking out.

I'm several steps down the staircase before I hear shouting. "Excuse me, sir, you can't go down there. Sir, stop!"

I'm running now. The staircase is long and devoid of turns. When I reach the bottom, it's almost pitch black.

Light.

I run past each cell, whipping my head to either side.

Empty, empty, not Diego, empty, not Diego, empty.

The cells seemingly never end. After a dozen empty cells, I hear the cock of a pistol. "Stop, or I shoot." A scrawny guard aims the pistol at my chest.

I stop, but I don't stand quiet. "Diego!" I shout down the hallway, hoping he hears and responds. "Diego!"

"Stand down." A large black man pushes past the scrawny guard. He has a tight, curly beard and wide, gentle eyes. The very tips of his ears curl outwards.

"Matt, my name's Octavian. Zane wanted me to bring you to him as soon as you awoke."

If Diego's not here, he's already hung. I nod, already crushed with my discoveries. First Velma, Tick, Enrique, now Diego too. *I can't keep doing this. I can't.*

153

I walk a few feet behind Octavian as he guides me to Zane's room. I've hardly the sense to look where we're going. All I can think about is Diego on the gallows. He followed his father's terrible fate.

I didn't even get to hear his last words.

Every little while, Octavian glances over his shoulder at me. "I'm glad to see you're doing well. He won't admit it, but General Zane was worried sick. He's hardly slept." When I say nothing, he continues. "In fact, you had the whole palace on edge. The king came by quite a bit… the princess nearly every night."

Lynn!

I've nearly forgotten about her. The girl I met in the garden. The girl who's mind I couldn't read. The girl who loved the commander. She saved my life. I don't know what it means, but it must mean something. If only as a friend, she still cares about me.

Octavian stops in front of Zane's door. I can hear voices within, but not with any clarity. It's only the muffled buzz of intonation. Octavian knocks once and retreats down the hall before Zane can answer. "I've got to get back to my post." He says, waving. "Best of luck to you, Matt."

Before I can thank him, the door whips open. Zane frowns at me through his bushy beard. His face is a blank page. "Matt, come on in. There's some... things we need to discuss."

He steps aside slowly and directs his attention to the other figure in the room.

"Diego!" I nearly choke on my tongue. "But… how? You're alive!"

"Hi, Matt." Diego's voice is almost sarcastic, hardly resembling a friendly greeting. His arms are crossed as he sits on Zane's desk chair. Strangest of all, he's wearing a guard uniform.

Zane steps between us and motions for me to sit on his bed. When I refuse, he sighs. "Matt, I know a lot of strange things have happened, but it will all make sense after I explain."

I take a step back, keeping a clear path to the exit. Now that I know Diego is safe, my worry dissolves, and all I'm left with is the pain of betrayal.

"He tried to kill me," I hiss. "If you hadn't come..." My emotions battle one another. I'm relieved he isn't dead, but at the same time, he shouldn't be rewarded.

Zane speaks slowly. "Diego was our spy, Matt. He's the one who leaked the maps. He—"

"He's loyal to the Holy One," I cry. "He told me himself."

Zane frowns, and his lips disappear within his beard. "It's true, he sympathizes with the Holy One, but that's why he made the perfect spy. Every new equalist must submit to a mind-reading. When Iris read his mind, she saw only his hatred of the king. I knew he would be the only spy that could survive her examination. Now that his cover is blown, the palace is the only safe place for him."

I let Diego see my indignation. "If he's on our side, then why'd he try to kill me? He was fighting for Iris. If we worked together, we could've taken her!"

"Because I told him to," Zane growls. "I told him to earn Iris's trust. To follow her wherever she goes." He groans and rubs his temples. "Your sister is the key to this, Matt. We didn't find the Holy One in the tunnels. He's still out there, and Iris will help us find him. But to get to her, we need Diego."

I turn my attention to Diego. "So what, befriending Iris is more important than my life?"

"Maybe you don't remember, but you passed out right in front of me. I had every chance to kill you, and I didn't," Diego stresses. "Don't treat me like something I'm not."

"And what if Zane hadn't shown up?" I ask. "What would you have done? Would you have killed me then?"

Diego sits up and looks me in the eye. His brown eyes used to be carefree, but now they're lifeless, like desert sand. "I would have done what I had to, same as you."

I know what he's thinking, and it boils my blood. "Same as me? What does that mean?"

"You shot my father," Diego shrugs. "You did what you had to."

"Your father was an accident, okay? An accident!" Now, I'm yelling. "You can't say the same. You knew exactly what you were doing."

His voice chokes and tears swell in his eyes, like a flash flood in a desert valley. "She would've killed you, and then she would've killed me. I didn't have a choice." He wipes at his tears, and like that, the flood is over, replaced with quiet determination.

Zane steps toward the door. "I'll let you two talk this out." I open my mouth to protest, but I'm too slow. He slips into the hall and slams the door behind him. Now, I have no choice; I must give all my attention to Diego, or blatantly ignore him.

I expand my lungs and try to see this as Judy would. *He's frustrated, Matthew. His father is dead, and he's trying to protect what family he has left. He wants to see you as a friend, so give him a reason to. Make the first move.*

I walk to the bed and sit down. "I'm sorry..." I finally say. "For everything."

Diego looks up, letting my words lie stagnant in the air. "When you came the other night to warn me, I only said that stuff to keep my cover. Equalist spies are all over the ring." He puffs his cheeks. "I really didn't want to fight you. I'm not proud of what happened, but I definitely don't want you dead."

"Did you mean what you said about bringing back Velma? That you'll help the Holy One if you can? Did you mean that?"

Diego looks to the window. "If I can bring them back, I have to try. I know about the risks, and I prefer them to a world without Velma... a world without all of them."

I don't argue with him. In some ways, I think he's right, but in other ways, he's so very wrong. An Adamic overlord would be a best-case scenario. The worst-case scenario is almost unimaginable.

"Well then," I say. "I hope I never get in your way again."

"Same." Diego's jaw muscles tense, but whatever he's think-ing, he doesn't say it.

"So... are we good?" I ask.

Diego chews his lip, and for a second, I think he'll turn me down. "I forgive you." He says it with a grimace. "But… I think don't we should be friends." The words hit me like a freight train, leaving me gasping.

"What? Why?"

Diego clenches his fists. "I know it was an accident, but it hurts too much to see you."

I look at him blankly and he groans. "Don't you see, dude? It's like if a rabid dog killed my dad. I wouldn't keep the freaking thing as a pet. A daily reminder is the last thing I need. It's better if we keep our distance." He looks away. "It's safer that way for both of us."

I'm stunned. "Uh… okay. Well then, I guess this is goodbye for now."

Diego pauses at the door, holding it open with one hand, "I wish things could've been different. Goodbye, Matt." He lets the door swing behind him without another word.

I stare at the door until it opens again. This time, it's Zane coming back in. "That looks like it went well."

"Can we really trust him?" I ask. "What if the Holy One asks him to kill someone in the palace… or the princess. Who's to say he wouldn't do it?"

Zane strokes his beard. "It's a possibility, but one I'm willing to take. Remember, Matt, the Holy One took Diego's mother. Diego may hate the king, but he hates the Holy One more. I trust he'll do the right thing when the time comes."

"Okay," I say. "I trust you."

Zane looks me over, noticing the way I slump in my chair. "You should probably get back to the healing loft." He says it like a suggestion, but I know it's an order. "They'll want to keep an eye on you."

"Actually, I have a few questions really quick."

"Hmmm?" Zane grunts

"Ummm... what can you tell me about the afterlife?"

Zane rolls his eyes. "I'm not the one to be answering this, Matt. Go ask a priest or something."

"Please, Zane."

"Fine." He looks down at his hands—at his wedding band. "They say the afterlife is a different plane of existence, whatever that means. It exists superimposed over our world, but it's all theory." His voice softens. "According to the ancient text, it's a place where people live in joy. Friends, family, all reunited."

"Is there a place..." I wonder, "where someone could get trapped between life and death?"

Zane straightens, suddenly more interested. "There's the veil. Some call it the bridge between worlds, but it's not a bridge, more like a barrier. They say that wicked spirits—those who fear the afterlife—sometimes try to return to the physical world, only to be trapped beyond the veil. They fear what heaven holds, and yet they can't return to earth. They call it purgatory. It's rumored to be a lonely, endless suffering."

I suck in my lip and look down.

Zane's eyes turn to slivers. "Matt, why do you ask?"

I say nothing. I don't even know how to say it.

"Matt?"

"When I was dead... I saw a big glass wall. And... Commander Elsborne was there. He wanted to return, but the veil wouldn't let him. He can't pass on because he's still bound to his body. He's stuck."

Zane grows still.

"What if I can bring him back?" I say. "You said that some mystics could speak with the dead. What if I learned how? Maybe I could untether my soul and go back."

"Don't even think about it, Matt; it's too dangerous. I'll speak to the king. Maybe he can think of something."

"There's one more thing. According to Iris, the Holy One said that you killed my parents. If there's any truth to that, I'd rather you just tell me now—"

"No!" Zane barks. "Listen to me, Matt." His brown eyes quiver like two tectonic plates. "I didn't kill your parents. You hear me? I would never do anything to hurt your parents. The Holy One is a liar. He will say anything to manipulate his followers."

"I believe you," I say. "I do. I swear… but that's got me thinking. Everyone says the Holy One is a mystery, but you said my parents fought against him, right?"

Zane nods. "Like I told you, your parents gave their lives to protect Hogrum."

"Exactly," I say. "To save Hogrum from the Holy One. You said it yourself; you were all fighting the Holy One, weren't you?"

Zane knows where this is going, but he doesn't let on. His brow creases down the center. "Your point?"

I suck in a breath, storing up the air to form my next question. "Zane, tell me the truth. Do you know who the Holy One is? If you tried to kill him, it only makes sense you knew who he was."

Zane turns so that I'm facing the side of his face. I follow his gaze to a small family portrait. It shows Zane standing beside a beautiful brunette. Each of them holding one of their daughters.

Zane swallows once. "Yes, Matt. I know who the Holy One is. He's the man who killed my family."

I'm stunned. I had my suspicions, but I didn't expect Zane to be so blunt. "Who?" I demand. "Who killed my parents?"

"I can't say." Zane sighs. "I promised someone I'd never tell."

"What? Who?"

Zane faces me, his beard unable to hide the pain.

"The king."

I quicken my pace on the gravel road, stepping farther and farther from the outer wall. I'm at the most dangerous place of my journey, exactly halfway between the city and the bunker, but I'm not worried in the slightest. Zane is by my side, and I've never felt safer.

His eyes move like windshield wipers, back and forth across the horizon. One hand rests on the hilt of his shortsword, and the other swings carelessly by his side. It's subtle, but every so often, his eyes dart my way. He's assessing me. Or maybe he's building the courage to ask me something.

Either way, I seize control of the conversation. "Zane, can you tell me a little bit about my parents?"

He looks down at me grunts. "I was wondering when you were going to ask that." He runs his fingers through his beard. "What do you wanna know?"

I don't have the slightest clue. "If you were me, what would you want to know?"

He must take my question to heart, because he thinks for a long while, all the while scratching his beard with his hand. "Well, you have your father's hair, blonde, but his was more curly. Yours is wavy like your mother's. Her hair was much darker." He stops scanning the horizon, lost in the fondness of the past. "You definitely have your father's knack for dominion. He tried to teach your mother once. She was full-blooded, but she didn't care much for it. She could barely manage a shield, and she rarely tried. She was one for the books. I guess you get that from her, your book smarts, I mean. She could read an old text about Adamic and have the characters memorized, almost photographic."

He taps the hilt of his sword. "She actually was the one who crafted me this. She was an amazing adalit, maybe better than the king."

"Seriously?"

Zane nods. "You're level-headed like her. She was always observant, sometimes even shy. But your father, humph, that man had a temper. Once he was angry, there was no stopping him, literally. Once, a feeder burned his favorite coat, and your father nearly leveled a forest. The man was powerful. When he'd get like that, only your mother could calm him down. They were good for each other… complementary."

"What was the coolest thing my dad could do with dominion?"

Zane smiles. "That's easy. He could turn any drink into wine. It was the greatest party trick. Got him invited to everything."

"You told me once that Kildron became a feeder. Can you tell me how?" I wonder.

Zane grimaces. "That's a long story. Better for another time."

"Alright." I don't press, grateful for the few answers he's already given. "I have another question, but this one's about you. Why do you go by Zane?"

"Huh?"

"All the other guardians go by their last names, but you go by Zane? Why? What's your real last name?"

"I first came to Hogrum because my uncle was a guardian there. Wingrin Alazar was his name. He's the only reason I'm a guardian today."

"He chose you as his apprentice?"

"Actually, no. My uncle already had an apprentice, but by the time Kildron and I were Lieutenants, General Cusp was looking for one. Your father was his first choice. He was powerful and well-spoken... opinionated too. He was perfect for the job, but my uncle insisted Cusp choose me. Eventually, General Cusp announced me as His guardian elect. The next year he died of a heart attack, and I was bonded to his soul-anchor. With my uncle on the council, I decided to go by Zane. Things would've been confusing with the same last names. When I arrived here, I stuck with it. General Alazar just doesn't sound right."

"Did your uncle, did he die in Hogrum too?"

Zane nods.

"I'm sorry."

Zane says nothing, once again scanning the horizon. The bunker is just up ahead, and with it, the safety of steel walls. "You go on," Zane says. "I'll stay watch out here."

"You sure?"

He nods. "Go on."

I jog the last 50 yards and rap my knuckles on the steel dome. A few seconds later, the hatch tips open from the inside.

"Matt, ole buddy ole pal. Welcome back." It's Ronald. He retreats back down the ladder, and I follow.

As I get to the bottom, he holds his finger to his lips. "Captain Renshu is sleeping in the dorms. He's a light sleeper so we have to keep it down."

I give him a thumbs-up, and together we creep into the communications room. Ronald eases the door shut behind us.

Klinton stands and gives me a hug. "Matt, I can't believe you're here. Rose told us what happened. You should be resting."

"Rose was here? Like, the princess?"

"She came by yesterday. She said you were in a coma for three days?"

"Yeah, I was pretty messed up, but I'm doing fine now. Don't worry about me."

Ronald shakes his head, his grin hints at both absurdity and admiration. "You seriously tried to use dominion without an amulet?"

I smile. "I didn't just try, I succeeded."

Ronald laughs. "Was it worth three days?"

"Best sleep of my life," I laugh. "What else did she say?"

"She also said that Vyle asked her on a date. Can you believe that?"

"No way? Vyle? What'd she say?"

"No, of course," Klinton says. "She hates him. I just can't believe he had the nerve to ask. He says he's changed apparently."

"Fat chance," I say. "The dude's trash."

"And Diego was a spy?" Klinton questions. "I still can't believe that. Rose says he's a lieutenant now. All three of you in the palace together. That's insane."

"It's not as cool as it sounds," I shrug. "Rose is always busy, and I work the night shift, so I never see anybody. You're not missing out."

"Still. It sounds like a good time."

"It's alright. Tell me about you guys. What have you been up to?"

162

"What is there to tell?" Ronald grows quiet and motions at the room. I hadn't realized it, but all the monitors are turned off. "The High Council had a meeting this week and decided to call off the convoy. With the Holy One still out there. It's getting too dangerous. The last group of guardsmen returned this morning."

"Seriously?"

"Yep." Ronald sighs and spins around in his roller chair. "We're supposed to stay for surveillance, but there's not much to do anymore. Klinton is the only thing keeping me sane."

Klinton shrugs. "Sanity's my specialty. We find ways to pass the time." Suddenly he goes rigid and glances between Ronald and me Like a sunburn timelapse, his face grows steadily redder. "But not like that. We play cards and stuff."

I wave my hand. "I know what you meant; you're fine."

"And what about you, Matt?" Ronald bounces his eyebrows. "The princess sure did have a lot to say about you. She's going to need a date for the Fall Ball. It's only a month away."

Rose told me about the fall festival weeks ago, but not a fall ball. "Fall Ball? Is that the same as the Fall Festival?"

Ronald looks dumbfounded. "Do you know anything about it?"

"It's a festival in the fall? Is there much else I'm missing?"

"Oh, you're missing everything. Allow me to explain. Fall Ball is the party of the year. It's both a feast and a ball. It takes place in the palace on the night of Hallow's Eve."

"Halloween?"

Ronald glances at Klinton, notably confused. "Did I stutter? I said Hallow's Eve. Anyway, only the elite are invited, and they each get a plus one—your date, assuming you ask someone."

"I can ask anyone? Even a laborer?"

"If you want to make a statement, sure. You can ask a maid for all I care, but this next part is important. Traditionally, to ask a girl, you have to bring her flowers. To accept, the girl places the flowers outside her door. That way, you know who's taken and who's available."

"Can't she just say yes?"

"It's tradition, Matt. Don't question it. Besides, I didn't finish. If you give someone white flowers, it means you invite them as a friend, but if you give them red flowers, it means you invite them as more than a friend. So, don't mess that up. Girls are very particular about their flowers. If a girl is into you and you give her white flowers, I can guarantee her friends will hate you forever."

"White flowers equal friendship, red flowers equal romance. Got it."

"So, who are you taking?" Klinton interjects. "You know the princess had quite a bit to say about you. If you don't ask her, who will?"

"Her boyfriend is in a coma. Isn't that kind of... disrespectful?"

"Then give her white roses." Ronald shrugs. "Just to play it safe. That way the commander doesn't kill you when he wakes up."

I think of his voice, the way he begged me to kill him. "Maybe." I soak the word with uncertainty.

Ronald frowns. "If not her, then who?"

"Well, there's this healer named Kendra." Before I can say more, Ronald interjects.

"Ohhhh, I've heard good things about the healers."

Klinton is smiling too. "Is she the one you were talking to at the graduation party?"

I nod, trying to keep from grinning like a child.

"I say go for it," Ronald says. "If you wait too long, someone else might ask her first."

Klinton's head slowly drops to the floor, "That'll be fun. You, Rose, and Diego will all be there together. You'll have to let us know what it's like." He tries and fails to hide his disappointment.

Ronald steps behind Klinton and puts him in a chokehold. "Klinton just needs to be grateful for what he has and his wonderful coworkers." He rubs his knuckles on Klinton's hair and then grunts as he's elbowed in the gut.

Klinton grins, obviously loving the attention. He runs his finger through his hair. "Klinton will be jealous when he wants to be, thank you very much."

Ronald exaggerates a glance my way. "Klinton shouldn't talk in the third person. It'll scare away the guest."

Klinton raises his chin and smirks. "Klinton knows the guest better than Ronald, so Ronald should shut his pie hole."

"Matt is going to go call his mom." I finally add. They look at each other and blush.

Klinton points down toward the exit. "If you want some privacy, you can use the bathroom. It's the first door on the right. Here, I'll just show you."

He walks ahead of me and opens the door to the bathroom. It's small, with a single sink and a dirty mirror. Fortunately, the toilet is modern.

Klinton leans in as I walk past him and whispers, "He kissed me yesterday."

"Ronald did?"

Klinton nods, giddy with excitement.

"Congrats, man. That's awesome. Are you guys official?"

"Not yet. It's still kinda new. Anyway, I just wanted to tell you. I gotta go before he gets suspicious. I don't want him to know I've told you. Keep it on the down-low." Klinton backs out of the bathroom, still smiling from ear to ear.

I give him a thumbs-up as he closes the door. Then, I sit on top of the toilet lid and turn on my phone. It still has some charge from last time at 19%.

I tap 'favorites' and then 'Mom.' Finally, I take a deep breath and press the phone to my ear.

Ring... ring... click.

"Hello?"

My heart drops. It isn't Judy.

"Hi. This is Matthew MacArthur, Judy's son. Is it alright if I speak with her?"

The nurse hesitates. "Ummm, yeah, I suppose this is a good time. Give me one second."

I hear shuffling, then I hear the nurse. "Hi, Judy, your son is on the l—"

"You give me that phone," I hear Judy demand.

I smile to myself as the phone is presumably passed to Judy.

"Matt? Matt... is that you?" Her voice is like sandpaper, and her eager rabbit tone moves at a turtle's pace. As painful as it is to listen, no doubt, it's costing Judy more.

"It's me, Mom. I'm doing well. I've missed you so much."

"I miss you too. It's so nice to hear your voice. Tell me, Matt, How are you doing? Are you healthy? Are you happy?"

"I'm doing well. I was actually pretty sick last week, but I'm almost back to normal now."

"And... are you happy?"

I hesitate for a moment too long. "Yeah, I'm happy."

Judy isn't fooled. "Is there anything you want to talk about?" she presses. "Your research? Or maybe your friends? If you want to talk about anything, I'm here."

I sigh. I don't want to stress her, but I need her wisdom. "I don't know, Mom. I just don't know what I'm doing anymore." I do my best to translate my situation into something Judy will understand. I have to remind myself she thinks I'm studying in Australia.

"They made me a supervisor for one of the research groups, and I think we're working towards a good goal, but I don't really agree with our... methods."

"Hmmm. When you say you don't agree, what exactly do you mean?"

The system is corrupt. The laborers are abused. But I can't say that. I try my best to translate it into non-Adamic terms.

"Honestly, Mom, some of the things they do here just aren't right. They exploit the test subjects. They don't get properly compensated. If I get promoted, I might be able to make some changes, but I have to do some things I don't agree with to get there."

"Hmmm," Judy thinks. "That is complicated. Does anyone else feel the same way you do?"

"I have one boss who I like." *Zane.* "He doesn't agree with the methods either, but he can't change anything on his own. And there

166

are a few other researchers." *Rose and Diego.* "Other than that, I think we're the only ones."

I can imagine Judy nodding her head slowly. "Hmmm. That's tough, Matt. You've always been smarter than me. What do you think is the right thing to do?"

"Well..." My voice trails off as I think. "If I refuse to do the research, I'll just get fired, and someone else will take my place. Either way, the subjects will be treated the same. So, maybe I should go along with it for now, and when I'm in a position of enough power, maybe then I can make a real difference."

Judging by her silence, I can tell she disagrees. "Perhaps, Matt. Or perhaps you're not as alone as you think. Perhaps the others haven't spoken up because they assume the same as you: that they're the only ones. It's not guaranteed, but maybe if you take a stand, others will do the same. You could be the start of something great."

"And if they don't join me? Then what? I get fired? I come back home?" *I let everything I've worked for go to waste.* I don't try to dampen my frustration. Instead, I let Judy bear the weight of my burdens.

"I'm sorry, Matthew." She soothes. "I know it's not easy. Both options come with risks but in my opinion, It's better to be fired from a cause you don't agree with than to dedicate your life to leading it." The line goes silent, and I hear her coughing away from the mic.

"If you do get expelled," she resumes, "you'll find a new school and a new cause. Life will go on, and odds are, you'll be happier for it."

I lean forward from my seat on the toilet and let my forehead rest on the empty towel rack. "What if I'm confident I can make it to the top? That way, I can actually help the people here. I'm friends with some of them. I can't just abandon them."

I hear Judy sigh—barely a puff of air. "That's a decision only you can make. You're a good person, Matthew. I've known that ever since you were little. I trust you'll do the right thing. But, if it's okay with you, I'd like to give you some advice. I'm not saying that the end can't justify the means—in some cases that may be true—but I will say this: never sacrifice doing good today, for something good that may not come tomorrow. It's just not worth waiting."

"Okay, mom. I'll keep that in mind. Thanks for listening."

"That's what I'm here for, baby. That's my job. Now, tell me about that girl you liked. Lynn was her name, right?"

This time I frown. "Uhh, I'm not really sure what to say. I haven't spoken to her in weeks. She got moved to a different project. I see her every now and then, but it's not the same." *I'm not sure she's who I thought she was.*

"Have you tried to talk to her?"

"Not really. Her, uh, boyfriend got in an accident. He's in a coma. I don't want to intrude. I figured if she really wants to talk, she'll come to me."

Judy scoffs, disgusted by the thought. "Or she's thinking the same about you. Sounds to me like she needs a friend now more than ever. You don't have to kiss her, Matt, but at least be there for her. She deserves that much. All great relationships are built on friendship. Why don't you start with that?"

"Thanks, Mom. I think you're right. I'll talk to her." I don't tell her that there's another girl: Kendra. I don't want to complicate things.

"And what about you?" I ask. "Tell me how you're doing."

"Oh, there's nothing to tell," she redirects. "Tell me some more about you. What are you most looking forward to?"

I don't have much, so I say the first thing I can think of. "Well, there's actually this dance coming up at the end of the month called the Fall Ball. It's a big feast. Apparently, I have to take a date. It should be fun. I'll probably need to ask someone in the coming weeks."

"Oh, wonderful, Matt. Promise me you'll ask Lynn. She'll need someone to keep her mind off things. Promise me you'll ask her. Next time we talk, I want to hear all about it."

I hesitate, but I can't bring myself to say no. "Of course, Mom. I promise."

"Good." Her voice is strained, but she sounds happy. "Well, I should get going. The nurse wants me to rest. But know that I love you, Matt. Please call again soon."

"Love you too, Mom, and I will. Bye."

"Bye-bye now."

I wait for the line to disconnect, but it doesn't. Instead, the nurse breathes in the mic, I can hear her heels clicking as she walks into the other room.

"I'm speaking with Judy's son, Matthew, correct?" She asks

"Yes, that's me."

"Well, Matthew, I regret to inform you that Judy's health is deteriorating rapidly. Today, she managed to hold a conversation, but some days she's hardly able to eat. To be completely transparent, I don't see her living more than a few weeks. If you can, I recommend you arrange to say your final goodbyes."

I'm speechless. I squeeze my eyes shut and press my head into the towel rack. *No! I need more time!*

Eventually, I have to respond. "Okay. Okay, I'll do that. Thank you."

"Thanks for calling, sir. Have a good day."

"You too."

The line clicks.

One month. I have one month to save Judy.

It's time I visit Kendra in person. It's time she teaches me how to heal.

Chapter 12

Rose

I tiptoe deeper into the pit. The silence feels like a blanket over my head, comforting and concerning at the same time. I miss my soul-anchor more than ever.

I pass cell after cell, most of them empty. Cavernum doesn't waste time with prisoners. They're seen as nothing but another mouth to feed. The only exception is those with information, and that's exactly what I'm after.

Finally, I spot him. He's facing away from the bars, sitting cross-legged on the floor. I'm about to speak when a nauseating Australian accent fills the pit. "Hello, princess. I was beginning to think you'd forgotten about me." He rests his hands on the stone floor and rotates his body to face me.

I brace myself for the hideous sight of his injuries, but the darkness hides them from view. The only thing I see with any clarity is his eyes. They reflect the amber torchlight, looking more yellow than green.

Where's Nevela? The question is clear, but I can't quite get myself to say it. I'm not sure I'm ready to hear the answer.

Jack lifts his head and lets out an amused snort. "I'm not a piece of art. You can't just stare at me. Go ahead. Ask your questions. What are you afraid of?"

"Where is she? You said the equalists had her, but you were wrong. We captured their base; she wasn't there."

"You see, the maid really is a tragic story." He grabs hold of his feet, leaning in closer. "You promised to come quietly in exchange for her life. Had you kept your word, she would've been freed days ago, but no. You just had to call out for big, strong Antai." He says the last words with a shrill, mocking tone. "Believe me, I wish it wasn't so, but you put yourself first, and there are consequences."

I don't want the answer, but I ask anyway. "What are the consequences? Can you at least tell me what I put her through?"

"The Holy One has her. She's serving a very special purpose, but don't worry; he'll keep her alive as long as possible. It's in his best interest." He smiles as if it's nothing but a game.

I feel my blood beginning to simmer, but I can't give in to rage. I need to keep a clear head. "If you tell me where she is, I promise I can make your stay more comfortable. Food, clothes, you name it. I can make it worth your while."

Jack shrugs. "It doesn't really matter where she is. She'll suffer the same. I'm sorry, Rose. I know you think I'm a monster, but I don't take joy in her suffering."

"Then let her go!"

Jack laughs. "As if I have any say. Look at me." He grabs the bars with each hand. "You think I'm in control here? I'm nothing but a zoo animal for your precious king to admire once in a blue moon. No, you'll have to ask the Holy One. Only he can set her free. He decides who lives and dies." He leans back, letting his fingers slip from the bars. "Even my own life is in his hands."

"How do I find him? He wasn't underground."

Jack smirks. "Don't worry, princess. He'll find you before long. I may have failed, but he hasn't forgotten about you."

This isn't the information I came for, but I fall for his bait anyway. "What does the Holy One want with me?"

Jack smiles. "You should ask the king. He can tell you."

"W-what do you mean?"

"Your Grandfather knows the Holy One better than anyone. Or has he not told you?"

"Told me what?" I demand.

Jack shrugs. "Why don't you ask him? Or... are you afraid that he'll lie?"

I bite my lip. *Give Grandpa the chance, Rose. Maybe he won't disappoint.*

I look to either side and lower my voice. "Two weeks ago, you said something after my grandfather questioned you. You said that he knows what the Adamic phrase meant, the one left in the inheritance box."

Jack grins, his teeth gleaming in the darkness. "That's correct."

"Even if he did know, how would you possibly know that he knew?"

Jack shakes his finger. "Now, you're asking the right questions." He lets me suffer his silence for several moments.

"Well?"

"The Holy One was taught the purpose of the incantation, but he never learned the phrase itself. That's why he sent me to discover the syllables."

"What does that have to do with my Grandpa?"

His lips stretch thin. "It was the king who taught him, and it was the king who refused to show him the verbal spell. Apart from myself, they may be the only ones in the world who know."

"You know it too?"

Jack grins. "If you let me out, I'll tell you what it does."

I don't give him the satisfaction of responding. He killed Antai, and he'll rot in here forever for it.

Jack suddenly stands, and I feel the mood changing. He wraps his raw, peeling fingers around the bars. "You know, Rose, you can still have him. If the Holy One succeeds, all can be undone. The only question is, what are you willing to do to bring him back?"

"If you believe that the Holy One will ever help you, you're a fool. You're just his puppet, and when he gets what he wants, he'll toss you aside."

"Now, Rose, how can you say that when you don't even know him? The Holy One understands. He shares your grief. He's lost loved ones, but they will live again. The Holy One is not your enemy."

"If he understands, then why kill Antai? He didn't have to die!"

"The Holy One doesn't do anything that can't be undone, Rose. Antai is no exception. All he needs is the book of life, and balance can be restored. Join him, and you will have everything you've wanted. Peace in Cavernum. Safety from the feeders. Equality for your people. These are not selfish desires, Rose. The world can be made perfect." He smiles in a way that could have been charming, but with his burns, it gives me chills. "Join us, Rose."

"If the Holy One wants me to join, why not invite me himself? Why hide?"

"He…" Jack looks down, and for the first time, I sense disappointment… shame in the Holy One. "He has his reasons for keeping his distance, but you will meet him soon. All things in his timing."

I've heard enough. I don't say goodbye, not to such a man as low as him. Without a word, I turn and walk away.

"You'll be back, princess. Pray I'm still here when you come. It won't be long before the Holy One has need of me."

I quicken my pace, tapping my way up to the ground floor. I don't stop until I'm in the Central Wing. I need to be free of his voice. I need time to think.

"Hello, Rose."

This voice is no better than the last. Vyle approaches slowly, almost cautiously. He's wearing a long tan cloak and his pale hair falls flat across his face like bangs. A crystal vase, the only beautiful thing about his appearance, is perched on his palm with a dozen white roses.

He smiles, not a victorious grin, but a smile of relief. "I was hoping I'd find you here."

"What do you want?"

"I'd like to apologize for some of the harsh things my father said at the hearing the other day. And I'd like to apologize for myself… for what I did. It was wrong. I'm hoping to make amends." He says it like a script, as if he's practiced a dozen times.

"I'm not interested in making amends. I want to be left alone." I take a step toward my chambers, but Vyle takes three and cuts me off.

"Please, Rose. You'll want to hear this; trust me."

"Oh yeah, because you know what I want better than I do." I roll my eyes. "Why are you even here?"

"Isn't it obvious?" He holds out the flowers. "I'm here to ask you to the Fall Ball. I figured we'd go as friends."

"Friends? How can you possibly call us friends after what you did?" I start to walk away. "We'll never be friends." *You belong in the pit.*

Vyle chases after me. "Rose, I'm not a bad guy. Just let me prove it to you."

"Not a bad guy?" I clench my hands. "You nearly killed me. You… you put your hands all over me, Vyle. Did you think I'd forget? It's unforgivable."

He takes a deep breath, expelling his anger as carbon dioxide. "Please, give me another chance. We'll go as friends, nothing more. I swear on the creation."

I try to move around him, but he sidesteps to block my path. "Please, princess. You don't have to go alone."

"Ughhh!" If he won't move, I'll take the long way. I turn around and start marching toward the eastern quadrant. Vyle trails behind me like a stray dog.

"Rose, I've said I'm sorry. What more can I possibly do? Whatever it is, I'll do it. Do you want me to beg on my knees? I'll do it."

I don't respond. Nothing I can say will penetrate his dense skull. I speed up to the threshold between walking and jogging.

"Rose, slow down, damn it… Rose. Stop being a—"

A shrill scream erupts from the hallway in front of us, followed by the clatter of a tin tray. Milk, eggs, and shattered glass spread across the marble. Failing to form words, the maid merely points into the room.

I can't quite see what the maid is pointing at, but I can see the blood-red door hanging ajar.

Judge Lumb! I hadn't realized where we were, but now I'm in panic mode. I sprint to the doorway, already anticipating the worst.

I gasp as I grab the doorframe to slow me down. On the far side of the room, Judge Lumb is lying face down in his bed. The white sheets are stained a sinister shade of red. The quantity is appalling.

"Guards! Sound the alarm!" I scream.

Vyle comes up behind me. "Demons! He's dead."

I can't see his face, but his amber curls are enough to convince me it's him. I nod as the pounding of boots grows nearer.

That's when I see the door across the hall; it too is marked with death. Strangely, the door is cracked open. I don't want to know, but my body moves for me, crossing the hall and pushing the door open.

I gag, retching on an empty stomach. The scent of burnt iron hovers in the air; I can almost taste it in my throat. I creep into the room until the bed is visible. I don't dare look directly, spotting the blood from my peripherals. It's enough to confirm my worst fears: another judge murdered in his sleep. I back slowly out of the room, wishing more than ever for my soul-anchor.

Down the hall, I see Octavian checking every blood-stained door. "You, sound the alarm!" He barks at a guard before entering another room.

175

He doesn't try to revive the dead. He opens the door only far enough to see inside. Then, he turns to me. "Come, princess. We need to get you somewhere safe."

"What's happening?"

Octavian's jaw quivers. "They're dead, princess. The palace is no longer safe."

Chapter 13

Matt

Kendra's hand is ice cold as it moves across my chest. It's been two weeks since the sewer raid, and not a day has passed without a healing session with Kendra. In all honesty, I hope the sessions continue.

Kendra presses her palm flat on my sternum. "Breathe in."

I take a dramatic breath, as if I'm about to go deep-sea diving. My cheeks inflate to maximum capacity.

"And out."

Her lips curl as I exhale. As dumb as it is, she finds my shenanigans amusing. "Lungs and vitals are normal, and your soul looks as strong as ever. You've healed up nicely. In all honesty, I don't think there's much else I can do for you." She steps back and jots a note on a clipboard. "You should be healthy enough to resume your dominion training. As long as you take things slow, I don't foresee any issues."

"Slow. You got it."

"Well, is there anything else you need from me, Matt?"

I look around the healing loft. It's almost empty. "I was actually wondering if you would still be able to teach me how to heal… and I could teach you how to use combat dominion like I promised."

Kendra leans in close. "I've been thinking about that, and it's complicated. I can't teach you during my shift, and I don't have my amulet when I'm off duty. Luckily, patients can request in-room visits from a healer. Hypothetically," she grins, "if you were to request an in-room visit, we could have the amulets and a private hour to ourselves."

I'm nodding along with every word. "Hypothetically," I bounce my eyebrows, "how would I make that request?"

"You can write a request and submit it to the head-healer. Be sure to specifically mention my name, and make sure you give a reason for the visits. For example, maybe you have chronic head-aches, and the sunlight of the healing loft makes it worse?" She winks. "Got it?"

I nod. "Okay, yeah, those headaches are terrible. I'll make that request. Thanks, Kendra."

"My pleasure. I look forward to treating you."

I hurry down the stone steps and head straight for my room. I'll write the request immediately. How soon should I request it? Tomorrow? Tomorrow morning?

I'm already formatting the letter in my head when I hear a woman scream.

"Let go of me! Please! You're hurting me!"

Two women round the corner, a taller pale woman and a shorter dark-skinned girl. The white woman is clutching a fistful of the young girl's curly hair, dragging the girl beside her like airport luggage. The poor girl stumbles along, craning her head to reduce the tension.

"You!" The tall woman points at me with her free hand! "I need a guardsman! Are you a guardsman?"

"I am, but I'm not on du—"

"Arrest this woman! She's an imposter! She needs to be arrested!"

178

I don't have to ask the woman for her name; I already know it's Karen. "What makes you think she's an imposter?" I ask. The girl is wearing the typical maid attire—a grey dress with white sleeves.

Karen steps closer, asserting her superiority. "Do you think I'm stupid? First off, she doesn't have her papers. Second, the girl is pregnant. I've never seen a pregnant maid in my life. And this... wench has the audacity to tell me that she's the princess's personal maid. Over my dead body!"

I half expect the girl to cry, but Karen's words seem ineffective against her. The maid ignores Karen completely and turns to me, her brown eyes pleading for support. "I'm telling the truth. I don't have my papers because I'm new. The princess is getting them arranged. Please, ask her yourself. She'll tell you I'm telling the truth."

I let my soul drift closer, grateful for my prescribed amplifier. Unsurprisingly, her words ring true. There isn't an ounce of deceit in her soul. All I sense is frustration.

I lock eyes with Karen, trying my best to sound official. "Why don't you let her go, and I'll take it from here. I'll take her to the princess and confirm everything." I take a step closer. "You can let go of her now."

Karen scowls, jerking the girl back. "No! I'm not letting go until she's arrested. She's an imposter!"

"Ma'am, please let her go. If you don't take your hands off her, I'll... I'll have to use force."

"No! Don't you dare touch me! I will not be threatened! You are verbally assaulting me!" She lifts her head and spots two royal guards at the end of the hall. They're far, but they're marching our way.

"GUARDS!" She wails. "Come here! Hurry! This girl is an impos—"

Before she can finish the sentence, I catapult my soul into her body. I splash into her swamp of a soul and wade my way deeper into her mind, trying not to collect her entitled, self-serving schmuck. Then, when I feel her body around me, I speak a single sentence.

"I feel woozy!"

Sleep!

The effect is instantaneous. Karen's hand goes slack, and her knees buckle. The maid moves out of the way just in time. Karen comes crashing down in the center of the hallways. I wince as her face slaps the tiled floor.

The guards triple their pace, arriving in a matter of seconds. Both are baffled. They squint at the woman and then look to me for answers. "What in the hell just happened?"

"Beats me!" I try my best to look exacerbated. "She said 'I feel woozy,' and then she just fainted. She was freaking out before she passed out. I think she was having a panic attack. She probably needs a healer." I glance down at the maid, barely containing my smile. "If you guys watch her, we'll go get help."

The guard on the left nudges Karen with his foot. She doesn't move. "Yeah, why don't you two get someone. We'll see if we can wake her."

"We're on it!" I start slow, giving the maid time to follow, then I pick up the pace until we're around the corner.

I expect her to look relieved, but if anything, she looks more panicked than ever. She twists at the waist to look back at Karen. "Did that woman just die?"

"Nah." I shake my head. "She probably had low blood sugar or something. They'll get her to the healers, and she'll be fine."

The girl soaks in my confidence, and I watch her worry melt away. A glimmer of a smile twitches on her lips. "What are the odds of that?" Her smile grows wider. "We're not going to get help, are we?"

"Not a chance." I look down at the girl. For someone who's just been manhandled, she's surprisingly calm. "Are you okay?" I ask. "That old hag was yanking on your hair pretty hard."

The maid pats her scalp where Karen held her hostage. "I'm fine. I've been through worse." Her voice is soft, yet sweet and optimistic. "Thanks for getting me out of there. I thought for sure I would end up in handcuffs."

"I'm sorry you had to go through that. If she hadn't passed out, I swear I would've sucker-punched her."

The girl frowns. "Do you really think she's okay? Maybe we should go check on her?"

"No! You're too nice. That woman will be pampered far more than she deserves. Trust me." I look the maid over. She's short—as short as they come, yet something about her looks familiar. "So, you're the princess's new maid? What's your name?"

"Wendy," squeaks her reply.

"Nice to meet you, Wendy. My name's Matt."

The maid slowly peers up at me, a hesitant smile driving her lips apart. "Matt? Your name is Matt?"

"Yeah, why?"

She stops in her tracks. "Like the refugee Matt? Friend of the princess Matt?"

Now, I'm smiling too. "Yeah... how do you know about me?"

Her face blinks several times. "Of course I know about you. The princess..." She blushes, suddenly self-conscious of what she's shared. "Let's just say she's told me all about you. My sister has too."

Now, I'm the one in shock. I snap my fingers as it hits me. "Your Velma's sister! Oh my gosh, that's why you look so familiar." *It explains everything.*

I notice her shoulders relax. I don't know what Rose has told her, but she seems significantly more comfortable in my presence.

"Where are you headed?" I quickly interject. "I'll walk you back if you don't mind."

"Yes, please. To the Royal Wing if that's alright."

"Yeah, of course." I take us down a flight of stairs to the ground floor, then we turn up the hallway leading North. "So." I pretend to be disinterested. "What's the princess up to these days?"

"She's on guard duty, most of the time. Right now, I think she's on the palace wall, but that might've been yesterday. I'm not really sure."

I nod as if I expected as much. "Cool." I want to ask more, but I don't want to come off as creepy. "And what about you? You live in the palace. How has it been so far?"

Her face is neutral. "It's been... hmmm. How do I describe it?"

"You can say it," I insist. "Boring, lonely, you have to deal with grumpy old hags like Betty Crocker back there."

"Different," Wendy concludes. "It's been different. Better than I expected in some ways, and worse in others. The other servants are nice, and the work isn't so bad."

"How's the princess? I imagine she treats you well?"

"Oh, yes! The princess is wonderful," Wendy gushes. "She's been amazing to my family. She also healed Diego's sister."

"Really? Mary's all better now?" I shouldn't be surprised. I remember seeing a memory from Kendra. It makes sense that Rose sent her. The Lynn I knew would do anything for her friends.

"That's not all. She has an idea to bring better health care to the ring. She says she's going to pitch it to the council."

"Wow. Hopefully, she can pull it off." I say. "It sounds like the princess is on top of things." *No wonder she hasn't stopped by.*

Wendy nods but doesn't elaborate. I take her silence as agreement. We turn down another long hallway. The Royal Wing is only a short stroll away. I can already see the point of no entry where Royal guards stand at attention.

"Thanks, Matt. I can make it from here."

"You know, if you ever need anything, feel free to swing by. I'm in the Eastern Wing, room 224."

Wendy stops and looks at the floor, "I..." her jaw snaps shut. "Never mind. Thanks again, Matt." She smiles graciously and turns away.

"Wait? What is it?"

Wendy's lips fold on one side and her cheeks pucker inward. "It's just... maybe you could talk to the princess for me?"

"For you?"

Wendy frowns. "Well, no, for her. I can tell by the way she talks that she misses you, but she's afraid or something. I think you should talk to her."

I know that fear. The fear that things will be awkward. The fear that a friendship is over. "Okay. I'll talk to her."

"Thanks, Matt. It was nice to meet you."

"Nice to meet you too. And tell the princess to get you those papers."

Wendy waves and disappears down the hall.

I turn around and shake my head at what just happened. Maybe it's time I visit Rose.

Tonight! I promise myself. *Tonight.*

The weight bench is sticky against my neck, most likely from other people's sweat. I don't even want to think about the last time it was washed. All the equipment could use refurbishing. The barbell is rusty, and the weight plates are chipped. There's a better gym in the palace, but I prefer the solitude of the trench. I have the entire cavern to myself.

I press the bar until my elbows lock, then I drop it on the rack. It's only 160 lbs, but the last few weeks have stripped my months of progress.

"You know, you should really have a spotter," Zane booms from across the cave. He has a small leather pack, and as always, his sword jostles on his hip. When he draws near, he squints at the bar. "What is that, 150? You can do better," he insists. "Yesterday, I saw Diego press 250."

I look down. "Yeah, well, not all of us have the luxury of self-dominion."

Zane laughs and takes a seat on the next bench over. "I know. I know. I was only joking." He grows serious. "You know, if you asked him, he might teach you. He really does have a knack for it."

"Eh, that's okay. Kendra's teaching me how to heal, and our first lessons cover self-dominion."

Zane scratches his beard. "That's good. How are things with your squadron? It looks like you have your men's respect."

"Yeah, I guess. They obey me for the most part." *Except Togum.*

"And how are things back home?"

Judy's gonna die any day now. "Fine," I lie.

Zane studies me with a neutral face. "Anything you want to talk about before we begin?" he double checks.

I shake my head. "Let's get this over with." I stand and follow Zane across the trench. We stop at the shore of the underground lake, the very place I once fought Vyle and his goons. "What do you have in mind?"

"The basics, Matt. You *have* to master the basics. Dual-dominion. We keep trying until you get it."

I sigh. "Okay, what do you want me to do."

Zane bends down and picks up an angular chunk of granite. "Don't let this touch the ground." He tosses the rock into the air.

I reach with my mind and intercept its descent.

Float!

The rock hovers there, perfectly still. It's only a few feet from my head, so the effort is minimal.

"Good." Zane grabs hold of his amulet. "Now, defend yourself."

The flames erupt in a circle around me. They start wide, but the circle begins to tighten around me, choking me like a noose—oxygen quickly consumed by the flames.

I stretch my consciousness, trying my best to think in two places at once.

Shield!

I command a sphere of force around me, but I quickly feel my will growing weaker on the stone. Like an old birthday balloon, it starts to slowly sink to the floor.

Lift!

I divert some of my soul back to the stone, but now my shield grows weaker. The flames converge on my feet, and I worry my pants will ignite at any moment!

Disperse!

The stone hits the floor as I battle back the flames! I've failed the task, but Zane doesn't back down. I feel his influence accelerating the molecules around me, and I desperately try to siphon away the heat.

Zane steps closer, and his influence grows stronger. "What are you going to do, Matt? I'm a feeder, and I've just fed on an entire family. My dominion can last all day. What are you going to do to survive? I'll give you a hint. I have no defenses."

I know what he wants me to do. He wants me to use dual-dominion—to maintain my shield and simultaneously lash out. *I'm not sure that I can.* Already, my body grows heavy. The familiar ache in my head is piercing.

While keeping a hold on my shield, I try to stretch my mind at Zane. My soul resists, like trying to look in two separate directions.

"C'mon! Attack me!" Zane bellows.

It has to be now! The longer I wait, the weaker I become.

In one final effort, I throw my soul at Zane. my shield disappears, and the flames lick at my skin. The instant before I'm burned, the heat dissipates.

Zane sighs, not even trying to hide his disappointment. "What if I were a feeder, Matt? I'm telling you. You have to master dual-dominion. It's going to save your life someday."

"I'm trying. It's not easy."

"I know," Zane says softly. "I just wish we had more time."

The sentence alone isn't alarming, but Zane's tone sets me on edge.

"Time for what? Why don't we have time?"

Zane plops down on a rock, the way a parent would when they have bad news. "The High Council has voted to make Commander Quill a guardian."

"What? Are they stupid?"

Zane silences me with his angled eyebrows. "It's out of our control. What matters is that his father needs a new apprentice. Each council member gets to elect one champion. The champions will engage in a series of tasks. The most qualified becomes the apprentice. It's not guaranteed, but you should have a decent shot against the other champions."

I don't want to disappoint him, but my lips curl down. "Risk my life to be Kayne's apprentice? I'll pass. I'd rather be the devil's butler."

Zane doesn't laugh. "It's an opportunity to regain your soul-anchor."

"Why can't I just be your apprentice. Isn't that the whole point of training me?"

Zane clenches his fists. "That's not the point, Matt. This is bigger than you. It's as much about bringing you on the council as it is about keeping others out. If you don't win the apprenticeship, someone else will. Do you want Vyle on the council?" His voice grows louder. "And say you do win. Then, I can choose a different apprentice—someone good, like Diego. Someday, you might actually have council majority. You might be able to fix things around here. But to have a chance at that, every spot counts, especially this one." He stops himself, lowering his voice and letting out a deep breath. "Can I count on you, Matt?"

"Screw the council," I snap. "Don't you get it, Zane? It's already over. Judy is going to die any day now. Even if I became your apprentice today, I wouldn't become a guardian until you die. And say, by some miracle, I make it to her with an amulet, I don't even know how to heal her. She's basically already dead. I've been lying to myself this whole time. I don't even know why I'm here."

Zane frowns, but something in him changes. He sees my confusion, and he empathizes. "Let me ask you something, Matt. What do you want with your life? Where do you see yourself in 10 years, 20 years?"

The question takes me by surprise. "I don't know. What does this have to do with anything?"

"Just think about it," Zane says. "I want a real answer."

I sit there for a moment, trying to imagine what happiness would look like. Who do I want to be in 20 years?

"I don't know. I guess I see myself getting married, having a family. I used to want to do research, but that's pretty much out the window."

"Okay. So, you want to raise a family. Where? Where are you going to raise them? In Cavernum? In the beyond? Are they going to be ring-born? Palace-born?" Zane talks fast, not giving me time to respond.

"And if you live in the beyond, how will you keep them safe? How will you make sure a feeder doesn't find them like the one that found you. Will you follow them to school? Will you ever let them out of your sight? You're Adamic, Matt. These are the options you have. You have to decide what you want to pursue."

I consider the question as honestly as I can. I can't imagine raising kids in Cavernum. Trying to explain the injustice. Trying to shield them from the cruelty. They deserve better than that.

But Zane's right. Raising a family in the beyond would be terrifying. Even if I had my amulet, I couldn't keep them safe forever.

"I... I don't know," I confess.

Zane throws his hands up. "If you want to raise a family in the beyond, I won't be angry, but if that's the case, you're going about it wrong. You should be in the beyond, getting an education, meeting girls, establishing a life. You shouldn't be here wasting your time."

"What's your point? What does any of this have to do with Judy?"

Zane sighs. "You say that Judy is going to die either way, right? So why haven't you left then? If you can't save her, why are you still here?"

I can't keep it in any longer.

"Because I'm happy here!" I shout it, and immediately, I feel guilty. Not only am I abandoning Judy, I'm rejecting the life she made for me. I can't shake the feeling that I'm dishonoring her somehow.

Zane watches me with worried brown eyes. "Talk to me, Matt. Tell me what you're thinking. I can't read minds."

"I feel terrible. It's like… if I stay here, Judy will become nothing but a memory. Her home will be sold, her gardens will be destroyed, and her legacy will die. I feel like I'm forsaking everything she taught me."

Zane nods as if he knows exactly what I'm talking about. "After my wife and girls died, I felt that way for a long time. I had this idea in my head that if I wasn't mourning them, I was forgetting them. And if I was forgetting them, it was because I didn't love them. I thought that way for a long time, and let me tell you, I was miserable. In those years, I learned something. Honoring someone isn't about remembering them… and it isn't about living the life they lived. Honoring someone is about being the person they'd want you to be. I ask you this, Matt… what kind of man does Judy want you to be?"

She'd want me to be happy. I've heard her say it a million times, but still, it feels so selfish.

I look out over the water, picturing her face. "If my mom were here, she'd probably ask me two things. Where am I the happiest, and where can I make the most difference? The answer to both is Cavernum. She'd tell me I belong here. She'd want me to stay."

The more I think about it, the more sure I become. "I want to be your champion, Zane. I want to join the council if I can. If you choose me, I'll give it my all. I won't let you down."

"I know you won't." Zane stands before I can change my mind. "If that's what you've decided, then we have some work to do. As a champion, the council will send you on tasks that only guardians should face. You need to be prepared for anything… and I mean anything."

He reaches into his bag and removes a stick of wood. It's only a foot and a half long with a wooden crosspiece nailed a third way up the shaft. I recognize it instantly as a toy dagger.

He tosses the wooden knife, and I catch it by the hilt. "What do you want me to do with this?"

"Fight me, what else?" He unclips his sword from his belt, wielding it safely within the sheath. He points the tip of his sheathed blade at my wooden dagger. "I modeled it after your Adamic blade. It's time you learn how to use it. The Holy One will be arming his followers, and it's only a matter of time before you fight against Adamic weapons. When you earn back your Adamic blade, I want you to be ready to use it. Now pay attention." He holds his sword at the ready, clasped firmly in two hands. "Your enemy comes at you with an Adamic sword. Show me your fighting stance."

I hold the blade on the thumb side of my hand and extend it directly out in front of me. My feet form a typical boxing stance, wide with my left foot slightly forward.

Zane looks me over. "That'll do, I guess. Now, swords have many advantages over daggers. They have a much longer reach, and they're heavier, so they carry more power. That said, those same advantages can be turned into weaknesses. A dagger is light and can change directions faster than a sword. The closer you get to me, the less effective my sword is, and the more deadly your dagger."

"Okay. So I want to get within your swing?"

"Exactly." Zane locks eyes with me. "Go ahead. Give it a try."

We circle each other for a moment. Zane holds his sword flat like a spear. I wait for what seems like a good opportunity, then I lunge.

With a minor deviation, Zane follows my body with the top of his sheathed sword. As I lunge forward, the scabbard tip jabs into my stomach.

"Hauh," I grunt as the air is forced from my lungs.

Zane chuckles. "Don't try to take the offensive. Use your dagger to defend, and then counter. You have a crossguard. Use it to immobilize my sword, and move close. Then, strike."

I nod my head, trying to ignore the nausea in my stomach. We circle for a second, then Zane raises his sword. He swings with his entire body, and the blade whistles through the air. I raise my dagger, and the two crash together.

Clack!

My wrist buckles, and the sword continues into my collarbone. It doesn't strike terribly hard, but the pain is enough to make my eyes water.

Zane frowns. "You can't wait for the sword to hit you. You have to counter. As soon as I start swinging, you need to step forward. The outermost tip of the sword is moving the fastest and therefore packs the most punch. You want to intercept me as close to the crossguard as you can."

"Got it."

Zane nods, raises his sword, and swings again. This time, I'm ready. I step into his swing and intercept his sword at the base of my dagger. Immediately, the two weapons lock together. I yank my dagger down, driving the tip of his sword against the ground.

"That's it. That's the stuff. You can't forget to follow through. Once you're inside my defenses, stab with your knife."

Zane squares up to me, and I see a glimmer of a smile. It hides like a panther in his jungle beard.

Feign!

He steps forward and fakes a swing. Halfway through, he diverts the sheathed sword across his body and follows through with a backhand.

Strike!

I twist to face the blade and raise my measly dagger to meet it. As soon as our blades meet, I twist my body toward Zane and drive my wooden stick into his chest. He hardly flinches as the wood jabs him in the ribs.

"Very good. Very, very good."

"What if they have a dagger?" I ask.

Zane rests the tip of his sword on the ground and leans on it like a cane. "That changes things. You no longer have the same advantage. It becomes about striking first, and striking fast." He takes the wooden dagger and flips it around so that the 'blade' is facing his pinky finger. "Hold it like this, and keep your dominant foot forward. Hold the blade high, and strike down like you're swinging a hammer." He demonstrates, lifting it above his head and swinging it down at my neck. "Aim for their shoulder level. That gives you maximum range. If you miss the neck, follow through into the chest."

I furrow my brow. "Is that really the best way? It looks kinda... primitive."

Zane grumbles. "This isn't some movie, Matt. It's not about finesse or looking cool for the audience. Often, simple is better. There's less room for error where errors are often deadly."

Zane looks me over once more. "You're going to do great, Matt. Just remember what I've taught you, and follow your gut."

"Wait, that's it?"

"For now, yes. We can go over some more techniques in a few days. Right now, you need to rest."

"What do I have left to learn?" I ask.

"There's lots really, but you've covered the basics. Much of the advanced stuff we only teach guardians."

My face lights up. "Like what?"

Zane shrugs. "Radiation dominion, poison dominion, combustion dominion."

My face lights up. "You can do all that?"

Zane grins. "You could learn too, given time. Remember when you dueled the princess, and you ruptured her eardrum with a loud explosion."

"Yeah."

"That was basically combustion dominion on a tiny scale."

"What's poison dominion like? Can you teach me?"

Zane's smile quickly disappears. "These techniques aren't to be attempted, Matt. Accidently fill a hallway with poison, and you could kill half the palace, yourself included. They're complicated techniques, with drastic consequences. Even combustion is risky. Explosions can be unpredictable. People have blown themselves up on accident. Or worse, blown up their comrades."

"I got it. I won't do anything stupid."

"Promise me you won't try them without me."

"I promise."

"Good." Zane stands. "That's enough for today. Keep practicing your dual-dominion."

He clasps his sword to his belt and turns toward the exit.

"Hey, Zane."

"Yes, Matt?"

"Thanks for the advice about my mom and everything. You're a good friend. I... I don't really know what I'd do without you."

Zane pauses, and I think I see his jaw quiver somewhere beneath his beard. "I'm sorry I can't do more. If I knew how to heal... if I could save her myself, I would. But I'll tell you this: if the day comes that you think can heal her yourself, I'll give you an amulet and let you try, and I won't let anyone stop you."

Chapter 14

Rose

As I do every night, I dream of Antai. But this dream is different. My assassin is nowhere to be seen, nor is Nevela. I'm somewhere outside, and all I see are pine trees. The moon is my only means of sight, illuminating nothing but silhouettes. Worst of all, I hear him calling for me—his voice, nothing but raw desperation.

"Rose! Kill me! Please!"

His voice taunts me, reminding me of what I did. No matter how far I run, forcing my way through bushes and trees, his voice never gets any closer.

"Antai! Where are you?" I scream at the top of my lungs, but the foliage swallows my voice.

I can't find him. I'll never find him. I know I'm wandering in circles, but I have to keep moving. I have the terrible sense that something is stalking me. The second I stop moving, the predator will pounce. I push through a large pine. "Antai!!!"

Then, something changes. I can't quite put my finger on it, but it's as I've put on glasses. The world around me crispens, suddenly bursting with details. The soil crunches beneath my feet. The air is cold, and goosebumps gather on my arms in mass. Then, I hear something else: the rustle of a branch behind me.

I don't have an amulet, so I do the next best thing: I duck under the lowest branches of a spruce and tuck my body in the shadows. The rustling grows closer and suddenly, a body emerges from between two trees, I attack before it can, swinging my fist at his blonde head.

I sock him in the back of the skull, and the blow jars through my wrist.

"Ow!" The man covers his face with his arms and recoils. His blonde waves glistening in the moonlight.

"Matt?" I ease myself from beneath the tree and step toward him, drawn to the gentle aura that emanates from his body. He's a lantern, and I'm a helpless moth.

"I uhh," he looks around, as if unsure why he's here. "I thought maybe you were lost, so I came to help."

Now that he mentions it, I realize the incongruity of my memories. "Wait, how did I get... what's going on."

Matt smiles at me, slowly gaining confidence. "Your dreaming, Rose. This is all a nightmare, or it was I guess. I don't really know what it is anymore."

"And you're..."

"I'm a part of your dream," he casually replies. "Nothing more than a figment of your imagination."

"Hmmm" I don't know what to say. It certainly explains how I got here. And why I can't escape. "So, what do we—"

"Rose! Kill me!"

Matt's head whips in the direction of Antai's voice.

"That's part of my dream too?" I shiver.

Matt falters, then slowly nods. His head lingers, looking toward the source of the sound. "Nothing but your own imaginations," he says. Somehow, he seems less convinced.

I step closer to him, inspecting what my mind has supposedly reproduced from memory. His hair is messy, wavy locks crisscrossing at odd angles, and his cleft chin is hard to see in the moonlight.

Even in dream form, he's more handsome than I care to admit. *Still, he's no Antai.*

As if he heard me, Matt recoils half a step. *Of course, he heard me.* He's nothing but a fabrication of my subconscious. *I'll have to think nicer.*

"I'm glad you're awake," I say. "You know, in the real world. I was really worried about you. You were unconscious for so long."

He smiles, his full lips stretching thin. "I'm glad to be back. It's been a while since we've talked. How are you doing? I'm sorry about the commander. If there's anything I can do, let me know."

"There's nothing you can do," I sigh. "And I'm doing alright. Much better than I was last week. I'm keeping busy now."

"Doing what, if you don't mind me asking?" Matt wanders to a relatively flat boulder and sits down. "I'm pretty bored these days. I could use some distracting myself."

I take a seat on the boulder, my hips a few feet from his. "I'm learning to write the armor-piercing spell, and it's turning into quite the challenge. Also, I'm going to be learning archery soon. Gideon is making me a longbow, and hopefully, it'll be ready soon."

Matt tilts his head. "Gideon?"

He may be a figment of my imagination, but he sure is consistent. "Gideon is one of the survivors from Lycon," I explain. "I don't know him well, but he seems like a good man."

"Archery, very cool. Maybe you'll be the next Katniss."

"The next who?"

Matt's eyes widen. "Oh, uh, never mind. Just forget I said anything."

I sit in silence for a second. I don't really know what else to say, and I'm glad this awkwardness is only a dream.

Matt looks down and straightens the leg of his pants. "Have you spoken to Diego yet?"

I tense. I'm ashamed of my answer. "Not yet. I'm afraid he still blames me for his father."

Matt shrugs. "Maybe he does, but you'll never know until you talk to him. And if he does blame you... all the more reason to set the record straight. Tell him you didn't have a say."

"And what if he doesn't believe me?" I worry.

Matt shrugs, as if to emphasize it's out of his control. "Who knows? But if you do nothing, you'll lose him for sure."

I breathe in through my nose and exhale my frustrations. "You're right. I know you're right. I'm just so afraid of losing more friends."

Matt glances at me and flashes a somber smile. "You know, that's how I felt about you. I've wanted to reach out, but I was afraid you wouldn't be the same person—that Lynn was only an act."

"You thought Lynn was an act?" I'm offended. "Those felt like the only real months of my life. Are other people saying that? Are they dismissing everything I did?"

Matt is stunned. "No, I didn't mean that... I just..." He hits the breaks and composes himself. "I don't know. I thought I found a friend, and then I found out she was someone else. I guess I was afraid your name wasn't the only lie." He looks down at the ground. "I figured if you wanted to talk, you'd take the time to come visit."

I had a lot on my mind, I think. "Why didn't you visit me?"

Matt raises his eyebrows at me as if to say 'really?' "You know, princesses aren't the most approachable. I tried once, but the guards wouldn't let me."

"Oh." Is all I can say. As much as I hate it, he's right. My position is a barrier, even to my friends.

Matt opens his mouth, then closes it again.

"What?" I ask.

"I don't mean to be bold, but it's likely that Diego feels the same way I did. I'm not saying he shouldn't reach out, but if you want him to know you care, maybe you should make the first move."

Suddenly, I smile. Matt notices, and I see a glimmer of his teeth in the moonlight.

"What?" he asks.

I look up at the night sky, relishing the reminiscence. "Remember the night before The Dividing, the night we first met? I was nervous about failing the trials, and you told me something similar, something Judy used to say. There's no worse pain than knowing you never tried."

"You remember that?"

"Of course I do," I say. "I'll probably never forget it. You know, I used to tell myself you'd make a great advisor. Even in my dreams, you give good counsel."

Matt seems pleased at that. As I stare, I can't help but notice how much has changed; he's not the hapless refugee he once was. He's lieutenant now—a lieutenant directly out of training. Any palace girl would be swooning.

Matt looks over at me. "I hear the fall festival is coming up this month. It's your favorite holiday right?"

"It's spectacular, Matt. Wait until you see it. They decorate the entire palace, and the feast is to die for. And the music, and the dancing…" Suddenly, my face falls. "I was supposed to go with Antai this year. We talked about it for years. He made me promise him he'd be my first dance at the festival."

"Maybe he'll still wake up. It's always possible."

"Maybe," I admit. Every night, I imagine the same fantasy. That upon waking up, Antai will be sitting at the foot of my bed. Upon waking up, I'll discover that Antai has been awake for hours, yet he didn't want to disturb me, so he waited. The moment I awake, he's leaning over my bed, taking my chin, and kissing me.

Every day, I wake up disappointed, and I can't keep it up much longer.

For a second, I think Matt will suggest we go together. I can almost feel him thinking it, but he never voices it aloud. He has feelings for me, it's clear, but I'm impressed by his restraint. He never makes a move beyond friendship. He respects me too much, or maybe he doubts himself too much.

It's just a dream, I have to remind myself. *This isn't real Matt.* Regardless, I'm grateful. My head couldn't handle a full-blown battle of attractions.

Suddenly, a gust of wind moves through the trees. I don't shiver, but I wrap my arms tighter around myself.

"Here, take this." Before I can resist, Matt wraps his guard jacket over my shoulders. It's warm with his body heat, and I happily nestle inside.

"Thank you." I look out over the forest. What once was the setting of a nightmare, is now a peaceful getaway from palace life.

"It's so peaceful when you're here," I explain, almost to myself. "I've been running through this forest for who knows how long, and I never once thought to stop and relax."

Matt stands up and gestures around us. "You know, you can change it."

I scrunch my forehead. "Change what?"

"This! Everything." Matt spins in a small circle, gesturing with his open hands. "When I was little, I could sometimes control my dreams. It was like I knew I was dreaming, and the dream obeyed me," he smiles. "Almost like dream dominion. Anyways, every time I would figure out I was dreaming, I'd fly. Every single time. It was all I wanted to do. Looking back, I think it was because I felt trapped. I wanted to escape my life. I wanted to find my birth parents. I wanted something more than my little life in Kentville." He looks up, his brilliant blue eyes sucking me in like a riptide I can't escape. "I think I can do it here too," he says expectantly.

He closes his eyes. For several moments, nothing happens. Then, I notice the trees are moving—entire trunks shifting horizontally across the ground, their roots dragging through the soil. Within a few seconds, Matt has created a small clearing, and a huge swath of the sky is visible.

"Demons, Matt. How'd you do that?"

The sky is speckled with the most brilliant array of stars I've ever seen.

"It's a dream, Rose. We can do whatever we want, go wherever we want." His chin dips ever so slightly, and he gives me a mischievous grin. "I'll leave it up to you. Where do you want to go? Anywhere…"

"Anywhere?" I echo.

"Well, anywhere I can imagine," he says

"Show me your home!" I don't know why, but it's the first thing that pops into my head. "What was the beyond like for you?"

"Okay." He takes my hand and the ground drops away. His hand isn't bearing my weight, but rather whatever force lifts him, lifts me in unison. I feel my stomach rising in my chest and for a second, I think I'm going to throw up. Then, I see the tree sinking next to us, and we're gliding through the air above an endless evergreen forest. His grip on my hand is light, but it somehow has a force over my entire body, dragging me effortlessly along with him. My hair flutters in my ears, and I'm suddenly self-conscious of my nightgown.

Time is irrelevant in my dream, and in a matter of moments, the sun creeps up over the mountainside. Together, we descend on a small meadow. A clear stream divides the meadow in two. Slowly, we start to sink toward the grass below. The second my feet touch the ground, gravity returns to normal.

"I think I've spent more time here than anywhere else on Earth."

"Is this where you used to hunt?"

"Yep." He points up at the far side of the meadow at a chain-link fence. "Right over there is Hogrum. My whole life, it was maybe a mile away."

I know it's just a dream, but I ask anyway. "Can you show me Judy?"

I expect him to be protective, but instead, his face lights up. "Judy? You want to see my mom?"

"If that's alright with you. You've already met my Grandpa. It's only fair you return the favor."

"You really want to meet her?"

"Yes. Why wouldn't I? I need to meet the woman who gave Matthew MacArthur all his wisdom."

"Alright, let me think. This is how I like to remember her." Matt closes his eyes, and suddenly the landscape warps around me. When the colors settle, I'm standing alongside a small, one-story home, the likes of which I've only seen in photos. The home is tan with small front windows and an orange-tiled roof. An odd square of shaved grass grows in front of the house.

"C'mon, she'll be around back in her garden." Matt leads the way.

I turn the corner and find myself at the foot of a modest garden. There are six small planters surrounded by a dozen fruit trees. The flowers catch my eye first: daffodils, lilies, tulips. They grow in a beautiful cascade of colors, rivaling the beauty of the palace garden.

Judy is at the back of the garden, kneeling on a small foam pad and tending to the vegetables. She has on a white visor, gardening gloves, and a jacket is tied around her waist. A white bucket sits next to her, filled with the weeds she's plucked from the soil.

She's on her feet the second she sees, dusting off her hands on her jeans. "Matt, oh my goodness, what a pleasant surprise."

Her hair is light brown, but some strands are beginning to fade. Otherwise, she looks vibrant and healthy. She tosses off her gloves and strides toward us.

"Mom, this is my friend, Rose. She's the princess of Cavernum, the one I told you about."

Before I can offer my hand, Judy pulls me into a tight embrace, rocking from side to side. "Oh, it's so good to finally meet you." She pulls away and gives me a modest distance of personal space. "Matt has told me so much about you." She glances at Matt, grinning as any proud mother would. "I've been waiting some time for Matt to bring a girl home, and I can say, you do not disappoint."

I blush, glancing accusingly at Matt.

"What?" he laughs. "That's what she would say, I swear." He holds up both hands. "I'm not controlling her. My subconscious is making this happen."

Judy frowns. "I'm sorry, I don't mean to embarrass. I just didn't think Matt had it in him." She flashes me a wink as Matt shakes his head.

"Mom, we're just friends."

"I know, I'm sorry. Come, can I get you a drink? Maybe some tea?"

"Some tea would be lovely," I agree.

She leads inside and motions to the table. "Well, why don't you both take a seat? I'll be right there." She grabs a glass pitcher from a strange metal closet.

"That's the fridge," Matt whispers. "It keeps things cold."

Judy pours the three of us a glass and finally takes a seat across from me. "Hibiscus mint tea. I hope you like it," Judy says. "Well go on. Try it. It won't bite."

I take a sip. "Mhhh." There's no ice, yet it's unbelievably cold. The tea itself is sweet and minty, with a slight tang of lime. "It's delicious," I emphasize. "Honestly, you'll have to give me a recipe."

Judy beams. "Of course, dear, remind me before you leave."

I take another sip as an idea enters my mind. This may just be a dream, but part of me is curious what my mind will come up with. "So, Judy, tell me. Does Matt have any embarrassing stories I should know about?"

Matt turns pale. "Maybe I should end this part of the dream."

Judy waves her finger at Matt. "Matthew, don't you dare, your friend has requested a story, and you will humor her. Didn't I raise you to cater to your guest?"

"Yes, mom."

Judy smiles. "Good. Oh, where should I begin? It was the summer Matthew finished 5th grade."

Matt groans and tucks his head between his elbows.

Judy hardly takes notice. She looks me in the eyes, catching me with her emerald green irises. "Matthew had never been to a water park before, so we visited one near steamboat springs. At the time, Matt was outgrowing his clothes every few months. We didn't have the money for frequent shopping, so I bought his swim trunks a little big; that way, he could grow into them. That's important to remember." She glances at Matt which only seems to animate her even more.

"Now, Matt wanted to go down one of those really big slides. It wasn't straight down, but it was too steep for me. So, I told him to go by himself, and I'd wait for him at the bottom. Now, this is the good part. Matt had a crush on the lifeguard stationed at the bottom of the slide. He would wave at her, and being a nice girl, she would wave back. So, to impress her, Matt decided he wanted to go down the slide headfirst."

She laughs, a bubbly rich laugh that urges me to do the same. "Well, I'm waiting at the bottom next to the lifeguard, and sure enough, Matt comes flying down headfirst." She suppressed a wave of laughter, covering her mouth. "As fate would have it, the second he hits the water, his trunks come flying off." She pauses between breaths to continue the story.

"From my vantage point, I didn't know this at the time. The bubbles from the water slide made it hard to see. The poor lifeguard was clueless too, but Matt knew they were gone. He dove straight down and started feeling around for his swim trunks. Mind you, the water was only four or five feet deep."

Judy laughs some more. "All I knew was that Matt wasn't coming up for air, so at this point, I'm screaming. 'He's drowning, he's drowning!'" Judy mocks herself with a high pitched voice. "The lifeguard dives in and she pulls Matt to the surface. At this point, people have heard me screaming and a small crowd has gathered. Well, she pulls Matt to the side, and before he can explain what was happening, a male lifeguard grabs Matt and hoists him out of the water!"

At this point, Judy is laughing hysterically. "Oh," she wails. "You should've the lifeguard's face when Matt's bum broke the surface. He dropped Matt back in the water faster than a hot potato! And poor Matt, he dove back underwater, as if we couldn't see everything."

"What was I supposed to do?" Matt laughs. "I had nowhere to go."

Judy wipes at her eyes. "What a good memory. Thank you, Rose. I'd almost forgotten about that."

"No, thank you!" I insist. "It's been a long time since I'd laughed like that." And it's true. I love Antai, but I already know everything about him. With Matt, there are so many untold stories. There's so much to share.

"And what about you, Rose?" Matt grins. "Any embarrassing stories to share?"

He may be a dream, but I'm not ready to embarrass myself. "Not today. Maybe next time."

"Okay, fine," Matt says, pretending he isn't disappointed. "Well, mom, we better get going."

"Of course. It was so nice to meet you, Rose." She glances at Matt. "Take care of my boy for me. He won't admit it, but Matthew needs all the friends he can get, you especially."

"Mom!" Matt protests. Before she can say more, he closes his eyes, and the scene morphs. Once again, it's nighttime and we're back in an unknown wood.

"Thanks for letting me meet her. I can see why you're so close. She's a special lady."

My mind wanders to my own mother, and I find myself dwelling in 'what ifs' and "maybes.'

My heart leaps as Matt takes my hand. He's never been so bold, but this is only a dream. He squeezes, and I can feel his thoughts. *Your mom would be so proud of you, trust me.*

He smiles, amused by whatever thought just popped in his head. "Rose, do you know if the king is looking for a girlfriend? Judy's single."

I snort. The concept is ridiculous, but that only makes it more amusing.

Matt takes a step away. "I should probably get going, but tonight was fun. I'll see you around, okay?"

"Wait." I don't know why I say it, I just don't want him to leave. I don't want the nightmare to return.

"Don't worry, I'm sure you'll dream of me again. Goodnight, Rose." Then, he's gone. His calming presence disappears with him and my dream slowly fades into everyday unconsciousness.

At some point, I awake to the sound of knocking.

Tap. Tap. Tap.

I slowly stir, expecting to see Wendy at the maid's entrance, but the knock came from the other door... the hallway door.

I feel in the dark for a matchbox and light the candle on my bedside stand. Then, I slip my feet into my slippers.

Tap. Tap. Tap.

"Who is it?" I call out. As long as I don't unlock the door, they can't get inside. *I'm safe.* I tell myself.

The knocking continues. Tap. Tap. Tap.

"Who's there?" I yell this time, certain they've heard me.

"It's your grandfather," his voice hisses. "We have a predicament. May I come in?"

"Grandpa?" He never interrupts me at night. For a second, I worry he's an imposter. If someone stole the morph mask, they could be impersonating Grandpa's voice. Or maybe he's possessed.

"Yes, Rose. I have my key. If it's alright, I'm coming in."

He doesn't wait for permission. I hear the clanking of the key and a short click. A moment later, the door swings open, and Grandpa shuffles inside.

At this point, I'm on my feet. "What's going on?"

Grandpa frowns, unhappy with whatever news he's about to bear. "Commander Quill has been marked with death. His father is afraid his life is at stake. We're going to perform the bonding ceremony tonight. I want you to be a witness."

"Tonight, as in right now?"

"Yes, Rose. Get dressed." He reaches into the fold of his robe, removing an amplifier. "And wear this." He tosses it into my bed, the gold chain streaming through the air like a shooting star. "Your room is now the only safe place in the palace. Whenever you leave it, I want you armed, the very least with an amplifier. I don't care if the council complains."

"Okay."

Grandpa grins, showing more teeth than I'm used to. "Tonight, Rose, you witness a guardian in the making."

I don't share his enthusiasm. Not only do I distrust Quill, I hate him. I hate his cruelty and I hate his power.

Tonight, my enemies grow stronger.

General Kaynes is waiting for us outside of Quill's quarters. The door, normally a deep, aged mahogany, is now sweating crimson drops of blood. The drops pool every few inches, suspended, but not quite heavy enough to run down the wood.

General Kaynes bows as we approach. "Thank you for making this possible, your highness. It's his best chance of survival."

"Of course," Grandpa says. "I know what it's like to lose a son. I'll do what I can to keep yours safe. At the very least, he'll be immune to possession."

General Kaynes nods, locking eyes with Grandpa in a brief moment of vulnerability. "I owe you, Dralton. I won't forget this." He steps aside and motions us into Quill's bedchamber, already lit with an assortment of candles.

In all honesty, the room is a mess. A pyramid of beer bottles are stacked on the window sill and a small mountain of linens are piled on the opposite side of his bed. Most disturbing are the paintings. Hanging on nearly every wall is a nearly-nude portrait of young, impeccably beautiful women, some barely of age. They're lying prostrate or standing with their arms raised seductively above their heads. Coiling tendrils of sheer white fabric are suspended at just the right angles to shield their womanhood. Whoever these girls are, their identities are redefined as sensual decoration.

Despicable.

I avert my eyes and spot Vyle standing along the wall. He smiles as if he's relieved to see me. When I don't smile back, he glances uncomfortably at his brother.

He's afraid of him.

I join Vyle against the wall, but I don't humor him with any attention. I press my back against the stone and watch Grandpa get to work.

He picks up a wooden chair, and using his cane, he carries it to the center of the rug.

"Quill, why don't you take a seat, and we'll begin. The ceremony will only take a few moments, but first, tradition states I say a few words."

Grandpa waits until Quill is seated. Then, he stands directly in front of Quill, never blinking as he speaks.

"Guardianship is the greatest gift God can bestow. With a soul-anchor, you will be immune to the flaming darts of the adversary. You will be a guardian angel, and ultimately, you will be representative of the Creator. By accepting this soul-anchor, you covenant to protect Cavernum with your life, and every one of its inhabitants. As a guardian, God will hold you to a higher degree of judgment. Quill Aradian Kaynes, do you make this covenant?"

Quill raises his nose to the ceiling. "I do. Bestow his power upon me."

I almost laugh at the theatrics, but I seem to be the only one amused. Vyle is paler than an onion, and Grandpa's face is stone cold.

"Very well," Grandpa says solemnly. He removes the Lycon soul-anchor from his robe and passes it to Quill. "You must be holding this as the spell takes effect. Now, give me your hand, and I will place the bond. I will be creating the tattoo via self-dominion. I will need your permission to continue."

"I give you permission," Quill says.

Grandpa turns his hand so that his palm is facing upward. Then, with his index finger, he begins to trace his fingers along the inside of Quill's wrist. Everywhere his finger makes contact, a deep, oily mark appears in the flesh. Grandpa moves flawlessly across Quill's wrist, and soon, the spell takes form.

Grandpa releases his wrist, and Quill promptly leaps to his feet. "Yes! I can feel it. It worked." He loops the amulet over his head and puffs out his chest. "I feel invincible."

Grandpa frowns. "You're a guardian, but you're still a man. You are no more invincible than the guardians of Lycon, who were slaughtered by the Holy One. Even with a soul-anchor, you must be prudent."

Quill nods, but I know he's hardly listening. "Of course, your highness. Of course." He clenches his fist, slowly uncurling his fingers. "Shall we go hunting for this intruder? The palace gates are sealed, they can't have gone far."

Grandpa nods. "Very well. We'll begin a full-scale sweep. But first, I must return Rose to her room."

"Your highness," Quill complains, "Every second we waste, the intruder could be further away. We don't have time to spare."

"And I won't risk her safety," Grandpa snarls. "I ref—"

"King!" A palace guard cries from outside the door. "There are more doors marked on the Eastern Wing. Whoever is doing it, they're still in the palace."

Bang! Bang! Bang!

The gunshots are distant—perhaps from the Northern Wing—but they're unmistakable.

Grandpa grimaces. He looks back at me, his wrinkles weighed down with worry. "Rose, will you—"

"I'll be fine." I wave for him to go. "I'll go straight back to my room and lock the door. Just go."

Grandpa hesitated a moment longer.

"I'll walk her back," Vyle volunteers. "I'll keep her safe. You have my word."

Grandpa nods. "Very well. Straight to the room and lock the door." Then, he turns and shuffles out the door, already moving toward the source of the commotion.

I leave immediately for my chambers, and Vyle follows at my heels.

"You know," I say, "you don't have to follow me all the way back. I'm sure I'll be fine on my own."

Vyle smiles. "I don't doubt you would be, but I promised the king, and I won't go back on my word."

I sigh and we walk a moment longer. Out of the corner of my eye, I can see Vyle glancing at me every few seconds. Finally, he builds up the nerve.

"You know, I'm sorry it couldn't be Antai. He would've made a better guardian. My brother doesn't deserve it."

"You don't have to flatter me. I know you don't mean that."

Vyle furrows his brow. "What, because they're my family I have to support them? To hell with that. I mean what I said."

Finally, I let myself look him in the eyes. "And why's that? What reason would you possibly have to choose Antai over your brother?"

"Well, I don't hate him, for one. He's not a total asshole."

"You hate your brother? And why's that?"

Vyle rolls his eyes. "It'd take me all night to answer that." He looks down at me, a glimmer of excitement in his eyes. "You really want to know?"

"Yes, please."

"Well, this isn't the only example, but I think it summarizes our relationship. I hate spiders, always have. I mean, I can kill them no problem, but if I walk through a spiderweb, I freak out. I just hate them."

"Okay, and…"

"Well, when I was little, Quill would search the castle for spiders. He'd catch them, and then he'd put them in my bed. He'd put them inside the covers so they wouldn't crawl away." Vyle shudders. "When I'd get in my bed, sometimes I wouldn't feel them until I was half asleep, and I'd feel something crawling up my leg."

I laugh, but Vyle only grows more serious. "You don't understand. He didn't stop there. When I started shaking out my blankets every night, he changed his tactics. He used his weekly allowance to pay the palace gardeners to catch spiders for him. Together, they had dozens. He put them everywhere. In my clothes, in my shoes, in my toilet. He'd even put them in my food when I wasn't looking. He did this for years. He liked to watch me suffer, and my dad did nothing to stop him. He said I had to defend myself, but there was nothing I could do to make him stop."

Now, I'm silent. "I'm sorry. That sounds horrible." *Traumatizing.*

"It gets worse. When he became a guardsman, he would stand outside my room and control them with dominion. He would make them crawl in my mouth and in my ears."

"My god!" It's almost unbelievable. "Why? He's your brother!"

"He's a psychopath, Rose. He's good at hiding it, but he doesn't care about anyone. He doesn't feel guilt. He doesn't feel anything."

"What did you do?"

"Nothing at first. I wore earplugs to bed and slept under the covers. Eventually, I started training with my dad. I practiced nonstop. I had to be stronger than him. Then, he just stopped one day. As soon as he felt I could fight back, he gave up. Now that he's a guardian, who knows what he'll do? Believe me, Rose. I wish it were Antai instead. I'd give anything to bring him back."

I remember what Tick once told me when I was a recruit. He said that General Kaynes enjoyed torturing feeders. That he relished it.

"Is… is your dad the same way?"

Vyle sighs. "No… well… not really. He doesn't enjoy suffering as Quill does, but he's far from sympathetic. He views kindness as a crutch. A hindrance. He'll do whatever it takes to get what he wants. His vision for Cavernum is…" Vyle looks away. "I'll just say we don't see eye to eye. I grew up fearing my own family more than I feared the feeders."

I want to ask more, but we're already at the Royal Wing. As I pass, Octavian steps in front of Vyle. "Royalty only," is all he says.

"Thank you, Vyle. Ummm… goodnight, I guess." I want to say more, but this isn't the place or time. I hurry into my room and lock the door.

After all the evil Vyle has done to me, I can't help but feel sorry for him. *Maybe he isn't as sinister as I thought.*

In the end, maybe he isn't my enemy after all.

Chapter 15

Matt

My soul drifts away from her body. As much as I want to linger, I force myself through the stone wall and into the hallway.

Did that seriously just happen?

Part of me feels guilty for invading her dream, but the majority of me is thrilled. I haven't had that much fun in ages.

I urge my soul back toward my bedroom, doggy-paddling my soul through the darkness. I move slowly, awkwardly. As I approach my door, I pause. Kendra's room is in the East Wing. It would take me awhile to get there, but it would be worth it.

I don't bother with the hallways. I fly directly through the walls like any ghost would do. Maybe after I visit Kendra, I'll find where Vyle sleeps and haunt his dreams. Then, I'll meet Casper and we'll have a friendly ghost play date. The thought makes me metaphysically smile.

I make it to the West Wing and begin searching the rooms on the ground floor. Most of the occupants are women—healers, no doubt.

I drift over their beds, extending my soul just enough to sense their identities. So far, none of them are Kendra. Then, in the darkness, I feel a woman thrashing.

She's just having a nightmare, I think. I probably shouldn't get involved, but regardless, I feel the urge to help. Without a second thought, I descend on the dream.

As our minds merge, I find myself standing in a dark room. The sensation feels real, from the cold, damp air to the gritty, stone floor. The woman's brain is creating the illusion of a physical body. As my eyes adjust, I hear ragged, fearful panting.

The only object in the room is a bucket in the corner. A barred window is perched far out of reach. Behind me, I find a long wall of rusty bars.

A prison cell!

The cell is wide enough for several prisoners, but I only see two people. In the corner of the room, a woman—maybe 50 years old—is chained to the wall. She's wearing a tattered black robe. She's helpless, but she isn't afraid. I can sense her defiance from across the room. It bubbles beneath her skin, sending hot emotion into the air.

The second figure is shorter than me and fairly slim, feminine in fact. She wears a long cloak, which conceals her features from head to toe. Perhaps most concerning, she's holding a long knife in her left hand.

The moment the cloaked figure speaks, I recognize her voice. "If you want to live, you must answer every one of my questions with perfect honesty."

Iris!

I bite my lips, and hold my breath, hoping she doesn't sense me. Whatever's about to happen, I want to be a witness.

"Who are you?" The prisoner tugs on the chains. "How did I get here?" Her nose is long and triangular, like the beak of a toucan. With her hollow eyes, she could pass as part bird.

Whatever is transpiring, it's only just begun. I retract my soul ever so slightly and hold my emotions as if they were my breath. Whatever happens, Iris can't know I'm here.

Iris ignores the bird-lady's questions. She looks at the knife in her hand, slowly spinning it with the tips of her fingers. "Tell me your name, woman."

Bird-lady narrows her beady eyes. "If you don't know who I am, then why am I here? What use do you have of a stranger?"

Iris doesn't look up from her knife. "Everyone must be judged for their crimes; you are no different. I'm here to assess your sins. Now, what is your name?"

"Like I'd tell you, witch!"

I can't see within her cloak, but something tells me Iris is smiling, excited by the idea of conflict.

Finally, Iris looks up from her knife and studies her prisoner. "Your life is in my hands, and yet you do not fear me. That is rare among the elites."

Bird-lady sneers. "If you think I'm any average elite, you're wrong."

Iris steps closer, "If you think I'm any average witch, you're wrong. You don't have to tell me anything, but let me assure you, the alternative is worse. I'll have to extract the knowledge myself, and I'll be sure to make it painful."

"Do your worst. You'll never get inside my h—"

Iris's hand lurches forward, stretching her fingers over bird-lady's face. The second their skin collides, bird-lady lets out a hideous screech.

"Ahhhhh!!!"

The scream, like a dying crow, continues until Iris retracts her hand.

Iris speaks slowly, her voice laced with scorn. "Chancellor Gwenevere: a woman of prestige and ambition. Hmmm." She sneers. "As I said, your secrets are mine for the taking, but I prefer to hear them from your own mouth. It helps me gauge your regret."

"What do you want from me?" Gwenevere gasps, still recovering from the mental assault. Now, I can feel her terror. It coats the air, like a cold early morning mist. "If you want palace secrets, I know nothing. The guardians manage the military. I know nothing of their escapades."

Iris feigns forward, and the chancellor flattens herself against the wall.

"I've already said; I'm here on behalf of the Holy One. You are to be judged for your works, whether they be good or evil."

Gwenevere laughs. "As if you have the right to judge me, witch. Bringing me here, putting me in chains. You're no better tha—"

Iris strikes Gwenevere, her hand clapping flat against the chancellor's cheek. It's only a slap, but it hits with enough force to buckle Gwenevere's knees. She slumps against the chains.

"I have already been judged for my crimes," Iris says solemnly. "Now, you must do the same. Answer me this one question, and I may just let you live. What is the most vile thing you've ever done?"

"Why in God's name would I tell you that?"

Iris raises her hand slowly towards Gwynevere's face. "Because you don't have a choice. If I have to extract the knowledge myself, I'll make sure every person in the palace knows your deepest secret. And then I'll kill you." Iris pauses, and a smug smile spreads across her face. "Besides, some people find the confession to be a healing experience."

Gwenevere swallows. "I've never spoken it to a single soul."

"Few people have," Iris says, "Trust me."

"If I tell you willingly, you'll keep this between the two of us. You'll let me live?"

"That depends on your sin," Iris says. "But yes, in theory. And don't try to spare the details. I'll know if you're lying."

Gwenevere nods. "Very well. Well..." she swallows again. Already, her shame is like a stench in the air. Whatever tale she's about to tell, it has ravaged her soul for far too long, rotting and molding along the way.

"I... uhhh..." She looks down at her feet. "I... I had a friend. She considered me her best friend, actually. Her name is Emira. 20 years ago, we were both judges in the upper court. Chancellor Eveckson announced that he was looking for an apprentice. There was talk that he was debating between Emira and I." Gwenevere stares at the floor. "I decided that I would spread a rumor, just something small and only to hurt her reputation. So, I concocted a lie. Emira's husband is much darker than she, yet their child is very fair. So, I told some of the maids that Emira was having an affair… that her child was illegitimate." Gwenevere chokes, the emotions beginning to seep into her voice—20 years of guilt accumulated like dust on her soul.

"They were so in love, I didn't think anyone would believe it, but soon the entire palace was talking. Her husband sided with the rumors. He too was a judge in the upper courts." Gwenevere falls silent.

"And?" Iris urges.

Gwenevere takes a deep breath. "Everything spiraled out of control from there. There's a little known Cavernic law against adultery. Her husband decided he wanted to make an example out of her. He accused her in the upper, and somehow, they convicted her of the crime. It all happened so fast, I didn't know what to do. She was expelled from the courts, and her husband disowned the child. They ended up in the fields."

"And you did nothing?" Iris asks. She doesn't sound too surprised.

"I tried everything to fix my mistake. I helped her build a defense. I begged her husband to reconsider, but I couldn't bring myself to tell the truth." She falls silent once more.

"That's not all," Iris announces. "You're leaving something out."

Gwenevere nods. "That same year, Emira's baby fell ill. It all happened so fast." For the first time, Gwenevere's voice cracks. "She died of smallpox before I caught word. If I had known…" she sighs. "Had someone told me, I could've saved the baby, but no one said a word until it was too late…" The chancellor clenches her jaw. "Emira took her life a few months later."

I'm stunned. Iris says nothing. She watches with what must be silent pity.

Eventually, Gwenevere continues. "It was just a rumor. One stupid rumor. I didn't know it would cost Emira her child. Or her life. If I could still save them someway... if coming forward could bring them back, I'd do it in a heartbeat. The High Council was never the reward I thought it was. Now, it's a prison, reminding me of the devil I am."

Gwenevere slumps against the chains. "Please, have mercy! I'll be better. I'm a Chancellor. I can make a difference. Give me a chance to change!"

Iris sighs. "You're despicable, but you won't be marked with death. You've suffered enough for your sins."

Gwenevere breathes a sigh of relief. "Thank you!" she gushes. "You won't regret this!" Suddenly, she grows solemn. Her smile fades, and she looks at her feet. "If you find the Book of Life, will you please bring back Emira? Her child's name is Keikum. They both deserve a new start."

Iris nods. "I'll see what I can do." Then, she turns her back on Gwenevere.

Gwenevere tugs against the chains. "So what? You're just going to leave me here?"

She doesn't know it's a dream.

"You'll wake up eventually," Iris calls. She moves toward the exit and her eyes shift until she's staring right at me. "Goodbye, Ezra. I don't suggest you stick around."

My jaw drops to the floor, and before I can say anything, her body steps out of the cell and vanishes.

I do the only thing I can think of: I chase after her, diving from the chancellor's mind. Once again, any semblance of a body disappears as I'm thrust into oblivion.

As I exit her mind, I land on top of my sister's soul. Before she can flee, I project my consciousness.

What the hell was that about?

She needed to be judged. Her thoughts vibrate through my mind. *So you're the one behind the killings? Tell me it's not true!*

The Holy One is no madman. He knows when to have mercy. Most are spared, Ezra. You can be assured that everyone I mark with death is more than deserving. I feel her soul grow bitter. *Can you say your king does the same?*

I don't know, I admit. *I'm just trying to do what's right.*

Her disgust diffuses into me. *Forget killing. What about whipping? Torturing? How can you say you're on the good side?*

I... I don't know!

Well, good luck with that. Her soul starts to drift away.

Wait! I beg, and to my surprise, she does. Her soul teeters at the edge of my mental sense.

I want to talk to you, I admit. *Not about the Holy One, just as your brother. Please. I don't want to be your enemy. Read my mind. You know I'm telling the truth.*

Fine, Iris says, *but we do it in person. Meet me at Bob's Brew tomorrow at noon. Don't go in the entrance, there is an alley on the left. Go down it. I'll find you. And come unarmed.*

Okay, Tomorrow at noon.

Just like that, she's gone.

My in-room appointment is scheduled for 10:00 am. It's 9:56 when Kendra knocks on my door.

"Come in!"

She pushes the door wide open so that she can slip inside without using her hands. In her arms, she's carrying a stack of textbooks. She pauses, waiting for the door to close behind her. "Alright, Matt, welcome to your first day of healing class. I'll be your professor, Miss Esecks." She lowers her chin and grins playfully. "But I let my favorite students call me Kendra."

"Esecks? That's your last name?"

Kendra smiles. "And you will say it with respect. I am your elder after all." She dumps the books on the desk, sending an ant-sized dust storm raging across the wood.

I should've dusted.

Kendra pretends not to notice. "These will be your study materials. I want you to read through chapter four by our next session. When it comes to healing, knowledge is everything. As a healer, you don't rebuild the body yourself, you simply help the body do its job. The more mechanisms you understand, the more you can take advantage of."

"Okay. ."

Kendra flickers her eyes at my bed and smiles. "Lie down."

Despite my best effort, I feel the blood rushing to my face. Kendra looks at me through her lashes and smiles. If I'm not mistaken, her cheeks get pinker.

"Don't worry," she laughs. "This is strictly business. Before you can heal, I want you to be the patient. Observe what healing feels like in your own body."

I reluctantly lie down on top of my sheets. Kendra hands me an amplifier and I drape it over my head. From her waist, she removes a small scalpel!

I stiffen, and Kendra laughs. "I promise I'm not about to stab you. If it's alright, I just need a small incision to heal. This is how we always did it in training. When I'm done, you won't even have a scar."

I imagine a room full of young healers, slicing themselves without a second thought. I refuse to look weak.

"Do it, I'm ready."

I hold out my palm, but she turns my hand over and hovers the tip over the middle of my forearm. "Fewer nerves here, the palm is painful, trust me." She presses down and my back arcs. I bite down to keep from making a noise.

"Alright. It's over. Sorry about that."

I look down. The cut is smaller than I thought, but it's already bleeding pretty decently. Kendra, obviously unaffected by the blood, places her hand directly over the incision and applies gentle pressure.

"Now what?" I ask.

"Now, I'll begin the healing. Normally, a person's soul is centered in the brain. The soul of a patient and the soul of a healer rarely interact directly, but that's the goal of today. I want you to focus your soul to the area of the wound. Find my soul there, and try to sense what I'm doing."

I nod. This is exactly how I learned dominion from Zane. "I'm ready," I say.

I move my soul, like a snake slithering through my veins, down to the source of my pain. Kendra's soul catches me by surprise, like a sudden burst of sunshine on a rainy day. Our souls collide and for a moment, our minds intercept, two separate colors instantaneously becoming one.

Our souls, as naked as a soul can be, collide. I don't see any memories, but I do experience a rush of her most recent thoughts. They're all directed at me.

In an instant, I feel all of her expectations. The hope that I'll make a move. That I'll find her attractive. That she'll find in me a lifelong ally. I feel her soul move closer, coiling around my own. Before she can learn too much, I retreat.

My eyes burst open, and I find myself gasping. Kendra's face is only a few inches from my own. Her face is pink and her chest swells in sudden breaths. The moment is fleeting, and I devour every feature. The strand of her blonde hair, the darkness of her lashes, the endless green expanse hidden within her eyes, like a forbidden forest.

Kendra brushes her hair from her face and leans back. "I'm sorry, That's never happened before. I..." She swallows and meets my gaze. "That was completely my fault. Normally, someone can't access your mind unless you give them permission. I... I must've given you permission by accident."

"No, it was my fault. I'll try to go slower this time."

"You want to try again?" Kendra questions.

I look down at my arm, suddenly reminded that I'm bleeding. I force a playful smile. "Of course, Miss Eseck. Show me how it's done."

Kendra offers a relieved glance. "Alright. Let's try again."

For a second time, I direct my soul into my arm, this time moving at a snail's pace. When I sense Kendra's soul, I hit the brakes. Her soul is condensed around the point of injury. I can sense her speaking to the cells, commanding them to replicate.

"The key to healing," Kendra narrates, "is directing energy to the right places. Your body can heal on its own. It has the potential to replicate cells at an astounding rate. You have 30 to 50 cell layers in your skin. And every month, you completely replace the skin on your entire body, 20 pounds of it. If we can shed 20 pounds in 30 days, then by condensing all that growth in one location, you can make an ounce of skin in a matter of minutes."

Replicate!

She speaks to the cells lining the incision, but the effect is so much greater. Nutrients and proteins are directed towards the wound from all over my body. Chemical messengers erupt into the bloodstream, and for a few unbearable seconds, the wound itches and burns. Clenching my fingers is all I can do to resist the urge to scratch.

Within a few seconds, the itching fades. I open my eyes, scanning my skin for the wound. The blood remains, but the skin is perfectly smooth.

"That's incredible. Can I try it now?"

"Oh no," Kendra laughs. "It might seem simple, but even healing flesh is fairly advanced. We're going to start you on the healer basics: Heart rate and blood pressure."

"Heart rate? 60 beats a minute? 120 over 80? What else is there to know?"

"How to control it," Kendra says. "Try with yourself first. Lower your heart rate. With dominion, you can make it unbelievably slow—a dozen beats a minute, sometimes less."

I close my eyes, focusing my consciousness around my heart. I can feel the muscle contracting, the valves opening and shutting.

Bum-bum... Bum-Bum...

Slow!

Bum-bum… Bum-bum…

Nothing happens.

"Use your biology, Matt. Your heart contracts because of electrical signals. It all comes down to the diffusion of ions, negatively charged particles in your heart. If you slow down those ions, you slow down your heartbeat."

I take two deep breaths, focusing once again on my heart muscle. I dig deeper, finding the flow of ions through the cells.

Bum-bum… Bum-Bum...

Slow!

Bum-bum……... Bum-bum………...Bum-bum…

My breathing stays steady, but my heart beats only once every few seconds. The feeling is unnerving.

I release the command to look to Kendra in my triumph. "What next?"

"Now, you try it on me. It's easy when you have dominion, now you have to learn to ask permission." She looks down at her chest. "Go ahead."

"You, uhhh." My face grows warmer. "You want me to…"

Kendra laughs. "With a patient, you can't worry about personal space, and you have to be comfortable with some physical contact. The more hesitant you are, the more awkward it'll be. You need to take control, announce what you're doing, make sure they're comfortable. The more confidence you have, the more at ease they'll be. Let me show you."

Kendra gives me a friendly, professional smile. "Alright Matt, if it's alright with you, I'm going to be placing your hand on my chest."

She takes my hand in both of hers and steps close to me, then, she rests my palm flat onto her sternum, lowering it until the base of my wrist is touching the top of her bra.

My face goes from warm to simmering uncontrollably.

Focus Matt. This is about healing. This is about saving Judy.

Kendra smiles. "You good?"

"Never better," I mumble, trying not to stare.

"Okay, go ahead and give it a try."

I close my eyes and let my soul drift directly through her chest. The best part is, I don't have to worry about permission. I'm a demon.

Bum-bum. Bum-bum. Bum-bum.

Her heart rate is racing, well above average. And for a second, I almost forget what I'm doing.

Slow!

Bum-bum……...Bum-bum………..Bum-bum.

Her trembling chest grows steady under my hand. I've succeeded, but now I don't want the moment to end. I should've let it take longer.

She looks up at me, as I lift my hand, the corner of her mouth curling up. "Impressive. Maybe you were meant to be a healer after all."

I know she's being extra nice, but I can't help but feel accomplished. With Kendra's help, I might actually save Judy after all.

"Well, that concludes our lesson. Now it's your turn." Kendra looks around the room. "So, what do you have planned to teach me Master MacArthur?"

"Honestly, I don't get why you need teaching. If you can heal, you should be able to do anything."

"I've never even tried an attack. Madame Xantone would flip her lid if she knew about this. Our number one rule is 'do no damage.'"

I clap my hands together. "Well, lucky for you, Master Mac-Arthur is accepting of all things violent and deadly. For our first lesson, I thought we could begin with fire. A bit of a cliche, I know, but it's easy for me to visualize your progress."

I point to a candle in the center of my desk. "See that candle. I want you to light the wick." I take Kendra by the shoulders and walk her back a few paces. "Stand…. there."

"You want me to light it all the way from here?"

I raise a finger, getting into the role of teacher. "That, my young padawan, is where healing and combat are different. From what I've

222

seen, healing is always within arms reach, while combat almost never is. If your enemy is that close, you're likely already dead. One of your biggest challenges will be to stretch your soul to its very limits. The same way you reach out to a patient, I want you to reach out to that candle. Go ahead and give it a try."

Kendra closes her eyes for a second and quickly opens them again. "I can't even sense it. How am I supposed to find it?"

"I struggled with this too," I admit. "You really have to commit to it. You won't sense the candle for a while, only the air, but you have to keep projecting your soul. It may even seem at times like you're leaving your body behind, but don't panic. Just keep reaching your soul into the unknown."

Kendra shakes her head and laughs. "If you say so, but if I strain my soul, it's on you."

"Worst case scenario, I give you the breath of life," I joke.

Kendra turns to me, raises an eyebrow, and laughs. "I'd like to see you try. You couldn't save a fly with the breath of life."

I grin. "Not unless you teach me."

"Maybe I will," Kendra smirks. She closes her eyes, and for several seconds, the room is silent. I'm about to offer more advice when, silently, the candlewick bursts into flame.

"Very nice."

Kendra curtsies once, still grinning, her lips a smooth arc of red lipstick. "You know, Master MacArthur, I was really hoping for a challenge." She taunts.

"I figured it would be easy for a prodigy such as yourself, so I came prepared." I grab a wedge of firewood that I stole from the commons. I walk to the middle of my room and balance it upright on the stone floor. "Now, do the same thing, but this time, expand your soul around the whole log. Command it to burn all at once."

I step back and fold my arms. Kendra narrows her eyes at the log until her pupils are entirely hidden. A few seconds pass, then a few more.

Eventually, a few embers eat away at the outermost slivers of wood, sending small streams of smoke into the air. Still, I don't see any flames.

"Don't think like a healer," I say. "It's not about precision. Don't hold back! Make everything burn! Command the molecules!" I'm shouting now, Kendra's personal cheerleader.

Finally, she sighs and opens her eyes. "Oof, It's harder than it looks."

I nod. "It's not easy, but you'll get it. Command heat into every atom of the wood, not just the outside. Make every atom burn. This isn't like with a body. You don't need permission. Be assertive. You're in control."

Kendra closes her eyes. *C'mon... you can do it.*

After a few tense moments, the bark begins to singe. White, cloudy smoke billows from the edges of the wood. Before Kendra gives up, I intervene. I reach forward until I find the log.

Burn!

Two wide cracks erupt in the log as it's instantly consumed by the flames. Each crack gives view of the orange ember center.

"Hey! I would've had it!"

She swipes at me, but I dance away. "Hey now, that's not how you treat your master.

"You know what?" Kendra eyes me mischievously. "I have some healing to teach you. How to give someone explosive diar-rhea."

"Nooo. You're joking... you're serious?"

Kendra shrugs. "As long as someone gives me permission to heal, I could do it, hypothetically."

I point my finger at her. "You know, you seemed innocent at first, but now I know the truth."

"Oh come on," she laughs, "you know I'd never."

She takes a step toward me, but I push her back with a gentle wall of air. "Remind me to never get on your bad side," I say, exaggerating a shiver. "I don't even want to think about what you've done to your exes."

224

"Nothing. I was kidding, Matt. I'm harmless."

"Okay, but if anything happens to my bowels, I'm blaming you first."

Kendra holds out her hand. "Truce?"

I shake it. "Truce."

Kendra sighs. "Well, I should probably be going, I have another assignment." She starts to collect her bag.

"Tell me, what's the worst thing you've ever had to heal?"

Kendra cringes. "Oh, I don't even know where to start. Honesty, Matt, being a healer has its downside. The runs is nothing compared to what we have to deal with. Technically, I'm not allowed to tell you any specific cases, but it's awful. I probably have blackmail on half of the High Council."

"What kind of blackmail?" I ask, unable to help myself.

Kendra shrugs, "Incontinence, STDs, abortions, stuff like that. Every year after the fall festival, we get a handful of secret visits."

"Dang, that's quite the blackmail." I look up. "And what about the best of being a healer? What's your favorite part?"

Kendra's lips lift in a subtle smile. "There's a lot of good. Helping couples get pregnant can be really rewarding, especially when I get to meet the babies."

"What else?"

"I'm working on a way to treat depression," she grins. "It's been a challenge, but I'm really excited about where it goes." She thinks a moment longer. "Honestly, I enjoy most of it. Helping the sick. Healing the injured." She looks up at me and blushes. "Saving you."

I glance down, suddenly more conscious of the space between us. I step closer, unable to look away from her lips. My soul drifts towards hers, and I can sense her longing.

Kiss me, Matt!

I want to do it, but I freeze. I've never kissed a girl like Kendra. What if she doesn't like it?

I step back, blowing the moment and instantly regretting it.

Kendra frowns but hides her disappointment well. She throws her bag over her shoulder and shifts her weight. "Speaking of the fall festival, I was wondering if you've already asked anyone. Someone asked me yesterday, and I haven't given an answer yet. I'm waiting in case someone else wants to ask me—someone I'd rather go with. Have you given it any thought?"

Already, nausea settles in my stomach like a stagnant pond. I hate disappointing people, especially a girl like Kendra.

Be honest or it'll only complicate things. I try to swallow my fear. "To tell you the truth," I press my sweaty palms together. "I was thinking about asking the princess... strictly as a friend," I insist. "With the commander being ill, I figured she'd have no one else to take her. I actually promised my mom I wouldn't let her go alone. If I had known..."

Kendra forces a smile, but her eyes droop with disappointment. "No, I get it. That's a good idea. I'll go ahead and tell him I can go. That's nice of you to ask her."

I force a smile as well. "I'll see you there, right? Maybe we can trade dates for a dance?"

"I would like that," Kendra says. "I'll hold you to it." She stands suddenly and moves toward the door. "Same time next week. Don't forget to read through chapter four."

"I won't. I'm looking forward to it."

She smiles one last time, and I try to capture the image. Then, she's out the door.

I stand, and my smile quickly fades.

It's time I visit my sister.

Chapter 16

Rose

The plentitude of rotten fruit is appalling. I told Wendy to ask the kitchen for their spoiled goods, and she returned with an entire basket full. Apples and peaches are pinned to the face of a hay bale. A single red melon teeters on the top. Together, they will be my target practice.

I stand 20 feet from the fruit. The bow, beautifully crafted by Gideon, feels awkward in my hand. It's longer than I expected—over four feet. I place my left hand on the leather grip. Then, I pick up an arrow.

"What do I do now? I've never done archery before."

Gideon smiles. "It is simple. The notch on the back of the arrow goes between the two beads on the bowstring, and that little notch next to your bow hand is the arrow rest. Place the arrow shaft so that it rests upon it. That helps ensure your shots are consistent."

I nock an arrow and rest the shaft on the wooden shelf as instructed. I look back to Gideon.

He motions to the fruit wall. "Pull and release, princess."

I groan as I yank back the string. It resists more aggressively than I imagined. "It's heavy," I note. "Is this a longbow?"

"A light-weight recurve." He grins. "The best for beginners. Still, you'll have to wrestle with it. If the draw weight is too much, I can reduce the tension."

I pull it back until the string is nearly touching my ear. My shoulder shakes, and I do my best to time the release with the tremors.

Twang!

The arrow disappears into the grass at the foot of the hay bale.

I look to Gideon, but he's already giving advice. "Several things. First, your body is not aligned. Your bow arm should make a straight line with your back. Point your left shoulder at your prey." He quickly nocks an arrow for me. "Go ahead and draw it back, but don't release."

I clench my teeth and pull the arrow back to my ear.

Gideon taps me on the right shoulder blade. "There needs to be tension here. Pull your shoulder back as if you're trying to pinch your shoulder blades together. And tighten your core. Everything must be taut."

I do as instructed, and instantly my shoulder stops shaking. I can feel the support running down my back.

"Good. Now, draw to your eye. Tilt your head if you need to, but keep your body straight. You want your right pupil looking down the shaft. The arrowhead will be your crosshair. Place it over your target. To release, simply let your fingers go slack. Try to keep the rest of your body as rigid as possible."

I aim the arrow at the center of the bale. At the peak of my exhale, I let the string slip from my fingers.

Twang.

The arrow disappears halfway to the fletching in the hay. It's three feet from the center—down and to the left. I can already feel the dopamine. "I hit it."

"You did. A great start. Try again. The more you shoot, the more natural it will become."

I knock an arrow, draw, and release. Over and over.

Twang. Twang. Twang.

After a minute, I have a wide grouping of five arrows. Had a feeder been standing in front of the bale, only two arrows would have hit home. I collect the arrows and repeat.

Twang. Twang. Twang...

This time, the grouping is closer together. It looks more like a vertical oval. By the next volley, my arrows are in a vertical line, only deviating from the center axis by a few inches. Yet for whatever reason, the height of each shot is unpredictable. "How do I aim up and down? I'm aiming the arrowhead on the same spot every time."

Gideon smiles as if he had been waiting for me to ask. "I've been watching your draw. Sometimes you pull back farther than others. The added power reduces the drop."

"How do I fix it?"

Gideon picks up his own bow and places his hand at the very peak of the grip. "I like to place my bow hand level with the arrow rest. That way, I can feel the arrow sliding as I draw it back. When the arrowhead hits my knuckle, I release. Assuming my arrows are the same length, my draw will be identical every time."

"That's really clever." I slide my hand an inch higher so that the top of my index finger is level with the arrow rest. I draw the arrow back, focusing on the wooden texture of the shaft as it drags across my knuckle. As soon as the metal arrowhead bumps my index finger, I release.

Twang. It hits just above the center.

I aim at the same point and repeat.

Twang. Twang. Twang.

The arrows hit high, but they do so consistently. They all land within the same foot radius. *You're doing it, Rose. You're an archer.*

I snatch the arrows from the bale and hurry back to my shooting spot. This time, I focus on the red melon perched on top of the hay.

The melon is out to kill you, Rose.

I let myself believe it. I imagine it as a feeder with sickly, leather-tight skin. I see the moldy patches as dark, bloodthirsty eyes. Rotten watermelon juice seeps like drool from an open mouth.

Time to die!

The bowstring digs into the crease of my fingers. I try not to groan as I yank it back and align the arrowhead with the base of the melon. Already, my arm is fatiguing. I give it one final tug and as soon as I feel the metal arrowhead graze my knuckle, I let the arrow fly.

The bowstring snaps, and the arrow pierces the melon, embedding itself to half-shaft. Watermelon juice oozes, the blood of a fresh kill.

"Beautiful shot, dauphine. You are a quick learner indeed."

"Thanks, Gideon. you have a knack for teaching." I nock another arrow and aim it at a rotten apple. It's large for an apple—about the size of a human heart, which helps my odds considerably. My elbow wobbles as I pull back the string. I exhale and release.

Twang!

My eyes follow the arrow as it strikes the hay only two inches to the left of the apple. I knock another arrow and let it fly. This time, it's four inches to the right. "Uhh!" I grab another arrow and pull it back. I hold this one longer, failing to steady my trembling hand. The longer I hold the string, the more exhausted my arm becomes. When I finally let go, the arrow strikes over a foot off target. "It's like I'm getting worse!"

Gideon encourages me with a gentle grin. "You are not getting worse, you are getting fatigued. As your muscles grow stronger, your aim will improve. You have my word, dauphine." He walks over to the bale and begins gently plucking arrows, like thorns from a child's foot. "Besides, your aim need not be perfect. The Adamic spells that tip the arrows make them significantly more deadly. Any hit to the torso will most likely be lethal." He plucks the last arrow from next to the apple. "This feeder would've been dead three times over."

"Should I try scooting back?"

Gideon raises his own bow and nocks an arrow. Up to this point, I haven't seen him shoot. He draws back the string, almost poking his eye with the back of the arrow. He holds the string drawn as he speaks.

"In my opinion, this is the ideal distance. At 10 meters, dominion is strained. You can shoot at a feeder while still being safe from attack."

Twang.

In the blink of an eye, the string whips, and the arrow splits the apple in half. Gideon draws an arrow from his quiver, and in a single, smooth motion, he nocks it and draws it back.

Twang!

The arrow dives at the foot of the hay bale. At first, it looks like a stray shot, but then I notice the apple. The second arrow pierces one of the halves, pinning it to the moist soil. Then, he shoots again, pinning the other.

Gideon lowers his bow. "Once you begin shooting at longer distances, flight time is increased. If a feeder is swift, they may dodge your arrows. It's happened to me before. The key is to find a balance between keeping a safe distance and hitting your target. For me, that balance is 10 meters."

Without warning, Gideon's bow snaps up. In the time it takes to take a breath, Gideon fires two more arrows, one into a peach and the other into an avocado.

"That's amazing!" I gasp. "How long did it take to master the bow like that?"

"Many years, dauphine, but I must confess: most of my progress was made in the first few months. You don't have to be a master to become a formidable foe. The real challenge will come as you master depth and movement. Perhaps we should try a new exercise."

Gideon removes three arrows from his quiver. Unlike the others, these don't come to a point. Instead, the tips widen, forming a fat rubber glob. Gideon taps one against his knee. "They may bruise, but they won't harm." He hands me the arrows and I pinch one between each of my fingers.

Next, Gideon lifts another rotten melon from the basket and sets it carefully at my feet. "Pretend this is your head," Gideon grins. "I will start at the wall and try to kill your melon. Your task is equally simple. You must shoot me before your melon dies."

"You want me to shoot you?" I reaffirm.

"Fear not, Madame. You will not hit me, but it will be good practice nonetheless."

He paces past the hay bale and stops when his back is against the palace wall 50 feet away. "Ready?"

I knock an arrow and take a deep breath. "Ready!"

Gideon breaks into a sprint, quickly erasing the space between us. 50 feet immediately becomes 30. The second I lift my arrow to my eye, he cuts sideways. I try to trail him, but he cuts back the other way. He's only 20 feet away.

In a panic, I aim and release.

Twang!

The arrow is true to my aim, but Gideon is already 3 steps ahead of the arrow. I fumble to nock the next arrow, but I'm too late.

Squash! Gideon stomps down on the melon. "The feeder wins today, princess. Tomorrow you can try again."

No. The feeder can't win. Already, I feel my disappointment weighing down on me. If the feeder wins, Velma dies. If the feeder wins, I can't protect the people I love. Archery was supposed to be the key. It was supposed to empower me, but it seems I was mistaken.

Gideon squints and hunches his shoulders until our eyes are level. "You are discouraged? For what reason are you discouraged?"

I force the frown from my face and shrug. "I suppose I assumed I would be able to defend myself. This was supposed to be my secret weapon."

Gideon is astounded. "Defend yourself? Of course, you can defend yourself."

"Yeah, if they were standing still. If an actual feeder charged me, I'd be as good as dead."

"Dauphine, if it were easy, everyone would do it. Be glad it's not easy, or your enemies could pick up your bow and have the same advantage as you. Be grateful it is your training that will set you apart. Hear my words, it will take sacrifice, but soon you will be able to kill any feeder, no matter how swift. Do not compare yourself to your goals, but rather to yesterday. Have you not seen improvement today?"

"Yes, I have."

"Good. And more improvement will come, but it will take effort. I want you to practice nocking your arrows as fast as you can, 100 times a night. Every evening, we train out here. It will take time, princess, but I will make you invincible. Feeders will fear your name."

"Thank you, Gideon. I appreciate it. You've gone above and beyond to help me."

"I do not do it for you alone, princess. I do it for Cavernum. Do not forget I need Adamic arrows, and it won't be long before you will be the only adalit alive. I need you to be a survivor, for my sake and yours. Do I have your commitment?"

I nod. "Of course. I'll do my best."

"I know you will," he grins. "And I know you will craft the armor-piercing arrowheads. The sooner you do, the safer Cavernum will be."

"I know. I'm making progress."

"Good. Now, go... Rest. I will clean up here. Remember to practice nocking. I will see you here tomorrow."

"Very well," I say. "Thank you, Gideon. I owe you."

He begins picking up his arrows. "And soon your debt will be paid, princess. Soon, it will be paid."

I leave him and briskly walk to the Central Wing. Normally, I like to think I would stay and help Gideon pick up, but not today.

Today, I need to be there for Antai.

I squeeze Antai's lifeless hand as Kendra presses her palms to his temples. Madame Xantone has already given an assessment, but for whatever reason, Grandpa only seems to care about what Kendra has to say.

After a long silence, her hands fall from Antai's head and sulk to her side. Kendra stands and looks back and forth between Grandpa and me. Whatever she's about to say, she dreads it.

"I'm afraid I must agree with Madame Xantone. I... I can't sense his soul. It's been long enough that, if he were going to recover, we believe he would have done so by now. I'm sorry."

Grandpa's lips turn down. More than anything, he looks confused, as if that wasn't the answer he expected. "How long will he live as he is?"

"A few more weeks, maybe a month or two at most." Madame Xantone solemnly says. "I would suggest you both think about removing him from the feeding tube."

How can she say that? If there's any chance he might awake, we have to wait it out. As long as it takes, we have to try.

"You said the odds are slim, but what exactly does that mean? 1 in 10 he wakes up? 1 in a 100?"

Kendra looks to Madame Xantone, who sighs. "I say this because I care, princess. Frankly, it's zero. His soul is gone. It would take a prophet to raise him from the dead. That's the kind of miracle you need."

No! She doesn't understand. Titan already tried that, and it didn't work. I feel despair beginning to drown me, so I let my anger rage instead.

"How can you say that? You've never seen this condition before. How can you make that claim as if you know?"

Grandpa puts his hand on my shoulder, unshaken by the somber prognosis. "Thank you both for your opinions," Grandpa says, "but we'd like to continue with his treatments regardless. At least for the present."

Madame Xantone's tone is gentle and motherly. "I know this must be painful for you both, but you'll only be delaying the ine—"

"I said we'd like to continue his treatments," Grandpa growls. "We'll inform you if we change our minds."

"Y-yes your majesty. As you wish."

"You're both excused," Grandpa says.

Without another word, the two healers hurry out of the room. The resulting silence is almost unbearable.

"Do… do you think he'll wake up? You can be honest with me."

Grandpa sighs. He props his cane under his chest and leans forward, staring intently at Antai's face. "I always felt that he would. It's not easy to ignore the facts, but I still believe he'll come through."

"How do you stay so positive? I want to believe, but it's getting harder. More and more, I feel like I'm lying to myself."

Grandpa doesn't look up from Antai. "I suppose it's just a gut feeling. I beg you, Rose. Don't lose hope. This is not the end of Antai."

"I'll try," I say. "Can I just be alone for a bit?"

Grandpa nods. "Of course. Take as much time as you need."

He shuffles away from the bed, and I hear Antai's door softly shut.

Now that I'm alone, I let myself feel the full force of the tragedy. Self-pity wells inside me until it spills out of my eyes. I keep my voice low, in case someone is listening at the door.

"Antai, I have no idea what to do. Everything is falling apart. You're not getting better. Quill is on the council. Grandpa…" I take a deep breath. "Grandpa knows who the Holy One is, and he's hiding it from me. I have to confront him, but I don't know how. I need you now more than ever, Antai. I'm losing my mind. I've been trying to keep busy, but… I just can't do it anymore. I need you to wake up. The Fall Ball is only two weeks away, and I need you to be there for me. I've been waiting for this day since our first dance lesson. I can't imagine a—"

Thump. Thump.

I hear two knocks on the door—short and firm, a heartbeat against the oak. "It's unlocked," I say. The nurse must be here to replace Antai's feeding bag.

The door opens slowly, and I catch a glimpse of wavy blonde hair. "The king let me back here. If this is a bad time I can come back."

"Matt!" I quickly dry my tears with my sleeve, but he already has a clear view of all my emotional madness. *Why now?* I consider turning him away, but some part of me craves his company. "Ummm, come in I guess, but I have to warn you, I might drip on you." I sniffle one last time, hoping my nose stops running.

Matt keeps his distance, loitering by the wall. His eyes fall on Antai's weakened frame. "I heard about what happened to him. I'm sure you must be going through hell right now."

"I…" I'm about to deny it, but something about his icy blue eyes sees right through me. "It's been rough. I'm barely hanging on."

Matt's lips pinch shut, and his eyes look deep inside me. His gaze carries a certain calmness. From his look alone, I feel my grief being pushed aside, my suffering soothed… shared.

"How are you doing?" I ask. "You look good. Last I saw you, I thought you might not make it."

Matt smiles. "I feel good, thanks to you. Whatever you did in the tunnel, it saved my life. So, thank you for that."

"It's the least I could do for when you saved me from that feeder." *The one who killed Velma.* "I guess we're even now."

"I guess we are," he breathes, watching Antai from the corner of his eye. "Do they think he'll make it?"

"No." As much as it hurts, I say it out loud. "The healers are convinced he'll never recover. The only one who disagrees is my grandpa. I don't know what to think, to be honest." I sigh. "They're giving me the option of cutting off his food supply. I have no clue what to do." I look down, eventually finding myself watching Matt once more. "What would you do?" I finally ask. "You understand better than anyone. What advice do you have?"

Matt straightens his back and extends his chin. He licks his lips once and looks back at me. "I guess it really depends. My first question would be, what do you think Antai would want? If he knew his body was being fed through a tube?"

I already know he would hate it. Antai would want his death to be meaningful—an epic sacrifice for a loved one—basically, what he's already done for me. He wouldn't want to slowly wither away as I watch him devolve into a living corpse.

"What's your second question?"

Matt sighs and frowns at Antai. The aura in the room changes to worry… or maybe guilt.

"I guess I would ask what you want. His life affects you too, and you shouldn't have to be selfless." Matt wrings his hands together like a rag. "If I were you, I would choose whatever you'll regret the least."

I let that sink in, his advice becoming dissolved in the very way I think. It's obvious what I should do. If there's any chance of Antai waking up, any at all, I have to try. If we pull the plug, I'll always wonder if things could've been different.

"Thank you, Matt. That's helpful. I think I needed to hear that."

"Happy to help, Rose."

The bridge of my nose wrinkles as I peer at Matt. "You know, I think that's the first time I've heard you say my real name."

Matt tilts his head, trying to see if he can conjure up a counter-example. After a moment, he nods in agreement. "You'll always be Lynn in my mind."

I smile. "I miss being Lynn. Everything was easier as a recruit. I took it for granted." *I took them all for granted.*

Matt nods. "I miss it too, being a recruit, I mean." He watches Antai for an oddly long time. "I don't mean to be insensitive, but what happened to him? He doesn't look injured. No one I've asked seems to know."

"Oh." I've rehearsed my story once with Grandpa, but this is the first I've had to use it. "When the equalists raided the vault, one tried to steal from my Grandpa's study. He has some amulets there. Antai tried to stop him, but he used poison dominion. He looks fine because the damage is internal."

Matt grimaces, as if it's not the story he was expecting. After a moment of obvious confusion, he recovers. "Poison dominion? Really?"

"What? You seem surprised?"

"No. I just…" He looks at me, and suddenly he's hyper-focused. "I thought that would be something they could heal."

"Yeah, me too," I admit.

He's quiet for a second. Shifting his weight from side to side. "Hey, Rose. Can I ask you something?"

"Of course."

"I don't mean to make this weird, but… you gave me the breath of life, didn't you?"

I'm grateful my complexion hides my embarrassment. "Yeah, I did. Why?"

"It's just that… when you did that, did you happen to see any of my memories?"

My eyes turn to slits. "No. Why, did you?"

His eyes shift as he nods. "Just a few. Some of it isn't memories. It's just… knowledge. It's like I just know things that I shouldn't. I know what you know."

My heart is pounding, but I don't know why. I don't have much to hide. "What kind of things?"

"I know how Antai really died. You were possessed, I think, and… you shot him. I know the Holy One was behind it, and that he wants the Book of Life."

I'm stunned. I don't know what to say, so I simply stare back.

"I don't want to freak you out," Matt insists. "I just… I felt like I had to tell you."

"What else do you know?" I demand.

Matt looks down at Antai. "I know he died, but was brought back. An old man spoke Adamic and resurrected him, only it didn't work." He hesitates a moment longer. "And I know you loved him."

238

"I… I'm sorry. I don't… this is just a lot." My chest feels tight. *This was your choice, Rose,* I remind myself. *You shared your soul. He didn't choose this.*

"If you need some space, I can go," Matt offers, keenly aware of my disgust. "I know this must feel like a major invasion of privacy. I just… it felt weirder keeping it from you. I felt like I could trust you with the truth."

I stoke my voice with acceptance. "I appreciate you being honest. It's just… you promise that's all you learned?" I don't even want to imagine the memories he might have seen. Gossiping with Nevela. Antai and I kissing in the cornstalks.

"That's everything," Matt insists. "And you, you didn't see any of my memories?"

"Not a single one," I say. "Swear to God."

His shoulders relax. "Good."

I wonder what kind of memories Matt might have to hide. Perhaps a secret girlfriend in the core? Hidden riches?

In addition to my curiosity, I feel a weight lifted. I feel understood. As weird as it is, I'm glad Matt knows about Antai's death. I'm tired of pretending I wasn't the one who shot him. I'm tired of all these secrets.

"You know," Matt turns to Antai. "I'd be dead if it weren't for him. He practically saved my life."

"He did?"

"Well, from what I've heard, he saved your life, and in the tunnels you saved mine. If he never saved you, I'd be dead too."

"I've been saved by a lot of people lately," I say. "I'm starting to feel helpless. I do nothing but stand at attention around the palace."

"I'll trade you." Matt smiles. "My platoon would love you, and I could sleep like a normal human being."

"Please, anytime." I insist.

At that, the conversation falls flat, Antai's heavy breaths filling the silence.

"Can I ask you something?" Matt looks over suddenly. "I've just been thinking a lot about some of those memories you gave me. That old man who spoke Adamic, who was he?"

"That would be great-grandpa."

"Your great-grandpa? Sooo, does that mean you can speak it too?"

"No, he's never shared how he learned. We didn't even know he was adalingual until that night."

"Adalingual?"

He doesn't know. Whatever knowledge I inadvertently gave him, it must have been very limited. "To be honest, I'm not really sure what I should tell you. Some of this is somewhat secretive in Cavernum, so you have to promise you won't tell anyone."

Matt raises his hand. "I promise. You have my word."

"Well, adalinguals are people fluent in Adamic. Technically, we don't know if Titan is fluent, but he knows a few spells at the very least. "

"Titan? As in crazy Titan?"

"You've heard of him?" I laugh.

"Some of the other guards mentioned him. I didn't expect him to be adalingual. They said he was senile."

Rose's amusement quickly disappears. "He is. His dementia is pretty severe. He's pretty much losing his mind."

Matt furrows his brow. "And he doesn't know any more spells? He can't try something else to save Antai?"

I shake my head. "His dementia is severe. He doesn't remember much anymore, and whatever he does remember, he doesn't share. My grandpa has tried over and over. He goes berserk anytime we mention The Book of Life."

"Bummer," Matt sighs. "I was hoping I could thank him. By saving you, he saved me as well. I owe Titan my life."

I glance at the clock. It must be getting close to sundown, but we might have enough time. "If you'd like, you can meet him. He's right down the hall."

"Seriously? I mean, if you're okay with that, I'd love to."

I guide Matt out of Antai's room and into the deepest recesses of the Royal Wing. "Like I said, whatever you do, don't mention The Book of Life. And I have to warn you. He might call me Clarisa. Supposedly, I look like his deceased wife."

"He must've been a lucky man," Matt muses under his breath.

I look away, trying to hide my smug smile.

When we reach his chambers, I knock softly before entering. "Titan, it's me. I brought a friend to say hi."

Titan is utterly unconscious in his armchair. One of the servants is sitting on the satin sofa, snoozing as well. He awakes the moment we enter the room.

"Princess!" He bows. "How can I be of service?"

"We're here to visit Titan. You may do as you wish for the next few minutes. I'll keep a close eye on him."

"Of course, princess. Thank you, princess."

The servant retreats, and I softly tap Titan on the shoulder, dodging the dandruff that has already settled there.

"Hmmm?" Titan stirs but doesn't open his eyes.

"Titan, it's your granddaughter, Rose. I brought a friend," I repeat.

His eyes flutter open, and he slowly sits up. "Clarisa, you came?"

"Hi, Titan. How are you feeling today?"

"Tired!" He's already dropping back into the chair, like ice cream melting on a hot day.

"Titan, can you stay awake? We want to talk to you."

He nestles his head against the back of the chair, and his eyes slowly close.

"Titan. If you wake up, I'll read you a page from Clarisa's diary."

Even with a bribe, Titan remains rooted in his chair, now snoring in slow, steady breaths.

"I'm sorry, Matt. This probably wasn't what you were expecting."

"Nah, it's fine," Matt brushes it off. "That's just the reality of aging. Honestly, he doesn't look too shabby for a grandpappy. A lot of people don't even get to meet their great-grandkids."

I wonder if he's thinking about Judy, and I feel the need to distract him from his sorrow.

"You know," I add. "Titan actually lived in the beyond for a while. He used to travel to all the different sanctuaries looking for… you know what. From what I've read in his journal, he's been to five or six."

When I look at Matt, he isn't looking back. Instead, he's oddly fixated on Titan's face. He stares, unblinking, at Titan's closed eyelids. He almost looks… hypnotized.

I'm about to say something when Titan startles awake. He lurches upright and the instant his eyes open, his lips part like theatre curtains revealing a toothless grin.

His voice is like a broken wagon wheel grinding against the dirt. "Matt? Is that you?"

The color drains from Matt's face. He takes a step back. "You know my name?"

Titan turns to me, his eyes are pink and veiny, yet they focus on me with alarming clarity. "Rose? You're both here." His head swivels back in Matt's direction. "It's so nice to see you again," he croaks.

Matt recoils. "I… I've never met you before in my life."

Now, Titan is the one who looks shocked. He looks at his feet and starts shaking his head, slowly at first and then violently. "I shouldn't have said that. I shouldn't have said that. I need to forget. I need to forget everything."

In a manic craze, he begins slapping his palm against his forehead.

"I shouldn't remember. I need to forget. He'll know. Forget. Forget. Forget."

"Titan. Look at me." I grab one hand, but he starts slapping with the other. "I need to forget. Help me forget." Finally, he squeezes his

242

head between his two hands, flexing his entire body at once. Then, as quickly as the tirade began, he slumps unconscious in his chair.

When I'm sure he's not faking, I glance at Matt, who's white as a ghost.

"Are you okay, Matt?"

Matt never takes his eyes off of Titan. "He doesn't have dementia, Rose. I think he erased his own memories. He erased them all."

Chapter 17

Matt

The cloak is more comfortable than I imagined. It's a matte black color, and surprisingly silky. It's not terribly thick, but it deflects the wind without issue.

I look down at myself and smile. I look ridiculous, but I didn't have a choice. It's getting cold in Cavernum, and a maid took my sweatshirt for cleaning.

The gust of wind parts my cloak and threatens to pull the fabric from my shoulders. I wrap the material tighter around me. *This better be worth it.*

I enter a slender alley and keep a busy pace, stepping around what looks like a broken barrel. I avoid a suspiciously dark puddle and tiptoe my way over some beer bottles. About twenty yards back, the alley takes a 90-degree turn to the right. I follow it and stop before a door. A sign reads: **Employees Only!**

Iris is no employee, I know that for sure. I'm beginning to wonder if I'm in the wrong place when I hear the metallic scrape of a deadbolt, one after the other. The door slides open, and Iris scowls at me.

"Any weapons?" she asks.

I toss open my cloak to reveal my empty hips.

Iris nods. "C'mon." As soon as I am through the door, she slams it shut and resets the locks. "Follow me."

She leads me into the next room over—not much bigger than a closet. A round table stretches nearly from wall to wall. There isn't a single window in the room, and the lantern on the table is struggling to illuminate much of anything. It looks like one of those rooms where the mob gets together to play poker.

"Sit," Iris commands, lowering herself into a chair. "Make yourself comfortable."

I want to sit as far from her as possible, but instead, I take the next closest seat. I'm here to be friendly. "What is this place? Is this part of Bob's Brew?"

As if on cue, Bob bursts through the door. He holds three beers between two hands and pushes the door with his belly. "Iris, my girl, how are ya?" He slaps the triad of beers onto the table. Then, he leans over and gives Iris a kiss on each cheek, European style.

Iris looks oftly young to be dating Bob, but love is love, I guess.

Iris senses my confusion. "Ezra, this is my dad, Bob. Dad, this is my brother, Ezra."

"Wait!" Of all the things I imagined Iris telling me, this was the absolute last. "You're serious?"

Bob leans over and shakes my hand. "It's a pleasure to meet you, Ezra." He turns to Iris. "I can see the resemblance. He has your hair and your ears."

"Bob… is your dad?"

Bob takes a swig from his beer. "After the tragedy in Hogrum, Zane spent an awful lot of time in my Tavern. When he heard that my wife and I couldn't have children, he brought us Iris. We raised her as our own." He turns to me, brushing his scraggly hair out of his face. "If you ever need anything, Ezra, you can come to us. A brother of Iris is a son of mine."

"Thank you…" His hospitality catches me off guard. "Uhhh, that's really kind of you."

"So," Bob lowers his brew and gives me a hopeful glance. "Have you decided to join us yet?"

My eyes widen. "You're one of them too?"

"One of them?" Bob bellows. "I was the first. 30 years ago we founded the equalists in this very room. Before they took to the tunnels, we met here every week."

"You?" I try to water down my disbelief. "You founded the equalists?"

"Dad?" Iris warns. "Careful what you say. He's not loyal."

Bob waves his hand. "Please, he's practically family. Besides," He turns to me with a sudden intensity. "If he spills, you can kill him in his sleep."

"I won't," I insist.

"Good." Bob rubs his belly before picking back up his beer.

I shake my head. "But… don't you run a tavern for the guard? Aren't you worried that they'll—" I wave my hands. "—find out about all this?"

Bob grins. "It's like they say, a spider spins its web closest to the water, not to take a drink, but to catch the flies." When I lift my brow, he chuckles. "The guardsmen are the flies, Ezra. They sit in my web all the day long, talking of their plans and of their secrets."

Bob tosses back his beer and his throat bulges as he swallows. "Besides," he roars, "It'll be a cold day in hell before they suspect me of anything. They think me a dull-brained drunkard. That's the beauty of the bar. When they come here, they want a break from the job. They'd never think to do any inspecting."

"That's… that's actually pretty genius," I admit. "You had me fooled."

"Aye, I've got the body of a drunk, it's not hard to act the part." He stands. "Well, Ezra, it was a pleasure. I don't doubt I'll see you again. I'll leave you two to chat."

"See ya, dad," Iris calls out

Just like that, he waddles out of the room and closes the door. Now, it's just the two of us and the small kerosene lamp.

"So," Iris starts. "What did you want to talk to me about?"

"I... I want to understand why you serve the Holy One. I don't quite know where I stand. The more I understand, the better."

Iris rolls her eyes. "I thought we already covered this in the tunnels. The Holy One can make the world right. He can make it fair. What more do you need to hear?"

"But how?" I say. "How will he make things fair? What will happen to the sanctuary? Will he make his own government? What's his plan?"

The corners of her mouth sharpen. "Actually, he has. He refuses to be a monarch. He'll form a council of his most trusted servants, myself included. Together, we'll remake society."

"And in this society, what happens to the wicked? They die?"

"Yes, Ezra. The wicked are punished. That's the way it's always been. Everyone I kill deserves death, or worse."

"So, you admit it? You're the one marking the doors? You're killing all those people? You use your invisibility ring, don't you? That's how you sneak in and out of the palace?"

"And what about it?" Iris asks. She crosses her arms across her chest. "I'm improving Cavernum. What have you done?"

"I..." I have nothing to say. Sure, I've saved a few lives, the princess included, but Cavernum is still the same mess it was when I arrived. Maybe this is the only way. Maybe they have to die...

No! There has to be another way.

"Well?" Iris waves her hand in a circle. "Spit it out."

"I just don't understand," I say. "How can you kill them? How can you murder so many people? Does that not feel evil to you?"

Iris shifts her shoulder away, growing defensive once more. "I've seen inside their minds, Ezra. I know they deserve it. The people I've killed belong in hell." She shudders. "If I didn't kill them, more innocent people would suffer at their hands. So, no, I

247

don't feel bad." She sighs. "Besides, they don't even suffer. I kill them in their sleep."

"But what about in the tunnels? You killed at least 10 men. You can't tell me they all deserved it!"

Iris's lips pull tight. "The Holy One will bring them back. What do I have to say for that to sink in? The Holy One will make it right."

"How?" My voice grows with my confidence. "How will he know who you've killed? Do you know their names? Do you even keep track anymore? How will he possibly know who to bring back?"

"He'll know." She slaps her hands on the table. I see the rage in her eyes—our father's rage. "The Holy One will make it right. He will!"

She's trying to convince herself. "Okay," I give up. "Maybe you're right." *Who knows, maybe she is right.*

She looks at me. "I'm not a monster, Ezra. I'm not. When I bring back our parents, you'll see the goodness of our cause."

I look away first, conceding the argument. After a few moments of silence, I point at her thumb. "How does it work?"

Iris instinctively buries her hand under the table to cover the ring. For a moment, she chews her cheek, a lie brewing on her lips. Finally, she lifts her hand from beneath the table and drops it on the hardwood. "It's a gift from the Holy One—the invisibility ring of the prophet Soronan," She boasts. "The children of Cain still tell legends of this ring."

The Lord of the Rings! I suppress a smile. She actually has an invisibility ring.

'How does it work?" I ask. "You're wearing it, but you're not invisible. How?"

Iris holds up her hand. The ring is flat and wide, taking up half the space between the two knuckles. I can see several Adamic symbols, but there's an odd gap between the center-most characters.

"It's made of overlapping segments that slide. When the symbols come together..." She rotates the outermost layer until the symbols are side by side. The instant they align, she vanishes.

"Wow."

In the blink of an eye, she reappears, twisting the symbols apart once more.

"Can I see it?"

Iris pulls her hand back, hiding the ring under the table. "It's a bar, not a brothel."

My eyebrows tip inward. "What?"

Iris grins, amused by my innocence. "Look, don't touch."

I look down at the table where I imagine the ring must be resting. "So... The Holy One just gave it to you?" I ask.

"It isn't free. He offered it in exchange for my service."

"Oh," I say. "That makes sense."

"That's not all he offers, Ezra." She looks disgusted by the thought. "I'm not doing this for power; I do it for love... for Jazon."

The name triggers a memory—not mine, but hers. I can see it as clearly as when I first possessed Iris. She's watching a body in the center of a small pyre. As the flames obscure his body, her vision blurs with tears.

"I saw him when I possessed you," I say. "Zane told me what happened. I'm sorry, Iris."

Iris turns away, facing the darkness. I watch the lamplight dancing in her hair. "What did Zane say?"

"He, uhhh... he said that he was shot by the guard. That he was unarmed. He said that it never should've happened."

"Did he say that Jazon got shot because of me? Did he mention that?"

"No." My voice is frail, barely loud enough to maintain its pitch. "No, he didn't tell me that."

Iris is quiet as her memory revives her emotions. Anger, despair, I can see it all in her demeanor.

"We were spending the night for the first time," Iris begins. "We had a storm that night. More rain than we've had in years. It wasn't long before his roof started to leak directly above our bed. We tried to move the bed, but the mattress was already soaked. That's when I suggested we go to my place. Initially, he refused, but I managed to convince him. I was a guardsman. I thought we would be fine. Guards back each other up. Well... we didn't go far before they spotted us, and they didn't wait for an explanation. They saw us creeping through the ring, and they shot him on sight, no questions asked. He died that night in my arms... and for what? Because of a leaky roof? Because I wanted to sleep on a dry bed? That's why I support the Holy One. Because he's the only one on Earth who can bring him back. Do you know how many other people have gone through the same hell I have? Diego sure has, and others too. The Holy One can make everything right."

"Have you met him?"

Iris scowls. "I... no, not yet."

"Then how can you say that you trust him?" I demand. "Especially after what he did to Diego's mom?"

Iris cock her head to the side. "What are you talking about?"

He didn't tell her!

"A few weeks back, when you were robbing the palace vault, there was a man with you. Not the giant, the other guy. He had a scar on his face."

"Torvik?" Iris asks.

"Yeah, him. Well, Diego recognized him as the man who took his mom. Diego tried to interrogate him, but the man wouldn't talk. All he said was that the Holy One has Diego's mom, and whatever he wants her for, it's worse than death."

I see a glimmer of recognition in her eye. Whatever she's realized, she hides it with a scowl. "That's... I don't know anything about that."

"And still, you trust him?" I press. "Who knows what else he's up to? They say he destroyed Hogrum. What if he does the same to Cavernum?"

"He won't!" Iris spits. "And... even if he did, he could fix it. He doesn't do anything that can't be undone. The language is everything, Ezra. Don't you see? If you put your trust in the king, you'll lose everything."

I shrug my shoulder. "No, I don't see, Iris. This whole thing sounds insane, and frankly, Cavernum is no better. I don't trust anyone. The king, the Holy One. I don't even trust you."

She looks at me as if seeing me for the first time. "I believe I misjudged you, Ezra. When I possessed you in the palace, I saw the princess—the way you felt about her. I thought you'd be an undying supporter. Turns out I was wrong."

"The princess isn't your enemy. She..." I hold my tongue. As much as I hate to admit it, I'm at my sister's mercy. I only leave this meeting alive if she lets me.

Iris brushes her choppy bangs off of her eyebrows and gives me a scowl. "Is this what you came for, Ezra? To lecture me about my loyalties? I don't care if we're kin, I won't waste my time." She begins to rise.

"Wait!" I beg. "Can you tell me about our parents? Maybe something that Zane is less likely to share?"

She rests her weight back on the chair, but she doesn't scoot it in. "Everything I know, I learned from Zane. As far as I'm convinced, it was all a lie. I have nothing to tell you."

"So, do you have your amulet from our parents? Zane said our mother made you one too?"

Her face contorts with disgust. "When I turned 12, the king came and took it away. Some birthday that was. I was hoping I'd find it when we raided the vault, but it wasn't there. For all I know, the king is wearing it himself." She glances at my chest. "What about yours, they take yours too?"

I nod. "Zane took it when I arrived. My Adamic blade too."

Her eyebrows jump. "They left you with an Adamic blade? Pfft, all I got was some dumb jewelry." She fishes into her shirt and removes a small hourglass about the size of my thumb. The hourglass is angular—two glass pyramids joined at the tips. Except for the sand within, the hourglass is pure crystal. It's bound to the chain at the hourglass's waist, making it hang horizontal. In all honesty, it's beautiful, sparkling like two conjoined diamonds.

"An hourglass? I've never seen one like that."

Iris looks unimpressed. "It's not even an hourglass. It's a minute glass, and it's not even consistent. It's virtually useless, but it's all I have." She closes her fist around the glass and drops it back in her shirt.

I can relate to that. I thought my amulet was useless my entire life, but still, it was my greatest treasure. "At least you get to keep it. If it was anything useful, the king would've taken it too."

Iris shrugs, taking one last swig, tipping the glass back until it's empty, then slamming it down. "That's all I have time for. It was nice to meet you, brother. Take care of yourself." She moves quickly, slipping out of her seat and reaching for the door. "You can help yourself out."

"Wait!" I open my mouth, but I don't know how to say it.

Iris studies me, and I know my thoughts are on display. I can feel her soul rifling through my thoughts. "I know you're thinking it," she says. "Ask me already."

"I'm supposed to stop you. The champions are tasked with protecting those marked with death."

"I'm not having mercy on them, Ezra they deserve to die."

"I know. It's just…" I sigh and look her in the eyes. "I know I can't stop you, but please don't hurt my friends. They're not the ones marked. They're good people. Don't hurt them if you don't have to. That's all I ask."

"Fine, but if they get in my way, I won't hesitate. That goes for you too. Don't test me, Ezra. Even as a demon, you're no match for me."

"How do you do it by the way? When I possessed you in the tunnels, you forced me from your body?"

Iris laughs. "What, you want me to teach you? To give up my one advantage? Hell no. The day you pledge yourself to the Holy One, I'll consider it, but not a day sooner."

She pulls open the door, looking back at me one last time. "I hope you join us, Ezra. I really do." She looks up at my eyes. "And don't try to stop me tomorrow. I've killed a lot of people, people I've liked more than you. I don't want to add family to the list." Without another word, she disappears out of the door, leaving me alone in the back of Bob's Brew.

I slowly rise and make my way back into the alley. After our discussion, I'd like to think something's changed—that we're on better terms. Deep down, I know we're not.

If I choose to oppose the Holy One, I must be willing to kill my sister.

I stand shoulder to shoulder with my squad, Kork to my left and Keizer to my right. Togum is two men to my left. Our job is simple: protect the stage.

The crowd is insatiable, especially those surrounding the stage. They're the drunkest, most opinionated of the lot.

One stumbles forward and spits a mouthful of beer from his blowhole of a mouth. My uniform catches most of it, but a cloud of beer mists my face.

"To hell with you!" the man mumbles.

Keizer steps forward and points the butt of his gun like a battering ram. Before I can stop him, he swings the stock forward, catching the laborer square in the chest. The drunkard flops to the floor where he lies for several seconds before groggily crawling away.

The crowd takes a step back, learning their lesson, but I hardly feel victorious. The man was never a threat. For all I know, he has every reason to hate the guard.

Keizer smiles and leans over. "So, Lieutenant, they're telling me you're gonna get chosen. Zane is basically your daddy, they say."

Togum snorts. "I'll believe it when I see it. MacArthur doesn't have the balls to be a guardian."

Keizer raises his eyebrow at me. "You gonna take that, lieutenant?"

I shrug, cracking a smile. "Why is Togum so concerned with my balls? It's kinda weird if you ask me."

Kork snickers. "Lieutenant's got a point."

Togum spits the tobacco he's chewing. "God, it's a figure of speech. You're all a bunch of children."

Suddenly, there's a change in the crowd before me, and their eyes dial in on the stage. I crane my neck to see the stage behind me. The entire High Council is seated in a row. Next to each council member is an empty seat.

General Kaynes steps forward, his black and silver robes swooshing around his legs. He approaches the podium. He runs a hand over his peppered grey hair and smiles.

"My dear citizens of Cavernum. We have gathered here for a truly monumental moment in our history. As you may be aware, survivors from Lycon have sought refuge in Cavernum. They brought with them a soul-anchor, the most powerful amulet known to man. An amulet so powerful, only the guardians are entrusted to wield one. Today, I am pleased to announce that the High Council has elected to bestow it upon another guardian."

To my surprise, the commoners cheer. I don't see how they benefit, but they seem to enjoy the theatrics. The laborers, however, look like they've had enough. Taut jaws and clenched fists tell me everything I need to know.

General Kaynes abandons the podium and ventures toward the edge of the stage. "As a council, we have already elected who this guardian should be. I assure you, he is a man of great strength and impeccable honor.—" I turn around just in time to see Rose roll her eyes. Her disgust brings a smile to my face. "—I've had the pleasure of training this guardian as my apprentice. He has demonstrated time and time again his undying love for this great city. Without further ado, I present to you my son, General Quill Kaynes."

Quill stands from his seat on the stage and holds both arms above his head like a boxing champion. His soul-anchor is displayed proudly on his chest. His lion's mane of hair blows elegantly in the wind. If I didn't know the guy, I might just believe all the bull crap.

The crowd is divided. While the commoners cheer, the laborers boo at the top of their lungs. They know his reputation in the fields: merciless, unquestioning cruelty.

King Dralton shuffles forward to a portable wooden podium that has been placed at the edge of the stage. He clutches the podium for support.

"This is not our only announcement. Now that General Quill is a full-fledged guardian, his father's apprenticeship remains unfilled. As a council, we have decided to fill this position according to ancient tradition. Beginning today, each council member will announce one champion. Each champion will compete in The Surviving."

A shockwave of whispers pulsates through the spectators. Whatever The Surviving is, it has a reputation.

King Dralton raises one hand to silence the crowd. "Let me be clear," he calls. "The Surviving will not proceed as tradition dictates. It will not be a duel to the death, but a series of tasks. Fail a task, and the champion will be eliminated. The last survivor remaining will be welcomed as a guardian's apprentice."

The crowd offers a half-hearted cheer. The guardsmen whoop and stomp their feet.

"These champions must be young, bright guardsmen. They must have many years of faithful service to devote to Cavernum." King Dralton turns his shoulders and peers proudly at his daughter. "As king, I will be the first to announce my champion. I present to you, Princess Roselyn Malik."

I turn around, completely ignoring the crowd I'm entrusted to repel. I watch as Rose stands and waves to the crowd as elegantly as her reputation demands. The king shuffles over to her, and they both take their seats in unison.

Next, General Kaynes steps forward once more. "My champion is one who, in his first year as a guardsman, has already saved the princess's life two times over. He is both a prodigy and a paragon of virtue. I present my youngest son, Vyle Kaynes."

The crowd stomps their feet out of nothing more than social norms. I keep my eyes riveted to the stage, trusting my men to watch my back.

General Katu takes the podium. "Hello, my brothers and sisters of Cavernum. My candidate was not the first in their class, nor the most well-known, but he is one to whom I would trust my life. He is a man of honor. I nominate Ekan Chaxby."

A guard comes running up the stage steps and gives General Katu a hug. The champion looks only a year or two older than me, with mocha-colored skin and a crooked smile. Together, they wave to the crowd and take their seats together.

My heart starts racing as Zane takes the stand. I know he'll choose me, but it's the part that comes after that makes me nervous. The odds of failure. The risk of disappointing him. Judy's life on the line.

Zane cracks his knuckles, the sound amplified by dominion. "My champion is a refugee, like myself. I actually had the pleasure of escorting him to Cavernum only a few months ago." Zane glances my way, and I find myself leaning toward the stage.

"In those short months," Zane continues, "he not only prevented a palace robbery, but his undercover operation brought us a great victory against the equalists. I present to you… Diego Ortega."

What… no! He can't be serious.

I watch speechless as Diego hops up the opposite steps and shakes Zane's hand. They both take a seat side by side. I stare at Zane's face, but he doesn't meet my gaze.

"Nice try, MacArthur," Togum taunts. "Looks like daddy adopted a new son. If you're in need of a father figure, maybe I can take you in."

I resume my spot in the defenses. Ready to smack Togum if he says another word.

Kork casts his eyes my way. "I'm sorry, boss. You'll get 'em next time."

But I won't. There won't be a next one. I need a soul-anchor now.

Why him? Sure, Diego is good, but is he better than me? Does Zane really like him more?

Chancellor Gwenevere takes the stage and I try to distract myself with her words. "My champion is a guardswoman of great potential. Not only did she excel in the field, but she was the first woman to rise to the rank of Commander. Should she triumph, I have no doubt she would be a valiant guardian of Cavernum. I present to you, Commander Kierstan Hunt."

A woman climbs the stage. She's definitely the oldest of the champions, maybe 30 years old. Several girls scream from the front row. "Whooo! You go, girl!"

Next, Chancellor Bolo hobbles forward. "This last week," he begins. "A dear friend of mine passed away. This man was an un-bending exemplar of justice. His daughter, I'm proud to say, shared his devotion to justice. She will continue her father's legacy as my champion... Crasilda Lumb!"

Crasilda? That's a name I hadn't expected. She flies onto the stage, her red hair bouncing. I don't envy her. Being sponsored by Bolo is the equivalent of being endorsed by bacon.

As soon as they take their seats, another chancellor drags his feet to the podium. He's a gray-haired man with a long, saggy neck, a cousin to the desert tortoise by the looks of it. Without an explan-ation, Chancellor Turtle announces his champion as Axelander Degoon, whoever that is.

Lastly, Chancellor Quine rests his palms on the podium. He adjusts his glasses and looks out over the crowd. I don't bother watching. I focus on the crowd, letting his words wash over me.

"My champion is one to whom I owe a great debt. I first met him only three months ago. At the time, my daughter was being dragged across the cornfield by a runaway horse. My champion saved her when no other guardsmen could. Again, when no other guardsmen could, he stopped equalists from raiding the palace vault. I present to you, Lieutenant Matthew MacArthur."

I spin around and gape at Chancellor Quine. Once again, I can't believe what I've just heard.

Keizer slaps me in the back. "Get up there, boss."

I stumble to the steps and hurry to Chancellor Quine's side. We shake hands once, and then he escorts me to my seat.

The crowd is still stomping as the king shuffles over to the podium. "Now, The Surviving has officially begun. For their first task, each champion will be assigned a citizen who has been marked with death. They are to protect that citizen at all costs. God's will be done."

Chapter 18

Rose

Matt pauses at the doorway, allowing me to enter before him. We're the last two champions to arrive. The chancellors are already scattered around the table, and Grandpa sits on his throne. The only member missing is General Quill. As the newest addition, he has no say in The Surviving. They're deciding his own replacement after all.

The eight of us champions line the wall, my shoulder blades grazing the frame of the city map. Diego's father likely stood in this very spot only weeks ago. Now, Diego is here as Zane's Champion.

So much has changed.

Grandpa stirs in his throne, angling his achy body to face us. "Welcome, champions. As announced, your first task will be a trial of protection. You will each receive a ward to protect. Currently, there are 12 people in Cavernum who have been marked with death and are still alive. Those persons are in this bowl."

Grandpa lifts a white porcelain bowl, overflowing with folded pieces of parchment. "You will each choose a ward whom you must protect. If they die, you will be eliminated from The Surviving. There will be no exceptions."

Grandpa sets the bowl on the table and slides it to the edge nearest us. "Draw your names, civilly, please. Read it aloud so that the council can account for your success or failure. Vyle, you may proceed."

Vyle lifts his chin and steps forward. Without any hesitation, he pushes his hand to the bottom of the bowl and removes a slip of paper. "Tigrinya Alamora. Eastern Wing, Room 364," he announces with a smirk.

He steps back against the wall, and from the corner of my eye, I see General Kaynes nodding his approval. I know why. Vyle's assignment lives in the palace, a much easier location to protect.

General Katu's champion goes next, plucking a name from the top. "The Qualimar family. Blessing Blvd 4231, 4th District." He frowns. "The Qualimar family... as in the whole family?"

General Katu sits up slowly and purses his lips. "I'm afraid so, Ekan. An entire family lives at the address. It is unclear who the marking is for. Therefore, you will be expected to protect them all. I wish you the best."

Ekan nods and steps back, obviously still upset with his assignment.

Diego goes next, swirling the bowl twice before selecting a paper. "Lieutenant Warren Blazer. Western Wing, Room 420." He snickers. For whatever reason, Matt snickers as well. I see him staring at Diego, hoping to share in his amusement, but when Diego finally notices, his face only darkens.

Still not friends, I guess.

Zane gives Diego a quick nod of approval and Diego resumes his place in line.

Crasilda is next. She fishes around for a long time before finally selecting a slip. She frowns as soon as she starts reading. "William. 4286 Charity Lane, 9th District. Who the hell is William? This doesn't even have a last name!"

I know she's not upset about the name. It's the location she doesn't like. The 9th District is in the outskirts of the ring, directly bordering the flats. Guard influence is weak that deep in the ring, and she'll have little support should she need it.

Chancellor Bolo clears his throat. "The names are reported by the commanders of each quadrant. Kierstan Hunt is the commander over District 9. Perhaps she knows?"

Kierstan steps forward. "Yes. The man at the address refused to give his full name. We contacted his landlord, and they also couldn't provide his identification."

"Whatever." Crasilda brushes the hair from her face and rolls her eyes. "Thanks for nothing," she mumbles under her breath as she steps back in line.

Commander Hunt goes next. Then, a guard named Axelander steps forward. Both read equally unmemorable addresses from the core. Finally, it's my turn. I take a deep breath and approach the bowl, the tiny piece of porcelain containing my immediate future.

I pinch the name off the top and use my nail to unfold it. "Rovik Manganara. Western Wing, Room 145." *Thank god!*

It's a palace address. Grandpa will only be a short walk away, as will a hundred palace guards. *I can do this.*

Matt waits until I step back before approaching the bowl. There are only five slips left at this point. They each lie bent on the bottom of the porcelain, like helpless humans curled in the fetal position. He eyes each one before removing a slip. He pauses for a second, glancing at General Kaynes and back at the parchment.

"Quill Kaynes, Eastern Wing, Room 404."

"That's not fair!" Crasilda cries. "He's a guardian. He can defend himself. Tell me how that's fair?"

"It is fair," Grandpa projects, "because you chose randomly. Some may be easier to defend than others; that was an inevitable aspect of this task. We didn't have the liberty of choosing the Holy One's targets. Let this be a lesson to you all. The guardians serve the laborers as much as the elites. Don't view it as a burden, but as a privilege."

"It's a disadvantage; that's what it is," Crasilda sneers.

I think of every laborer I've ever known, of Diego's family—Mary and his brothers. I think of Wendy and the family she left behind. They deserve better than Crasilda. They deserve a protector who sees them as something more than a human hindrance.

"I'll do it!" I say. "We can trade, Crasilda. If we both agree, that would be fair, would it not?"

Crasilda is shocked at first, but she quickly joins in the pitch. "Yes.... yes, that would be fair. The princess said she's willing, and I'm willing as well."

Grandpa raises a graying eyebrow. "Rose, are you sure about this? Once you make the trade, you won't be able to take it back."

His tone is screaming at me, *Don't do it, Rose!* But I don't listen.

"Yes, I want to trade." I don't wait for further permission, I extend my paper to Crasilda, and she does the same. Just like that, I hold a new name in my hand.

Grandpa sighs, his voice dead with defeat. "Very well. What's done is done. You each have your wards. Protect them. We will readjourn in two day's time."

As I exit the council room, I look down at my paper.

William.

Whoever he is, his life is in my hands now, and as much as I hate it, my life is in his.

I stare at the door, wondering what to do next. There isn't a knocker or a bell of any kind. The blood is dry, but regardless, I'd rather not touch it. After some debate, I kick the door with the toe of my boot.

Thud, thud, thud.

I wait for a long while, then I kick the door again.

Thud—

"Go away!" A voice calls back. "I told you yesterday, I don't get paid until Friday. You'll get your damn rent."

"William? Am I speaking to William?" I lean disturbingly close to the bloodied door and yell.

"Who wants to know?" I hear floorboards creaking on the other side of the door as he approaches.

"My name is Roselyn. I'm here to offer you some help."

"What kind of help?" I hear the familiar sound of metal sliding against metal and the jingling of a chain. Finally, the door cracks open a few inches. When he sees my uniform, William recoils. He tries to slam the door, but my boot is already wedged in the crack.

"William, please just let me explain. I'm here to protect you from the Holy One. I promise I'm on your side."

William doesn't relent. He throws himself into the door and heaves. I push back. He's scrawny and seemingly malnourished, and for a moment, I think I might be able to muscle my way in. Then, the door swings back, snapping against my boot."

"William! I'm here to help you. If you don't let me in, the Holy One will slaughter you."

"Go away!" he screams back. "You can't fight the Holy One. You'll only make it worse. Let me die in peace!"

I've had enough. I can feel the icy metal of my amulet against my chest. I need to conserve my energy, but it appears I don't have a choice.

Push!

The door lurches inward, tossing William onto his back. I expect him to rush to his feet, yet he lays there, wallowing in defeat. He rubs his temple, groaning as he slowly crawls to his feet.

William is smaller than I thought. He's average height, but his thinness makes him look much smaller. His clothes are unkempt, and his hair glistens with grease. His eyes are red, and his dark beard is an unflattering hybrid between scruff and fluff. Even breathing through my mouth, I can smell the sour scent of alcohol.

"I'm sorry, Mr. William, but I'm assigned to keep you safe. You're not going to die. That's my promise to you."

"Keep your damn promise. I don't want it." He shuffles back into what looks like a small studio apartment. There isn't furniture of any kind, only a pile of blankets in the corner and a long counter built into the opposite end.

"Is this where you live?"

"This is where I die," he says before collapsing onto his pile of blankets. After some squirming, he manages to get the majority of his body covered.

"You're not going to die," I insist. "I won't let that happen."

"Woman, if you have any decency, you'll walk out that door and let me die."

"No, I will not," I assert. "My *decency* is the reason I'm here. It doesn't matter what you've done. You have value. You deserve to live."

The man rolls over, flinging off his blanket. He stands and faces me. "Don't you tell me what I deserve. I've done things… terrible things." His entire body shudders at the very thought of it. "And I'll do them again. I know I will. The Holy One is my savior. He'll save me from myself. He'll make my mind clean. I beg you, let him take me. I don't want to live like this, and I don't have the strength to change." With that, William crawls back into his pile of blankets.

I watch, pity expanding within me until the pressure is unbearable. "You must have something to live for? Family? A friend who needs you? A wife?"

William responds with a wet cough, spitting his phlegm onto the stone floor. "My wife left me years ago. I have a brother, but he wants me dead... probably more than the Holy One. Everyone I love wishes me dead. The least I can do is give 'em what they want. This is the will of God."

"This is the will of a psycho." I cry out. "How can the Holy One judge you? He doesn't even know you."

He rolls over so that he's staring directly into the wall. "The Holy One knows what I've done. His angel came to me in a dream. I wouldn't tell her, so she stole it from my mind."

"She?"

William nods.

"Wait." I step closer. "You're telling me the Holy One is a woman?"

William shakes his head. "No... you're not listening. She was his servant. His angel. She does his bidding. She made it clear I would die for my sins. The next day, my door was covered in blood. I can't go against the will of God. Maybe this way, I can be cleansed. I want it all to be over."

I feel odd standing, so I crouch down next to William, making our faces more level. "Whatever you did, William, this isn't the end. You can find redemption. You can fill your life with good."

"No!" He hisses, and I hear anger for the very first time. "You're wrong! There's no forgiveness for what I've done. I've hurt people. Really hurt them. Strangers, family... even my own niece."

Niece?

Bile fills my stomach and I suddenly feel light-headed. I take a step back and reach for my amulet.

"William, what's your last name?"

William rolls over, still shivering beneath his blanket. "It's Venderson. William Venderson."

Venderson! As in Velma Venderson and Wendy Venderson.

"It's you!" I gasp. I take another step back and clutch my amulet even tighter. "You..." I struggle to say the words. Even just speaking it feels dirty... sinful. "You raped her. You..." *You don't deserve to live.*

In an instant, I want to take back everything I've said. He does deserve to die. I want to kill him myself.

Then, I remember Velma's words. The night she died, she told me about her uncle—this very man. *If she were a high-born, he would've been hanged, but instead, he goes free. How's that for equality? How's that for changing times?*

Dying at the hand of the Holy One isn't enough. He needs to be made into an example. He needs to be tried by the High Council and hanged. Wendy deserves that much.

265

"William, as of now, you are under arrest. You will receive a trial, and you will confess before the High Council. Then, you will be hanged."

Normally, I would handcuff him, but I don't bother. Should the Holy One attack, I want him to be able to defend himself. As much as I despise him, I can't let him die. I need to see justice in action. I need some evidence that Cavernum can change.

"Stop torturing me and let me die." William buries his face in the pillows. "Just let me die! I want to d—"

His chest lurches, and his face immediately turns red. He coughs twice more, as if trying to clear something from his throat. Then, he rolls onto his back and falls silent.

"William?"

I step closer and gasp. A red gash, like a thin-lipped smile, stretches across William's throat. The gushing blood is immediately absorbed by his blankets, pooling in the folds. I keep watching, but he doesn't stir. He's dead.

How? How is this possible?

I don't have time to worry about The Surviving or about William; my adrenaline prompts survival.

I stand perfectly still as my eyes tear the room apart, searching for the killer. A sinister dread spreads through me like a sickness. The windows are shut. The door is locked. I'm completely alone.

No! It's not possible!

Just as I'm about to surrender to the supernatural, I hear the jingle of the deadbolt. Without a soul in sight, the chain unlatches itself swiftly and precisely. Untouched, I see it fall. Next, the wooden latch lifts, and the door swings open. I would suspect a ghost if it weren't for the sound of footsteps echoing down the alley.

Invisibility! It's the only explanation. Whoever killed William was invisible.

Whoever killed him was here the entire time.

Chapter 19

Matt

I should be excited. I'm tasked with guarding a guardian. Even saying it sounds ridiculous. Like watering water or feeding food. In theory, it should be a piece of cake, but I've learned enough about my sister to know otherwise.

Quill is in constant danger.

Worst of all, Quill isn't making it any easier on me. He won't allow me in his room, so I stand outside like some Secret Service agent. Should Iris attack now, he'd be dead before I could get inside to help. *Maybe that wouldn't be so bad.*

I wait patiently, standing at attention. Every time a royal guard meanders past, they snicker to themselves at the sight of me. It must look ironic, like a little chihuahua guarding the kennel of a pitbull.

After 30 minutes, Quill emerges from his room, fully adorned in a new cloak. It's a creamy tan color, with olive-green designs lining the hem. They look decorative in nature—not Adamic.

Quill spots me staring and does a little twirl. "It looks good, right? It was the only armor I could find in the vault."

"Armor?" I question.

Quill spreads his cloak like the wings of a griffon, revealing the familiar pattern stitched into the inner layer of fabric.

Before he lets the fabric fall, I catch a glimpse of a knife on his belt—no doubt Adamic as well. He's armed with the most powerful weapons an adalit can supply—as a guardian should be.

Be careful, Iris.

"Come," Quill says, striding down the hall toward the Central Wing. "I have something special planned for us this evening. We're heading to the ring."

I follow silently behind him. Other than keeping him alive, my only goal is to stay on his good side. That means staying out of his way and staying quiet.

Quill moves quickly, swinging his arms with purpose. Every few moments, he glances at the sky. The sun is already set, shielded by the distant mountains. A soft glow of salmon is the only evidence it was ever in the sky. Technically, curfew doesn't begin until dusk, but the streets are already bare. No one wants to risk the lashings.

"You know, Matt. I was happy to hear you drew my name."

"You were?"

"I was," Quill insists. "I've been meaning to ask you. What do you know about demons?"

My chest constricts. *Does he know?*

"Well," Quill continues, "One demon in particular. I read your report about the vault thieves. You were possessed by a woman. You described her as tall with short blonde hair. I was hoping you could tell me more about her."

Iris.

"Of course," I say, trying not to look relieved. "Pixie-cut girl. What do you want to know?"

I need to earn his trust.

"Anything you didn't include in your report," he says. "Any detail at all. Any memories you might have acquired."

"How did you know?"

Quill smiles. "Because same as you, I know what it's like to have your body taken over. Don't you remember? To be forced to kill your own men. It was your quick thinking that saved me. Your threat to collapse the tunnels saved us both. Anyway, while she was in my head, I saw some things. I was hoping you had as well."

"Yeah, I did actually." *Say something useless.* "I saw her boyfriend. His name was Jazon, I think, but he died. And I know she has a necklace. An hourglass. That's about it."

"An hourglass. Hmmm." He considers this a moment. "Did you see any memories about a ring? Or traveling unseen? Going into dreams?"

How does he know so much?

I shake my head. "No. I didn't see anything about a ring."

Quill frowns. "Shame."

"Do you think you'll catch her? Bring her to justice?"

A devious smile speaks over Quill's lips. "I believe so. And soon."

"Do you know where she is?"

"I don't have to find her, Matt. She'll find me. You see, before I was a guardian, she possessed me in my sleep. She threatened to kill me. Something tells me we'll be meeting very soon."

I force myself to smile, as if the notion of revenge is too good to be true.

"To tell you the truth, Matt. I'm very impressed with your resume. First, you survive a feeder bite. Then, you save Quine's daughter. Then, with a single bullet, you took down a carriage, preventing amulets from being stolen. And on the sewer raid, you kept your head. You refrained from attacking me directly. Your threat to collapse the tunnels might be the only reason I'm still alive. You see, Matt. When someone helps me out, I like to help them out back."

"Help me out how?"

"My father is convinced you'll join the council someday, and I agree. I want to help you get there. I just have one little concern."

"What's that?"

"That you're too soft. That when it's time to enact justice, you won't have the stomach. That maybe… you favor the pickers over your own comrades."

"No," I lie. "I've killed equalists when I had to. You can count on me."

Quill shrugs. "I guess we'll see."

We'll see?

We pass through the core, following the main roads. The path we take is familiar, and it takes me a second to realize why. We're heading directly to my zone, District 14. At first, I doubt my own hypothesis, but soon it becomes clear. We're only a few blocks away.

No, not there. Anywhere but there.

We continue south on Zedekiah Way, finally turning into a small side street. It isn't a main road, but it's much too big to be an alley. Each side of the street is lined with doors, leaving a 15-foot travel space between the apartments.

We stop in front of a door, the wood still splintered from being kicked in. I know this apartment. It's the home we raided a few weeks back. It's where I put Togum in his place.

"What's going on?" I demand. There are no windows, but I think I can hear crying from somewhere inside.

I told them to never come back.

Quill only smiles wider. "Togum. Bring him out."

After a brief pause, the door bursts open. Togum drags out the son by the scruff of his shirt and tosses him into the cobblestone street. When the boy starts to stand, he kicks him back down.

Nathan!

I follow the sound of sobbing and spot the mother in the doorway. She holds a daughter under each of her arms, hugging their heads against her hips. Her shoulders shudder with silent sobs, but she doesn't move to intervene. Her husband is painfully unpresent.

Keizer and Kork are here too. They squeeze past the mother and position themselves directly outside the doorway. Each of them looks uncomfortable. They didn't ask for this either.

Togum smiles at Quill and dips his head in a pathetic bow. "General Quill, we're in your service." Keizer and Kork don't bow.

"Quill?" I ask, hostility cracking my composure. "Why are we here?"

Quill paces back and forth, his hands clasped behind him. "You see, during my brief station as Commander, I was tasked with viewing complaints. Togum here—good, faithful Togum—informed me of a certain occurrence. According to him, you have been neglecting your duties. One specific account alarmed me. Togum claims he was shot by a picker, and yet the picker was absolved of all guilt. It may be true that Lieutenants are given the discrepancy to alter such punishments… alter, adjust perhaps, but they can not eradicate. When he told me you pardoned the boy of all crimes, I knew I had to intervene."

"The kid is what, maybe 13!" I emphasize. "He's just a kid! He was trying to save his dad, who Togum was torturing. Togum probably would've killed him if the boy hadn't done something. The boy isn't a killer. He doesn't deserve this."

"It doesn't matter!" Quill barks. In an instant of instability, spit sprays from his lips. He matches my anger with ease. "Punishment keeps the peace, MacArthur. Without punishment, there is no peace… there is no order. If you can't manage the mantle of your office, perhaps you don't belong in the guard."

"But… he's just a kid. The gun was his dad's. He shouldn't be responsible."

"I realize that," Quill retorts. "And that is precisely why he's not before the council. Don't you see, Matt? I'm being merciful. He won't be hung, but he can't go unpunished. Denying a lawful order. Resisting arrest. Assaulting an officer. These habits must be eradicated, and you must be the man to do it."

Now, I'm getting nervous, terrified even. I can't whip the boy. I won't do it. I have to stop this another way.

271

"C'mon, Quill. This isn't smart," I try to reason. "You're marked for death. Hanging out in the ring at night is the last place you want to be. The demon could—"

He stalks over to me, protruding his chin until it's in my face. He's so close, I can smell cherries on his breath. "I don't fear demons," Quill hisses. "I will not hide from her. Mention it again, and it'll be the last thing you ever say."

I want to fight him. I want to put him in his place the same way I did to Togum, but I know I can't. With a soul-anchor, he's too powerful. I can't possess him. I can't overpower him. I'm at his mercy.

"Yes, sir." I lower my gaze and bite my tongue.

"Good." Quill stands and looks at the boy. "Alright, MacArthur. You take it from here." He tosses me his whip, the frayed leather darkened with what can only be blood.

I shake my head. "I'm not doing this. This isn't justice."

Quill tightens his fist. "This is your job, MacArthur. If you can't do this, then you shouldn't wield that amulet."

Reluctantly, I take hold of the whip. All I can think to do is buy myself some time. "Nathan, I need you to remove your shirt."

The boy ducks his head and goes into a kneeling ball, almost like a turtle. "Don't hurt me. Please, don't hurt me."

My heart breaks. *I can't do this.*

Quill is getting impatient. "It's easy. Like this." He squints his eyes, and the faded fabric of Micah's t-shirt separates down the length of his spine, sliced by dominion. The cut is unnaturally clean, and the fabric falls open like a curtain, revealing his unharmed skin.

"Good. Now, you have a proper workspace. Now do it."

"Please!" The mother begs from the doorway. "Please, have mercy!"

Quill pretends he doesn't notice her. "Alright, MacArthur. Let's see it. Announce the punishment."

I raise the whip. "You said it yourself; as Lieutenant, I have the power to adjust the severity of the punishment." I exaggerate a glance at Quill. "Not eradicate, but adjust. So, within the bounds of my authority, I declare his punishment to be one lashing."

His mother makes a squealing noise. "Oh, thank you. We won't forget this mercy. God bless you."

I hold my breath, waiting for Quill to protest. A few seconds of silence ensue.

"Well…" Quill waves his hand in a circle. "Get on with it."

I'm speechless. I can hardly believe that worked. *It's just one lashing,* I tell myself. *At least with me, he only gets one. It's better this way. It's for the greater good.*

I take a deep breath and raise the whip. Then, I urge my soul into the boy's mind. I feel his heart racing and the icy tendrils of terror that pierce his mind. The least I can do is offer one last moment of comfort. *It's going to be okay.*

I swing the whip.

Crack!

I bite down on my tongue as the boy screams. The pain courses through my back like a branding iron. With each passing second, I think it'll subside, but the pain flares with every heartbeat.

I'm so sorry.

I retract my mind, and the pain dissipates, but not for Nathan. He curls up on his side and claws at the stone with his nails. After another few seconds, his breathing slows and his muscles relax. "It's over, Nathan. You can go home now."

I move to help him up, but Quill holds up his hand. "Not so fast. You gave your punishment. Now, as guardian, I extend 19 more lashings, to be delivered at the hand of Lieutenant MacArthur."

"Nooo!" His mother screams from the doorway! "Don't do this. Please, I beg of you! He's just a boy! Please. Take me instead. Whip me instead." The mother wrestles to break free, but the Keizer and Kork hold her back.

"You can't stand for his crimes," Quill says coldly. "Justice must be met."

"Please, Quill," I echo. "One is more than he deserves, just let him go."

"What's wrong, MacArthur? You already did one. The rest gets easier and easier. 19 lashings and you'll be a better man for it. The quicker you go, the easier it is."

"I'm not whipping him again," I say quietly… fearfully.

Quill frowns. "Show me your strength. Prove to me I was wrong about you. Just do it. The quicker you go, the easier it is. Finish this, and I'll never doubt you again. You'll have my respect."

I won't be a villain. I won't do it.

"No!" I say it louder this time. "I won't do it. He doesn't deserve this."

Quill's jaw tightens. His masseter bulges and his brows tip down. "I've given you your chance, MacArthur. Disobey me one more time, and I'll have you tried for insubordination."

Diego's dad once warned us of insubordination. He warned me of this exact scenario. He refused to whip a child, and he was expelled. If I don't do it, my future in Cavernum is finished.

"Think hard, MacArthur. You won't just get lashings; you'll be a picker by morning. And it won't stop there. I'll be watching you for the rest of your miserable life, lashing you for every mistake. So I'll give you one last chance to change your mind."

My stomach rises in my throat and my arms begin to tremble. I try to steady my breathing, but I feel helpless, like I'm back in the jaws of a feeder.

Finally, when I muster the courage, I shake my head. "I won't do it. He doesn't deserve it."

Quill sneers as he glances at the boy. "Oh, please, don't think you're doing the boy any favors. If you don't whip him, I will, and I guarantee I'll swing harder. This is about you, Matt. This is about your future."

I hesitate another moment, my moral compass swinging in all directions. Amid my confusion, Judy's words come to mind. *Some things aren't worth the greater good. Sometimes, you have to take a stand.* Still, I'm not so sure I believe her. *If you don't do it, Quill will.*

I take a deep breath and face the boy.

I'm helping him. I tell myself. *It'll be worse for him if I don't.*

The boy looks at me, his entire body shivering out of sheer fear. As I raise the whip, he tucks his head and whimpers. Slowly, a dark stain spreads from his crotch and diffuses down his legs. He's wet himself.

I can't do this. I straighten my shoulders. "General Quill, I... I refuse your order. I submit to any punishment you inflict on me." I kneel, bow my head, and hold out the whip.

"You refuse?" He takes the whip, looking at me in utter bewilderment. Finally, he grins. "Very well. Insubordination it is. You always struck me as a picker." His voice is calm and controlled —sinister in the most appropriate way possible. "You're excused."

"I... I can go?"

I hesitate. His passivity unsettles me, like the calm before a storm. Quill turns his back to me. "Sleep tight, MacArthur. Enjoy your last night in the palace."

Not knowing what else to do, I give the boy one last glance.

I'm sorry.

Then, I turn and walk toward the palace. I'm barely out of sight when I hear the boy scream. It penetrates the frigid air and jars me to my core.

I hurry, desperately trying to get out of earshot. With each scream, I find myself fantasizing about what Iris might do to Quill. I don't care if she kills him anymore. In fact, I hope she does.

I pace back and forth in my room. I have my clothes packed and my boots laced. My life in Cavernum is officially over. Tomorrow, I'll be expelled, and I refuse to stay as a laborer. I won't spend my life on the fields. I'm going to make a run for it tonight.

My plan is already in motion. I never returned my amulet. As a champion, the armory expects me to have it all night as I try to protect Quill. The rest is easy. First, I'll possess as many people as necessary to make it out of the palace alive. Then, I'll steal the keys to one of the trucks, and drive my way home, possessing whoever I have to to get there.

It's better this way. With an amulet, I can at least attempt to heal Judy. I can protect myself from feeders. I can live a decent life. I highly doubt any guardsmen Will hunt me down. They have much bigger things to be worrying about.

There's really only one thing holding me back. Well, several things. *Kendra, Rose, Diego, Klinton.*

My friends.

Every thought of them is a stab to the heart. I don't know if I can leave them behind. They're my family now. I can't ditch Rose before the Fall Festival. I can't leave Diego before we fix our friendship. I just can't give it up.

As my anger dissipates, I start to rethink my plans. I take a deep breath and close my eyes. I don't know what to do. I need help.

I grab my candlestick and push open my door, walking down the hall and descending a flight of stairs.

"Name and business?" A royal guard barks.

"Lieutenant MacArthur, Chancellor Quine's Champion, on my way to General Quill's chambers."

The guard laughs. "Oof, what a mouthful. Carry on."

I let out a sigh of relief. I am heading to the High Council Wing, but not to Quill's quarters, to Zane's. Now that Quill is a guardian, they're practically neighbors.

I stop at Zane's door, relieved to see candlelight through the seams.

Tap. Tap. Tap.

Zane cracks the door open, and upon seeing the look on my face, he pulls me inside.

"What's wrong? Why aren't you with Quill?"

"Umm about that. I kinda have something I have to tell you." I tell him everything, from the first search of the home to the whipping and my own insubordination. Zane's frown drags lower and lower the more I share.

When I finish, he shakes his head, staring at the floor. "This is not good, Matt. This is not good at all."

"Do you think I have a chance? What if I can convince the council?"

Zane shakes his head. "Insubordination doesn't go before the High Council. It's not punishable by death. He'll take you before the lower court, and he'll choose a judge he knows will side with him. You don't stand a chance."

"Well, couldn't the council undo his decision? Couldn't you bring it before them?"

"You don't get it," Zane growls. "We don't have a majority. You have me and the king... Maybe Katu if you're lucky. That's three. We need five. The council can't save you." He stands there, seething in silence. Suddenly, he turns and slams his hand onto the desk. "Damn it, Matt. It wasn't supposed to happen like this."

"I did what I thought was right."

Zane takes a deep breath, extinguishing some of his anger. "I know. I'm sorry. I ... just give me a second to think."

"I was planning on running," I admit. "That way I can keep an amulet. I think I can escape easily enough. Do you think I should do it?"

Zane shakes his head pacing back and forth in front of his bed. "No... that's not it. You can't leave. This is where you belong."

"I'm not staying as a laborer. I'm not."

"I know... I just... there has to be a way." He stands there for a moment, looking at the rug and anxiously tugging on his beard. Finally, he looks up, hope in his eyes. "You have to beg."

"What?"

"You have to beg, Matt. You have to go to Quill and beg him to forgive you. Beg him to give you another chance."

"That's not going to work," I say.

"It might," Zane insists. "Quill is driven by his pride. Why do you think he favored Togum so much? Because Togum is a kiss-ass. You have to submit yourself. Acknowledge his power. Tell him how great he is. And if you're lucky, he might have mercy."

I shake my head. "What if he just kills me instead and says the Holy One did it? I don't think it'll be that easy."

Zane grows still, engrossed in a memory. "Matt… you told me a few days ago that you wanted a life here. If you don't do this, that life, everything you worked for, it's gone."

I throw my hands in the air, unable to contain the frustration. "I know! I know. Just let me think for a second." I don't want to run, but I'm terrified of what Quill will say. I'm terrified of what else he might make me do. I'm terrified that if I stay, I'll become just like him.

What would Judy say?

Don't give up so easy, Matthew. A guardian threatened you? So what? You can't just run away from your problems. You have to face them, and facing your problems doesn't always mean fighting. Sometimes, it means admitting defeat. Humble yourself, my son. You need to look outside yourself; do what is best for your friends. Cavernum still needs you. And don't worry about me! I'll be fine a little while longer.

I smile. I know it's my own imagination, but I want to thank her for the advice. Imaginary Judy is right. I know what I have to do.

"Okay. I'll do it."

Zane nods. If he's worried, he doesn't show it. "Good luck."

With a deep breath, I exit Zane's chambers, running through my plan in my head.

I'm going to fall down on my knees and beg him for forgiveness. I'll tell him that I'm weak, that I need his help to be a better guardsman. That's the key. I have to stroke his ego until he sees me as he sees Togum: a faithful, devoted servant. Only then will he want me around. Only if I serve him.

But the plan doesn't end there. Earning his forgiveness is only the first part. The next is much riskier. I'll need to turn the council against him. Surely, Iris has some dirt on him. She didn't mark him for no reason. If she can help me get evidence, we can bring him before the council. Best of all, I'll technically pass the task. It's a plan I think Judy would approve of.

Please, God, let this work.

I hurry down the hall, anxiety rising within me. I'm walking into the dragon's keep, hoping it doesn't burn me to a crisp. I stop at his door and take a deep breath. *Just get it over with.*

I'm about to knock when I hear the muffled grunts of a feminine voice behind the door. I'm about to retreat, my mind already jumping to conclusions, but then, I hear a cascade of shattering glass.

SCREECH!

It's dampened by the door, but I hear it loud and clear.

Iris!

As quickly as it starts, the screeching stops. Something heavy hits the floor, followed by another anguished cry.

I tug on the handle, but it doesn't budge. I'll have to use dominion. I wedge my soul into the lock until I feel the pins.

Unlock.

The latch clicks, and I shove the door open. It takes me a moment to register what I'm seeing. Quill stands next to his bed, his soul anchor gripped in his fist. The dome of an energy shield vibrates in the center of the room. Within the dome, I don't see anything except a small puddle of blood. Every few seconds, another drop of blood, seemingly coming from nowhere, splashes on the marble floor.

She's bleeding!

Quill sees me and smiles. "Welcome, MacArthur. Close the door behind you. You're just in time to meet the Holy One's little assassin."

"What? Shouldn't I go get help?"

"If you want to redeem yourself, you'll do as I say. I have some questions for our intruder. I want you to be my witness."

I have no choice but to submit. If he can take Iris, I don't stand a chance. "Yes, sir." I pull the door shut, sealing us inside.

Quill returns his gaze to Iris. His eyes are half-closed with concentration. Suddenly, his smile stretches wider. "There it is." I hear a chain snap, and a glimmering gold amplifier appears from thin air.

The amulet hovers for a moment in the center of the energy dome before bubbling and boiling. As the molten gold drips, it falls several inches before disappearing from view. At the same time, Iris screams.

Throughout the entire event, Quill maintains the energy dome. "Reveal yourself," he calls to Iris. "Remove the relic, or I crush your body like an olive press." I see the dome begin to grow smaller and smaller, now, it's hardly big enough to hold a human. With the added pressure, the blood puddle grows even faster.

"Fine," Quill snaps. "Let's speed this up." He approaches the energy dome and points the tips of his dagger into the shield. Slowly, he plunges it inside. It barely moves an inch when the entire knife turns invisible.

"Ahhh," Iris cries.

Quill inserts it deeper. "Show your—"

Iris materializes, the knife clearly protruding from her side, just above her hip bone. She's clutching the invisibility ring in her fingers and blood is oozing from a wound in her thigh.

Retracting the knife, Quill smiles. "Good girl. Now, drop the ring."

It clatters to the floor, twirling once or twice before resting on its side. Quill extends his hand. The ring briefly slides along the tiled floor before slingshotting into his palm. With a technique I don't quite understand, it passes unaffected through the energy shield.

He squints at the ring before slipping it onto his pinky. After a brief moment of invisibility, he removes the ring and slips it into his pocket. "A powerful weapon for a servant," Quill sneers.

"I'm not a servant," Iris responds, but her words are weak and strained. "How do you know I'm not the Holy One myself?"

"Because my father fears the Holy One, and you're nothing more than a nuisance."

Iris narrows her eyes at him, somehow looking menacing even as she bleeds out. "The Holy One defends his kind. If you harm me, he'll come for you!"

"That's actually what I want to know," Quill says excitedly. "The Holy One has a style I admire. I would love to make him an offer. Where do I find him?"

"I'm not telling you anything."

"Very well. MacArthur, this is your chance to make amends." He points to Iris's knife on the floor. "Take that and cut her hands off. If that doesn't work, we'll do feet and eyes next. But don't take too long. We don't want her to bleed out."

I don't hesitate. If I hesitate, he'll only raise his guard more. The element of surprise is all I have. "Right first or left first?" I ask with a trembling voice, as if I'm terrified of displeasing him.

"Left first," Quill commands.

I approach the energy dome from Iris's left. When I'm close, the shield dissolves, appearing twice as large. It now contains us both, trapping us like lab mice. At the same time, The air ripples around Iris's wrists, stretching them wide and pinning them to the floor.

"Don't be shy," Quill calls. "She has no amulet. She can't hurt you."

"Do your worst," Iris seethes. Either she thinks I'm prepared to kill her, or she does a good job of hiding our allegiance. "Whatever you do to me, the Holy One will do worse."

My hand is shaking as I position the knife against her wrist. My mind is in overdrive. Iris has already lost a lot of blood. If I take her hands, it'll almost certainly be fatal.

If I don't do it, Quill will. I've already learned that lesson. My only choice is to retaliate.

I won't let her die. I have to fight.

I can't defeat Quill in a duel, but maybe I can win in a single move. His energy shield still surrounds us. It's meant to keep us in, but it also keeps things out... even an explosion.

"Prove yourself, MacArthur. Redeem yourself."

I don't put pressure on the blade. Instead, I stretch my soul behind me, passing through Quill's energy dome and into the open space between us. I make sure my mind is focused closer to us. If the shockwave hits Quill first, his shield will dissolve. I can't let that happen, I fix the focal point immediately outside his shield. Then, I scream at every atom I can find!

Combust!

KA-BOOM!

The world erupts around us, and I feel my body being thrown across the room. Pain punctures my bones from all sides, and my skin feels tingly, almost numb. When I open my eyes, all I see is darkness. The blast put out the lantern and filled the room with a cloud of suffocating dust. The ringing in my ears lasts an eternity, but overall, I'm okay. No missing limbs or ruptured lungs.

His shield actually saved us.

Iris is right next to me, squirming in the rubble. I offer my hand and pull her to her feet, still clutching the Adamic dagger in the other.

"We have to run," I say. "Come on!"

"Wait. I need my ring." She stumbles through the dust, searching for Quill's body.

"You won't find him," I whisper. "He was invisible."

But she does. Oddly enough, his body is in full view, slumped on the ground next to his bed frame. The blast must have knocked the ring out of alignment. His face is battered, and much of his lion's mane is singed to a crisp. His tan robe, however, almost looks untouched.

"Is he dead?" I ask.

As Iris moves closer, I hold my breath and watch his chest. Up... Down.... Up... Down. He's alive, but he isn't moving.

"Hurry," I hiss.

Iris bends over and reaches for Quill's hand. At that moment, Quill's eyes snap open, and his hand leaps for her throat. He pulls Iris to the ground and rolls so that his body is sitting on her waist, and both hands are pressing down on her throat.

His eyes are mad and murderous. He doesn't care if she's unarmed. He's going to kill her. He's going to kill my sister.

My heart hardens, and I tighten my grip on the blade. I focus on the only unarmored flesh I can find. Then, I swing.

Thunk!

The knife enters his skull with eerie ease, and like turning off a switch, his body goes limp. He falls on his side as I recoil.

Now that I've done it, I wish I could take it back. I want his body to move. I want to know it isn't permanent, but it's too late.

I killed him. I killed Quill.

Iris gasps for air and clutches at her throat. For a few seconds, we just sit there and breathe. Before long, I hear voices from the hallway. I look to the door but find an empty doorway instead. The door has been unhinged from the blast, and lanterns are approaching.

"Seal the exits, no one leaves the palace." It's Commander Noyen of the royal guard. He isn't far. "Don't get too close, the floor might be unstable."

Zane's voice grumbles back. "I don't care. Move!"

That's when Iris bursts into action. "If you want me to live, give me your amulet, now." As soon as I fish it from my shirt, she snatches it and bolts for the opposite side of the room. She runs straight for the window, whose glass is nowhere to be found, and dives through the gap. I wait to hear a thud, but something tells me she never hits the ground.

I'm still looking at the window when Zane bursts into the room, a brilliant glow emanating from his hand. He shines light at me like a flashlight. "Great gods! You're alive. He takes one look at Quill and hardly bats an eye.

He kneels down and grabs me by the shoulders. "What happened?" He whispers. "Is she still here?"

"I…" I close my mouth. I can't tell him. *I can't admit what I've done.*

Before I can say anything else, General Kaynes stammers into the room. "No." The word is barely a whisper. "No. no." He shakes his head as he falls to his knees, gingerly feeling the knife in his son's head. Then, the sobs overtake him. "I'm so sorry, my son," he gasps. "I should've done more. I failed you."

He turns to me, and his beady eyes quiver. "You… you!" He struggles to his feet. "Why are you alive? You were supposed to protect him!"

He makes a move at me, but Zane intercepts him and wraps him in a hug. "I'm sorry, Benton. I know what it's like." He holds him, and they rock back and forth as he cries. "I know…I know."

As I watch, I find tears running down my cheeks.

I didn't want to. I didn't have a choice.

Chapter 20

Rose

I take another sip of my ginger beer, watching the torch lights twinkle in the distance. I've been rationing the final sips, savoring the sting of the ginger. Despite my hopes, it does nothing to curb the crushing disappointment.

Maybe Matt will win. It's the only thing that consoles me. If Matt wins, he'll someday join me on the council. Such a future doesn't seem so bleak.

Don't give up, Rose. You'll still be a guardian.

It sickens me to think, but if Antai never wakes up, I'll certainly take his spot as my Grandpa's apprentice. The thought only makes me feel worse.

"Princess." The voice yanks me back to reality. Octavian stands a few feet behind me. His face screaming concern. "Princess, there's been a murder in the Eastern Wing. Tigrinya Alamora is dead. We need to get you back to your chambers."

Vyle! That was his assignment. *Matt might win this after all.*

I follow Octavian, carrying my bottle and myself back to my chambers. I turn the Adamic key and slip silently inside.

"What happened? What are you doing back so early?" Wendy greets me as I enter my chambers. She's perched on my reading chair. In her hands, she holds the second Harry Potter book—one of the few I didn't burn.

I had told her I'd be in the ring at least until morning, but all that changed when her uncle died.

"I'm fine," I say as I remove my boots. "My assignment was killed, so I guess that means I lost."

"What?" Wendy drops the book. "They died? Are you okay? Do you need to talk about it?" She drops the book and climbs to her feet, reaching to untie my boots.

"You don't have to do that, Wendy. You're pregnant."

"As long as I can, I will. I want to feel like I earn my keep." Once she unties the laces, she steps back, letting me pull them off myself.

"Are you sure you lost? What if everyone fails? Maybe you still have a chance."

"Maybe." I sit on the edge of my bed and use the heel of each boot to pry off the other. "I'm not sure. As far as I know, only Vyle and I have lost."

"So what happened? Did you see who did it?"

Rip it off like a band-aid, Rose. Just get it over with.

I pull off my armored coat, leaving only my black undershirt. "Maybe you should sit back down, Wendy. I think we both need to talk about something."

Wendy purses her lips. "Uhhh, okay. Are you breaking up with me?"

Despite the seriousness of the situation I snort. "Wendy, did you just make a joke?"

Wendy smiles proudly. "What? I can be funny when I want to be."

I smile too. We're practically roommates, but she's so much more reserved than Nevela was. In some ways, she still feels like a stranger.

She sits back in the armchair. "So, what was it you wanted to tell me?"

"Oh, I…" I sit down at the edge of the bed. "Wendy… my assignment was someone named William."

Already her eyes widen, and the corner of her lip twitches.

"When I arrived, he told me his name was William Venderson. I just wanted you to hear it from me first."

Wendy doesn't look at me. Her eyes are fixated at the corner of the rooms. "What happened to him?" She whispers.

I start at the beginning. "When I arrived, he said he wanted to die. He said he deserved it. He didn't want me to protect him." My mouth is dry and I have to swallow twice to wet my throat. "He basically admitted to what he did. I tried to protect him anyway, but then he started choking, and by the time I could get there… someone had slit his throat."

"So… he's dead?"

"He's dead."

Wendy stares at the corner. "Huh."

I lean in closer. "What?"

Wendy shrugs. "I thought I would feel better. He can't hurt anyone. He can't hurt me. He can't hurt my daughter. I thought I would feel… free. Instead, I just feel empty. I don't know what else to say."

"You don't have to say anything," I assure her. "Healing is a process, not an event. It'll take time."

"Yeah, I guess." She kicks her feet which are suspended a foot above the floor. Then, I notice a glimmer of a frown. Her legs stop kicking.

"What?" I ask.

"It's just… doesn't it bother you?" she sighs. "The Holy One did it. He brought my uncle to justice when the guard couldn't. They said they didn't have any proof. Frankly, they didn't care. And then the Holy One comes along and makes him pay. Doesn't it make you wonder? Maybe he really is good?"

"Maybe," I admit. *Maybe.*

Wendy tugs her feet to her chest, repositioning the book on her armrest. "Thanks, Rose, for telling me all this."

"Of course. You deserved as much."

For a while, neither of us talk. I sit on the edge of my bed, kicking my feet to fill the silence. "You know, Wendy, we've never really talked about the whole baby thing. I'm not talking about what happened, but the fact that you're going to be a mom. I mean… are you nervous about it?"

Wendy smiles and wraps her arms around her stomach. "I try not to think about it. My mom says it comes naturally. Besides, babies aren't that complicated. Sleep, drink, poop. That's pretty much all they do."

"Sounds terrifying if you ask me."

Wendy nods. "It was at first. I worried about everything. I worried I wouldn't survive the birth. My mother said one in ten don't. I was afraid that my daughter would grow up without me. Or, I was afraid that she wouldn't survive. I was born premature, and so was my mother. She says it runs in the family. Most preemies don't make it in the ring. I was one of the lucky ones." Wendy leans back in the recliner and sighs. "Being in the palace, I don't have to worry about that anymore."

"When are you due?" I wonder. "I can't believe I never asked you that."

"Eight weeks."

"A new year's baby?"

Wendy nods. "I'm excited, but I know it'll be tough. I'll understand if you want me to change rooms. The baby would probably keep you up at night. Or I can stay with my parents?"

"If it really bothers me, maybe I can ask my grandpa about a soundproofing spell. There's no way I'm kicking you out. I don't care how loud your baby is."

"I hope she'll be an easy baby." Wendy laughs. "I don't do well without sleep."

"Can I ask you something? I've noticed you always call your baby she? How come? Is it a maternal hunch?"

Wendy's face darkens. "Actually, no. It's more of a preference. I really hope it's a girl." She doesn't sound excited when she says it.

"How come?" I ask.

"My worst fear is that the baby will be a boy, and that when it grows up, it'll look like my uncle. I don't know if I could love a baby like that. It scares me more than anything. Or even worse, that he'll act like him." She looks at me for comfort. "What do you think? Do you think that could happen?"

I'm tempted to say it's impossible, but instead, I have another idea. "Your father, is he like your uncle?"

"No!" Wendy reviles at the thought of it. "Not at all. My dad is the opposite of my uncle."

"Exactly! And yet they were born from the same two people. Same genetic source, and yet totally unique souls. I'm not saying there won't be similarities. Boy or girl, your baby will resemble him in some way, but that doesn't mean they'll be good or bad. They're unique. All you can do is teach them the good, and hope they follow it."

Wendy nods. "I hope so. Thanks, Rose, you'll make a good mother someday."

I smile. "You know, I don't think I've ever held a baby before. I don't even know how to do it."

"What?"

"Mmhhmm. To be honest, I'm afraid to try. I have this hunch that I'll make them c—"

Ka-BOOM!

My entire room shakes. Nearly knocking over the candlestick and sending my heart into plummet. I grab onto the bedsheets and squeeze my eyes shut.

Then... everything is quiet. I hear guards running past my door. Shouting down the halls.

"What was that?" Wendy shudders, clutching her stomach.

"I have no idea," but I'm lying. The Holy One used a bomb on Lycon. *Is this it? Is he attacking?* I don't let myself believe it.

Come on, Rose. You're overreacting. Whatever it is, Grandpa will handle it.

Wendy comes and sits next to me on my bed, and I put my arm around her. "Don't worry. Our door is Adamic. We're safe in here. Eventually, someone will come to tell us what's going on."

We sit in silence for what feels like an eternity. When the knocking finally comes, I flinch.

"Who is it?" I yell. "

"Rose!" It's Octavian's voice. "The council requests your presence..." He pauses for a moment. "The first trial is finished. It's time to report."

Octavian escorts me to the base of the west tower. I climb the steps alone, giving myself plenty of time to replay my anxieties in my mind. I've failed my task. What will grandpa think of me? What if I never get back my soul-anchor?

As I summit the steps, I find a gathering of downtrodden guardsmen. The small landing is filled to capacity. Crasilda is closest to the steps, and Diego is a bit behind her. Vyle is against the door, and Matt is in the far corner. All of them seem utterly depressed.

"What was that explosion?" Katu's champion asks—Ekan was his name.

"I heard it was the Holy One," Crasilda says. "Supposedly, a council member died or something?"

I glance at Vyle for any inkling of a clue, but he stares unblinking at the oak door. Matt turns his face to the wall and hunches his shoulders. The longer I look, the more I notice. His uniform looks freshly changed, but his pasta gold hair is peppered with dust. His eyes are swollen, and he's favoring his right foot.

The explosion!

Matt must have been close enough to get hurt, and not just physically. Whatever happened, it's weighing heavily on him.

"Do you think—"

Suddenly, the oak doors swing inward. "Champions," Grandpa calls from his throne, loud but unenthusiastic. "Please enter. Line up along the wall."

Everyone shuffles in, and like last time, Matt and I enter last.

The council table has two empty seats. One is Quill's, which doesn't surprise me; he has no say in champion matters. The other is his father's.

Grandpa's own face is distraught. His lips are pursed and pulled down to one side. "I'm afraid I have some dismal news. As you likely already know, none of your assignments survived the night. In addition to the deaths in the ring, the palace has been breached. Those who had been marked were murdered... among them was General Quill Kaynes."

The air is filled with uncertainty. The champions glance at each other, hoping to find some kind of solace. To kill a guardian and escape? It means no one is safe.

Grandpa continues. "Before falling victim, Quill managed to confront the assassin. Matt was a witness to the interaction." Grandpa nods his head at Matt. "Matt, would you share with the council what happened, and please, give as much detail as you can remember."

Matt steps forward. "Well, I was in Quill's room. He was getting ready to go to sleep. He told me that if I had to use the bathroom, to do it then, because he didn't want me waking him up. So I went. I was only gone a minute or two. Then, I came back, I was almost to the door when I heard some glass break in Quill's room. I rushed inside and found Quill making an energy shield. I couldn't see anyone, but it was rippling as if someone was inside. Then, Quill used his knife to cut through the field. He..." He swallows and makes an effort to look the king in the eye. "Stabbed her twice."

"Her?" Bolo mumbles.

Grandpa holds up his hand. "Silence. Proceed, Lieutenant."

"That's when she became visible. She had been wearing an invisibility ring—an Adamic ring. Quill took the ring and put it on. The next thing I remember was the explosion. I got thrown against the wall. When I opened my eyes, she had already taken my amulet. Then, she killed Quill and fled out the window. I tried to stop her, but without my amulet, there was nothing I could do."

The king slowly spins his cane like a top. "This girl... what did she look like?"

Matt looks down. "Short blonde hair, about this tall. Blue eyes I think. It was the same girl who tried to steal the amulets from the vault."

Grandpa frowns, his worst suspicions confirmed. "Does anyone else have any information to add, anything that hasn't been mentioned?"

When no one responds, he addresses the council. "Very well. Fortunately for us, the assailant wasn't able to recover her ring. It is in the possession of General Kaynes. Without the relic, I imagine she'll have trouble gaining access to the palace. We can only hope that these killings will cease."

He turns his attention to the champions. "As stated, not one of your assignments survived. Because you would all be disqualified, we have decided to nullify the entire task. All of you will be allowed to compete in the next trial."

I feel guilty for feeling relief—for benefitting from such a tragedy, but Wendy was right. In failure, we all proceed.

Grandpa holds up two fingers. "In two days, the lumber haul will take place beyond the outer wall." Grandpa glances at Diego and Matt. "For those of you who aren't familiar with the lumber haul, it is a three-day event. Laborers are allowed the opportunity to restock their wood supply before winter. They are brought into the beyond to fell trees. One half of what they chop they keep; the other half is distributed to the palace and the core. As always, the guard will be responsible for providing protection. This year, each champion will be given a region to supervise. You will be free to direct the guard in your respective regions. If any of your subjects pass away, you will be disqualified. Any questions?"

No one says anything.

"Very well. One last matter of business. Because of the dangerous nature of this task, we will be arming you all with Adamic blades. You will be allowed to select these before the lumber haul begins."

I don't want a blade; I want arrows. Still, it's better than nothing.

"Lastly," Grandpa says, "there is the matter of Quill's death. Once again, we are left with an empty seat. General Katu's apprentice will be accepting that office as soon as he finishes his studies. That leaves a second apprenticeship to be filled, one for General Kaynes, the other for General Katu."

Grandpa looks directly at me. "In light of this change, we will be accepting two winners of The Surviving... two of you will join the council someday."

Two days of rest. It was a tempting offer, but one I had to refuse. There is too much to do, and too little time. During the lumber haul, I'll be at the mercy of the feeders. An Adamic blade is useful, but it won't do me much good. Velma had an Adamic blade when she tried to save my life. Still, the armored feeder snapped her neck like a twig.

A dagger isn't enough. I need arrows.

I hold the arrowhead in my hand. It's the size of my thumb, flattened just enough to provide a surface for symbols. I've already dipped the tip in wax. Now, it looks like an arrow-shaped candle. All I have to do is complete the spell. I drag the wooden stencil in an elliptical spiral, finishing with a thick circle in the center.

"Done." I hold up the symbols for Grandpa to see.

"I'm impressed. It looks flawless." Grandpa smiles.

"You think it'll work?" I hope.

Grandpa shrugs. "We can't know for sure until the acid treatment." He stands and shuffles to the back corner of his study. Bending down, he lifts a small plastic bucket. On the side of the bucket is a strip of tape with the word: **ACID**.

I watch as Grandpa lugs the bucket to the table. "That's the acid?"

Grandpa nods. "Sulfuric Acid. It doesn't take much to dissolve steel." He peels off the lid and motions to the clear liquid. "Toss it in."

I drop the arrowhead, and Grandpa quickly replaces the lid. "The fumes are toxic," he warns. "Now, we wait."

"How long?"

"The acid is concentrated. 10 minutes... maybe 15." He sets down his book and smiles at me. "It's been a while since we've talked. Anything on your mind?"

I try to think of something casual, a history question, or maybe a comment about the weather. In the end, all I can think about is what Jack told me in the pit. *The king knows who the Holy One is.*

Grandpa frowns. "What is it? And don't say nothing. I know that look."

"I..." I bite my lip. "Grandpa, can I trust you to tell the truth? About anything?"

Grandpa grows somber. "You can trust me, Rose. I promise I will not lie to you."

"Do you know who the Holy One is?"

Grandpa rears back, blinking his eyes excessively. "Who... what gave you that idea?"

"It doesn't matter. What matters is that you tell me the truth. Do you know who it is?"

Grandpa takes a deep breath and sighs. "Yes, I know who the Holy One is. I... I've known for a long time."

"Is it that girl? The invisible one? Is she the Holy One?"

Grandpa shakes his head. "I'm afraid not. She's only a pawn—a dangerous pawn, but a pawn no less."

"So, who is it?"

Grandpa matches my gaze, pain comprising much of his emotion. "I'm sorry, Rose. I won't lie to you, but I can't answer that question either."

"What? Why?"

Grandpa looks away. "I… I'm afraid you aren't ready for the answer. When you learn the truth, you'll understand why I had to hide this from you."

"Just tell me," I demand. "Whatever it is, I can handle it. You have to trust me!"

"I do trust you," Grandpa insists, "but I also must protect you from yourself."

"So what, knowing who the Holy One is puts me in danger? How does that make any sense? If I don't know who he is, how can I protect myself from him?"

Grandpa says nothing, his grip tightening on his cane. "I'm sorry, Rose. Someday you'll understand."

My rage burns within me. "No, I understand perfectly. If you can't trust me, how do you expect me to trust you?"

Grandpa's eyebrows turn down—a look I'm not used to. "I don't need you to trust me, I need you to obey. Everything I do is in your best interest."

"How can—"

"ENOUGH!" His amplified voice tears through me, severing any last strings of trust. "Enough… This is getting out of hand. I will not discuss the matter any longer."

I'm angry, and I'm confused. *Why? Why wouldn't he tell me who?*

Tap. Tap. Tap.

"Your highness." It's Octavian's voice. "Zane wishes to have a word with you."

Grandpa sighs. "Very well, I'll be right there." He groans as he stands and shuffles toward the door. Halfway across the study, he stops, depositing a skeleton key on the corner of the table. "Lock up on your way out."

"Wait. What do you mean?"

"It's a spare key to my study." He turns just enough to make eye contact. "I do trust you, Rose. I trust you as an adalit. I trust you with my relics. I trust you… I just need time before I tell you about

295

the Holy One. Please, have faith in me this once. Soon, it will all make sense."

Ugh! Just when I'm convinced I can't trust him, Grandpa wins me back. A key to his study is no small gift. It grants me access to his Adamic collection, the morph mask, everything my Grandpa values most. "Fine. I trust you. I don't understand you, but I trust you." *I have no choice.*

"Thank you, Rose." He turns and shuffles out the door. "The arrowhead should be done," he calls as he disappears around the doorframe.

I turn back to the bucket of acid trying to distract myself with my work. *At least one good thing came from today.* I peel open the lid and using tongs, I drop the arrows in a bowl of water. I give it a few good stirs before plucking the arrowhead by hand and peeling off the protective wax.

Amazing!

The symbols are strikingly precise, etched nearly a pencil tip deep. *I have to show Gideon.* Our lesson starts in just a few minutes, and he'll be ecstatic.

I grab the key, careful to lock up on my way out. Then, I run to the northern reaches of the palace grounds.

Gideon is near the palace wall, shooting a tight cluster in the haybale. When he hears my flurried footsteps on the path, he cocks his head and loops the bowstring over his shoulder like a single-stringed knapsack. "Good evening, dauphine. What has you so merry this afternoon?"

"I did it!" I hold up the Adamic arrowhead. "See for yourself."

He eyes the arrowhead as a mother would her own infant. "So soon?" He accepts the arrowhead and squints down at it. "You are sure it is effective?"

"Positive."

Gideon draws another arrow and places the two arrowheads nose to nose. As he applies pressure, the Adamic tip quickly sinks into the other. "Oh, yes. This is very good news." He peels his eyes from the arrowhead and smiles at me. "You can make more, correct?"

"It might take me some time, but I should be able to replicate it."

"How long will it take to make 20?" Gideon asks.

"20? Oh, God. I don't know. It would probably take me all day. Why?"

"Excellent. With your permission, I suggest we cancel the lesson," Gideon says. "I must prepare the arrows tonight if we wish to begin in the morning. If all goes well, you'll have a full quiver in time for the lumber haul. You must be armed in the beyond. You are Cavernum's future adalit. We must make sure you are prepared for anything. Tonight, we make Cavernum safe. I will bring you more arrowheads tonight. 10 for you, and 10 for me. By morning, you will be untouchable."

His enthusiasm is contagious, and I find myself nodding along "Very well. Bring them to the Royal Wing. I'll collect them from you there."

Now, I almost hope the feeders come. Now, I can get my revenge.

Chapter 21

Matt

I'm running out of time.

It's October 25th. The lumber haul starts tomorrow, and the Fall Festival is only two days after that. If I'm going to ask Rose, I have to do it now.

The temperature is quickly dropping in Cavernum, and the wind outside the walls is unrelenting. *I should have worn gloves.* The glass vase saps the heat from my hands like a never-ending ice cube. A servant was nice enough to find it for me. I've already filled it with water and a spoonful of sugar.

Now, all I need are the marigolds.

It's the end of their season, and I'll be lucky to find some in full bloom. I follow the road, knowing it's my best bet. Marigolds thrive in sunshine, and along the open road is the only unshaded soil in sight.

Is this too weird? Her dad used to pick marigolds for her mom. I'm not trying to say I'm husband material; I just thought it would be a nice gesture. She's been cooped up in the palace for so long, who knows when she'll see more marigolds—at least until next summer.

298

Ten minutes in, I've passed the turnoff for the bunker, and I'm still flowerless. That's when I hear it.

Shluuurp.

It sounds like someone finishing the last of a smoothie through a straw.

I scan the forest floor, but all I see are orange and brown leaves. Still, the slurping continues. It sounds like it's close. I snake my eyes to the source of the sound, a wide oak tree. I approach as quietly as I can.

Quiet!

I command the air around me, silencing all of my footsteps. Then, I creep closer. I don't walk toward the tree but parallel to it, granting myself a wider view of what's behind. Three steps... five steps. A bare foot slowly comes into view. Then, a leg, lying flat on the floor. As I move closer, I see a torso covered in a tattered black cloak. A separate set of legs kneel on top of the victim's back. Now, I can see everything.

One man is face down on the floor, his head turned to the side. Another man—a feeder by the looks of it— is kneeling on the first man's back. He's keeled over, his mouth pressed to his victim's throat.

The creature on top doesn't stop drinking. I can hear every disturbing gulp. He drinks like a child at the elementary school fountains, sloppy and loud, lips suctioned onto the faucet. The victim moans in response.

He's still alive!

Squeez-

I'm about to choke the feeder when I see the victim's face. It's Aramaias, the feeder I met a few weeks back, the one who called me master. I told him to stay away, yet here he is, being fed on by another feeder.

The Archangel!

As if he heard his name, the man lifts his head and sucks in a breath of air. The gaping mouth of his hood pointing right at me.

He sees me!

I hold my breath as the Archangel stands, suddenly fighting the urge to run. He studies me, the cloud of his steamy breath hovering before his face. Then, he strikes.

It isn't a physical attack, but a supernatural one. He rams me with his soul, nearly knocking me out of my body. My muscles spasm, arching my back and contracting my limbs.

"Aaaagh!" I cry out before crumbling like Aramaias. I try to move, but I'm disconnected from my body. My soul has been displaced by another. I can't see, I can barely feel what my limbs are doing. I'm at the mercy of the archangel. His soul walks over mine like a dirty doormat, then, he's gone. I climb my way back to my brain and open my eyes.

I'm on my back, leaning against the base of the tree. Two thick tendrils of tree root are coiled around each arm, cutting off the circulation to my hands.

The archangel is holding my amulet, staring down at me. He must have removed it while I was possessed. Now, I'm at his mercy.

Archangel removes his hood with the sweep of his hand. He's a feeder alright, but a young one. His skin isn't sickly like the others. He has pale blue eyes and a mountain range of a nose—tall and broad. Except for the blood on his lips, he almost looks normal. Then, it dawns on me.

It's him! It's Mystery-man!

I feel the roots tighten around each wrist. They pull my arms back, threatening to dislocate my shoulders.

"Who are you?" he hisses. His voice is rough and grainy, the voice of someone who's hardly spoken in years.

"I'm Matthew. I'm a lieutenant in the guard."

I feel his consciousness encircling me, eating up my every thought. If I lie, he'll know immediately.

Archy lets this sink in. "A demon in the guard? Interesting. Do you serve the Holy One?"

"No." *Not yet, anyway.*

Mystery man frowns, bewildered to the core. "Really? I have a memory from Aramaias that says otherwise."

"What? No!" *It's the truth!* "What I told him was a lie. I told him what he wanted to hear."

Mystery man grins. "Let me get this straight. You overpowered a feeder, and then let him go free?"

"It's the truth!" *I just couldn't kill him.*

"Hmmm." Mystery Man takes this to heart. "You asked him a lot about me… why?"

"Because you saved my life."

His eyebrows knit together.

He doesn't remember.

"There was a graduation party in the meadow." I recount. "Feeders attacked. I possessed an armored feeder, and I couldn't control him. You stabbed him before he could kill me." I point to his Adamic blade.

"I remember. You were protecting a girl. Your girlfriend?"

I shake my head. *The princess.*

"The princess," Mystery Man laughs. "Wow. That's one I haven't heard." His gaze softens, and the roots retract back into the ground.

I sit up and rub my wrists, trying to work the blood back into my fingertips. Still, Mystery Man keeps a tight hold on my amulet.

"So," he coils the chain around his index finger. "If you aren't here to kill me, what are you doing alone in the beyond?"

"I was looking for marigolds."

"Flowers? You've got to be kidding me."

"I'm asking a girl to Fall Ball."

Mystery Man rocks his head in disgust. "The Holy One is on the verge of war, and you're looking for marigolds. You know they symbolize death and misfortune?"

"Yeah, I know." *They're for the princess.*

Mystery man sighs. "God, you are a different breed. A word of advice, ditch the princess. Avoid her at all costs. The second she finds out what you are, you'll be burned at the stake."

She's not like that.

Mystery Man shrugs. "Suit yourself, but don't say I didn't warn you."

The man steps back and shakes his head in disbelief. "You know, an unpledged demon such as yourself, you could go places. If you weren't so stupid, maybe I'd train you myself." He tosses me my amulet and begins walking away.

I scrambled to my feet and follow after him. "Wait. Where are you going? Who are you?"

"I'm a damned soul, seeking redemption." He calls back as he walks. "That's all you need to know."

"How do you do it?" I demand. "How do you feed on other feeders?"

Mystery man stops in his tracks. His shoulders are hunched and defensive.

I elaborate. "The king told us feeders can't feed on each other. Their souls are too broken. It's like sand through fingers or something."

"Don't be fooled by your king, it's definitely possible. Not many do it. It's like eating crumbs. You're never really satisfied, but it's enough to get by."

"Best of luck with your princess." He sneers one last time as he ambles into the brush. "Oh, and if you're looking for marigolds, try a quarter-mile west of here. Just don't let her learn what you are."

I hurry through the Royal Plaza, dodging the craft stands and the food carts.

Everything is working out.

The marigolds were right where Mystery Man said they'd be, and they were in nearly perfect condition. I tried to deliver them myself, but the royal guards denied me entrance. A guard named Octavian promised me he'd get them to her.

I swear, if he forgets…

I stop at the southern end of the Royal Plaza, right where Kendra instructed. To my left is a tent, selling tables and chairs. Next to it, a woman is holding up hand-knitted baby socks, shouting at every passerby.

"Get ready for winter. Keep your babies warm."

I quickly adjust my hair and toss a piece of peppermint bark into my mouth. Kendra should be here any minute.

We've been meeting daily for the last week. My healing has progressed rapidly, and so has our friendship. Still, nothing major has happened, but her parents invited me for dinner, so I don't know what to think. *We're still just friends... aren't we?*

"Matt!"

I spin and spot Kendra approaching. She's wrapped in a long scarlet coat that nearly reaches her ankles. Her black winter boots are overflowing with fluffy white fur. I trace her curves up to her face. The dress has thick black buttons that cinch it tight around her waist. My eyes are drawn to her lips, a deep mesmerizing red just like her dress. Her blonde hair, residually wavy from yesterday's curls, flutter in the fall wind.

"Kendra! You look..." I hesitate. "You look beautiful."

She gives a quick spin, the dress flaring around her feet. "You like it? I bought it yesterday with my mom."

"I do." I'm suddenly self-conscious of my own attire. It's palace clothing, black pants and a baggy olive shirt that feels more like a sweater. A black cape hangs from my shoulder, the furry collar a symbol of my status. I thought it looked ridiculous, but Wendy insisted she liked it.

"What do you think about mine?" I grab one end of my cape and throw it in the air like a bullfighter.

She grins. "I love it. Handsome and professional, but not over the top." She turns back the way she came "Follow me; my family lives right over here."

I walk at her side as we weave through more of the shops. Seeing our attire, craftsmen and women crowd to offer their goods and services. Kendra takes the time to politely decline every one.

She points up at a balcony overlooking the plaza. "See the balcony with the rocking chair. That's theirs."

"Wow, right against the plaza. That's nice."

Kendra nods. "My dad bought it up when an old lady died." Her lips curl into a smile. "Some say it's haunted. You a believer, Matt?"

"Haunted by a nice old lady? What does she do, bake you cookies?"

Kendra laughs. "I wish." She hurried ahead to open the stairwell door for me.

"Oh, thank you." We both step inside and begin climbing to the 3rd floor. I take a deep breath. "Now, remind me. Deklin is ten, right?"

Kendra raises an eyebrow and laughs. "It's not a test, Matt. You don't have to memorize their names. It's just dinner."

" I know," I insist. "I just want to make a good impression. The last family I met was Diego's, and I told you how that went."

Kendra reaches over and gives my hand a quick squeeze. "It'll be fine. My parents are pretty easy to please. Trust me."

"Okay."

Before we even crest the last few steps, I hear the door open. A woman stands in the doorway. "Welcome home, Kendra. And you must be Matt."

She holds out her hand and I shake it. She's a beautiful woman. She looks a lot like Kendra, only a bit heavier set. Or maybe it's just the coat. It's hard to tell under all the fur.

"A pleasure to meet you, Mrs. Esecks."

She turns to Kendra and gushes. "Kendra, you never told me he was this handsome."

Kendra lightheartedly rolls her eyes. "Yes, mom, I actually did."

"Well, I guess I doubted you," Mrs. Esecks laughs. "Why don't you go say hi to your father in the kitchen. I'll tell Deklin you're here."

"This way, Matt." She takes me by the arm, pulling me past her mom and into the house. We walk past two small bedrooms and into a wide living room lined with windows that overlook the plaza. As we walk to the kitchen, I can help but notice the differences between Diego's home. Here, the floor is layered with simple orange tiles, and the ceiling is sanded stone. The windows are wide and freshly cleaned.

Mr. Esecks stands next to a small brick oven, an oven mitt on each hand. He's balding above both temples and wears simple wireframe glasses. When he sees us, he gives a toothy grin. "Well, my my." His voice is nasally and flat, but ultimately friendly. "Look what the cat dragged in."

"Hi, dad." Kendra skips over and gives him a hug. "This is Matt, the Lieutenant I told you about."

"Welcome, Matt. It's a pleasure to have you in our home." He shakes my hand. "Now don't be shy around here. What's ours is yours, alright. We expect you to make yourself right at home."

"I will. Thank you, sir."

"Kendra tugs me back toward the hallway. C'mon, let me show you Deklin's room."

"Don't go too far," Mr. Esecks reminds. "Dinner will be ready in just a few."

"We won't." She leads me into the hall. "Just a warning," she whispers. "Deklin can be a little hyper some—"

"Put your hands up!" A small kid bursts into the hallway with an L-shaped block of wood. He points it at Kendra like a pistol. "Die, feeder scum! Pchew! Pchew!" He shakes the gun with every pretend bullet, spit spaying like Windex.

"Ahhh." Kendra shudders and drops to the floor, clutching her shoulder. Like a zombie, she jerkily begins to sit up, still clutching her shoulder. "I want blood. Give me your—"

"Pchew!" Deklin gives the gun one last shake as Kendra slumps back to the floor and sticks out her tongue.

So this is what a brother is like.

Deklin turns to me, his lips pressed in a frown. "Die, feeder!"

Before he can shoot, I drop to my knees and clasp my hands together. Mimicking a raspy, monster voice, I beg for my life. "Wait.

305

Don't kill me. Spare my life, and I will serve you, master. I will be your feeder slave."

Deklin doesn't miss a beat. He grins, looks at Kenra, then turns back to med. "Okay," he agrees. "What do you ask in return?"

I hear Kendra laughing behind me, and my face burns red. Still, I force myself to do the voice. "All I want is food, master." I turn and point at Kendra. "Feed me her blood, and I will be loyal."

Deklin thinks for a moment before unleashing a snaggle-toothed grin. He points his gun where Kendra still plays dead. "Eat her liver!"

"Yes, master. Liver is feeder's favorite." I crawl on my hands and knees and look down at Kendra. I see her eyelids peek open, and the ghost of a smile tugs on her lips. Somehow, she stays in character.

In our healing sessions, Kendra and I have grown pretty comfortable with each other. Still, I hesitate. Before I can chicken out, I press my face into her stomach. "Nom, nom, nom."

Kendra laughs and thrashes. "Stop! That tickles!" She pushes my face away and kicks to keep me at bay.

"Dinner!" Mr. Esecks calls.

I break character before Kendra's mom walks into the hall, my face red enough as it is. I hold out my hand and help Kendra up.

She wipes at her eyes. "I'm sorry, Deklin. I can't let him eat my liver."

Deklin doesn't seem too disappointed. He prances over and looks up at me. "Who are you?"

"I'm Matt, Kendra's friend. A pleasure to meet you, Deklin."

"His face lights up and he looks at me in awe. "How do you know my name?"

"Because I told him, silly." Kendra teases. "Now c'mon. It's almost time to eat."

We take our seats around the table, a sturdy, glossed piece of wood wide enough to fit a feast. Mr. Esecks pulls two pot pies from the brick oven and sets them on the table next to the cornbread and the pomegranate juice. Every dinner plate has already been served a helping of each dish.

"This looks delicious, Mom. I'm starving."

"Hi, starving. I'm dad," Mr. Esecks chimes with a perfectly straight face.

I find myself choking back a laugh. Apparently, I'm the only one amused.

"See, at least someone appreciates my humor," Mr. Esecks says.

Mrs. Esecks puts the pot pie on the table with a buttered pan of cornbread. "Alright, let's dig in."

Immediately, everyone grabs their utensils, and I do the same. Just as I imagined, the food tastes delicious. The cornbread falls apart in my mouth, and pomegranate juice is irresistibly tart.

"You know Matt," Mr. Esecks chimes in, waving his cornbread through the air. "I bet you'd be great at baking bread."

"Hmmm? Why's that?"

He's already smiling. "Because you're proficient with dough-minion."

It takes me a second to get it, and I can't help but snort—a violent sudden laugh. "That's good. I'll have to tell that one to some of my men."

Kendra smiles. "You don't have to humor him, Matt."

I shrug. "I don't know. Sounds like your dad will be doing the humoring."

"That's the spirit," Mr. Esecks chimes through bites of pot pie. "So, Matt, you're Chancellor Quine's champion?"

"Yes, sir."

"Wow, a future guardian in our midst," Mrs. Esecks hums.

Mr. Esecks taps his spoon on the table. "You know, Chancellor Quine founded Cavernum University. You could say we have the same boss."

"Kendra told me you're a professor. Sociology, right?"

"That's right. Hang out here enough, and you'll hear me preach all about it. You know, sometime I'd love to pick your brain about the guard."

"Dad…" Kendra's voice is a warning.

"Oh, alright." He turns to me, disappointed. "I promised I wouldn't talk about politics."

"I don't mind. I'd be happy to chat anytime."

Mrs. Esecks looks down at Deklin. "Deklin wants to be a guardsman someday. Deklin, do you have any questions for our guest?"

Deklin looks at me with wide, hopeful eyes. "Can you make fire?"

"I can."

"Can you make a shield?"

"I can do that too." I smile, trying not to act too cocky.

Deklin pulls his knees underneath him, bouncing up and down. "Can you fly? Can you shoot lightning?"

"I don't think I could fly," I admit, "but I've been practicing with lightning. I don't have an amulet today, but if it's alright with your mom, maybe someday I can show you a thing or two."

"Really?" Deklin is practically vibrating.

"That's kind of you, Matt, but you don't have to…" Mrs. Esecks starts.

"No, it would be my pleasure."

She smiles graciously. "Well, we would love that, wouldn't we Deklin? What do you say to Matt?"

"Thank you," Deklin squeaks.

"My pleasure."

Deklin is still watching me with boyish delight. "Kendra said you were bit by a feeder. Can I see the scar?"

"Deklin," his mother scolds. "That's a personal question."

"It's fine. He's not the first to ask." I pull down my collar a few inches until the pink ridge of skin is exposed.

"Wow." He kneels on his chair and leans closer to get a better view. "Did you kill it?"

"Deklin!" his mother scolds.

"I'm not really sure. I stabbed him, and he ran away."

"Have you ever killed anyone?"

His question takes me by surprise. His mother scolds him once more, but I don't hear her. Instead, I see Quill on the floor before me. I feel the gentle jolt of the knife as it enters his skull. I see his body go limp as his life is snatched away before my eyes.

"Matt?" Kendra takes my hand, pulling me back to the present.

Mr. Esecks is watching me, clearly concerned.

"Oh, uhhh, I… I…" My heart races and the words feel stuck in my chest. I want to say no, but the words won't come. *I have. I have killed.* "I'm sorry. Please excuse me for a second."

I push back my seat and hurry down the hall to the restroom. I'm opening the door when I hear footsteps behind me. "Matt, are you okay?" Kendra whispers.

"No, I feel like an idiot. I was so awkward. Your family is going to think I'm a psycho."

She takes my hand, and as I try to pull away, she squeezes harder. "Hey, it's not a big deal. My parents won't even care. Trust me." Her green eyes demand my attention, sucking me into a viridescent pool. "Are you okay? Is it about what happened with Diego's dad? Do you want to talk about it?"

"No. It's not about that; it's something else. I… I think I'm good now. We can go back before they think I'm having an episode."

"You sure? You can trust me if you want to get anything off your chest."

"I know I can, Kendra. Thank you. Let's just get back."

"Okay." She squeezes my hand once more. "Whenever you're ready."

She holds my hand until we're almost within view. Mr. and Mrs. Esecks smile as we take our seats. They watch with sympathy, and maybe concern, but I don't sense any hostility.

"I'm sorry," I say as I take my seat. "I just got a little over-whelmed with a memory." I scoot in my chair and take a deep breath.

"Nothing to be ashamed of," Mr. Esecks smiles. "We all have those moments."

I nod. "The truth is, Deklin, I have killed someone. I did it to save a friend of mine, and even though the person I killed was a bad guy, thinking about it still makes me...well, sad I guess."

Mr. Esecks nods his head. "Death and sorrow are inseparable, regardless of our relationship with the victim. Thank you for sharing, Matt. And thank you for your service to this city."

The proceeding silence is unbearable, and Kendra quickly comes to my rescue. "What's for dessert, Mom?"

"Oh, I'm glad you asked," Mrs. Esecks sings. "No one get too full. I made pumpkin pie."

Mr. Esecks scans his eyes across the table. "It'll give us *pumpkin* else to talk about!"

I snort out of sheer surprise and stifle a laugh. Kendra shakes her head in playful disgust.

"What?" Mr. Esecks laughs, knowing exactly what he's doing. "You can't tell me that isn't comedic gold."

The rest of the meal is easier. We talk about the coming winter. Mr. Esecks asks me all about the education system of the beyond. Before I know it, it's almost sunset.

Kendra glances at the window and frowns. "Mom, is it alright if we take dessert to go? We have to be back in the palace before dark, and I want to give Matt a quick healing lesson."

"Of course, honey. Whatever is easiest for you."

"Thank you." Kendra stands. "This way."

She leads me down the hall, stopping at the room closest to the front door. She opens the door and gestures for me to enter. A small window offers mediocre lighting, but it doesn't take much to see the posters on the wall. Each is a different part of the body, hand-drawn and life-size. One shows the muscles of the legs, another shows the facial bones. The walls look more like a doctor's office than a bedroom.

"Did you draw these?"

Kendra grins, flattered by the awe in my voice. "They're nothing special. It was part of my training. All the other healers had to do the same."

"You call this nothing? These are incredible." I turn to her and smirk. "I'm only bummed there's not any of me."

Kendra looks away, trying to hide her look of guilt. She struggles to suppress a smile.

"No!" I gasp. "You didn't."

For the first time ever, I think I see what embarrassment looks like in Kendra. "It was a few little sketches. It's nothing."

"Where are they? You have to show me." I beg.

"Next time," Kendra says. "I promise I'll show you next time."

"What could be so bad about them? Did you give me a mustache or something?"

Kendra laughs, but it's an uncomfortable laugh. "No, You look fine. It's just...."

"Fine, how about we play hot or cold?" I walk toward the bed. "Am I getting hotter or colder?"

"Matt..."

I don't have an amulet so I can't read her mind. I focus on her body language instead.

"No? How about now?" I move toward a small dresser by the window. It has a single drawer, the perfect place to store drawings. "Is it over here?"

"Matt." As I keep walking, her voice intensifies. "It's not that simple."

I reach for the drawer, but Kendra is faster. She grabs my wrist, her chest heaving in a panic. "Alright! fine! I'll show you. I just... I have to tell you something first. You have to promise not to get mad."

Now, I'm really confused. "Why would I get mad?"

Kendra brushes her hair aside and grows serious. "When I gave you the breath of life, I know you got a look inside my head. That's how it works. Well, when I was healing you those three days, you opened your mind up to me, maybe more than you realized. It helped me heal you, but... I saw some things."

"What kind of things?"

She tugs open the drawer and hands me a stack of papers. As I start to flip through, my blood turns cold. The first drawing shows a chain-link fence in the woods. A small sign hangs on the fence. It reads: **High Radiation Zone. Do Not Enter.**

I turn the page and find a sketch of Judy. She's in a hospital bed, the blankets pulled up to her chin.

I turn the page. This time, I see myself. I'm standing in front of a mirror, craning to get a look at the symbols on my back. They're sketched in perfect directly between my shoulder blades.

I begin flipping frantically through the pages. A sketch of Remmy, my rifle back home. A sketch of my amulet.

Kendra waits until I'm on the last page. "I drew just about everything I saw. I promise I didn't go snooping; the thoughts just came." The words keep tumbling. I've never seen her so flustered. "But this doesn't change anything. I don't care if you're a demon. I know you. You're a good person. I won't tell anyone about this. You can trust me, Matt. If you don't believe me, you can read my mind. I have nothing to hide."

"Kendra. It's okay." I laugh. I should be terrified, but all I feel is relief. I can finally tell the truth.

"It's okay?" she echoes.

"It's fine. This is good." I run my fingers through my hair. "I just can't believe... I mean... you've known this whole time? You knew I was reading your mind?"

"I didn't know for sure, but I figured you wouldn't be able to resist." She steps back and looks at the floor. "I was hoping you'd tell me on your own, but I understand your hesitancy. Why risk your life for a friend?"

The words punch deep. *She knows about my feelings for Rose.*

"You know," I say. "You're the first person to find out about this. No one knows except for Zane." *And technically Diego.* "I'm glad it was you. There's no one I trust more." And as weird as it is, I know it's true. Diego's loyalty is unknown. Rose is focused on her own struggles. Kendra is the only one I can count on.

Kendra relaxes, finally regaining her usual confidence. "So, we're good?"

She opens her arms for a hug, and I lift her off her feet, arching my back. "We're good," I whisper in her ear. I relish the weight of her body against mine before lowering her back to her toes. I hope she'll look up at me, but instead, she steps back.

Kendra looks down, plucking the sketch of Judy from my hands. "I see why you're so desperate to master healing. If you want, we can focus on cancers for the next few weeks. I'm not an expert, but I know enough."

"I think that sounds perfect." I set down the rest of her sketches on the desk. "What do you have in mind for tonight?"

Kendra purses her lips. "We don't have an amulet, but I'd be happy to cover a new technique. We could look at burns. Or maybe neutralizing poisons. You tell me what interests you."

"Can you teach me the breath of life?"

"Oh!" Kendra brushes her hair out of her face and blushes. Her lips part in a dazzling flash of white. "Of course. Why don't you lie down on the bed?"

Already my heart is racing. Something manlier than butterflies stirs up my stomach. Kendra sits on the bed next to my waist. "The breath of life is simple in concept but complicated in execution. Essentially, you have to split off a piece of your soul and breath it into the other person. Breaking the soul can be painful. A lot of people can't find it in themselves to do it."

She leans over me until her emerald eyes hover above my own. Her lips are so full of life, I find myself contemplating their texture.

"From there," she says, "all you have to do is breathe out."

Her lips drift closer, but then they stop, peeling back into a gorgeous smile. She's teasing me, and she knows it.

"Read my mind," she whispers. "Guess what I'm thinking."

I can't take it any longer, "I know what you're thinking." I rest my hand on the back of her neck and guide her face to mine. That's all the permission she needs. Her lips close over mine, vivacious and hungry. I lean in, relishing the gentle pressure between us. I'm about to pull her on top of me when a knock echoes through the room, jolting us apart.

"Kendra, it's almost dark. You and Matt may want to get going," her mom calls through the door.

We share a guilty glance as Kendra tosses the hair out of her face. "Thanks, Mom, we'll be right out."

As we grab our coats, all I can think about is the kiss. The warmth of her skin. The way her eyes crease when she smiles. All I want is another moment alone.

But one looming thought spoils everything. *What about Rose? What about the Fall Festival?*

Chapter 22

Rose

I'm exhausted. I spent the entire day in Grandpa's study, attempting the armor-piercing spell hour after hour. Gideon supplied me with a batch of 20 steel arrowheads, of which only 16 Adamic ones remain. The other four were either too defaced with symbols or mangled by the acid—unusable either way.

I want to sleep in more than anything, but Gideon depends on me. Before tomorrow, he has to fasten each arrowhead to its shaft and prepare the fletching. Only then will I be armed for the lumber haul.

I drag myself out of bed and get dressed in a grey winter coat, complete with fleece stockings and a sturdy pair of fur-lined boots. Then, I grab the leather sack of arrowheads. They clank like coins all the way across my chambers.

I open the door and freeze.

Marigolds!

I blink, look around the hallway, and blink some more. *Could it be?*

There's a small note placed gingerly in the bouquet. It's folded in half.

Antai?

I snatch up the letter and unfold it. My heart sinks.

The handwriting is unfamiliar.

> *Rose,*
> *The royal guards wouldn't let me give you this in person, so I have to write a note instead.*
> *I was going to give you white roses, but I decided marigolds might mean a little more to you. You've already taught me so much about Cavernum, I would be honored if you would be my date to the Fall Ball.*
> *Also, because I can't go in the Royal Wing to see if you put the flowers on your doorstep, I thought I'd show you how we do it in the beyond.*
>
> *Rose, will you go to Fall Ball with me?*
>
> *Check yes or no.*
>
> *Yes [] No []*
>
> *Your friend,*
> *Matt*

It's cute. I should be enthralled, but there's a bitter taste in the back of my mind.

They were supposed to be red. They were supposed to be from Antai. *He wasn't supposed to die!*

I want to say yes to Matt, but I don't know if I can. Attending Fall Ball with Matt would mean accepting Antai's fate.

C'mon, Rose. Don't give up so easily.

Octavian holds up the flowers. "Where should we put these? On your doorstep?"

"No. Give them to Wendy, please. Have her put them on my nightstand."

He raises an eyebrow. "Very well, princess. As you wish."

The sun will set within the quarter-hour, so I have to be swift. I hurry to Gideon's room in the West Wing. In exchange for his deceased brother's soul anchor, Grandpa granted him the status of captain.

I knock, wait, and knock again. When he doesn't answer, I already know where to look next. The temple.

As I suspected, Gideon's bow is leaning against the wall next to the temple entrance. I hesitate at the door. Technically, I'm not supposed to bring weapons into the temple, but these are only arrowheads, and I don't trust them to be out of my sight.

I turn the crystal handle and step inside, finding Gideon kneeling before the sacrificial fire. He doesn't stir at my entrance.

A single priest is stationed in the corner of the room. "Welcome, princess, to God's sacred edifice. How may I serve thee?"

"Actually," I say, "would you mind giving us some privacy?" I motion to Gideon. "We have some sacred matters to discuss. It'll just take a moment."

"Oh, I see." The priest is obviously insulted, but he obeys regardless. "Very well. May God bless you with His peace." He tosses back his robes and struts out of the temple.

"Sacred matters?" Gideon opens his eyes and laughs, climbing to his feet. "Are you referring to the sacred matters of warfare?"

"I am." I hold up the leather pouch. "I finished the arrowheads. Do you think you can complete the arrows by tomorrow morning?"

"For you, dauphine, I'll work all night."

"Thank you, Gideon. You truly are a godsend."

"I serve how I can, nothing more."

I look towards the exit, but I can't bring myself to leave. Gideon's company is so calming, alleviating my uncertainty. I take a seat on the first pew. And look up at the Adamic script on the walls. I wonder what wisdom those words would offer, could I understand.

"Dauphine, I sense you are troubled. If you wish to unburden yourself before the Lord, I will happily leave you in privacy."

"No. Don't go. I don't feel like praying much."

"Of course. Then stay, I will."

Through the opaque walls, I can see that the sun has nearly set.

"Gideon, can I ask you something personal?"

"Anything you wish, dauphine. I am an opened book."

"I've been thinking a lot about what you said. About how God answers our prayers through us. We are responsible for our own protection, right?"

"Mmhhmm," he hums.

"Well, I wanted to ask you how you make peace when you can't protect the ones you love. I know you lost loved ones in Lycon. I have someone I couldn't protect as well. I mean, does it ever get easier?"

"Only when life becomes loveless will death become painless. And my dear, I hope that day never comes."

"So what? We just have to suffer forever?"

"You can't take the pain away," Gideon says. "You can only dilute it with love. You see, I think sometimes we refuse to love. We fear that loving someone new will erase the love we once felt. But that's not the case. Love isn't just admiration, love is service. As one recipient passes on, we have time to serve others. In that way, our love is never reduced, but reborn."

I wrinkle my nose. "Our love is reborn?"

Gideon nods. "Precisely. We must transition our love to new recipients. This might sound morbid, but the dead do not need attention. It is those around us who need attention. We cannot live in the past. We must let love live in the present," Gideon sighs. "Do not misunderstand what I am saying. If I could serve my brother for my entire life, I would happily do so. If I could have him back, I would. I would be with him instead of being here with you. But that is not God's plan. God's plan involves tragedy. In the absence of my

318

brother, here I am, serving the princess. The only question you must ask yourself is who will you love next?"

I think of Nevela. Obviously, I want her back, but I know if she were here, Wendy would still be in the ring. In the face of tragedy, I let myself love another.

"That… that makes sense. Thank you, Gideon. I think this time, you were my consolation."

Gideon smiles, a simple satisfaction on his face. "It was a pleasure, dauphine." He stands. "If I'm going to finish these arrows by morning, I must get to work."

"Of course, thanks again. I owe you my safety and my sanity. I'll see you in the morning to retrieve the arrows."

I push open the temple door and march my way toward the Royal Wing. I'm walking across the Central Wing when I find Vyle loitering by the Central Staircase. He's wearing a formal black suit coat with sharp lapels and a ruffled black shirt. Polished like a family heirloom, his leather shoes glisten in the fading daylight. He spots me immediately, relief filling his face. He holds a vase of white roses in his hands.

"Rose! I've been waiting for you all evening. Can I have a moment to ask you something?"

I groan, not to be intentionally rude, but because I want nothing more than to fall into bed. "Vyle, I already told you no. I'm not going to Fall Ball with you, and I never will. I shouldn't have to say that twice."

"What?" He looks down at the flowers and his mouth falls open. "Wait… you thought…" He laughs. "No. God, no. These are from my brother's service. We just finished cleaning up. Besides, I already have a date to Fall Ball," He looks at me, still smiling despite my rash response. "No, I wanted to ask you something else." He reaches into his pocket and pulls out two golden ticket stubs. "I have two tickets to the The Leaves of Change. They play the morning of Fall Ball, but I'm sure you know that."

I do. I know all about it. The Leaves of Change is one of the most prestigious performances in the palace. It's a traditional performance, played only once a year—the morning of Fall Ball. I've been so distracted with Antai, I never got tickets. They likely sold out days ago.

Vyle sees my mind churning. He grins. "They're 2nd-row seats. B-12 and B-13. I'm sure you could use a break from everything. I could too. It wouldn't even be a date. Just two friends on an outing. You have my word."

I'm tempted. I'm actually tempted to say yes. If it had been anyone else, the gesture would be beyond thoughtful. But it's not. It's Vyle, the man who nearly killed me. The man who held me down and reached under my shirt.

Don't give in, Rose. He can't make amends with money.

"I'm sorry, Vyle." I try to say it sternly, but it only sounds depressed. "The thought is nice, but… I'm going to have to decline." *This doesn't make up for anything.*

"I get it, Rose. I hurt you… but don't forget that I apologized. I'm a different person now. I won't ever hurt you again. I just need one chance to prove it to you."

"I don't need your friendship, Vyle. And frankly, I don't want it. Save us both the struggle, and stay away from me. Please."

"So, that's it? You're never going to forgive me?"

"Even if I forgive you, I'll never forget. My advice is to find a friend who doesn't know what you've done." I turn to walk away, but he grabs my wrist.

"Rose!"

I jerk my hand away. "Don't touch me! Ever again!"

"Rose, don't do this. Just gi—"

"She said to stay away." Matt is coming from down the hall, a charcoal cloak elegantly trailing each stride.

Vyle grimaces, his face contorting as if in response to a foul odor. He opens his mouth for a snarky response and then closes it. He blows out through pinched lips. "Fine." He holds out the tickets. "You can take your grandpa. Or you two go. I don't care. I was just trying to do something nice."

When I don't take the tickets, he thrusts them at Matt, who hesitantly accepts. "Enjoy the show," he sighs. Without another word, he sulks away.

Matt looks at the tickets in his hand, his face brushed with bewilderment. "What was that about?"

"I don't know," I groan. "He's set on becoming my friend."

"Hmmm, that doesn't surprise me," Matt says.

"What do you mean?"

Matt's eyes widen. He wasn't expecting to elaborate. "Oh, I mean. You're a beautiful, smart princess with the promise of the Cavernic Throne." He shrugs, trying to make light of the compliment. "It's nice that you got to go undercover in the guard. It let you see how he'd treat you if you weren't the princess."

"And you," I say. " I got the marigolds by the way. Where did you find them?"

"About a quarter-mile past the bunker, there was a small meadow. There's a bunch of them there. If you ever want more, I wouldn't mind."

"Well, they're beautiful. Thank you, Matt."

"It was nothing." There's a subtle pause, just long enough to be awkward. "Here." He hands me the tickets. "I won't be offended if you want to go with the king."

"Thanks. Actually, I have something for you too." I reach into my jeans and pull out his letter. "I don't have a pencil, but I hope you'll accept this as an answer." I fold the paper so that the crease falls over the yes box. Then, I make a perpendicular tear directly over the box. I unfold it and hand it to Matt. "I'd love to go to Fall Ball with you."

He grins. "Awesome. I can't wait." He looks happy, but not ecstatic. I probably look the same. "Is there any color I should wear? Do dates match or something? I have no idea what it'll be like."

"I'll be wearing gold. If you want to match, feel free."

"Gold. Got it."

"Well, It's pretty much curfew," I say. " I should get back to my quarters, but I'll see you soon.

"Bye, Rose. Goodnight."

"Goodnight, Matt."

I stroll down the hall to the intersection with the Royal Wing. I look back once only to find Matt doing the same. He smiles and waves before disappearing up the staircase.

A girlish excitement takes root within me. For the first time in weeks, I have something to look forward to. The night won't live up to expectations of Antai, but it will be something. I'm going on a date with Matt.

But first, we have to survive the lumber haul.

The clouds carry the promise of snowfall, marching slowly through the atmosphere. In a matter of days, the forest has shed its skin, leaving a blanket of freshly molted leaves. The woods are now a graveyard of skeleton trees. The cold adds certain challenges, but now is still the ideal time to haul lumber. The wood is significantly easier to chop without leaves.

I feel like a sheepherder, walking in front of a multitude of men. They carry axes and guide donkeys. In the two days, they've amassed a small forest worth of wood. Today's the last day, and everyone is frantic to finish strong.

Thunk... Thunk, Thunk... Thunk.

"Timber!"

The tree crashes down, branches snapping against the frozen earth. Immediately, men fall upon it like vultures, amputating branches and splitting the log. Once the wood is cut, it's piled into the wagons and hauled off by the mules, which are in constant circulation with the sanctuary. The entire process is surprisingly efficient.

At the moment, the laborers cover an area of about two acres. I have guards stationed on each border, keeping a constant watch on the horizon. I, on the other hand, stay in the center. If anyone sounds the alarm on either side, I should be within earshot.

I can't lose a single man.

Even our location was strategically selected. We're less than a mile west from the sanctuary, and while we're in the thickest section of woods, we're also sandwiched between two other groups. Matt's workforce is to our south, and Ekan, Katu's champion, is to our north.

Just one more day.

I sit down on a freshly severed tree stump and watch two laborers take swings at a pine, resin dripping like blood from the trunk. They're only a stone's throw away from me, much less than the height of the tree. Should it fall my way, I'll have to be ready to run.

The younger of the two laborers catches me watching and calls out to me. "Hey, princess, like what you see?" He's in his early twenties, neatly trimmed beard and nonexistent sliver lips. When he's sure he has my attention, he tosses his axe in the air, catching by the hilt after a full rotation.

I don't smile; it was a stupid stunt—one I shouldn't endorse.

"Oh, c'mon. Like an elite could do any better." He takes a few steps toward me, leaving his buddy to chop alone. "We're hard-working men. You can't tell me you wouldn't want a husband like us. Strong. Intelligent…" He raises an eyebrow in a pitiful attempt to flirt. "Some would say, handsome even. I'm Clorock by the way."

I say nothing. Scanning the horizon for the umpteenth time.

"Don't be like that baby girl, tell me you wouldn't want some of this."

"TIMBER!" His buddy jumps back as the trunk creaks. Almost in slow motion, the top of the tree teeters our way. In less than a second, the trunk splinters, and the tree rushes directly at us.

I dash to the side, distancing myself from the crash zone, but Clorock is much too slow. Rather than run, he freezes at the word "Timber," turning around to face the falling foliage. In an unfortunate stroke of fate, the tree tips directly toward him, thousands of pounds about to crush his bones.

He's going to die.

I extend my consciousness, finding the rushing wood moments before impact.

STOP!

I command the organism directly, my mental screams piercing the bark and penetrating the entire trunk. The wood strains against my soul but ultimately stops, hovering an arm's length above Clorock.

I try to hold on, but the strain is unsustainable. I sever my command a moment after Clorock dives to the side.

Crash!

The trunk strikes the ground, the majority of its mass missing Clorock by a few yards. Still, he isn't in the clear. He's buried under several thin branches—nothing heavy enough to break bones, but enough to immobilize him.

I catch my breath as Clorock struggles to crawl out. He's ultimately unsuccessful. "A little help!"

I'm about to go give him a piece of my mind when I hear frantic footsteps behind me. It's one of my guards, and their face is flushed, completely consumed with panic.

"Princess, I was scouting near the northern border. I saw a feeder. I... I think it had Adamic armor."

With those last two words, my mind goes into a spiral. "Is it coming? How long do we have?"

The scout shakes her head. "It was heading north," she stammers. "It didn't see me. I think we're safe... for now at least." She looks at me, her eyes dilated with desperation. "What do we do?"

"We should—"

A blood-curdling scream, dampened by distance, silences my very thought. It carries in the wind for several seconds before trailing off at the end of a breath.

A newfound panic empowers me. "Take everyone and go south. Find Matt and his men. They'll help keep you safe."

"What about you?" the scout asks.

I pull an arrow from my quiver, nocking it in a single motion. I'm going to help. "Get everyone south. Do it now!"

I don't wait for a response. I turn and run north, blindly moving into the trees. I haven't even been running for a minute when I see a figure coming towards me. Then, another. I raise my bow but quickly lower it again.

Laborers.

They're running for their lives, stumbling toward me with wide, trauma-stricken eyes. "Run!" a man gasps as he passes me, and I do. I run toward the scream.

This is what you've been training for, Rose.

"AAAHHHHH!"

Another scream, this time a man's gargling cry. It falls silent a second later, but not before I've pinpointed the source. I angle my body slightly to the left and keep running up a small incline. I step carefully, careful not to make too much noise. I need the element of surprise. As I crest a small hill, I freeze. The scene before me is otherworldly.

I'm at the edge of a small clearing, tree stumps dotting the leaf-strewn landscape. Scattered throughout the clearing are laborers, at least 30 of them, each buried up to their knees in the soil. At the center of the clearing, a mule is still strapped to a cart, sunk up to its axle in the earth. The mule thrashes and whinnies, trying to pull its legs from the ground.

My god!

One, two, three, four, FIVE! Five feeders are spaced on opposite sides of the clearing. Dark Adamic symbols tattooed over every inch of skin.

They move methodically through the captives, feeding on one after the other. The surviving laborers claw maniacally at the soil, trying to uproot themselves before it's too late. One man uses an axe to dig at the ground. He manages to get one leg free before a feeder pounces. It grabs him by the throat, pressing the back of his skull into the leaves. The bite is swift, and the hand on his throat silences any screams. The man succumbs without a sound.

The primitive portion of my brain begs me to run. One armored feeder I can handle, but five?

That's when I see them. Diego's brothers, Jorge and Javier, are digging around their ankles in the center of the clearing. Any second, a feeder could claim them as their next course. The only question is, can they free themselves first?

Do something, Rose!

I can't kill them all, but maybe I don't have to. I simply need to stall them until everyone escapes.

Preoccupied with their feast, the feeders still haven't spotted me. As quietly as I can, I draw back the string and position the arrow-head over the nearest feeder's heart. He's 40 feet away—far, but stationary. I think I can hit him.

Twang.

The arrow whistles as it flies, piercing the feeder's forearm! "Arrrgh!" His head snaps up, but I'm already behind the tree, renocking my arrow.

"What happened?" Another feeder demands. Its cloak conceals its features, but the voice is undeniably feminine. *A woman feeder?*

The injured feeder lifts his arm to inspect the arrow. "I don't know. Some little shit shot me." With his other hand, the feeder snaps the arrow in half, yanking it from his arm. He holds the arrow at eye level. "It's… Adamic?"

Twang.

I step out from behind the tree, releasing my second arrow. This one strikes home, embedding itself in the center of his stomach.

The wounded feeder spots me, and with an arrow in its gut, it raises its hand. A flicker of flame, no bigger than a matchstick, flashes on his fingertips. Then, the creature falls flat on its face.

I killed one!

I duck behind the tree and frantically nock my third arrow. I know I have their attention now.

"If you leave," I shout from behind my tree, "I'll spare your lives. You have three seconds before I send you all to hell."

I peek around the tree trunk, hoping to see the feeder's flea. Four of the feeders slowly step back, but not the woman. She advances like a shadow, black linen billowing around her legs.

"One!" I count.

She moves closer. Walking right over Javier.

"Two!"

She stops, bringing her arm parallel to the ground.

"Three!" I aim and release.

Twang.

Ka-Crack!

As I release the arrow, a brilliant blast of lightning surges from the feeder's hand. Like a cannonball, it strikes the tree I'm sheltered behind. A wave of hot air rolls over me, vibrating my ribcage. As soon as the flash dissipates, the tree begins to tip, nothing but embers to support it.

Crash!

I scramble behind the next tree and fumble for an arrow. As soon as the arrow is nocked, I peer from behind my new defense. The female feeder meets my gaze. As soon as she knows I can see her, the feeder pulls back her hood, revealing a hairless head and dark leathery skin. Her teeth are like needles, black pillars of space between each tooth. Seeing my disgust, she smiles.

She doesn't fear me. I draw back the string and release.

Twang!

The feeder lifts her foot the instant before my arrow passes underneath and into the soil behind her. As I reload, she bends down and picks it up.

"Adamic arrows indeed. I haven't seen these since the Roman Empire. What a pleasant surprise." Her voice is silky smooth, the exact opposite of her skin. "It's a pity you're only a novice, I haven't had a real hunt in years."

This time, I adjust for distance, aiming the arrowhead just above her head. I pull the string until I feel the arrowhead graze my bow hand. Then, I release.

Twang!

The arrow whizzes directly at her chest. In a blur of movement, she snatches the arrow out of the air. Now, she holds an arrow in each hand.

As I reload, a few of the laborers are beginning to break free of the earth. Jorge yanks his boots free, and scrambles to his brother, clawing at the soil with bloody, battered fingers.

Just a little longer.

Two others take off towards the treeline. For a second, I think they're about to escape, but the woman won't have it. She holds the arrows like a dart, and lobs them at the laborers.

Shlink. Shlink.

They both tumble in the leaves, arrows protruding from their backs.

No! I want to scream, but I need to stay focused. *You can't save them all, Rose.*

The tallest feeder turns to the woman feeder. "This is a waste of time, Cassia. I came to feed!"

Cassia! I've never imagined feeders having names. A name implies an identity... relationships and friends. In my head, they were little more than animals—solitary, heartless killers.

"Then feed," Cassia sneers. "I don't need your help."

I need to keep them busy, but now that they know my location, I have to be more cautious.

Shield!

A bubble of pure force ripples around me. Fully protected, I lean from behind the tree, ready to release another arrow. The woman feeder is waiting, and at the first sight of my shoulder, she launches a fist-sized stone. Exactly as designed, it collides with my shield, deflecting into the forest.

In an awful attempt to remain unpredictable, I aim at the tallest feeder on the left side of the clearing—the one most eager to feed.

Twang!

My arrow looks accurate at first, but accuracy isn't enough, the feeder twists to the side at the last moment, the arrow only grazing his hip before it disappears into the brush.

Meanwhile, another laborer bolts for the treeline and disappears into the trees. With Jorge's help, Javier finally gets his feet free, leaving his shoes behind in the soil. Lopsided socks flash above the forest floor as they sprint into the trees together.

"Go south!" I scream. "Run!"

The tallest feeder gives chase, and a second feeder follows suit. I release a quick shot in their direction, but it whizzes above their heads.

I'm sorry! Deep down, I know they'll die. *I'm so sorry.*

"Go then," The woman feeder, Cassia, spits in their direction. "I'll enjoy the girl myself."

Only two feeders remain. Cassia turns to the other. "It's just you and me, Caesar."

The feeder nods. "I'm with you, mom."

Mom?

Before I can give it much thought, Cassia raises her hands and the surface soil erupts into the air, forming a blinding cloud of dust.

If I can't see them, I can't shoot them.

Wind!

I command the air behind me, creating a gust of wind moving through the clearing. It displaces the dust, but not as fast as I'd like. My visibility increases at a snail's pace. 10 feet. 20 feet.

I see a blur of motion to my right, but it retreats into the dust. Then, I hear the trees snapping.

The air ripples like a tidal wave, rolling through the trees, snapping them like twigs. They fall like dominos, inevitably closer. Before I have time to think, a ten thousand pound tree trunk is barreling right for me.

Shield!

I dive into the clearing, as the trees smash down behind me. I hear half of my arrows clattering out from my quiver, but I can't risk picking them up. I clutch my bow and scramble to my feet as lightning erupts around me.

KA- CRACK.

The bolt is short-lived but potent. It takes all of my willpower to divert it into the ground. Leaves crackle and burst into flames as the lightning passes through them and into the earth. From the corner of my eye, I see an older man convulsing, his feet buried just a few feet away. When the lightning recedes, his limbs go slack... dead.

I'm sorry! Another tally to the list I couldn't save.

I don't have time to feel remorse. I have my own survival on the line.

Rise!

I command the soil in front of me, forming a defensive slab of clay. I reform my shield as I feel for an arrow. I've barely nocked it when I hear the hiss of flames behind me.

My shield reflects the heat, but it's unsustainable. I can feel the strain tearing at my mind. My hands are going numb. Before the flames consume me, I do the only thing I can think of. I aim into the flames and let my arrow fly.

Thunk.

The flames instantly dissipate, revealing a gasping feeder. His hands drift to the arrow in his chest and a moment later, his eyes roll to the back of his head.

"Noooo!" Cassia wails, the heart-wrenching cry of a loving mother. She's on the other side of my earthy slab, but that doesn't stop her. In the blink of an eye, I'm drifting into the air.

Gravity dominion!

My first instinct is to resist. I command gravity to resume, but her grip on nature is unshakable. The longer I resist, the weaker I become. My soul is being slowly worn down.

I'm an emaciated prisoner, banging against her iron bars.

"You're going to die for that." She froths at the mouth. "He was my everything! And you killed him!"

As she stalks closer, I reach for my arrows, but my hands swipe through empty air. My arrows have already drifted from my quiver and out of reach. I crane my neck just in time to find them floating behind me. A second later, the shafts incinerate.

No!

My last hope is nothing more than a few embers and melted metal drifting in the wind. *I can't give up.*

Energy wave!

The air ripples, but my soul is already strained. The attack is nothing more than a slap against her chest.

I'm going to die!

I look around, hoping to see grandpa emerging from the tree, but there's no one. Not only will I die, but every one of these laborers will be devoured soon after.

C'mon, Rose. You can't give—

Gravity returns with a vengeance, slamming me into the soil. My vision swims, and a hand closes down on my hair.

"You took everything from me, so now, I'm going to take everything from you. I'll consume you slowly, and then you'll be a part of me, suffering my son's loss until the end of time."

The worst part is, I believe her. No one is coming to save me, not grandpa, not Titan with his resurrection spell. No one. This is the end.

As the feeder bites down, I think of Antai. I think of him lying dead on the palace marble floor. I think of the spell that saved my life, the one that nearly killed my assassin.

Her teeth dig deeper into my neck. I can feel my soul dissolving, getting washed away in an ever-rising tide of darkness. It's now or never.

Please don't kill me! Please don't let me burn!

I use the last of my sanity to scream two simple words.

"Havaknah Ra!"

Chapter 23

Matt

I spin my Adamic blade in my hand. It's not my actual Adamic blade—not the one from my parents—but it's better than nothing.

I've enjoyed being out of the city. It's given me time to think about the last month: killing Quill, kissing Kendra, my sister's escape, my mother's certain demise.

When it becomes too much, I focus on the laborers. Despite the horrible hand they've been dealt, they chant as they chop.

> *Man was born to work*
> Chop.
> *The holy never shirk*
> Chop.
> *But wicked men*
> *Take more than ten*
> *And trap us in the cirque.*
> Chop.

Yet, God, he sees us pray
Chop.
Their sinful tithe we pay
Chop.
Our Lord will know
And home we'll go
At the end of the wretched day.
Chop.

They repeat the song, each verse more catchy than the last, until I find myself humming along. The lyrics are laced with hope while the situation is undeniably bleak.

As terrible as it is for the laborers, I'm almost sad it's ending. The next task will no doubt be even more deadly. For all I know, they'll have us face the Holy One himself.

I'm still daydreaming when I hear the footsteps in the distance. It's not one or two, but a stampede. Bodies come flying through the trees, hundreds of them, sprinting at us full-speed.

Feeders! I fear the worst, but it doesn't add up. They're coming from the north, from Rose's territory.

As they get closer, I can make out their clothes. Sweat-stained shirts and tattered jeans. *Laborers!* But I don't feel much safer. *They're running from something.*

I race to meet them, hoping to see Rose among their ranks. A guard greets me instead, through staggering gasps.

"Lieutenant… There are feeders… with Adamic armor. They attacked the northern group… we ran south to get away…"

"Where's the princess?" I demand.

"She went north to help… She told us to find you."

I rack my brain. If any of my men die, I lose The Surviving. But if Rose dies, I'll never forgive myself.

I make up my mind, hoping there's no ambush at Cavernum's entrance.

"Keizer, Kork. Take everyone and get them inside the sanctuary. Alert the king immediately."

"What about you?" Keizer worries.

"I'm going to help. Just get them there. I trust you to keep them safe."

Keizer nods and begins shouting orders. As the crowd moves west toward the sanctuary, I run due north, my Adamic dagger swinging in my arm.

The longer I run, the more I worry I'm heading in the wrong direction. I should be in Ekan's territory by now. Finally, I spot movement on a hill to my left. Several laborers are sprinting down the hill at breakneck speed. One stumbles, rolls twice, and manages to regain his footing.

"Matt!"

I can't believe my eyes. At the back of the pack, Jorge and Javier race toward me. Two feeders follow 50 feet behind. What seems like a safe lead is quickly disappearing. In a matter of moments, they'll be feeder food.

No!

I pump my arms until I can't go any faster, my muscles amplified by dominion. I'm almost there, but the feeders are faster. One extends his hand, and the air ripples. Jorge and Javier both go down, sliding to a stop in the leaves. The other feeder holds out his hand, and flames erupt.

Shield!

A wall of flames crashes against my energy shield, splashing ten feet in the air. I struggle to maintain the force field as Jorge and Javier scramble to get behind me.

Once the flames dissipate, I get a better look at the feeders. One is a tall, hairless creature. Despite his armor, he's bleeding somewhere on his right side. I can see the blood dripping onto his feet. The other has a scraggly black beard, dripping with the blood of a recent meal.

Both are cloaked, and both are ugly.

Think!

I have to act fast if I want to survive. Both are armored with Adamic symbols, and both have freshly fed. Dominion will only save me for so long. As much as I hate it, my dagger is my only hope.

Or is it?

"Hello, boys." I stuff my voice with maximum confidence. "Why don't we start with introductions? Most people know me as the archangel."

Their eyes widen, only to squeeze back to slivers. "The archangel is a guard?" Bloodbeard laughs. "You expect me to believe that?"

Hairless Henry steps forward. "You're just a boy."

"Stick around, and I'll prove it. Which one of you wants to go first?"

They look at each other, and smile. "You know," Bloodbeard hisses. "The archangel would be quite a prize. The Holy One would reward us well."

They stalk closer. Energy crackling on their fingertips.

Shoot.

Time for plan B.

"Fine," I say holding up my hands. "You win. I surrender." I dissolve my shield. "Here, catch!"

I toss my Adamic blade peacefully to Bloodbeard, and then I throw my soul at him. He catches the hilt a moment before I ram my soul into his body.

Memories flash before my eyes. I'm in a clearing with four other feeders. Together, we liquify the earth, trapping the prey up to their knees. I'm going through them, feeding one at a time. The blood is salty, and the sensation is ecstasy. The dominion of a dozen lives is thrashing just beneath my skin. Everything is as it should be.

Then, another memory. A girl. She's shooting Adamic arrows as I take cover behind a tree stump. I only catch glimpses of her as she leans around the tree.

Rose!

Her name reminds me who I am. I open my eyes just in time, taking control of Bloodbeard's body. The other feeder dives at my abandoned body, but I'm faster. I lunge, driving the blade into his spine. He thrashes for a moment, but I hold the blade steady until he falls still in the undergrowth. Finally, I stand.

Jorge and Javier stare at me, perfectly petrified. Their jaws hang dental-office wide.

"I'm sorry you guys had to see this," I mutter, my voice strangely sinister.

Now comes the part I dread. I press the Adamic blade to my chest, feeling Bloodbeard writhing within me. He knows what I'm planning, but he's helpless to stop it.

"Ahhh," I scream as I plunge the knife into his heart, as much from pain as from anticipation.

I don't have to push hard. The knife is made for this, slicing effortlessly into his heart. My body—his body—shudders, and the walls of his mind collapse like a jungle temple. Just when I think I'll die along with him, I'm ejected back into my own body, dragged back by the tether that connects me.

"Ptugh!" I take a gasp and fall back, disoriented by the sudden change in scenery.

"What the hell just happened?" Jorge breathes.

"Run! Find Diego!" I command. "He'll explain everything. I have to help Rose."

"But—"

I take off before they can ask any more questions. I know the way now, the memory imprinted from possessing Bloodbeard.

I race through the trees, praying she's still alive. My breath is ragged, but I press on, pushing my lungs to their limit. I'm not far now. The clearing is just over this incline.

WHOOSH!

The horizon turns red with flame, a 50-foot fireball expanding into the sky. I turn away and dive to my knees as the blast engulfs me, cinders and smoke tearing at my uniform. Then, the air rushes back, filling the void created by the blast.

I'm alive!

Where I'm standing, the trees are intact and the foliage untouched. Whatever just happened, it didn't reach me. However, when I look up, trepidation takes control.

Rose!

Not ten feet in front of me is the beginning of the kill zone. What used to be a thriving forest, looks like the bottom of a fire pit. The trees are corpses, the charred remains of a failed cremation. The rocks are charred, and the air tastes of soot.

I stumble, half in a daze, through the smoking forest. The heat emanates from the earth, expelling what it just absorbed.

Then, I see the clearing.

Oh my...

The scene before me is straight out of hell. Charred bodies, still buried up to their knees are scattered through the clearing. I stumble past them, trying not to look at them directly. Even from my peripherals, the images are scarring. I step over a hole where someone must've escaped and step deeper into the clearing.

Impossible!

Rose is lying in what appears to be the epicenter of the blast, her skin and clothes entirely untouched. Like the eye of a hurricane, the earth directly beneath her is also unscathed, a collage of orange leaves cradling her body.

I study her, expecting the worst. Her chest, ignorant to the massacre around it, lazily rises and falls. In fact, she looks flawless. Her only wound is a bite mark on her neck. It's bleeding, but not enough to be life-threatening.

Strangest of all is the body. Next to Rose is a scorched carcass, it's arm threateningly outreached. It's blackened fingers tangle in Rose's hair.

Without touching the body, I untangle Rose's hair from the hand. Then, I lift her into my arms. I use a method Kendra taught me to help the wound clot. Once I'm sure she won't bleed out, I hurry toward the sanctuary.

Whatever happened here, whatever hell was unleashed, I don't want Rose to ever see it.

We wait outside the High Council Room, crowded on the small landing. Only this time, there's a little more room. There are only 6 of us. Ekan obviously isn't here, and neither is Rose. When I last checked the healing loft, the healers said she had already left.

I hope she's alright.

I'm still thinking about her when Diego looks up at me. He shuffles over to me until we're shoulder to shoulder. He's still looking at the floor, but I know he's talking to me.

"Hey, dude. I uh… I wanted to say thank you. My brothers told me what you did."

"Don't worry about it," I say. "I know you would've done the same."

"Well, It's a big deal to me, okay. I don't know what I'd do if I lost more family. So, thank you. I won't forget this."

"Of course."

Diego lingers as if he's about to say more, then he nods and shuffles along. He moves to one of the windows and looks out over the sanctuary.

Rose still hasn't arrived when the council doors swing open a minute later. We know the drill now, marching in and lining up in front of the map.

"Welcome!" The king slouches on his throne, deep bags beneath his eyes. "General Zane will debrief you on your previous assignment."

Zane stands, dressed in a striped flannel and faded blue jeans. "Hey everyone, quite a bit has happened since we last met. As you can see, Ekan is not with us today. He gave his life in defense of his peers."

Katu sniffles. His face is composed, but the signs of mourning are obvious. His eyes are inflamed, and a damp riverbed of darkened skin marks the trail of past tears.

"Five armored feeders attacked his group," Zane explains. "Most of the laborers escaped, but the feeders managed to kill 26 of them. The princess went to assist, as did Lieutenant MacArthur, and fortunately, they made it out with their lives. As you can see, the princess isn't here today. She was wounded by one of the feeders and is still in recovery."

He looks around the room, his scraggly face unreadable. "Because Ekan was the only one to lose any of his workforce, no one else will be eliminated from The Surviving."

We're still in this. While Rose and I failed to save those 26 souls, they weren't technically our responsibility. Still, it doesn't feel like a victory.

"Seeing that tomorrow is Fall Ball and the kickoff of the Fall Festival, we won't be issuing another challenge at the moment. Enjoy the festivities."

Zane looks to the king, who shakily climbs to his feet. "Meeting adjourned."

As I shuffle past the throne, the king clasps my arm with his knuckle hands. "Thank you, Matt," he whispers in my ear, "for what you've done in defense of my granddaughter. I am in your debt."

"Of course."

The king pats me on the back. "Now go, before the others grow wary."

I exit last, following Diego down the spiraling staircase. I'm eager for my bed, and not just because I'm exhausted.

Tonight, I'm going to dream of Kendra.

I'm nervous.

This is the first time I've infiltrated Kendra's dream. She invited me, of course, but it's still nerve-wracking.

I soul-walk through the void, sensing Kendra's bed beneath me. I take one metaphysical breath and urge my soul into her mind. At first, all I see is darkness, but slowly a scene appears.

Kendra is standing in the healing loft, her girly white healer's skirt as tantalizing as ever. Her hair is flawlessly curled, and her lips glisten with a gloss of some kind.

"You made it!" she gasps, leaping into my arms.

I spin her around twice, dream-world adding to my confidence. "I have something for you." I reach behind my back, imagining a bouquet of red roses. When I feel the thorny stems materialize in my hand, I extend them to Kendra. "These are for you."

"What!" She snatches them from my hand and inspects them. "How do you do that? Is it really that easy?"

"Pretty much." I alternate hands, snatching bouquets from behind my back. I hand each to Kendra, piling them into her open arms. "For you... for you... for you..."

"Matt, too much," she laughs. "Matt!"

I stop when the roses reach her chin. "Now for the tulips..."

"No!" Kendra drops the roses onto the floor. "No more flowers. I only want flowers if you pick them yourself."

"Alright." I imagine a field of tulips like the one at the city fair. Once the image is crisp, I imagine us at the center. Colors swirl around me, and I feel my shoes sinking into the soft soil.

"What the..." Kendra's eyes widen as I bend down and pluck the nearest tulip and hand it to her. "How did you do that? Teach me how," She waves her hands excitedly. "I want to do it too."

"You just have to command it. It's kind of like dominion but with a little more imagination. Picture it from memory, and then make it appear. Let your subconscious do most of the work."

"Hmmm." Her lips compress, lifting in one corner. Then, she closes her eyes.

Woof!

A small bushy-haired dog materializes, wagging its tail in a frenzy. Its hair is straight and long, as if a mop and a duster had a baby. Kendra drops to her knees as the dog pounces on her, licking her fingers like mad.

"Kitty! Who's a good girl! Yes, you're a good girl!" She ruffles its fur as it darts circles around her.

"Kitty?"

Kendra grins, well aware of the irony. "Yeah, when I was ten, I wanted a cat. For my birthday, my parents got me a dog. I named her Kitty as an act of rebellion."

"Is she still around?"

"No. She died two years ago." She turns back to the dog, her sad voice instantly rejuvenated. "But now she's back, aren't you Kitty!"

Eventually, Kitty catches sight of me through her furry bangs. She barks several times before jumping against my shins, pawing at my pants. "Hey there, Kitty." I crouch down to pet her. "I'm surprised you can even see me with all that fur in your face." As soon as my hands are within range, she licks my fingers incessantly. I don't resist. Dog saliva isn't my favorite, but it's better than Kendra's wrath.

"Awww, she likes you." Kendra scoops her up and holds her like a baby. "I'm sorry, Kitty, but we have to go now. Matt planned a fun date for me." She sets the dog down, only for it to quickly disappear.

"Alright, I'll be your beyond tour guide on this date. Name your destination and your tour will begin."

Kendra scrunches her face. "What is it you called Hallow's Eve the other day?"

"Halloween?" I ask.

"Yes! Halloween. Show me what Halloween is like in the beyond."

"Hmmm, it's kind of dark and twisted, to be honest. To celebrate, people dress as monsters and creatures and try to scare each other. They decorate their houses with skeletons and fake blood. Is that what you want to see?"

"I want pure, uncensored Halloween," Kendra says.

"Alright. Just know that everything you're about to see is fake, okay?"

I take Kendra's hand, imagining our destination. I let my memory take control, building the environment from my subconscious. We're in a dirt parking lot at the edge of the forest. The headlights provide the only light.

"Where are we?" Kendra says, spinning in a circle.

"This is the haunted hayride. The beyond can be a bit overwhelming, so I figured this should be a good transition date."

"What's a haunted hayride?"

"Basically, we get pulled in a wagon through the forest, and people try to scare us," I explain.

"Hmmm," Kendra says. "Sounds… interesting."

I guide us to a semicircle of hay bales where people wait for their ride. There are a few highschoolers waiting and a family of four. I wouldn't normally do this under normal circumstances, but this is a dream after all.

"Hey guys, we're on our first date. Do you mind if we go next?"

The couple shakes their heads. "Not at all."

"Only if you kiss her!" one of the teenagers shouts. He looks to his friends, most of which snicker.

"Grab her butt!" another laughs.

Another friend, the only girl in the group, frowns. "Stop it, guys. That's literally like sexual harassment. Just let them go."

"Your mom's like sexual harassment," the first boy repeats. Everyone laughs.

They're still cracking jokes when two horses pull up to the hay bales, a small carriage in tow. To be honest, it's not much of a carriage, more like a trailer piled with a few hay bales. We climb on and sit facing forward.

"Geez, I know they're not real, but is that really how kids act in the beyond?"

"Not all of them obviously, but yeah. That wasn't unusual."

"Were you like that?" Kendra asks accusingly.

"Not quite. I was more on the nerdy spectrum." I admit.

The further we move from the parking lot, the darker it gets. The moon is concealed behind clouds, and the forest is pitch black.

"So... what are we looking f—" Suddenly, she grabs my arm. "Oh my God!"

Up ahead, a human-shaped silhouette is hanging from a tree. The closer we get, more and more bodies appear in the trees, each hanging by the neck.

"They're just dummies," I whisper. "They're fake!"

Kendra relaxes, her hand hovering over her racing heart. "Demons! That scared me. They call this fun?"

"In the beyond, death is something abstract. These kinds of horrors only feel imaginary to them." *They used to feel that way to me too.*

"So, how does this whole dream thing work? Are you making it up as we go?"

"No, I only picked the scenario. The rest is happening on its own. I assume it's drawing from my subconscious memory. I went on this hayride a few years ago, and it was exactly like this."

"So you know what's going to happen?"

"I think so."

Suddenly, the carriage stops. Two men, ski masks covering their faces, stand in the center of the road. Each one holds a shotgun in hand.

"Everyone out of the carriage, and don't even think about running."

Kendra squeezes my hand with all her might. She looks at me, eyebrows raised, as if to say *there's no way this is staged.*

"It's all fake," I whisper.

"No!" She shakes her head. "Seriously?"

"Just play along," I laugh.

We hold each other's hand as the two men march us into the woods. Every few feet, Kendra looks to me for reassurance. I squeeze her hand each time.

After a minute or two, we reach a new trail with another carriage waiting.

The two men stop. "Continue at your own peril. Vampires hunt these woods. We go no further."

"What are vampires?" Kendra asks.

"Bloodsucking monsters."

"So… feeders?" She looks concerned.

"Imagine if a feeder joined the royal theatre. That's basically a vampire. We'll be fine."

Once we climb onto the second carriage, the shotgun-toting men disappear back into the trees. The carriage driver shakes the reins, and we bumble down the road.

We don't go far before I see movement in the trees. A few feet off the road, something is following us. Whatever it is, it's dressed in all black.

"Did you see that?" Kendra is facing the opposite side of the road. She squeezes my hand, only this time, she's smiling. "They really thought this through, didn't they?"

Suddenly, the carriage slows, preparing for the next scare. On each side of the carriage, a figure emerges from the forest. They're each wrapped in a black cloak, half running, half crawling toward the trailer.

Kendra squeezes my hand as the actors tiptoe around her, hissing dramatically and feigning as though they're about to grab her.

I know the actors aren't supposed to touch us, but sometimes they grow bold. One of the men puts his hands on Kendra's shoulders and acts as though he's about to bite her in the neck. At that same moment, I get a glimpse of his face. He has a bushy black beard, with fake blood dripping from his lips.

Bloodbeard!

In that instant, everything transforms. The carriage vanishes. The actors vanish. Even Kendra vanishes. When I open my eyes, my heart goes into free fall.

NO!

I'm back in the field, trapped inside Bloodbeard's body. All around me are the laborers, planted up to their knees in the soil. They fight for their lives, but I know they can't escape me.

I can feel it. My body vibrates with the souls I've consumed. I can feel the urge. It promises more power... more pleasure. I kneel down next to one of the laborers, smiling as he contorts his body away from me. Then, I grab his head, pinning his skull against the ground. Without another thought, I bite down.

"Matt!"

I hear her voice, but I want to keep feeding. I'm absorbing the soul now, and my mind is swelling with new capacities. It's euphoric.

"MATT!"

Kendra!

The dream dissolves, transporting us back to the healing loft. For a moment, she stares at me, pure panic printed on her face.

She's terrified. And I can't blame her. What I just did, even in a dream, is bone-chilling. It's murderous.

"I'm sorry. This was a mistake." I want to explain, but I can't think with her looking at me like that. Just like I did at dinner, my mind grows cluttered and I can't think.

"I-I should just go." I'm about to ditch the dream when she grabs my arm.

"Stop. You can trust me, Matt. I know that wasn't you."

I regain my composure as she guides me to one of the patient cots. We both sit.

"I... sometimes I..."

"It's fine," Kendra says, squeezing my hand. "Take your time."

I nod, taking another deep breath and holding it. "You might understand this because you're a healer. When someone gives you access to their mind, you can accumulate some of their memories, right?"

"Mmhhmm," Kendra agrees.

"Well, when I possess people, I don't need permission, so their entire mind is instantly accessible. Even if I don't want to, I usually pick up memories along the way. Sometimes a lot of them. During the Lumber Haul, I possessed a feeder. He had just fed on several laborers. That was the memory you just saw. The memories are so vivid, sometimes it's hard to remember they aren't my own. It probably sounds psycho, but I feel like I've fed before. I know what it's like. When I go to bed, I have nightmares about it. And it doesn't stop."

I feel the muscles in my throat begin to cramp, and tears saturate my eyes. I stop talking to let it all pass.

My eyes are on the floor, but I can see Kendra watching me out of the corner of my eye. To my surprise, she scoots closer.

"Maybe I can help. Share the memories with me. Maybe we can stretch it between two people. Two minds versus one memory."

"No," I insist. "I don't want you to have to carry this."

"And I don't want you to carry it," she argues. "Not alone, anyway. Please, Matt. I want to."

Before I can argue, she takes my hand and urges her soul towards mine.

I want to resist. I want to protect her pure, precious mind, but I need relief. I can't do this alone.

I let my mind fall into hers, taking in a deep breath of her benevolence. Her desires, her memories. They're all filled with goodness. We're two paints, black and white, slowly turning grey.

"Ugh... Ahh!" She gasps as the parasitic memories infest her mind. For a moment, I fear I've done her harm, but her soul grows still.

When I open my eyes, I'm laying on her lap, my arms coiled tightly around her waist.

"That wasn't so bad," she laughs as a bead of sweat drips down her forehead.

"You okay?" I ask.

"I'm fine," she says. "What about you?"

"Much better." *Much much better.* "Thank you, Kendra. I... I don't know what I'd do without you."

Kendra smiles. "Probably go mad, feeding on the entire sanctuary."

"That's not funny," I say. "It could happen."

346

Kendra scolds me with her eyes. "No, it couldn't. When you let me in, all I saw was goodness, Matt. You've got nothing to worry about."

"Thanks, Kendra. I needed this." I look around, sensing the end of our date. "So, same time tomorrow? This time, I'll let you set the scene."

Kendra shakes her head. "Tomorrow is Hallow's Eve."

"And?"

Kendra tilts her head. "You know nothing about Hallow's Eve, do you?"

"I know it's the eve of hallow, whatever that is."

Kendra shakes her head. "Oh, we have to fix this right now. Hallow's Eve is the greatest night of the year. Every girl's wildest dream takes place on Hallow's eve."

"What's it celebrating?" I ask.

"Alright, where do I begin?" She beams, making her look that much more beautiful. "Hallow's Eve is a celebration of blessings and gratitude. We celebrate the creation and the blessings of this year's harvest."

"So it's like Thanksgiving?" I muse.

"It's more than that," Kendra gushes. "It's centuries' worth of tradition. The holiday is ancient. It's the night when the veil is thinnest between the physical world and the spiritual world."

"The thinnest how?"

She shrugs. "We don't understand how the veil works, only that it's weakest on Hallow's Eve. That is the only night of the year that spirits are known to visit."

"Wait… you're serious."

"The veil isn't gone, it's only weakened. The spirits have no power on earth, but they can enter our dreams. People say they have the most terrible nightmares on Hallow's Eve. People say the dreams are more vivid. Sort of like this dream right now."

"So… does that mean people can see their loved ones too?"

"No, heaven is a paradise," Kendra explains. "No soul would willingly leave heaven. It's only the wicked that return, hoping to flee eternal judgment. The spirits are evil… every one of them. That's why, every Hallow's Eve, no one sleeps. It's the only night of the year that we don't have a curfew. Everyone stays up until dawn."

"Wow. That's gotta be some night."

Kendra nods. "You'll see tomorrow."

"So, in two days then?" I offer. "You choose the dream?"

Kendra's lips compress. "Actually, I wanted to talk to you about something first."

The way she says it, I know it's not good news. "Ummm, okay, what is it?"

She spins her hair around her finger. "Matt, I don't know how to say this. I don't want you to take it the wrong way… it's just that… I really like you, Matt, but I also know you have feelings for the princess."

"Oh." Of all the things in my head, I was hoping that had stayed private. "Just to be clear, nothing ever happened between us. We're just friends."

Kendra nods. "You don't have to pretend, Matt. I'm not upset. I know you can't simply make your feelings go away. I just… I don't want us to get serious while she's still on your mind, you know? Say the commander doesn't wake up, and Rose decides she's into you. I don't want you wishing we never happened."

"So… what are you saying?" I ask.

Kendra takes a deep breath, as if she's going to regret what she's about to say. "I'm saying… if you need to explore your feelings with Rose, I understand. I don't want to win you by default. I don't want to be your second choice. I want to be with you because there's no one else you want. So, if you need to go find closure with her, I won't hold it against you."

"What? You want me to test things out with her?"

"No." Kendra drags her palms down her face. "I don't know. I want you to be sure about us. If you think you need to test things out to do that, then so be it. Do whatever you need to do to figure out your feelings. And until then, maybe we shouldn't be doing this dream thing. I feel really close to you, and I don't want to get hurt."

I know this is my chance to reassure her. This is my chance to say I only have eyes for her, but I can't bring myself to say the words. The truth is, I am confused. Every day, I secretly hope I see Rose in the hallways. I still care. I still have feelings.

"Okay," I say. "I'll, uh… keep that in mind."

"Okay," Kendra says, clearly disappointed. She twirls her ankle. "I'll see you tomorrow, I guess. We might be on a dream date break, but you still promised me at least one dance."

"Of course. I haven't forgotten."

"Okay. Goodnight, Matt."

"Goodnight, Kendra. And thank you for everything you did for me tonight. You're too good for me."

She forced a smile, and I can almost hear her thoughts. *Not good enough, apparently.*

Reluctantly, I distance myself from Kendra's soul, and the world around me darkens.

As I'm moving back towards my room, I can't get Rose out of my head. Medically, I know she's fine, but the feeder dream is making me doubt everything. I worry about her.

If Kendra hadn't given me permission, I might not visit, but she told me herself that she wouldn't be mad. The more I think about it, the less I'm able to resist.

I have to see Rose.

I have to know she's alright.

Chapter 24

Rose

The last thing I remember is saying those words.

Havaknah Ra.

I remember the power I felt as they slipped from my tongue. I remember the heat, not painful, but soothing, like being wrapped in a blanket. Like a warm summer's breeze. Like the hug of a loved one.

Then, nothing.

I know I've died. The spell killed me, or maybe the feeder consumed me. Regardless, I don't mind. My death was a peaceful passing.

When I open my eyes, I hope to see Antai smiling at me, welcoming me into the great beyond. I want it more than anything. Instead, Grandpa grins, his wrinkles tripling in size.

"Grandpa?"

Immediately, I try to stand, but Grandpa puts his hand firmly on my shoulder. "Go slow. You've exerted your soul a great deal."

I push with my heels until I'm sitting against my headboard. My thoughts swirl like alphabet soup. "Am I alive?"

Grandpa takes my hand. "You are. You're perfectly fine." He answers with as little information as possible—an interrogatory diet.

"How'd I get here? I was in the woods..."

"Matt. He arrived moments after your spell and carried you all the way back to Cavernum."

Matt! I should've known he would be the one to save me.

"So... my spell worked?"

"Grandpa frowns, his chest swelling as he inhales. "It worked, yes... but not in the way you intended."

"What do you mean?"

Grandpa looks down. "Rose, I know this will hurt you, but you need to know the truth. When you uttered the spell, it affected everything within earshot. Everything was burned... the laborers included."

"No!" I push past grandpa and leap out of bed. "No! I couldn't have. No! It was the feeder. It must've been the feeder."

Grandpa reaches for my arm. "Rose, you must under—"

"I have to see. This is a misunderstanding. Maybe Matt was mistaken." I grab my boots and a coat from my wardrobe.

"Rose!" Grandpa's voice cuts me to the core. "It's nearly midnight. The bodies have all been disposed of. There is nothing left to see."

"No." My eyes dance wildly around the room as my mind flounders for comfort. "No," I whisper as my knees grow weak. I fall into the corner of the wardrobe and the wall, clutching my knees. "I was supposed to save them. I was trying to save them."

"Rose, listen to me." Grandpa's voice is stern, doing nothing to comfort me. "You couldn't have known what the spell would do, and even if you did, it would've changed nothing. The feeders would've taken your life, and then they would've consumed those laborers, possibly Matt as well. You offered them a merciful escape."

"I killed them!" I wail, blinded by my tears. "I'm a murderer."

351

"Rose, please. It was inevitable."

I refuse to believe it. "I could've saved them. I could've done something different." Villains rationalize. I won't make an excuse for what I've done. For now, I want nothing more than to hate myself.

Grandpa doesn't relent. "Rose, you—"

"Get out!" I scream. "Leave me alone!" *Let me suffer what I've done.*

Grandpa hesitates, and for a moment I fear he'll ignore me. Then, he sighs. "So be it. I'll be in my chambers if you wish to talk." He shuffles out of my chambers, locking the door behind him.

As soon as he's gone, I run for my bed and bury my face in a pillow.

"AHHHHH!"

I scream until I taste blood, collapsing in a shivering heap of self-loathing. For the first time in my life, I want to die. Not to be with Antai. Not for any noble reason. Simply because I deserve it. I deserve to suffer whatever fiery end my victims suffered.

My pillow is soaked by the time I hear the maid-door creak open, followed by the pitter-patter of Wendy's footsteps.

For a moment, I'm afraid she'll try to talk to me, but she climbs silently into my bed without a word.

Stroking from my scalp down to the base of my neck, she runs her fingers through my hair. It's soothing... comforting. If my mother were alive, I'd imagine her doing something like this.

Wendy will make a good mother.

I focus on her fingertips, letting them distract me from the chaos in my mind. For a while, it's effective, but eventually, I grow restless. *I don't deserve this.*

I sit up, leaning away from Wendy's hand. "You don't have to do this."

"I know. I want to. You're my friend, and you're hurting."

"I'm not your friend. I'm a murderer. I killed them, Wendy. Hasn't anyone told you? 26 people. 26 lives destroyed. How do I come back from that?"

"By embracing the truth," Wendy says. "You didn't know. That is the truth. The spell killed them, not you. Murder is a choice, and you never tried to hurt anyone."

"My Grandpa warned me not to use it. He said it would be dangerous, but I didn't listen."

"You. Didn't. Know." Wendy persists.

I flip back into my bed, facing away from Wendy. "If I had just thought it through, I could've prevented all of this. I should have seen it coming."

Wendy sighs. "Rose, do you know how many times I've told myself those very words? That I should've seen it coming. I should've been more careful. Knowing what I know now, I could've avoided all of this." She motions at her stomach. "But that's the thing, I couldn't have known. I couldn't have! As terrible as it sounds, sometimes tragedy is the only teacher. You don't hold the blame any more than I do. The feeders made this happen, Rose. You only tried to stop them."

I want to deny it, but another part of me is desperate to believe it's true. *I couldn't have known. It isn't my fault.*

Still, the pain persists. The guilt hurts, and there's nothing I can do to fix it. "How long does it take?" I choke.

"Until what?"

"To feel normal again?"

Wendy looks away. "Our situations are pretty different, so I'll only speak for myself." She clasps her hands in front of her stomach. "My uncle is dead, and I still don't feel the same. I don't think I ever will. Life has a new normal, but that doesn't mean I don't feel happy." She looks over at me and offers a half-smile. "I think that might be true for you too. You'll feel happy again, Rose. You just have to give it time. The sun will rise. It always does."

The sun!

I wrestle my arm out from under me and glance at my wrist. The tattoo is still there.

I think of Velma and our discussion that night in the beyond. When she was at a breaking point, and I like to think I gave her hope... hope that the sun would rise again.

Now, I'm on the fringe of self-destruction. I'm hopeless.

I roll over so that she can see my face. "Wendy, do you think you could tell me your mother's story—the one about the moon?"

Wendy shifts in the bed, subtle surprise sketched on her face. "You know that story?"

"Your sister told it to me once, but it's been a long time."

"Of course. I would love to."

She begins, with Adam and Eve describing their first night on Earth. She details the darkness and the fear they felt, ultimately ending with the symbol of the moon: a reminder that the sun will rise again.

When she finishes, silence ensues—not an awkward silence, but a peaceful one. For the first time all night, my heart rate feels steady. My eyes are fatigued from shedding tears, and I let them slowly close.

The moment I drift off, the nightmares converge.

I'm back in the forest, only this time, it's a wasteland. The earth is scorched and barren. Bodies are littered everywhere, blackened and defaced by the flames. In my heart, I know I caused this.

I'm sorry! I'm so so sorry!

I'm running now, nearly sprinting, trying to escape the God-forsaken scene. I don't make it ten yards before I trip over something heavy.

"Oof!" I hit the ground hard, soot smearing across my side. When I finally climb back to my feet, I look back and gasp.

"Antai!"

He's lying in the ashes, his body blistered and burned. Beneath the seared flesh, his face is nearly unrecognizable.

"Rose," he croaks, somehow still alive. "Please kill me. Please! Kill me!"

"No." I want to hold him, but I'm afraid that touching him will only cause him more pain.

"Please!" he cries. "I want to die. Kill me, Rose! Put me out of my misery!"

"No! I can't!" I choke, tears streaming down my cheeks and into the corner of my mouth. "I can't kill you. You have to live. I can save you."

His eyes are desperate. "I can't, Rose! It's hopeless. If you love me, kill me!"

I'm about to refuse when I sense a presence appear behind me. It's more than just a premonition; it's as though I can feel their emotions. A wave of repugnance wafts over me.

"Rose!"

"Matt?" I turn around, and sure enough, Matt is standing two steps behind me, his face horror-stricken.

"You!" Antai's body trembles as he recognizes Matt. "You said you would kill me! I trusted you! You were supposed to set me free!"

Before I can make sense of anything, Matt takes my hand and the scene transforms.

In the blink of an eye, the sky darkens and the trees fall away. I find myself standing on a small sandy beach, a wide expanse of water stretched out before me.

"No!" I rip my hand away from Matt's. "We have to go back! We have to save him."

Matt looks at me, his glacier blue eyes unnaturally bright in the starlight. "It's a dream, Rose. It's not real. Everything you see is a dream. Antai is in his bed in the palace. I promise you."

With each passing second, my confusion fades. I was just with Wendy. I fell asleep.

I'm actually dreaming!

As my mind jumpstarts my memory, I take a step away from Matt. "But it's true, isn't it? I killed those people! That part wasn't just a dream. That really happened."

"Take my hands," Matt commands. "It'll help, I promise."

I do as he asks. The moment our fingers touch, I feel the anxiety drain away, diffusing into Matt. He grits his teeth and bites down, but he doesn't let go. I can feel his thoughts all around me, becoming so intertwined I can no longer keep them apart.

You did all you could.

You're a hero.

Everything will be alright.

Deep down, I know some of them are lies, but in this very moment, I let myself believe it. I let him draw out the pain.

When I open my eyes, a tear is clinging to his lashes. He turns away and wipes it with his uniform sleeve.

"Better?" he asks.

"Actually... yes. How did you—"

Matt shrugs, a sly smile flickering on his face. "It's your dream. You tell me."

When I can't think of a response, I just smile. "Thank you, Dream Matt. I don't know what I'd do without you." Now that my mental anguish is bearable, I find myself looking around. Behind us is a steep incline, mostly cleared of trees. In front of us, a lake stretches into the distance, separating us from the next mountain range. We're only a few feet away from the water's edge. The stars reflect like glitter floating on the water. The scene is quiet and calming. My mind grows still as my eyes explore the beauty around me.

"What is this place?" I ask.

Matt extends his arms. "Welcome to Green Mountain Reservoir, Colorado. As a kid, my mom and I used to camp here. I would fish while she read. Right over there—" He points to a small stone ring by a picnic table. "—my mom taught me to make a campfire. It was one of my favorite places."

"It's beautiful," I say.

He looks out over the water. "If only you could see it in winter, everything white and spotless. Sometimes, the reservoir would freeze over and we'd go ice skating."

"Ice skating?"

Matt whips around, gaping at me as though I French kissed a feeder. "You don't know about ice-skating? We're going to fix that right now."

"What?"

"Come here!" He takes me by the hand and pulls me toward the shore. "Observe."

I stare in disbelief as the entire lake crackles. A seamless sheet of ice extends over the water. When I turn back to Matt, he's holding two leather boots, each with a menacing steel blade protruding from the sole.

"Demons, what are those?"

"Ice skates," he laughs. "You wear them like shoes to glide across the ice. Watch."

He fastens his skates and steps out onto the ice. I half expect them to slice through the surface and into the water below. Instead, the result is spectacular. He glides, magically frictionless, across the ice. To propel himself, he angles the blade into the ice and kicks off, soaring on the other foot. He skates onto the lake and turns around, rocketing toward the shore. Just when I'm positive he'll barrel me over, he twists his blades to the side, showering my ankles in snow.

"Hey!"

Matt smiles, proud of his little performance. "C'mon, I'll lace you up. Put your feet out." He kneels down at the edge of the ice and guides my feet into the blade boots. As if by magic, they're a perfect fit. After double knotting the laces, he holds out his hand and pulls me onto the ice.

"Whoa!" My feet immediately fly out from under me, but Matt effortlessly bears my weight, keeping me from crashing into the ice.

His arm wraps around my back, holding my ribs just under my armpit. I find myself disappointed when he finally lets go.

"Want some tips?"

"Yes, please."

"Keep your knees bent, and keep your weight over your skates." Matt squats down to demonstrate. "Lean forward. Don't worry about stopping or steering. I'll take care of that."

He pulls me lightly by the hand, and somehow it's enough to move me. I feel unsteady, but his hand makes me feel safe. I know he won't let me fall.

For the next few minutes, we glide around the lake. I'm astonished by the amount of ground we can cover. The longer we skate, the easier it becomes. I can almost feel Matt's mind instructing me, transferring its own muscle memory. Before I know it, I don't even need his support.

"This is amazing. We have to introduce this to Cavernum," I decide. "What if we made an ice pond in the palace? Or maybe we could freeze the fountain."

"I bet we could do it," he muses. "The hard part would be making the skates. A blacksmith would have to do it or something."

I frown. "Yeah… I guess you're right. Shame."

Matt guides me back to the beach where we started. When I step onto the shore, my skates are instantly replaced with my shoes.

"I have one more thing to show you. He leads me up the beach to a cluster of small trees. A rope hammock is tied between two of the trunks."

"This is where I used to sleep," Matt beams. "The bugs ate me alive, but the stars were worth it." He crawls into the nylon cocoon and offers me his hand. "Don't be shy. There's room for two."

"Can it hold us both?"

Matt sneers. "Please, this puppy could hold Bob no problem."

I snort, unable to stop myself. "Bob from Bob's brew?"

Matt grins, pleased I appreciated his humor. "The one and only," he laughs.

I climb inside, gasping as we begin to sway. The trees creak, but we manage to stay suspended. I turn onto my back and settle in, the fabric forcing me shoulder to shoulder with Matt.

"Cozy?" Matt asks.

"Surprisingly." I can feel the bulk of his arm resting against mine. Our hip bones are side by side, and his body heat radiates through his clothes.

Matt looks up to the sky. "Not bad, huh?"

The sky is a glittering patchwork of stars, a never-ending field of silver dewdrops. I begin to think of my last date with Antai, but I don't let myself go there.

"Do you know any constellations?" Matt asks.

I shake my head. "No, teach me."

Matt laughs. "Oh, I don't either. I was hoping you could teach me. I thought maybe Cavernum had their own constellations. You know, that circle of stars right there..." he points to a small ring of stars. "That could be Baby-face Bolo for all I know."

"Could be," I laugh. I want to respond with my own clever constellation, but nothing comes to mind. Then, I notice as a red star moves slowly overhead. "Is that a shooting star?"

Matt laughs. "I wish. But no, that's a plane."

I've read about them, but I never imagined they could fly so high. "It looks like it's in space."

"Yeah, it kinda does. They fly at 30,000 feet or something like that."

"Demons, that's absurd!" I stare in awe as the blinking dot disappears behind a tree. I nestle closer to Matt. Letting myself lie my head on his shoulder. Matt knows so much. He's part of this exciting world of wonders. While Antai is amazing, I already know everything about him. With Matt, there seems to be an endless mystery. There's always something new to uncover, and I'm craving more.

I tilt my head to look at Matt. "What is something you've always wanted to see in the beyond, but you've never had the chance?"

"Oh, gosh. There are so many things. I've never been to the ocean. I've never been to the Grand Canyon. And then there are the northern lights."

"What are those?" I ask.

"They're these crazy lights in the sky, but they only happen way up in the North." His eyes narrow, and I know he's planning something. "I've never seen them in person, but I bet I could give you a little sample."

He looks out over the lake, and I follow his gaze as dazzling bands of neon-green light snake their way through the sky. They ripple and bend, as if being blown by a high altitude breeze.

"How! Is it dominion?"

"I don't really understand it," Matt admits. "Supposedly it's radiation hitting the atmosphere. Something like that."

"It's beautiful," I gasp. I feel like a child, seeing the world for the first time. For the next minute, we watch in silence. Every few seconds, a new color is introduced, vibrant pinks and violets.

When I finally look up at Matt, I see he's already facing me. He has this stricken smile, as if I'm the real show. For all I know, he's been watching the whole time.

Something about his eyes, something about the way he looks at me, makes me feel wanted. It makes me feel like I'm irresistible.

Desire begins to swell within me, and my imagination runs out of control. I want something new and exciting. As crazy as it sounds, I want Matt to kiss me. I want it so bad.

For a second, I fear Matt will shy away. I can sense his inhibitions, but he buries them deep. The next thing I know, he's turning onto his side.

"Is this too much?"

His body is facing me, and his arm gently rests across my stomach, scattering the butterflies that already reside there.

"Not at all." I lift my chin towards him, my lips twitching in anticipation.

"Good," he whispers, his voice silky and deep.

I close my eyes and his lips envelope mine. It's like he knows everything I want. His hand finds the small of my back, and he turns my waist to face him. One of his knees moves between my thighs, and next thing I know, we're chest to chest, limbs tangled together.

His hunger radiates as we kiss, and I'm sure he can sense my desire as well.

It doesn't last long. His kisses grow more deliberate until finally, he pulls away. The hammock doesn't let him move far. I can still feel his chest expanding with every breath.

"I'm sorry... I just. What about Antai?" he asks. "I... thought you loved him."

"I did," I say... "Or I do. I don't know. It's complicated." I turn back to the stars, trying to make sense of myself. "The healers are sure he won't wake up, and I can't keep waiting for the dead to rise. Not when I have you right here."

He looks at me, almost as if he doesn't believe me. "And what if he does wake up? You would choose him, wouldn't you?"

"Probably," I admit. "But that's not going to happen. They removed his feeding tube today. In a matter of days, he'll be gone."

"Oh," Matt looks at me, both concerned and relieved. "I didn't know."

"I'm ready for this, Matt," I insist. "Tonight was the first happy night I've had in forever, at least since the graduation party. And I know it's just a dream, but... I'm happy now. I like you, Matt. I want to keep being happy with you."

"You're sure?" he asks.

"Yes, I'm sure." Then, it dawns on me. "Oh, I see what's going on here. Okay..."

Matt's eyes widen, and he seems genuinely nervous. "What?"

"This is my brain's way of making me figure things out before tomorrow. I was worried about betraying Antai, so my mind made up this little facade. Well, it worked. Are you happy?"

Dream Matt smiles, amused that I figured out his plan. "So you're excited for tomorrow? We're going to have a good time?"

"We better," I say, climbing out of the hammock. "If you don't kiss this good in real life. I'm going to be very disappointed."

"Well, Dream Matt will be disappointed too. Trust me," he teases.

"Now," I look around. "How do I end the dream?"

Matt frowns. "You want to end the dream?"

"Dream Matt is fun, but I want to talk with the real Matt. The sooner the dream ends, the sooner I wake up. For all I know, it could already be morning."

"Alright, I'll let you sleep then," Matt says as he climbs out of the hammock. "Trust me, Real Matt is excited for tomorrow too. He'll see you soon."

He hugs me one last time, warm and firm. Then, he's gone, his presence whisked away in the wind. Ever so slowly, the landscape he created disappears.

The only thing that lingers is the feeling of his lips on mine.

Chapter 25

Matt

I adjust the collar of my coat. It's wool and not the most comfortable, but it wasn't really my choice. Zane picked it out for me.

He insisted I get one of the most expensive suits. The fabric is navy blue with gold trim lining the collar and sleeves. Elegant gold leaflets decorate the breast and shoulders. There aren't any lapels on the jacket. It's more streamline, flaring apart at the waist—almost medieval.

If you want to court the princess, you have to look like a prince. That's what he had told me.

Normally, I'd be on duty right now. Fortunately, only a few royal guards have to work tonight. The rest of the officers get the night off. The only catch is that we must attend the ball armed—a way to make up for the lack of defenses

My amulet creates an ugly bulge in my shirt, so tonight only, I wear it on the outside. I wait at the mouth of the Royal Wing, trying not to make eye contact with the guards. Already, I'm beginning to sweat. Thankfully, my heavy suit coat conceals most of it.

Tip. Tap. Tip. Tap.

I turn to see Rose strutting toward me. The hallway is long and gives me plenty of time to admire. The gown is unlike her others. It's intricate and more elaborate, layers of gold satin and shimmering ruffles. The material hugs her waist, then erupts at the beltline in a mass of fabric, leaving everything to the imagination. As heavy as the dress looks, it appears to hover, precariously balanced on the ends of her shoulders.

I feel awkward with the guards listening, but I say it anyway. "Wow! Rose, you look gorgeous."

"Why thank you, Matt. You look dashing as ever. The navy was the right choice."

I extend the crook of my elbow, and she takes it.

"So," I say, guiding us toward the palace entrance. "Klinton and Ronald will be waiting in the plaza. They said they'll be by the sacrificial fire. I figure you know what that is?"

Rose laughs. "It's huge. You'll see it as soon as we leave the palace."

As we move through the corridor, people are already spilling toward the ballroom. The outfits are phenomenal, and the atmosphere is buzzing with excitement.

"Are children allowed at the ball?"

"They're allowed, but they have to stay on the terrace. You have to be of age to join the dancing."

As we exit the palace gate, I spot it immediately. A roaring bonfire illuminates the plaza. I scan the crowd for Klinton and Ronald, but I don't see them yet.

Instead, I find myself watching the festivities. A puppet show is taking place on the plaza stage, and commoners run in all directions. The sun has nearly set, and the roaring flames burn bright against the dimming horizon. People approach the fire, tossing pumpkins and food into the open furnace.

"Why are they burning food? Aren't people starving?"

"They think it'll bring blessings. Legend has it, whatever you sacrifice on Hallow's Eve, you receive tenfold the next harvest."

"You believe that?"

Rose shrugs. "It gives people hope… something to look forward to. Maybe that alone is blessing enough."

"Hmmm." I let my lips part in a playful smile. "So, if I toss you in, I get ten of you."

"Yeah, ten angry mes." She laughs. "You're better off with one happy one."

We circle the fire once, but still no Klinton. "Looks like we're early," I say.

We stand by the bonfire, but soon I'm sweating once again. I know it's not the case, but I feel like I'm getting sunburned from the blaze.

"Want to take a lap?" Rose suggests.

"Yes, please."

I reach for her hand, relishing the softness of her skin. We walk toward the apartments that border the plaza. Immediately, I'm astounded by the number of laborers, most of them are young—not quite teens. They pace along the plaza edge, stopping at every door. If I'm not mistaken, each of them is holding a small bowl. Some have plates.

"Why so many kids? What are they doing?"

"They're prayer beggars," Rose says. "They offer their prayers to each household in exchange for a prayer cake. It's like a cookie, only not as good. I've always wanted to do it, but as a palace-born, I never had the need."

Rose slows as we approach another group of beggars. They knock on one of the doors and hold out their bowls. The moment the door opens, they chant.

"Bread or treat, fruit or meat, we'll pray for just a bite to eat," the children chant.

"Oh, aren't you all just darling?" an older woman responds. She holds a baking sheet of bite-sized cookies. "My grandson is being divided this coming year. Can you all pray for him?"

The oldest boy nods and bows his head. "Oh, God, bless this nice woman's son, that he will be divided and get the job he wants. Amen."

"Amen," the other children echo.

"Oh, thank you. And happy Hallow's Eve," the woman says. She drops one cookie in each of their bowls and closes the door as they run off to the next house.

"You know," I say, motioning to another house. "We could totally do that."

"No, no, no." Rose shakes her head. "I would be too embarrassed. Dressed like this, they'd think we're mocking them."

"Are you kidding me?" I say. "Imagine the stories that person could tell, saying they gave a prayer cake to the future queen of Cavernum. That would be legendary."

Rose smiles but shakes her head. We loop back toward the bonfire, and this time, I spot Klinton immediately. They're standing a few feet away, watching the dance of the flames. As soon as he sees us, Klinton waves, and Ronald bows.

"How kind of you to grace us with your presence, oh, champions of champions." He looks up and laughs. "I'm just playing. You both look stunning!"

"You really do," Klinton agrees.

"Right back atcha," I say. "I love the orange." Klinton is wearing a plain black suit with an orange pocket hanky and a burnt orange dress shirt underneath. Ronald's clothes are the same colors, but inverted. He wears a black dress shirt, with an orange accented long coat.

"Well, shall we?" Rose asks. "They'll probably be serving the food soon."

"You sure this'll work?" Klinton asks as we approach the palace wall.

"I'm positive," Rose insists. "Follow my lead." Rose extends her arm to Klinton, and Ronald wraps his arm around my shoulder. In our respective pairs, we approach the palace gate.

"Princess," The guard acknowledges.

Rose smiles courtly. "I'm here with my guest, Ronald Wicker."

The guard scribbles something on his parchment and turns to me.

"Lieutenant Matthew MacArthur," I say, "here with my guest, Klinton Enemary."

The guard looks at Klinton for an uncomfortable amount of time. "Hmmmph," He jots our names down before motioning us through.

Once we're out of earshot, Klinton and I switch places.

"Well, that was easy," Klinton says.

Ronald is hardly listening. He's fixated on the Central Tower. "Klinton, I can't believe you grew up here. It explains so much."

"Oh, shush. As if you're not the spoiled one. Let's not forget I'm borrowing your suit."

We enter through the main doors and cross the central corridor, directly into the ballroom. The orchestra is already playing prelude music as hundreds of elites mingle in the open.

Servants, both young and old, meander the crowds, offering drinks and small appetizers.

"Cider?" A servant extends the platter in my direction.

I hesitate.

"It's non-alcoholic," Rose mentions as she takes two and hands me one. "It's pretty good. Try it."

I take a sip, and it's not what I expected. It's hot, more sour than sweet, with a hint of caramel. "Not bad," I admit.

I've barely finished my drink before a man comes up to me. I can't tell if he's a guardsman or a judge. "Princess, Lieutenant, you both look lovely tonight. If there's anything I can do for either of you, let me know."

"Of course. Thank you for your consideration." Rose responds.

We barely take two steps before Commander Noyen meanders past. He stares the entire way, his head turning to follow us. Then, he chuckles to himself. "Looks like we have ourselves a future king."

Rose frowns but says nothing.

"It must be hard always being in the public eye," I say. "Everyone watching you all the time."

"Yeah, it definitely has its drawbacks," Rose agrees. "It usually gets worse the drunker everyone gets."

As we explore the ballroom, I peer around in search of friendly faces. I see Diego by the food, chatting with a performer girl. Not far from him is Kendra. She's wearing a deep red dress, much more simple and sleek than Rose's. Her hair brushes against her bare shoulders and her lipstick is distractingly red. I let myself stare a moment, following her with my eyes. Then, I see her date.

Vyle?

Vyle stands beside her in a ruffled white shirt and bow tie. His blonde hair is slicked black, forming rows of oil-soaked hair. His smug smile only makes his square jaw that much more boxy. With every movement, an amulet swings below his bow tie.

Vyle? Seriously? Of all the people, it had to be him.

"Come, let me show you my favorite game." Rose's voice pulls me back to reality. She takes me by the hand and leads me onto the terrace. It's massive, nearly the size of a football field, and it's covered in carnival games. I see a bean bag toss, and a corn-on-the-cob eating contest. Young children dash in all directions, wrapped up in their tiny dresses and suits.

We walk to the edge of the balcony, where a servant sits next to a wooden barrel. It's filled to the brim with water and two dozen apples float on the surface.

"I used to play this as a kid every year," Rose whispers as we approach.

One teenage girl already leans over the barrel. She opens her mouth wide and begins biting at the apples like a human claw machine. Most bounce off her chin, but eventually, she manages to snag one between her front teeth.

"What's it say?" her friend squeals.

The girl takes the apple out of her mouth, rotating it until she finds the letter carved in the side.

"H!" the girl exclaims.

Her friend covers her mouth and squeals. "That could be Haxton!"

"Or Hevai!" The girl grimaces. They continue naming every H name they can think of as they wander away from the barrel.

The servant grabs a new apple, whittling an H to replace the old one. He tosses it in the barrel. "Princess, come to see what fate has in store?"

"We have," Rose replies. "Can you explain to my date the meaning behind it?"

"Certainly." The man stirs the water with his bare hand, sending the apples spinning. "This tradition dates back to Adam and Eve. When Eve partook of the forbidden fruit, she was thrust into the mortal world. In order to remain with her, Adam did the same. It was this fruit that united them in their mortal journey. Today, we don't have forbidden fruit, but we believe that God can guide us to our soulmates. You must take a bite of an apple. Whichever letter the apple holds will lead you to your true love."

"Sounds fun," I say.

"I'll go first," Rose suggests, approaching the barrel. "Watch and learn." She pulls her hair into a tight wad, holding it in one hand. With the other hand, she grabs onto the rim of the barrel. Lastly, The air ripples around her eyes."

I scowl. "Hey, no dominion. That's cheating."

"It's to protect my makeup," Rose laughs. "Wendy worked hard on this." Her chest swells as she takes a quick breath. Then, she opens her mouth wide and submerges her face in the water.

She doesn't thrash. She moves with purpose, using the buoyant force of the apple to position it in her mouth. Then, she bites down. When she comes up, her lips are stretched so wide, they barely have the elasticity to smile.

"Ta-da," she brags through a mouthful of fruit. She drops the apple in her hand and after turning it twice, she finds the carving. "E," she whispers, her previous excitement replaced with sorrow.

Elsborne! That's what she must be thinking. Then it dawns on me. I've almost forgotten my own birth name.

Ezra.

She turns to me. "Your turn."

I lean over the barrel as the servant quickly whittles another 'E' and tosses it in. I close my eyes and lunge at the nearest apple.

I bite down, getting nothing but a mouthful of water. I come up, open my eyes, and bite at the next.

This time, I keep my eyes open. I bite at one of the apples, but it only dips under the surface. "Dang. This is hard."

"Maybe you just have a small mouth," Rose laughs.

"I do not!" In a flurry of indignation, I push down on an apple. It sinks deeper, so I push my face deeper. Finally, with half my head submerged, I manage to pin it against the side of the barrel where I can finally sink my teeth into it.

My head splashes from the barrel, water pouring from my hair. I spit the apple into my hand. "All that work for a 'B.'"

"Remember." The servant shakes a finger at me. "If you want your love fortune to come true, you must consume the apple as Adam and Eve did."

"We will, thank you." Rose moves toward the terrace railing, making sure I'm behind her. "So, you never told me you and Bob had a thing."

I laugh. "Yeah, I've actually been waiting to break the news. He even named a brew after me. Matt's Brew. It's a ginger beer. You should try it."

Rose takes a look at her own apple. "Don't worry. I never believed the superstition. Every year the letters are different. Besides, I never eat the apples anyway. The whole public barrel thing always grossed me out." She tosses her apple into a trash bin.

"I'm sorry, Bob." I toss my apple in as well.

"Want to go grab some food?" Rose suggests.

"Sounds good to me."

We make our way back into the ballroom, where Rose flags down a servant, who hands us both a small plate of roast pig, and some baked sweet potato.

"Attention, everyone!" Chancellor Gwenevere is swaddled up to her neck in an olive green gown. "I would like to welcome everyone to this year's Fall Ball. Now that the sun has set, we are going to open up the dance floor. Enjoy."

The royal orchestra begins playing a classical piece full of snare, violin, and resonating tuba. The tune isn't fast, but it's actually pretty catchy. In small bursts, couples surge the dance floor, each new pair giving confidence to the next.

Rose's face lights at the melody. "We call this the Zion Waltz. Everyone learns it in primary school. It's my favorite part of the Fall Ball."

She watches longingly as the other participants form two massive circles in the center of the ballroom. The women stand in the inner circle facing out, and the men stand in the outer circle facing in. Kendra and Vyle join in as well.

Ronald stands and holds out his hand. "Let's go, Klinton. It'll be fine."

"I'm good. I feel like it'll be weird."

"It'll only be weird when we're the sexiest ones out there, c'mon! I'll stand in the woman's circle. It'll be fun."

Klinton rolls his head in a circle before taking Ronald's hand. A smile spreads across his face. "Oh… alright." They jog over and fill in a gap in the almost complete circle. "Excuse me, ladies." Ronald towers over the women of the inner circle, but he's not the only man. I spot one or two others.

Rose wistfully watches the circles form. I know she wants to be out there. I let my mind press onto her consciousness.

If only Antai were here…

The thought pains me, and not just from jealousy.

"Let's do it," I say.

Rose shakes her head. "That's sweet, Matt, but don't worry about it. You're an excellent dancer, but the dance is choreographed. It would be impossible without practice."

I bite my lip. "What if I told you we have the Zion's Waltz in the beyond. I'm a little rusty, but I think I've still got it."

Her face lights up, and she looks at me with parted lips. "You're serious? You really know it."

"Let's do it. Unless you don't think you can keep up with me."

Rose is already on her feet, pulling me to a small space next to Klinton and Ronald. We stand facing one another, waiting for the music to start. My heart races.

Ronald keeps looking my way. "I'm about to be very impressed, or very disappointed, Matt."

"You and me both," I nervously laugh.

The music starts, and I expand my mind to the men on either side of me, letting their thoughts seep into my own. If I'm going to pull this off, I need perfect concentration.

I hear a long chord on the violin, and then the rest of the orchestra joins in. The moment they do, the circle comes to life. I need to know every move before they make it.

As the music picks up, their intentions start to pile into my mind.

Step, step, drag the foot, bow.

I manage to do it in sync with the men. I take two exaggerated steps toward Rose, drag my foot in a wide arc, and bow. As I bend at the waist, I leave my hand suspended in the air—an open invitation.

Now it's the women's turn. Rose skips forward curtsies and shuffles back. With the long draw of the violin, she slowly lowers her hand into mine.

Rise, step, turn.

The outer circle contracts as the men straighten and take another exaggerated step toward the women. Rose and I are chest to chest, our fingers interlocked between our collarbones. As I rotate my left shoulder toward her, she pulls her right shoulder away. I follow my mental cues, taking a step back until our arms are fully extended.

Rose shakes her head in disbelief. She's both thrilled and stunned.

I cross my feet as the outer circle rotates to the right, then we shuffle back the other way until we're realigned with our dates.

Arm up. Spin.

I place my right hand on Rose's shoulder and she does the same, mirroring me. The world blurs and we spin. Our hands are the only thing keeping us aligned. After two full rotations, my hands move to her waist, and we spin the other direction.

"You know it!" Rose laughs. "I can't believe you know it."

Hand on her waist, we skip left, gaining speed. The entire circle is spiraling. Faster and faster we go until everything is a blur. The only thing in focus is Rose's smiling face. Her dress billows beautifully behind her, and my amulet sways with every skip.

For the next minute, I'm lost in the dance. I twirl her and pull her close. Then, we break apart, shuffle around, and come back together again.

As the music intensifies, the moves become more elaborate. I take her hand and spin her twice, like winding up a music box. Then, I spin her back the other direction, catching her hip with my hand.

Dip.

Rose steps in, and I place my hand between her shoulder blades. The violin trembles one last time and then suddenly stops. In that instant, I lunge and she arches her back. I hold her there, bearing her weight, the length of her body elongated before me. I'm hunched over her chest, her lips close enough to kiss. My mind races, reverting to last night's dream.

Blood fills my face as I lift Rose back to her feet.

"That was amazing! I can't believe you know Zion's Waltz. What did you think?"

"It was exhilarating. The first time I've done it with anyone like you."

The orchestra begins anew, playing something slow and romantic. Most of the couples have migrated off the dance floor, but a few remain, swaying from side to side.

"Do you want to dance some more?" I ask.

"I'd love to."

I lead her deeper onto the dance floor, finding a quiet place away from anyone I recognize. I rest my hands on her waist, inhaling the subtle scent of lavender. I position my shoes under her dress so that I don't step on it, and we sway back and forth.

She looks up at me, and I find myself hypnotized by her hazel eyes. Her dark eyebrows, and the small ridge between her nose and her upper lip. It's all so delicate. So distracting.

"What?" She asks, brushing her fingers over the corner of her mouth. "Is there something in my teeth?"

"No," I laugh. "No. I was just admiring."

"Oh, really?" She teases me with a smile before tucking her head under my chin. For the first time tonight. Her body relaxes, molding against mine.

"How about we play a game…" I suggest. "Truth or Dare."

Rose lifts her head to look up at me. "Truth or Dare? What's that?"

"No!" I pull away so that Rose can see the exacerbation on my face. "Truth or Dare! It's only the most infamous middle school party game of all time. The game is simple. I ask 'truth or dare?' You choose which one you want—a question or a dare. Then, you have to follow through."

"And what if I don't want to answer it?" Rose asks.

"Then you become the queen of Loser Town, and I become the Truth or Dare master."

"Fine." Rose grins, her nose wrinkling with competitive charisma. "You go first. Truth or dare?"

"Dare!"

Rose bares her teeth, releasing a subtle growling sound.

"You wanted me to say truth?"

Rose nods. "Fine. I dare you to…" she looks around before eyeing Chancellor Bolo's drink. "Freeze Bolo's wine."

"Easy." Still slow dancing, we maneuver our way closer to the tables. Once he's within range, I project my soul on the tiny glass of wine.

Freeze.

The translucent red wine quickly solidified into a misty pink block. Bolo, still oblivious, lifts the glass to his lips. He continues to tilt higher and higher until he finally lowers the glass. "Hey!" He spins around, but we've already averted our eyes, snickering as we sway our way across the dance floor.

"Alright. Truth or dare, Rose."

"Truth."

"Would you rather lose your dominion, or lose all of your teeth... and you can't just regrow them or replace them."

"What? What kind of question is that!"

"An important one," I insist. "No teeth or no dominion?"

"I..." she looks at me defeated. "I guess no dominion. I can't live off of applesauce. Ugh. That would be a nightmare. And smiling... or kissing! No, thank you." Finally, she stops grimacing. "And what about you? What would you choose?"

"Nope nope nope." I shake my head. "That's not how the game works. If you want to ask me, you have to use your turn."

"Fine. Truth or dare?"

"Truth," I grin.

"What... is your favorite part about Cavernum?"

"Hmmm." I think for a moment. "This might sound weird, but it's feeling like I belong. I don't know. My whole life I felt like an outsider. I was adopted. I was different. And when Judy got sick, things got really hard. I felt like I was the only one struggling. But when Zane brought me here, all of a sudden everyone understood. It sounds kinda messed up to say, but I found people with problems as big as mine."

Rose hovers her hazel eyes over mine. "It's always nice to feel understood."

I smile, trying to shake the funeral vibes. "Alright, truth or dare?"

"Truth."

"Hmmm..." I let myself stare into her eyes as we rock back and forth. "This is kinda personal, but what would you ask your parents if you could talk to them tonight?"

Rose bites her tongue as she thinks. "Oh, that's a tough one," she sighs. "I don't know if I have anything I'd want to ask. Mostly, I just want to tell them stuff. I want to show them who I am. You know? I want them to see everything I've done to get where I am. I want them to see what they created—to appreciate me, you know?"

"I do." I know exactly what she means. *I just want to know they're proud of me.*

"Truth or dare?" Rose asks.

"Truth."

"This one is similar, but if you could ask God anything—if you could know anything in the world—what would it be?"

"I would ask… what's up with that Rose girl? Why did you have to make her look so good?"

"Stop it." Rose blushes and looks away. "That doesn't count. Honestly?" She moves a little closer. The fabric of her dress brushes against my jacket as we sway.

"Okay, fine. Hmmm." I think for a second, and then it hits me. "I would ask if the Holy One is right."

Rose furrows her brow, bordering a look of condemnation. "What?"

"That's what I would ask. I know it sounds crazy, but… don't tell me you haven't thought about it. Judy is probably going to die before I see her again. Odds are, the only way I'll see her again is through Adamic. I'm not saying I'd for sure do it, but I'd be curious what God would have to say."

Rose responds, suddenly a little more solemn. "Let me know what he says."

I'm about to open my mouth when Vyle taps me on the shoulder. "Matt, would you mind if I borrow your date for a song?"

I'm thrown off by his manners. "Oh, uhhh." I look at Rose, and she nods. "Yeah, of course."

Vyle extends his hand to Rose, and I interlock fingers with Kendra. Resting my hand on her waist, I begin a gentle sway back and forth.

"First things first," Kendra says "and don't you dare lie to me." She holds my gaze, and I dread whatever question is about to come out of her mouth.

"What…" a playful grin blooms across her face. "letter did you get in the barrel bob?"

I let out a hard breath. "Geez, Kendra! You almost gave me an aneurysm. I got a B."

"B?" Kendra frowns. "Did you eat it?"

"Nope."

"Good. I got a K, as in Kaynes. You should've seen Vyle's face when I threw it in the trash."

I grin. "You know… my surname by birth is Kaimor." I shrug. "Could mean something."

Kendra puckers her lips. "Hmmm, what do you know. I always believed in apple bobbing destiny."

I glance across the dance floor at Rose and Vyle. They look like they're having a civil conversation.

"Vyle treating you well?"

"He's fine," Kendra says. "He's not as bad as you described him, but he's no Kaimor." She grins at my name. "What's your first name… your birth first name."

"Ezra."

"Ezzzra." She stresses the E and lets the Z simmer on her tongue. "Ohh, that's a good one. I like that." She shimmies her shoulders. "Ezzzra Kaimor, slayer of women."

"Stop." I roll my eyes, but she knows I find it funny.

"You're lucky you don't go by Ezra, or every woman in a ten-mile radius would be after you."

"Two can play that game, Kendrrrra!" I roll my R's as dramatically as I can manage. "How many men do you have begging to be healed?" I fake my best dumb jock voice—deep and dopey. "Kendra, I hurt my bicep, I think you need to feel it, I-I mean heal it."

"Okay, fair enough. You've made your point."

Before I can ask her anything else, the slow song comes to a long, drawn-out ending.

"Already?" I turn and find Klinton and Ronald approaching. When they see Kendra they frown.

"That…" Ronald points at Kendra. "is not the princess."

"Date swap," I explain. "Ronald, Klinton, this is Kendra. Kendra, these are my friends Ronald and Klinton."

"Kendra?" Ronald bends his knees and covers his mouth. "Healer Kendra! Oh, it's my lucky day." He shakes her hand enthusiastically. "It's a pleasure to meet you. We've heard great things."

"We really have," Klinton adds.

Rose comes up alongside us. "Matt, I'm going to head to the lady's room. I'll only be a minute."

"Count me in," Kendra says. She glances at Vyle "Be back in a bit."

Side by side, they move toward the exit.

Once they're out of earshot, Vyle looks back and forth between Ronald and Klinton, laughing to himself. "What, you guys aren't going with them?"

Ronald narrows his eyes. "Excuse me?"

"Don't feel bad," Vyle laughs. "I didn't suspect a thing until tonight. Would've never guessed Klinton was gay, just thought he was scrawny."

"Why? You interested?" Ronald asks. "I mean, not that you have a chance with a guy like him, but we're pretty close." Ronald points back and forth between himself and Klinton. "If you'd like, I could put in a good word for you. It'll definitely help your odds."

Vyle narrows his eyes at Ronald's outfit. "Shut up, pumpkin. No one asked you!"

Ronald looks Vyle up and down and then, his jaw drops open. "Oh, pardon me. I could've sworn you were gay. I mean, with that hair… and the way you walked. But don't worry." Ronald slaps him playfully on the shoulder. "It's nothing to be ashamed of."

Vyle leans into him, puffing out his chest. "You better shut your mouth before I break it. Don't act like you're better than me. I know you're both dry-bloods, and now I know why. God cursed you for your… unnatural lust. Maybe if you repent, he'll give you your dominion back."

"Don't talk to me about cursed," Ronald spits. "Remind me again what happened to your brother. Now that's a curse. Something tells me you might be next."

Ronald must have struck a chord. Vyle's face is turning a deep shade of red. I can see the vein building in his forehead. He puffs out his chest, his pecs bouncing Ronald back. "You don't want me as an enemy. I can hurt you. One little thought, and I can—"

"Hey!" I put an arm between them in a pathetic attempt at peace. "Just back off, Vyle. What's the deal? Rose told me you had changed. Was she wrong?"

Vyle snorts like a bull, finally stepping back. "I'll let this one slide, but don't you ever insult my family again. Ever." He turns and starts walking away.

"Asshole." Ronald says it just loud enough to be heard.

"What did you call me?" Vyle spins, nostrils flaring. "If you really have balls, you'll say it to my face. Go on. I could break your arm right now, and I wouldn't even have to lift a finger."

"Oh, yeah," Ronald taunts. "I could break your nose right now, and I could do it with my eyes closed." Ronald closes his eyes. Then, like a cobra strike, he rears back and drives his forehead into Vyle's nose. I don't hear a crack, but the blood immediately starts gushing.

"Aghhh!" Vyle's eyes water as the blood drops into his white shirt. "I'll kill you for that!" Vyle roars. In an instant, everyone is watching.

"Vyle!" General Kaynes hisses from a dozen yards away. "What in God's name is going on?"

"It was an accident," Ronald says innocently, we bonked heads while dancing.

"Vyle, are you alright?" Kendra rushes over, her healer's instincts in hyperdrive. "Here, I can heal this. Come with me."

Without looking back, she takes him by the hand and leads him toward the exit.

He doesn't deserve that. Part of me is jealous. He gets alone time with Kendra for acting... well, like an ass.

General Kaynes gives our group one last glare before wandering back to where he came from.

"Demons, I can't believe you did that," Klinton laughs. "That was insane."

Ronald lifts his chin in victory. "Someone had to do it."

Klinton clutches Ronald's hand as he looks around. "Maybe we should get going. Everybody's watching us."

"Maybe you should," Rose hesitantly agrees. "Knowing General Kaynes, he might try to charge you for assault or something ridiculous."

"Okie Dokie, we're dipping," Ronald announces. "Thanks so much for getting us in here. You guys are seriously the best."

We wave as they head toward the exit.

"What do we do now?" I ask. I look around and see Diego on the far side of the ballroom. He's chatting with Wendy, who holds a plate of drinks in one hand. Otherwise, the room is full of strangers.

"We could always head somewhere more private."

"I'm down."

"I know just the place." Rose takes my hand and leads me to the royal palace. She waves at Octavian as we enter, and he waves back.

We don't stop at Rose's room, or king Titan's chambers. Instead, we continue all the way to the end of the hall and up one last staircase.

"This is the king's study. It's where he teaches me dominion. There's something I want to show you."

Rose hikes up the side of her dress and fishes around underneath. Finally, she removes a key and unlocks the door, coaxing me inside. The room is simple, a large wooden table with bookshelves on all sides. There's a reading chair in the corner and a wide dresser with three rows of drawers.

Rose goes immediately for the dresser, she pulls open the bottom left drawer. It's full of papers and a few maps. The second drawer has something that looks like a sundial, and a few metal trinkets. Rose tugs the third drawer, and I suck in a gasp.

My amulet!

It's lying in a pile of its chain, crammed between two leather-bound books. It's circular and hollow in the middle, like a flattened doughnut. It's lying on the side that shows my bonding spell.

Next to it is another amulet, completely identical to the other. *Or maybe that's my amulet.*

Then, It dawns on me. *Iris.* Her amulet wasn't in the vault, because it was here the whole time. Both of our amulets are right in front of me.

"What is it?" Rose asks. She sees the shock on my face.

"Nothing. Sorry. I just… those amulets took me by surprise. You can close it now."

Rose gives me one last suspicious glance before closing the drawer. She opens two more before finding what she was looking for.

"My grandpa calls these seer-glasses. It's a relic. You can think of anyone you know personally, and it will show you them in real time."

"Seriously?"

"Seriously." She hands me the glasses, nothing but thick metal bands and clunky white glass, like virtual reality goggles from the Bronze Age. Then, she motions to one of the chairs. "It can get disorienting. You might want to sit down."

I pick the seat closest to her and slip the glasses over my head. "So, I just imagine them?"

"Pretty much. The more details the better, it needs to be more than just a physical description. Personality too."

"Got it."

I imagine Judy. Her elastic pale skin and her bright green eyes. I imagine her hearty laugh and her nurturing hand.

The image forms slowly, colors swirling and taking shape. When I blink, she's there. I can't see the bed, but I can tell she's lying down, her upper body angled at a slight incline. I do, however, see the tubes. The IV feeds into her wrist, and the oxygen tube runs along her upper lip like giant translucent whiskers.

"Mom?"

I don't mean to speak out loud, but it looks so real. I feel like I could reach out and touch her.

"Is she okay?" Rose asks.

"She's alive... but barely." I can see her chest lurching up and down. It looks ragged and painful. Her eyes are shut, and they don't look like they'll be opening anytime soon.

I can't look any longer, but I don't remove the goggles. I imagine Kendra, her curly hair, and her girly healer's dress. I imagine her gentle touch and her playful smile.

Creams and reds swirl before my eyes, forming into Kendra. She's sitting with her legs crossed, nodding her head to an unseen conversation. I only watch for a second before feeling guilty.

"Thanks, Rose. This... this really means a lot to me." I pull them off and hand them across the table.

"Happy to help," she sighs.

Suddenly, a thought crosses my mind. "Out of curiosity, have you ever used this on me?"

Rose immediately blushes. "One time, and all I saw was you walking. I swear."

I laugh. "I wonder if it comes with a built-in censor. If someone is changing, it just blurs it out."

Rose grins. "Maybe. These relics can be pretty advanced."

"Well, we still have the whole night," I say. "What do you want to do?"

"I have an idea. Follow me."

She leads me out of the study and back toward her chamber where she grabs a giant blanket—more of a quilt really. Then, we climb the Central Tower. Five flights up, I have no doubts about where we're headed.

"The Tower Garden?" I ask

Rose nods. "Like old times."

We emerge on the balcony, the cold air nips at my skin. There's a slight breeze blowing that rustles the tree leaves. We make our way past the planters to the railing. Scanning the garden, I spot one other couple cuddling in the corner. Upon seeing the princess, they quickly retreat down the stairwell.

"Looks like we have the place to ourselves," Rose sings. She takes a seat on the bench overlooking the city. She unfolds the blanket and gives it a shake. "Scoot close, we can both fit in the blanket."

I obey, sliding until our hips are side by side. Her dress spills over my legs, and Rose tosses the blanket over the both of us. Just like in the hammock, she leans her head on my shoulder. I try to keep my racing heart under control, afraid she'll feel it through my shoulder. Slowly, I let my head rest on top of hers.

"You know," Rose starts. "So much has changed since we were last here."

"I couldn't even use dominion," I laugh. "I can't believe it's only been four months. It feels like forever ago."

Rose smiles at the thought. "Imagine how much will change in the next year. And the next."

"Someday," I imagine, "We might just be in the council together."

Rose rocks her head. "I've been thinking a lot about that actually. With there being two spots for The Surviving, you and Diego could both win. Think about how perfect that would be."

"What about you?" I ask.

Her eyes lower, and her lips sag. I let my soul creep closer. Her thoughts are laced with pain.

Now that Antai's gone... "My Grandpa will choose me as his new apprentice," Rose assumes. "Besides, the queen automatically presides over the council. That means all three of us can make it. Imagine what we could do."

"What would you change first?" I ask.

"Everything," Rose raves. "I would change the wages. I would cut back on consumption in the palace. I would get rid of all the terrible laws. I would expand the council to the lower class."

I can't stop the smile from overtaking my lips. Her passion, her commitment, I adore it.

"What?" She asks defensively.

"Three months ago, you were defending the oligarchy. You thought the most educated should make all the decisions. Now... I don't know. You've changed a lot... and I really like the new you."

"Well, thank you," Rose blushes. "And what about you? What plans do you have for Cavernum?"

I look out over the city. "I don't know. I'd love to get better healthcare for the ring. More healers... maybe fewer guardsmen, or better ones at least.. And who knows," I point to an empty section of the palace grounds. "Maybe I'd put a pond in the palace so we can ice skate in the winter."

"Ice skate..." Rose whispers to herself, then she stiffens. I feel her slowly leaning away from me. "Did you say ice skate?"

"Yeah, like..." *like the dream.* I freeze. *How could I be so stupid?*

"It was real," Rose shivers. "Oh my God. It was real. But... how?" She doesn't run, but she scoots until she is on the far end of the bench. "How? How were you in my dreams, Matt?"

"Listen to me. I have a perfectly good explanation, but you have to promise you won't freak out. You have to let me explain everything."

She stands, sending the blanket sliding to the floor. Her hand is pressed against her amplifier. "Tell me, or I get my Grandpa. How did you get inside my head? Tell me!"

The archangel warned me not to, but I have no other choice. I take a deep breath and let it out.

"Because, Rose... I'm a demon."

Chapter 26

Rose

"Because…. I'm a demon."

The word sends tendrils of ice down my spine. *Demon!*

I've feared that word more than any other. My father died fighting demons. Antai died fighting demons. There's not a creature on Earth I despise more.

My throat constricts, and I feel like I can barely breathe. He'll possess me at any moment. He'll enter my mind and enslave my body.

Run, Rose!

I turn to escape, but my dress slows me down. Matt races for the stairwell and cuts me off. "Please, Rose! Just listen to me. I didn't choose this! I—"

"Let me go!" I clutch my amulet and aim a shaky hand at Matt. "Or I'll…"

I don't know what I'll do. Matt is my friend—was my friend. Some part of me wants to trust him, but another part of me isn't so foolish. For nearly a year, I thought Nevela was my friend, then I discovered she wasn't Nevela at all. It was a demon the entire time. Now, it's happening all over again.

It was all a lie, Rose. You don't really know him. Attack before he does!

I lunge with an outstretched hand.

Electricity.

Before I even form the command, Matt is in motion. He twists out of reach, holding up both hands.

"Rose, I'm not going to hurt y—"

Fire!

Matt forms a shield an instant before the flames engulf him. I don't relent. The fiery current diverges around him, scorching the stone and singeing the nearby shrubs.

Stop! His voice erupts in my head.

I feel him, just like I feared, slithering his way into my skull. His soul presses against mine, taking control of my limbs.

You have to believe me, Rose. I'm on your side.

You're a demon! I scream back! *If you're really on my side, you'll let me go.*

Not until you trust me.

I'll never trust you! I wail. *You deserve to rot alongside the Holy One.*

I'm sorry, Matt sighs inside my head. *Then, you leave me no choice.*

I sense him digging deeper into my mind. Then, he speaks a single command.

Sleep!

I awake slowly, rolling over in a nest of silk and satin. My sheets are tucked tightly under my limbs, and my pillow cradles my neck in just the right places. Oddly enough, I'm not in my dress. I'm wearing my usual nightgown. Then, I remember.

He's a demon!

I bolt upright in bed. It's pitch dark. My curtains must be drawn because I can't see any stars where my window should be. I don't know how I got here, but I'm in my room. Matt would need an Adamic Key to get to me.

I'm safe.

I feel around on my nightstand until I find the box of matches. I strike it and quickly light the candle before putting out the match with a flick of my wrist. When I hold up the candle, I scream.

Matt is standing in the center of my room. The candle illuminates his reflective blonde locks. Instantly, my heart pounds against my ribcage, and my blood runs cold. I scramble to the top of my bed, my candle nearly blowing out in the process. With my back pressed against the headboard, I reach for my amulet, but it's nowhere to be found.

"HELP!!!" I scream, hoping someone hears me. "HEEEEELP!"

"Shhhh!" Matt holds up both hands. "It's okay. I'm not here to hurt you." He watches me, not with malice, but with concern. "You're safe. You don't have to scream."

He's a demon! He can't be trusted!

"H-how did you get in my chambers?" I stammer. "My door was locked… and what about the royal guards?"

Matt takes a timid step closer. "I'm not in your chambers. You are, but I'm on the other side of the palace in my own room."

"What? I don't understand."

"You're dreaming, Rose. I put you to sleep and carried you to your room. The king unlocked the door."

"No! You're lying! Grandpa… Grandpa would know better."

"I told him you drank too much. He watched me lay you in the bed, then he walked me out and locked up. I promise you, Rose. You're safe on your bed."

"Then… then how are you in my dream? Are you possessing me?"

Matt looks down, and he almost looks ashamed. "Technically, yes. It's called true possession. I can leave my body and possess long distance. But it's not what you think. I only did it to help with your nightmares. I'm telling you, Rose, I'm on your side. I can explain everything."

"Explain what? You're a demon! You've pledged yourself to the devil. What is there left to say?"

"But I haven't!" Matt says. "I didn't choose this. I'm not like other demons. I swear! Just give me five minutes, and this'll all make sense."

I don't have much of a choice. I'm trapped in a dream—a dream that Matt controls. "Fine. Say what you want, but the second I wake up, I'm reporting you to the council."

Relief flushes over Matt's face. "Thank you." He takes a deep breath. "Okay. Everything I've told you about myself has been the absolute truth. Judy, her cancer, not knowing about Adamic, all of it. But… there are a few things I haven't told you. The first being that I have tattoos. They were already there when Judy found me as a baby."

I can't help but sneer. "Do you think I'm stupid?"

"No!" Matt exclaims. "I don't. I know it sounds crazy, but this has been my life. Earlier tonight, I told you I felt like I didn't belong. This was why. I felt like I was marked at birth to be different. Kids made fun of me for my tattoos. They wouldn't let me swim with them at the pool. I knew I was different, but I had no idea I was a demon until Zane explained it to me."

My brows turn down with incredulity. "Zane?"

Matt nods. "Once I got an amplifier, I started noticing it. I would get glimpses of people's thoughts. Zane put it together. It turns out, he knew my parents in Hogrum."

My jaw drops open. "Zane… knew your parents?"

He nods. "According to Zane, my dad was a demon too; my mother was an adalit. They both fought against the Holy One, but they were killed. I only survived because I was left on Judy's doorstep."

I frown. "So, you received the tattoos as a baby, and everyone responsible has died. You expect me to believe that?"

"I do," Matt says. "Because it's the truth. You can ask Zane yourself." He sighs, growing more and more discouraged. "You know, I wanted to have the tattoos removed. Zane convinced me not to. He said that it could be a tool for good. And he was right. You would be dead if I wasn't a demon."

My nose scrunches, and my eyes narrow. "Why's that?"

"At the graduation party, there was an armored feeder. The one…" He swallows. "The one who killed Velma. It was about to kill you when I possessed it. I was holding it back. I saved you."

A demon saved me? I want to refute it. I want to say it's impossible. *Demons are killers, nothing more.*

Matt can sense my prejudice from across the room. "I know how you feel about demons, Rose. I know what Jack did to Antai. But I'm not one of them. I'm not evil for having a tattoo. I've only ever used it for good."

Dad! I'd almost forgotten. My own father was a demon. He was trying to infiltrate the demon cult. He did it to earn their trust.

My father wasn't evil!

"How do I know this isn't an act?" I ask. *Jack stayed in character for nearly a year.*

"Because I'll prove it. I'll open up my soul to you. I trust you with my secrets, Rose. All of them."

Matt approaches slowly, coming up along the side of the bed. He reaches out his hand, leaving it hovering before me. "You can trust me, Rose."

He radiates sincerity. I can feel his desperation. He wants to earn my faith—not to deceive me but because he cares. He's frantic for my approval.

I take his hand.

Instantly, I'm overtaken by his soul. The memories surge—a psychic jolt to the mind. I find myself looking out of his eyes—living his memories.

I blink, and I'm in the trench, surrounded by Vyle and his goons. Vyle swings at my face, but I sense his intentions. *Left hook.* I rear back, barely dodging the blow.

I blink, and this time, I'm in a laborer's home. One of my men, Togum, has a gun to a child's head. I read his mind, disarming him a moment before he pulls the trigger.

I blink, and I'm underground. A girl is inviting me to join the Holy One. *My sister!* I refuse.

His entire mind has enveloped me, and the memories keep coming. I see Judy in a hospital bed. I see Kendra leaning over me. I feel her lips on mine.

And then, from Matt's eyes, I see myself. I watch as I strut down the Royal Wing, dressed in my golden gown. I feel the stirring in his stomach. I feel his affection filling me.

I blink, and we're dancing. I see myself standing before me as I expand my mind to those around me. I have no idea what I'm doing, but I use their knowledge to perfect the Zion's Waltz. I have to get it right for her. She deserves as much.

Finally, I'm lying in the hammock. As strange as it sounds, I'm lying next to myself, admiring every feature. I see my hazel eyes and my athletic frame. The way I laugh. The way I talk. I adore it all.

He adores me!

Finally, Matt removes his hand, staggering back. His eyes meet mine, and a smile slowly blossoms on his face. "You believe me!" It's not a question but a fact.

"I… I believe you." *You're everything I thought you were.*

Just like that, the tension in the room dissolves. Matt looks like he couldn't be happier. "I'm sorry about the dreams. I really am. I—"

"It's okay. You had good intentions."

I move to the side of my bed so that I'm sitting next to him. "So, that embarrassing story Judy told me… and the reservoir…"

"All true," Matt grins. "Judy really would love you by the way. I know she would."

"You're a demon. I still can't believe it." I lean back and interlace my fingers, dragging them down the back of my neck. "Can I see them… the tattoos."

It takes Matt by surprise. "Sure... I can show you." He stands, removing the jacket. Then, he grabs his shirt at the hips and pulls it over his head.

Wow!

Matt is strong. He isn't as bulky as Antai, but he's toned. The candle's light causes shadows to fill the fissures of his form. Small canyons divide his abs into their six angular sections.

Then, I see the symbols on his right shoulder. It's a bonding spell.

"You have a soul-anchor?"

"I do," Matt says. "Zane says my mom was an adalit. He confiscated my amulet when I arrived. It's in the king's study. My dagger is there too."

Does Grandpa know?

I don't have time to think much of it. Matt turns around, and I get a full view of his back. Three symbols are evenly spaced between his shoulder blades.

The mark of the beast.

Ever since Grandpa showed it to me, I've hated this spell. I've hated these symbols. But here, on Matt, they don't strike me as vile. I'm not as repulsed as I've been in the past. I reach out and trace my finger along the inverted triangle.

I don't see a demon; I see Matt. I see a man who has the power to possess. A man who can take anything he wants from anyone, yet chooses to use his power for good.

I can't get those memories out of my head. The way Matt looked at me. The way he felt. I've seen myself through his eyes, and I'll never be the same. I've never felt so cherished.

Matt faces me, still shirtless, and I find myself gawking. He's kind. He's powerful. He's smart. In all honesty, he'd make a great king. I want him to know how much I admire him. I want him to feel it the way I did—to see himself through my eyes.

Matt sees me staring and steps closer. He glances down at my nightgown, then to my lips, a smirk spreading across his face. "I really care about you, Rose. I don't want to lose you, especially not over some stupid tattoos."

I put my hands on his shoulders and feel myself leaning in closer. His soul is like a magnet; the closer I get, the stronger the pull becomes. The instant our lips meet, a single thought sours the moment.

Antai.

I turn away, tearing my lips from his. I want to kiss him, but this doesn't feel right. I love Antai. At this very moment, he's down the hall, wasting away on his bed. Without his feeding tube, he only has days to live.

"I'm sorry, Matt. I can't. I mean, I think I could," I ramble. "I think soon I'll be ready for this, but not tonight of all nights. The veil is thinnest, and I feel like he's watching. If there's ever a night for him to come back. It'll be tonight. I'm sorry, Matt."

"It's fine," he lies, pulling back on his t-shirt. "I understand."

"Thank you, Matt, for everything. Tonight was amazing. And I'm glad I know who you are. Your secrets are safe with me."

He nods, his expression neutral. "Well, I'll see you soon, I guess. Thank you, Rose. I'll wake you up now."

"Alright. Goodnight, Matt."

He takes my hand and commands my very mind.

Awake.

My eyes flutter open in an instant. One second, I'm standing beside Matt. The next, I'm on my back, staring at the ceiling. My ball gown is pooling in the sheets around me.

I'm barely sitting up when the walls reverberate with the ringing of brass bells.

Ding! Ding! Ding!

Three distinct bells. *Danger!*

I climb out of bed and fumble for my key, unlocking the door. I open it and find Grandpa hobbling down the hallway, his cane clacking on the marble at double speed.

"What's going on?" I call out.

"It's our prisoner, Jack. He's escaped from the pit."

Chapter 27

Matt

I direct my soul through the darkness, passing like a phantom through wall after wall. I'm moving toward my own room, but I'm drifting slowly. I need time to make sense of what just happened.

I told Rose I'm a demon. At first, she wanted to kill me, but I finally earned her trust. I opened up my mind.

When our souls intertwined, I felt her attraction to me. I felt the excitement and the infatuation.

It was incredible!

And at the same time, I felt her longing for Antai. I saw her crying for days by his side. I saw her wildest dreams. She wanted to be queen. To be his bride. To explore the beyond with him at her side. In a lot of ways, she still does.

I stop, hovering aimlessly in what must be a stranger's chambers. I tried to keep these memories from Rose, but I can't ignore them any longer. Especially not on Hallow's Eve.

Antai.

I remember him banging his fists against the veil. I remember him begging that I kill him. He was desperate. He was in mental agony.

Rose is right. If there were ever a time to bring him back, it would be tonight.

I have to try. I owe her that much.

I urge my soul back toward the Royal Wing, finally arriving at Antai's chambers. I drift over the bed and let my soul descend on his corpse. For a brief moment, I open my eyes, seeing the ceiling of his bedroom. Then, I descend deeper into his mind. I don't hear any thoughts. I don't sense any memories.

He's dead.

When I'm about to give up, almost by mistake, my soul stumbles upon it. In the farthest recess of his body, I feel his lifeline—a current of spiritual energy descending into the unknown. I can't sense the end, but I know it will lead me to the veil.

I know what's at stake. If I bring him back, I'll lose Rose. There's no question about it. I have to be positive. I have to be ready to give her up.

She deserves happiness.

I take a deep breath and repel my soul along his lifeline, lowering myself into the spirit world. I'm not falling like when I died; I'm neutrally buoyant. I only sink or rise if I choose to.

In a matter of seconds, the nothingness consumes me. I don't have any inclination of what's up or down. There's no gravity to guide me. Without the lifeline, I would be beyond lost. I continue down it, placing one metaphysical hand in front of the other.

"You're worthless. You may as well die!" It's a sinister voice, not Antai's. A moment later, it's replaced with another.

"Hello, demon. Welcome to death."

Demon?

The next voice sounds like it's right next to my ear. "The devil be praised, welcome master."

Master?

Even in the spirit world, my tattoos take effect. Then, I remember. *My lifeline.* Parallel to Antai's, my own lifeline ascends behind me, bonding me to my body.

"Welcome to hell," the voices breathe. "You're one of us. Embrace it."

"Go away!" I scream into oblivion. Maybe it's because I'm a demon, but the voices scatter.

After what feels like an eternity, a scene materializes before me. The veil emerges from the void—an endless pane of glass in a sea of darkness. Sure enough, Antai's lifeline continues in front of me, passing through the veil and into his back.

He doesn't notice me arrive. He's sitting—or rather floating—with his legs crossed, on the opposite side of the veil. All I see is the back of his head as he stares at the light in the distance.

I follow his gaze, and instantly I feel the pull. An ancient part of my soul begs me to move toward it. The light promises peace, serenity. The sensation is stronger than a feeder bite and innocently pure. I know I'll be happy there. I belong there.

Home.

I pull my eyes away and take a deep breath. Once the urges fade, I focus on the figure before me.

"Antai!"

He turns at my voice. "You." The longer he looks at me, the more anger builds behind his brow. "It's you!" He lunges at the veil, pounding his fist into the translucent wall.

Like last time, the wall ripples with each blow. However, unlike last time, the veil warps around his hand, flexing toward me. A little further, and he might just break through.

It's weak!

"You were supposed to kill me!" Antai screams. "Why am I still here?"

"Antai, listen to me. I have something important I h—"

"Tell me why!" He steps away from the glass. "Why do you torture me like this?" His brown eyes never look away. They harbor a battered and broken soul—a man going mad with longing.

"It wasn't my place to kill you," I say. "I don't decide who lives and who dies."

"Who does? God? If it were up to him, I'd already be in paradise. Don't you see? This is what happens when we mess with the laws of nature. I was never supposed to come back. It wasn't Titan's choice to make. And so, unless he's going to kill me himself, I'm asking you. Fix the wrongs that have been made… Kill me!"

"Quiet!" I shout into the abyss. To my surprise, Antai obeys. "If you'll listen to me for two seconds, you'll know that you don't have to die. Tonight is Hallow's Eve. The veil is weak. You were just bending it. If you try, I think you could break free. With your lifeline still attached, you could repossess your body. You can live, Antai!"

Antai stares at me a moment longer, his face flat with disinterest. "I don't want to live."

"What?" *Has he gone crazy?* "How can you say that? You can go back. Isn't that what you wanted?"

Antai looks away, noticeably ashamed about what he's about to say. "It's not that simple, MacArthur. I'm supposed to cross over. I feel it inside me. It's the natural way of things. I don't belong with the living. Frankly, I don't want to go back."

"But…?" I'm dumbstruck. I stare at him until he rolls his eyes.

"I can't explain it, MacArthur. It's just how I feel. You wouldn't understand. I belong in heaven."

"And what about Rose?"

Antai grimaced, a mix of rejection and betrayal. "Obviously, she's taken to you just fine. I saw you in her dreams. Don't pretend like you don't remember. Looks like she doesn't need me anymore."

"That's bull crap. She does need you. Every day you think you've been suffering in here, she's been suffering just as much. She won't even kiss me because the thought of betraying you is too much. She's hurting, Antai, and she needs you. You make her happier than I do. So what's stopping you?"

"What happens if I die again?" Antai says. "Or what if I go back, and she dies. I don't want to go through this again. I saw her suffering, Matt. I know she was in pain. It's easier if we both move on. No more heartache. Only happiness."

"What do you think it's like over there?" I ask. "What do you envision heaven being like?"

He turns toward the light, falling into a trance. "Peace. Tranquility. Everyone I love will be there. They'll take care of me, and I'll take care of them. We'll never have to say goodbye again."

"And who do you love most?" I ask.

Antai frowns, seeing my intentions. "She'll join me someday. We'll be reunited beyond the veil."

"What will she think of you when you tell her you chose not to come back," I ask. "What will she think when she learns you put your own pain before hers? How will eternity be when the girl you love despises you?"

His jaw quivers, and he clenches his fist. "She'll understand," he hisses.

"How will eternity be without her? If you choose to die, she'll never forgive you. You'll be giving up a piece of heaven."

"Shut up!" He swings at the veil, causing the barrier to bulge with each blow. "You don't know her. She'll forgive me."

"She wants you to come back more than anything. How can you deny her that? You could be in her arms tonight. How can you do this to her?"

Antai says nothing. He sits in silence, staring into the distant light.

"So, this is it? You're just going to die?"

Still, he says nothing. If he's contemplating coming back, I have no way of knowing it.

"Fine," I hiss. "Die here. I don't care. You know what, maybe it's better this way. I thought you were better for her. I thought you could make her happy in a way that I couldn't. Obviously, I was wrong. If this is the real Antai, then she's better off without you."

With that, I take hold of my lifeline and begin to climb.

I can only hope that something I said resonates.

Another part of me hopes it doesn't.

Chapter 28

Rose

The High Council has never looked worse. Chancellor Bolo is drunk, and I'm fairly certain Zane is high on Laughing Leaf. It's well past midnight now, but the festivities ended hours ago when Jack escaped.

"Bring them in," Grandpa commands.

Octavian walks in first. He's still wearing his white guard uniform, only this time, a stream of dried blood runs down his temple.

Behind him, two guards drag in Commander Noyen. His hair is disheveled, and he no longer wears an amulet.

Jack, unfortunately, is nowhere to be seen.

Once they are aligned against the wall, Grandpa clears his throat. "I'm sorry for such an abrupt meeting, but this matter couldn't wait. For those who don't know—" He glances at the non-guardian council members. "—I'll set the scene. At some point after sunset, the guards of the pit were given drinks that we believed were drugged. Soon after, the guards fell asleep. They have no recollection of the night, nor who gave them the drinks. During the time they were unconscious, someone entered the pit and released a demon we had imprisoned. As soon as this was discovered, the alarm was sounded. Unfortunately, after searching the palace, we were unable to locate the demon. We did, however, find Octavian unconscious behind the palace stables."

Grandpa motions to Octavian. "Octavian, if you would please, give us your account of what transpired."

"Of course, your highness. Well, at 7:00, I finished my shift by the Royal Wing. I decided to join my family in the ballroom. I was walking toward the Central Hallway when I saw commander Noyen exiting the pit. I thought it was strange because he was dressed for the ball. I was about to brush it off when another figure emerged from the pit. He was wearing a cloak, and he was moving toward the eastern side of the palace. I decided to follow him. He went north along the Eastern Wing and exited towards the stables. He looked like he was going to board a carriage, so I tried to intervene. He possessed me and made me walk behind the stables. That's the last thing I remember."

Grandpa nods. "Thank you, Octavian. That is most helpful. You are excused."

Octavian exits as Commander Noyen begins looking wildly around the room. "I didn't do this, I swear. It was just a coincidence. It's true, I brought them drinks to celebrate. I care about my men. They were ciders, non-alcoholic. Then, I left. I did nothing wrong."

"You are the commander of the royal guard. Not only do you have a key to the pit, but you have the trust of your men. They wouldn't think twice to accept a drink from you. All evidence points to you."

"I have proof," Commander Noyen claims. "Octavian said that he was possessed. Well, to possess him, he would have needed an amulet. The demon probably got it from whoever set him free. I still had my amulet when you arrested me. It couldn't have been me."

"I'm glad you brought that up." General Kaynes grins as he rifles through a stack of parchment. "I have this month's armory logs with me. Two weeks ago, you filed a missing amulet report. This was just days after the demon was imprisoned. You've never lost an amulet in your life, so I decided to let it slide. I figured it would show up in the palace laundry. Now, I'm a bit concerned. My theory is, you never misplaced your amulet. You stashed it, knowing you would give it to the demon. You knew that if you filed a report weeks earlier, it would likely be forgotten by Hallow's Eve."

"No... that's not what happened." His eyebrows lift as his desperation rises.

"And what was the drug?" General Kaynes asks. "Sleeping tonic? A lot of it? You stole it from the kitchen, didn't you? If we ask the kitchen staff, would they remember seeing you?"

Noyan's face is whiter than fresh snowfall. "I went to the kitchen for other things. I wanted some ginger to soothe my stomach. It had nothing to do with sleeping tonic."

"The evidence points to you," General Kaynes smiles. "Who else would you have to blame? Your guards? Unless they released the demon immediately after you left and then drugged themselves, it just isn't plausible."

Commander Noyen slowly closes his mouth. "I have nothing left to say," he squeaks.

"Very well," Grandpa says "I propose Commander Noyen be held for questioning. Upon completion of all questioning, he is to be hung. All in favor, please manif—"

"Wait!" Noyan throws up his hands. "If you lessen the charges, I'll confess. I'll tell you everything I know about the Holy One. It's not much, but it may be useful."

Grandpa raises an eyebrow. "And what is this information?"

Noyan looks around, his heart visibly pounding. "A girl... a girl came to me in a dream and asked me to release him. She told me how to do it. She said that he needed to escape back to Hogrum— that he needed to join the others. That has to mean something, right? That can help you!"

Grandpa chews on this information a while longer. "And why did you agree? Do you believe in his cause?"

Noyen shakes his head. "I'm dying, your highness. My liver is destroyed. The healers can only keep me alive for so long. The Holy One promised to heal me. I want to be in my children's life. I... I was stupid to ever fall for it."

Grandpa nods. "Very well. Does any council member propose an alternate punishment?

No one speaks.

"No?" Grandpa asks. "Very well. Jeddah Noyan will be hung. All in favor?"

The entire council raises their hands.

"It is decided then. Take him away."

"No!" Noyen yells, falling to his knees. "Please. I'm still loyal. I can still serve you. Don't do this!"

They drag him on his knees out of the High Council Room. His cries are cut silent as they shut the doors behind him.

"Hogrum?" Katu wrinkles his nose. "Do you think it could be true? Why would they be in Hogrum? There are no Adamic there. It's abandoned."

"I believe it," Zane grumbles. "I visit there every year to honor my family. I go to the royal plaza where they were cremated along with the other dead. In the past 15 years, I've never been back in the palace, that is until this year. This last July, I found Lieutenant MacArthur there. He had been attacked in the palace by a feeder. I saw it myself. The thing had Adamic armor. It nearly killed me." He drags his fingers slowly through his beard. "If there's one, there are possibly others. I believe he's telling the truth."

Grandpa nods. "I'm afraid you may be right, Zane. We should send a guardian immediately to investigate. They w—"

"No!" Chancellor Quine cries out. "We will not weaken our sanctuary over a traitor's word. If we really think demons may be hiding there, send the Champions. That's why we have them."

"They'd be slaughtered," Zane barks. "We're talking about demons here. The champions don't have soul-anchors. They'd be lambs to the slaughter."

"I don't know," General Kaynes coos. "Quine has a point. A demon has just escaped, and could be anywhere for all we know. We don't want to weaken Cavernum now. Perhaps this will make a good lesson for the champions. They need to learn caution and restraint. They must learn to pick their battles. We inform them this is a scouting mission only. The champions are to keep a distance. Should feeder or demons be spotted, they report back. Then, we can feel justified in sending forces."

Grandpa hesitates, glancing my way. "Fine. I don't oppose. All in favor?"

Hands lift around the table.

Grandpa nods. "The champions haven't slept. I propose they leave first thing tomorrow morning. That gives them a day to prepare, and a night to rest. Any opposed?"

No one says a word.

"Excellent. As for our final matter of business—"

Suddenly the council doors swing open. A royal guard timidly peeks his head inside. "Your highness, we have urgent news."

"Speak!" Grandpa commands.

"Your apprentice, Antai Elsborne... He's awake."

Antai!

I'm nearly to his room now.

Brace yourself, Rose. I warn myself. *You don't know what condition he'll be in or what he'll remember.*

Still, I can't contain my excitement. Nothing could spoil the joy I'm feeling.

Antai is alive!

I burst into his room and glance at his empty bed. His feeding tube, like a severed snake, is hanging from the translucent bag, bleeding mush onto the tile.

"Rose!"

I turn and find Antai standing beside his wardrobe. He's pulling on a suit coat. His hair is damp and combed, and his face is freshly shaved. He looks… amazing.

"Oh, Rose." He breathes the words as though he can hardly believe them! "I thought I'd never see you again."

I walk over slowly, afraid at any minute I'll wake up from a dream. "You're here? You're actually here?"

"I'm here, Rose. I made it back."

Suddenly, I'm laughing, and then the tears are filling my eyes. My thoughts are bogged down by so many emotions. All I can do is tenderly wrap my arms around Antai.

"You can squeeze me, Rose. I'm not going to break," he laughs. As if to prove his point, he gives me a firm squeeze, lifting me momentarily into the air. His body. His voice. It all feels right. I don't have to feel guilty hugging him. I feel at peace.

"I can't believe you actually made it. I thought you were dead. It's been a month."

"I know," he breathes. "I'm sorry. It's over though. I'm here.."

"You changed your clothes," I note. "And shaved. How long have you been awake?"

"Nearly an hour."

"And you didn't come find me?" I accuse.

"I hadn't brushed my teeth in weeks. I wasn't ready to see you looking like that. This is so much better."

He pulls my waist against his, and his lips fall upon mine. It's a timid kiss. A kiss of uncertainty, as though things have changed since I shot him in the back.

I don't let myself doubt. I kiss him hard, pressing my body against his. Even after the coma, his frame is firm and strong. My fingers find his sides, moving along the gloves of his obliques.

"I love you, Rose. I didn't say it enough before I left."

"I love you too!" We kiss for a long time, but still, it doesn't make up for our time apart. As soon as we stop, I crave more contact.

As always, Antai pulls away first. He looks down at me and smiles, soaking in the moment.

I let my head fall in the crook of his neck. "God, I've missed you. So much has happened, Antai. I don't even know where to start."

"Start with that night. Tell me what happened," he says.

I lean away and gather my thoughts. "After I shot you, Titan came and spoke Adamic. Turns out he's adalingual. Only, he's erased his memories. It's a miracle he managed to save you. We captured The demon and stopped the equalists. From there, things only got worse. The Holy One has been killing across Cavernum. Quill became a guardian and then was murdered. And now, Jack has escaped."

Jack!

Matt admitted that some demons can possess from afar. The thought works its way into my head like a parasite, feeding on my fears and growing stronger. It can't be a coincidence. Jack escaped on the night of Hallow's Eve. He wanted it to look like it was plausible. He wanted me to believe it.

Antai is possessed!

Antai tilts his head to the side, watching me carefully. "What's wrong?"

Play it cool, Rose. I tell myself. "Nothing, I just can't believe you're back." *Don't let him know you're on to him.* "Wait here. I have a surprise for you."

I push open the door, praying he doesn't follow.

As soon as I'm out the door, he's moving after me. "Rose, is something wrong? You can talk to me."

No, I can't.

"One second," I insist. "I'll be right back." I move toward grandpa's study, practically jogging. I can hear Antai's feet thumping behind me.

Almost there!

I charge up the steps and fiddle with my key to the study. The lock clicks, and I stumble inside. I turn to swing the door shut, but Antai's foot jams the doorway.

"Rose!" Antai pushes the door wider and slips inside as the door slams behind him. "What's gotten into you?"

I back up until I'm pressed against Grandpa's dresser. Before Antai can attack, I open the inheritance box, push the morph mask aside, and grab hold of the demon amulet.

Antai watches me, still playing dumb. "Rose, what's going on? You're shaking!"

Once again, Jack and I are face to face in my father's study. Last time, he was disguised as Antai. This time, he's possessing him. Last time, I was naive. This time, I see right through him.

Antai holds up his hands and speaks quietly. "Rose, put down the amulet. It's me. I'm not going to hurt you. I can prove it. Ask me anything."

I grit my teeth. Jack has access to his mind. He'll know the answers either way. There's only one way to know for sure.

I tighten my grip on the demon amulet and throw my soul at Antai.

I collide directly with his consciousness, tumbling deeper inside. To my surprise, I don't sense madness. I don't sense malice. I sense...

Antai?

What did you expect? His thoughts laugh at me.

It's really you! I embrace his mind, letting my identity dissolve in the hot springs of his soul. I know I should leave his body, but his thoughts are warm and comforting. I find myself nestling in.

Memories swirl around me, saturating my soul. Suddenly, I'm sitting in an endless expanse of darkness. I'm banging my head against the veil. Then, a man appears... Matt. He's begging me to come back, but I refuse. I don't want to return. I want to pass on.

I retract my soul, a look of horror forming on my face.

Antai looks stricken, a mixture of anger and shame. "Rose, let me explain."

"You wanted to die?" I ask.

"Rose, it's not like that. I wasn't in my right mind. That place messed with my head."

I shake my head. "You didn't want to come back. You practically said so. You—"

"I thought you moved on," he yells, and I can see the torment in his eyes. "When you fell asleep, I could feel you. It was like you were sinking closer to me. Sometimes, if I pushed against the veil, I could see your dreams. I know what went on. I thought you had forgotten about me."

"It's not like that, Antai. I was trying to cope."

"You kissed him," Antai accuses. "Had you been in a coma, I would've never. I know I would have never. I only wanted you. I guess I found out you didn't love me the way I thought you did."

"I do love you, Antai!" I declare. "But you don't know what it was like for me. You were dead. I thought our future was over. I wanted to die right alongside you. And Matt, he was a distraction. In those brief moments together, it didn't hurt so bad. But I never chose him over you. I chose him over nothing. I chose him over giving up like you did."

Antai swallows and looks down, his forehead wrinkling with frustration. "Do you love him?"

I hesitate, but only for my own closure. I need to be sure this is what I want. "No. I don't love him, Antai. I love you. I want to be with you. One month won't change that. Please, tell me you feel the same."

Antai lunges forward, wrapping me in his arms. For a while, he says nothing, breathing deeply into my hair. "I do... I love you, Rose. We're a team. Whatever comes next, we're in this together."

He holds me, and my heart swells with joy. Still, the tiniest bit of guilt clings to the back of my skull. Whatever I had with Matt, it's over.

I choose Antai. Nothing can change my mind.

Nothing.

Chapter 29

Matt

It's noon, the day after Hallow's Eve. The entire palace is sleeping. The hallways are bare, and my footsteps echo off the walls.

"Name and business." The guards at the Royal Wing show no emotion.

"Lieutenant MacArthur. I just want to have a few words with the princess."

"She doesn't accept walk-ins," one of the guards laughs. "If you like, you can leave a message with us."

"No need for that," the king's voice calls from behind me. "I'll walk him over. I'm on my way to my study. It'll be no bother."

The guards bow. "Oh, thank you, your highness."

I amble beside him as we shuffle down the hallway toward Rose's chambers.

"I want to thank you again," the king praises, "for everything you've done for my granddaughter. You were there for her in a very dark time, and I cannot express what it means to me. I would hope, now that Commander Elsborne has recovered, that you remain a friend to her. I have a feeling she'll be needing more of you."

"I mean, sure," I stammer. "We're still friends and all."

The king nods. "I'm glad to hear it." When we arrive at Rose's door, he continues shuffling toward his study. "I wish you the best."

"Thank you."

I pause, letting him get further away. I don't want him overhearing what I'm about to say.

Tap. Tap. Tap.

I knock as quietly as I can, while still making a noise. I don't want to wake Rose, but if she's awake, I want her to answer.

It's a while before I hear some fumbling and the click of a lock. The door cracks open, and Rose squints at the bright hallway sunlight. She is wearing a white nightgown. When she sees that it's me, she glances back into the room.

"Matt? What are you doing here?" She quickly steps outside and shuts the door behind her, still holding the handle in her hand.

"I need your help with something."

"What?"

I hesitate, hoping I still have her trust. "I want to read Titan's mind, but I can't creep around by myself," I whisper. "I'll get arrested. Do you think you could escort me to his room?"

"Why do you want to read Titan's mind?"

"I know his mind is messed up, but last time, I got a glimpse inside, and there were still memories. They were broken, but I could see things. I saw this book. It was written on silver pages, bound in gold. I think it was the Book of Life."

Rose wrinkles her nose and finally sighs. "Fine. Wait right here." She closes the door, and after a few minutes, returns wearing a simple tan dress. "Alright, let go."

As soon as we start walking, Rose glances over at me. "Thank you, for bringing him back. I can't thank you enough."

"Oh, you know about that?"

She nods. "I'm sorry again for how I reacted. You were right. It is a tool for good."

I bite my lip. This is already growing uncomfortable. "So we're good? Can we just be friends? Forget about the stuff that happened?"

"Friends," she affirms.

We stop at Titan's door, and Rose knocks once before entering. "Titan, I've brought a visitor again."

Normally, Titan is lounging in the sitting room, staring at the fireplace. But this time, the room is deserted. His wife's journal is open on the coffee table, but there's no Titan nor any of his servants.

"Hmmm, he must be in his bedroom." She takes a timid step toward a massive oak door. "Titan?" She sings.

She pulls on the handle and freezes as the door swings open.

Octavian's body is lying unconscious by the base of the bed. Titan is lying on his back under the covers. His body convulses in small quick jolts.

"What's going on?" Rose gasps. "Is he dying?"

I run over to the side of the bed. If he's having a seizure, I can heal him—or at least I can try. I place my palm on his forehead and let my soul sink into his skull.

Immediately, I'm met with another soul. It rams me, forcing me from Titan's mind. My first thought is Iris—she's done something similar to me before—but this soul was different. Conniving. Apathetic.

"Get back!" I scream. "He's possessed!"

Rose stumbles out of the doorway. She still has a line of sight to the bed, but hopefully, she's at a safe distance. "What do we do?"

"Get the king!" I command. I form an energy shield wide enough to protect us both.

Rose takes one step toward the exit when the seizing suddenly stops. A moment later, Octavian sucks in a gasp, climbing to his feet.

"Now, that was a nightmare," he laughs as he slowly turns to face us. The voice is Octavian's, but there's something off about it. He gained an accent… an Australian accent.

"Ello princess. What a lovely surprise."

A piece of my soul—a piece Rose gave me—recognizes the accent immediately.

Jack!

"What do you want?" Rose demands from behind me. I keep my eyes trained on Octavian.

Octavian—or rather, Jack—shrugs. "I want what the Holy One wants. This little sack of dust doesn't know much anymore, but I think I found something useful."

"It won't be enough," Rose shouts back. "He knew you would try this. That's why he erased his memories."

Jack shrugs, removing his pistol from the holster. "You know, he happened to cause me a great deal of grief. Do you know what it feels like, princess, to have every inch of your flesh burned at once? I should do the same to him, but I'm not a monster like he is. I'll give him a merciful death."

Rose says nothing.

"In his day, I imagine he was quite the adversary. You know, it's really quite ironic. He could resurrect others, but in the end, he couldn't save himself."

Bang!

Jack fired directly at Titan's head.

"No!" Rose rushes forward, but I grab her shoulders and hold her back. If he possesses her, it's all over.

I hear a cane shuffling behind me, and the king appears at the door. The moment he does, Jack waves his hand in a salute.

"That's my queue. I'll see you soon." Then, Octavian's body crumples to the floor, an empty puppet.

The king wastes no time. He hobbles over to Octavian's side. After taking one solemn look at his father, the king draws an Adamic blade from his belt—a blade I never knew he had. The knife has a small needle nose blade, too small to be called a dagger. He kneels down next to Octavian and lifts the dagger. "I'm sorry," he whispers.

"Nooo!" Rose throws herself to the ground, covering Octavian's body with her arms. "He was possessed. It wasn't him!"

The king sighs. "Listen carefully, Rose. Jack is using true possession. His soul is bound to Octavian. If we kill him now, Jack dies with him."

"You can't," Rose cries. "He has a family. He's a good man. We can't kill him. We're better than this."

"Jack will kill others. Now is our chance. It's for the greater good." I can see the rage in the king's eyes. Part of this is about saving lives. The other part is about avenging Titan.

"No." Rose shakes her head. "If you kill him, you're no better than the Holy One. If Jack kills again, that's on him. If you kill Octavian, his blood is on your hands."

The king doesn't move for a long time. Finally, he lowers the knife. "So be it." He stands and finally looks at his father.

"I hoped this day would never come. Farewell, father."

Chapter 30

Rose

I've read about helicopters. I've seen pictures, but the noise is something I never anticipated. I don't understand how a few spinning blades can create such a constant, deafening roar.

The helicopter awaits us in the meadow by the bunker. It's black and sleek, shining like obsidian. From what I can see, it holds around a dozen passengers, including the pilot.

As we draw closer, Captain Renshu comes out to meet us. "Everyone in! Hurry, before the feeders come crawling." He's screaming, but his voice is like a whisper in the wind. "Get in, and put on a headset! C'mon!"

I use the metal steps and ascend into the back of the contraption. Rows of seats are facing both directions. Matt sits down first and unhooks a horseshoe-shaped headset from the ceiling. Without any hesitation, he fits it over his ears. Diego does the same, as does Vyle. I follow suit.

Instantly, the roar of the chopper is muffled by the synthetic leather, and Renshu's voice crackles loudly in my ear. "Buckle up, everyone. We're taking off."

My seat is forward-facing, and I can catch a glimpse of Renshu's head in between the seats. He fiddles with some switches as the engine whines louder. I gasp as the helicopter lurches, pressing the base of my thighs into my seat.

"Here we go," Renshu shouts. The steel frame tilts forward, and my seat belt digs into my chest. From my periphery, I can see the trees rushing past. They disappear from view as we gain altitude.

I catch Matt watching me, smiling like he did at the Fall Festival. "It's kinda fun, right?"

"Fun? This is terrifying. How do you control it?"

"You don't have to worry about that. Renshu's got it under control. Just enjoy the ride."

"Alright, everyone," Renshu's voice appears in my ear. "This is your captain speaking." His crackling laughter bursts in my ear. "We're approaching cruising altitude. We have 1284 miles to cover, so get comfortable. Total airtime should be about six hours." The headset clicks, and his voice is replaced with the hum of the helicopter.

I rest my forehead on the glass, but I refuse to sleep. I watch the clusters of lights as they drift down below. It's as if the Earth is a flowing river, continually drifting by the window.

After a few hours, Vyle distributes lunch. With a full stomach, the lull of the aircraft becomes too much. I let my eyes slowly close. I awake to Renshu's voice.

"Attention passengers: we are about to make our final descent over Hogrum. We will be passing directly over the palace in about 5 minutes, where you will make your departure. Please secure your parachutes and prepare for deployment. Remember, the longer you wait to deploy the parachute, the smaller your odds of being spotted."

Parachute!

Renshu explained it a dozen times, but I still don't trust the concept. Supposedly, a piece of cloth is supposed to save me from free fall. All I have to do is pull the string.

You'll be fine, Rose, I remind myself. Should the parachute fail, I can always stop my fall with dominion.

On the horizon, I can see the cascading stone building of a sanctuary. Even deserted, Hogrum is a site to behold—a stone needle hidden in a haystack of a forest. That's where my parents died. *That's where my dad was murdered.*

As I unbuckle, I see that I'm behind schedule. Matt already has his parachute on. Diego is fiddling with the final straps.

"A few reminders," Renshu says over the headsets. "This is a scouting mission only. Do not engage the enemy. Those with useful intel will proceed with The Surviving. The trial will only last one night. Tomorrow at noon, I'll be picking you up from the southern flats. Don't be late, or you'll be left."

"Are we going to pass over Kentville?" Matt asks Renshu.

"Kentville is on the far side of Hogrum. I'll be refueling and sleeping there tonight. Why?"

"No reason," Matt says.

I tighten the parachute straps until my thighs bulge on either side of the nylon. Then I put on a pair of goggles and hang my headset.

I'm ready.

"Alright, We're over the target!" Renshu screams. "Go! Go! Go!"

Diego tugs on a metal latch, and suddenly the helicopter wall slides open. Hurricane-force winds tear through the cabin, and my hair whips onto the exterior of my goggles. I can barely hear anything over the roar.

Diego jumps first, instantly getting whisked away by the wind. Crasilda jumps next, then Commander Hunt.

I grab a handle on the ceiling, lean out the door, and look down. Thousands of feet below us, the stone rooftops rush past. My stomach twists in a knot, and my heart rises in my throat. We're impossibly high. I never considered myself afraid of heights, but this is different. The Earth is an eternity away. Jumping looks like suicide.

Jump, Rose! Jump!

I try to move my muscles, but they refuse to budge. A primitive part of me takes control, acting out of self-preservation. Finally, when I've exhausted the last of my willpower, I shimmy away from the door.

Matt watches me. "You okay?" He shouts above the wind.

"You go first," I plead.

He shakes his head. "I'm going to Kentville to see Judy."

Vyle moves next to me and holds out his hand. "Take my hand," he suggests. "We can jump together. You'll be fine."

"No. That'll make it worse," I worry. "What if our parachutes tangle?"

"You have to jump," Matt shouts. "On three, you do it no matter what, okay?"

I nod, shimmying back over to the door. The sanctuary is almost gone now. This is my last chance. It's only Matt, Vyle, and me left.

I grab the handle and scoot my feet until the toes of my boots hang off the helicopter.

"One!" Matt shouts. "Two!"

Before he says three, Vyle shoved me out of the plane. My insides somersault, and I scream a terrified wail as I tumble toward the Earth.

Sky.

Earth.

Sky.

Earth.

Finally, the air resistance slows my spin. I manage to get in table formation, my belly button aiming at the Earth. After a few seconds of controlled free fall, the panic begins to subside. I'm okay. In fact, I feel like I'm floating.

I look down, and a new fear overtakes me. Directly below me is a thick forest. I'm going to miss the flats by over a hundred yards. If

I'm lucky, I'll get tangled in the branches. If I'm unlucky, who knows...

I bend my knees and angle my chest towards flats, but I'm falling too fast. I'm not going to make it. As the panic rises within me, I pull the cord.

There's a great whooshing sound above me, and the straps tear into my thighs, dragging me to what feels like a standstill. Then, I'm drifting slowly towards the sanctuary. I'm falling slower now, covering more horizontal distance. I'm still still a hundred yards up as I pass over the outer wall.

I made it!

For a moment, I enjoy the view. Never in my life did I think I'd have the chance to jump from a helicopter. However, as the ground rises to meet me, the urgency returns.

50 yards. 25 yards.

Thicken!

The air around me pushes back, and the tension on my parachute intensifies. When my feet finally make contact with the field, I barely have to jog to keep myself upright.

That wasn't so bad.

That's when I see Vyle. He's 50 yards overhead, spiraling tightly around where I landed. It's not an accident; he's aiming for me. As he lands, I press my hand to my chest to ensure contact with my amulet.

"Told you you'd be fine." His grin is unbearable as he effortlessly unclips his gear and steps out from the deflating bundle of cotton.

I take off toward the ring, desperate to put some distance between us. Before long, I hear Vyle's hurried footsteps behind me.

"Hey, slow down. Do you even know where you're going?"

"I'm going to the plaza. I want to get eyes on the palace."

"Think about it, Rose. Every champion and their great-aunt Lila will be at the plaza. They all want eyes on the palace. If we want to report something worthwhile, we have to do something different."

"And what do you suggest?" I ask.

"Well, Zane told my dad some things about Hogrum. Supposedly, there used to be this demon cult. They had a hidden room beneath a slaughterhouse in the southern ring of Hogrum. They would sacrifice the animals in their rituals. If demons are really here, I bet you they're using that slaughterhouse. All we have to do is find it."

"And where in the ring is this slaughterhouse?"

Vyle smiles. "Come along, and I'll show you."

"And why would you help me?"

"Don't you see, Rose?" Vyle backpedals in front of me. "I'm investing in our future. I'll win The Surviving, and become my father's new apprentice. Then, the king will no doubt assign you to be his apprentice. I'm not stupid. I know we won't be together. You'll marry Antai, and that'll be that. But we can still be friends. I want to be in your council, and that can't happen if you die today." Vyle shrugs. "I just have to keep you safe until then." He winces, recognizing his mistake. "Or rather, we'll keep each other safe. We're stronger together."

"Why in God's name would I trust you to keep me safe?"

"Because no one else is going to do it. Look around, Rose. It's just me. As hard as it is for you to believe, I'm the only one who cares enough to look out for you. Why can't you just once let me prove myself?"

His voice is strained—the pent up frustration of living with a bad reputation. As much as I hate him, I can't help but believe him.

"Fine. I'll go with you," I agree, "but don't get used to it. As soon as I see someone else, I'm going with them."

"You won't regret it, Rose. I promise." He's excited, almost like a puppy. He starts toward the building, glancing back every few paces. "If my dad is right, the slaughterhouse should be up this way. Follow me."

The snow is packed from sitting in the sunlight, and my boots crunch with every step. It's only a few inches deep, so the walking is light. Still, I can see storm clouds on the horizon. If it's not snowing soon, it will be by tonight.

"So." Vyle slows his pace to walk beside me. "How's the archery coming along? You're getting pretty good from what I've seen. Maybe you could teach me?"

"You want me to teach you archery? You're kidding?"

"I'm serious. Honestly, I think the whole guard could benefit from it. Feeders wouldn't stand a chance. I'm telling you, Rose, things are going to change when you're queen. I want to be a part of it."

We walk in silence for a bit. As stubborn and proud as Vyle is, maybe Antai was right all those weeks ago. Maybe he isn't so bad deep down.

As we pass the outermost buildings, Vyle begins scanning.

"What are we looking for?" I ask.

"My dad said it's in the Southern Quadrant, along a main road. It should also be by a canal."

I nod. It makes sense. Slaughterhouses produce a lot of animal waste. The river is an easy place to dump what isn't used.

For the first hour, we search street by street, never losing sight of the other. We find three slaughterhouses, but in none did we find a secret room underneath. As the storm clouds darken the sky, I begin to lose patience. The first snowflakes of a storm fall around me.

"It was a good effort, Vyle, but we're not going to find it. I'm heading to the plaza."

"C'mon, Rose, just give it another hour. We can find it. We have to be close by now."

"This is stupid," I say. "What if we find it and the demons are inside? We won't stand a chance. I'm going to the plaza with the others."

"You're making a mistake," Vyle calls after me. "Please, don't do this."

"I'll be fine." I head north, marching to the core. I'm walking parallel to the canal. It's 20 feet across and nearly full of slow-flowing water. The overcast sky makes it hard to gauge the depth, but it's definitely too deep to stand.

"Rose, C'mon. Just trust me. This is stupid."

I keep marching, heading for a bridge just up ahead.

Vyle bites down. When I don't turn around, he snaps. "If you go, you'll die. The Holy One will kill you."

I freeze mid-stride. "What did you say?"

"Don't you get it? I'm protecting you. If you go to the palace, you'll die. The Holy One is waiting for us there."

"What?" I stumble back. "How... how do you know that? How could you possibly know that?"

Vyle clenches his fists. "Let's just say... someone warned me about the Holy One. They told me to stay away from the palace."

"The Holy One is in the palace, and you didn't warn anyone? Are you mad?"

"You're my priority, Rose. I'm risking everything to save you! Don't you see? If the Holy One finds out I warned you, he'll want revenge. I'm putting my life in the line."

"Don't pretend you're noble!" I seethe. "You're abandoning them! I have to go warn them!"

I step toward the bridge, but Vyle sidesteps to block my path. "You're no match for him, Rose. I'm not letting you throw your life away."

"I don't care. I'm going to warn them with or without you. If you're really so worried, come and keep me safe."

Vyle throws his hands down. "You don't understand. Even my father fears the Holy One. We can't take him alone. If the Holy One has them, they're already lost."

"If you're so afraid of him, why save me? Why not join him?"

"Because I'm trying to do what's right. Dammit, Rose. I'm risking everything. You have to trust me on this."

"I don't have to do anything except save my friends." I turn my back to Vyle and step onto the bridge.

Vyle raises his hand—threatening to use dominion. "Don't make me fight you, Rose."

I spin around. "That's your problem, Vyle. You think you know what's best for everyone, but you don't. You can't control me. I'm going to warn them."

I take a few steps backward, training my eyes on Vyle. When he doesn't attack, I turn back around.

Crack!

A schism erupts in the stone just an arm's length in front of me. It's only an inch wide, but I feel the entire bridge shudder, threatening to crumble at any moment.

"What the hell, Vyle? Are you trying to kill me?"

His gaze hardens, and the air reverberates at my feet. It sweeps my ankles, and like a fulcrum, my head rotates toward the ground. I put out my arms, but I can't stop my momentum; my chin crashes against the bridge.

Fire!

I blindly command as tears fill my eyes. The burning vortex hisses where Vyle stood, but he's already moved to my side. His hand grabs me by the throat, and for a second, I'm afraid he's going to choke me, but his hand clasps onto my amulet instead.

Snap!

The chain breaks, and Vyle holds my amulet in the air as a hostage. "Let it go, Rose. You're powerless now. Forget about your friends, forget about the palace."

"No! You think taking that is going to stop me? I don't care if I'm powerless. I don't care what happens to me. I'm going to warn them."

"Rose, just stop this madness! I'm trying to save your life."

I don't turn around. I march my way over the bridge.

"I'm trying to save your life. I'm the good guy."

"No!" I should leave him, but my emotions get the best of me. "No! You don't get to call yourself that. If you were a hero, you would've warned us before we left. Even in your best moments, you're still a heartless killer, Vyle. When we get home, I'm going to tell the council everything, and then, if you're lucky, you can spend the rest of your life in the fields."

I don't care what he has to say. I turn and crest the peak of the bridge. I'm about to descend the other side when the stone beneath my feet gives. Immediately, I begin to fall.

Stop!

But I'm not wearing my amulet. I ride the stone all the way into the water, never really breaking the water's surface. For a brief instant, the water is suspended around me. Then, it all comes crashing down. The concussion of the water knocks the breath from my chest. My senses are instantly silenced by the cold.

It was an accident! The bridge simply collapsed, I tell myself. At any moment, Vyle will pull me from the river, but with each passing moment, the thought becomes less likely.

I flail until my shin hits something solid—a slab of stone resting at the bottom of the river. I plant the ball of my foot on the tip of the boulder and propel myself toward the surface. Just as I expect my head to break the surface, the crown of my skull hits solid stone.

I'm about to turn around when I notice the light. A dull grey glow emanates from the stone above me. Only it isn't stone; it's ice.

Vyle froze the river.

Vyle is trying to kill me.

Chapter 31

Matt

I approach the house slowly. A blue Honda sedan is parked out front. I feel my shoulders relax. It means the caregiver is here.

Judy is still alive.

I knock on the door, not because I have to, but so that I don't give the hospice nurse a heart attack. I wait for a second, and then I step into the house. "Hello? I'm Judy's son, Matt. I'm here to visit."

"Coming," a woman calls from Judy's room. Her heels click on the tiled hallway before her head appears from the corner. "Hello, Matt, I'm Barbara. I'm glad you could make it."

We shake hands. "Is she in her room?" I ask.

Barbara gives me a sympathetic frown. "I want you to be prepared for what you're about to see, Matt. Your mother is very close to death. She hasn't spoken or eaten all week. She won't be as you remember her."

I swallow, and instantly I feel nauseous. Dread wells in my stomach like a clogged drain. "Alright. I understand."

"Take as much time as you need. If you need me, I'll be in the kitchen."

The nurse steps aside, allowing me to enter the hallway. She doesn't follow. At the end of the hallway, Judy's door is already ajar. I take a deep breath and step inside.

Judy is laying on the bed, looking more dead than alive. She has oxygen tubes plugging her nostrils, and her skin is ashen grey, like cold, dead coals. Her joints protrude at odd angles, threatening to burst through the skin. As horrid as it sounds, she looks like a feeder.

She looks dead.

Judy doesn't stir as I take her hand. It's so cold, I almost drop it in surprise. "I'm so sorry, Mom. I should've come sooner."

As I stare at her, I sense something stirring beneath her skin. It's friendly and funny and wise.

Judy!

She may be on the brink, but her soul is still within reach. I can speak with her, if only in her dreams. I close my eyes and let my head slump. If the nurse sees me like this, she'll assume I'm mourning.

Hesitantly hopeful, I force my consciousness into Judy's mind. As I drift through the darkness, I expect to find pain and fatigue—at least suffering of some degree—but I don't find it. Instead, a sense of excitement buzzes through her thoughts. I feel contentment and peace. It puts my worried soul at ease.

Then, the darkness forms colors, and the colors form shapes. I'm standing on a street corner, familiar Colorado mountains on the horizon. Behind me, I see a chain-link fence with a playground on the other side. Children run through the wood chip and hang from the monkey bars, shrieking and laughing. Beyond the playground is an aged brick building. A sign reads: **Broadman Elementary School**.

My old school?

Judging by the time of day, school must have recently ended. Apart from the playground stragglers, the last of the students are getting picked up by their parents.

"Matt, is that you? I must be losing my mind."

Judy is sitting on the curb, her back resting against the steel pole of the bus sign. She's young, so young I almost didn't recognize her.

"It's me, Mom. It's really me."

She stands up and looks me over. "But... how are you here? I thought I was dying." Her face grows frantic. "Are... are you hurt, Matt? Is everything okay?"

"I'm fine," I assure her. "I'm totally fine. Consider it a miracle. I can't explain it, but I'm here."

Judy looks me over once more, and her suspicions dissolve. "Well, what are you waiting for? Come give your mom a hug."

For the first time in years, I don't feel her bones through her flesh. She squeezes me tight, pinching my shoulder with her chin. "Oh, it's so good to see you, Matt." Suddenly, her face lights up.

"I have something to show you." She bends over and flattens her hands on the sidewalk, forming a plank position. With a wild grin on her face, she starts doing push-ups, one after the other.

"Push-ups?" I laugh.

Judy giggles to herself. "Before you left, you told me you wanted to see me doing push-ups. Well, are you impressed?"

I laugh. "They look good, Mom. You look... so young."

"Only in here," she laughs. Judy stands up, dusting her hands on her jeans. "This is what I looked like back before Dave died." She looks down at herself. "I'm maybe 40 in this body." She turns around. "Do you remember when you were in my class? Those were the days."

I smile. "Remember when we went on the zoo field trip, and those parrots pooped on my head?"

Judy nods. "And you made me wash your hair in the drinking fountain because you didn't want to go in the girl's bathroom." Judy sighs, "Oh, I'd give anything to spend another day as your teacher."

"Maybe not as my teacher, but this doesn't have to be the end. I think I have a way I can save you."

"Save me?" Judy frowns. "I don't want to be saved, Matthew. I want this. I'm ready. When the bus comes, I'm going to get on. It'll take me to see Dave."

"But…" I shake my head. "I have a cure. I'm here in Kentville. You don't have to die."

Judy closed her eyes and inhaled through her nose. "Oh, Matthew. I don't know how to say this, but I'm ready for this. I want to be with Dave. I'm excited to go, Matt. Death is my next great adventure. Besides you, this life has nothing left for me. I'm ready to move on."

"But…" my lower lip quivers. "There's still so much to live for. You have to be at my wedding. And what about when I have kids? Don't you want to meet them?" Like a balloon, I feel my voice rising. The string is already out of reach, and I can't pull it down. "Don't you want to be a part of their lives? Don't you want to be a part of my life? You can't leave me now, Mom. I still need you. I can't do this alone." I try to swallow, but my emotions are caught in my throat. My eyes fill with water, sending the dreamscape into a blur of colors.

"Oh, Matthew." She pulls me into a hug, and I let the tears fall on my mother's shoulder. She holds me until my breathing steadies, and then she steps back. "Take a seat, Matt. I have a story I want to tell you." She pats the curb next to her. When I'm seated, she looks down the road and starts talking.

"The night Dave died was the worst night of my life. He was my everything, Matthew, and the world without him was a sad and lonely place. At first, I tried to go on. I tried to keep teaching, to find meaning in the mundane. For a while, I managed to ignore my pain, but eventually, it overwhelmed me. I started thinking about ending my life."

My jaw falls open, and I gape at Judy. She offers a thin-lipped smile and looks down at the road. "I didn't have anything to live for at the time. And I was sooo lonely, Matt. I had no one. And so, I made a plan. I picked a night, and I loaded Dave's shotgun, and that's when I heard you crying. It was the same night that the power plant exploded. God saved my life, by giving me you. You became my purpose, Matthew. You were my reason to live, and I loved it. I loved being your mother, and I'll always be your mother, but…" Judy sighs. "The truth is, you don't need me like you used to. From now on, you'll be doing research, finding love, you'll be off on your own adventures, adventures I can't be a part of. I hope you understand when I say, I feel like my work is done. I'm ready to move on."

"So what? You… you want this?" I can't bring myself to say it.

"I want to progress, Matthew. I want to explore whatever life comes next. I want to be with my husband. For 20 years I've missed him, and finally, I'm on the verge of being reunited. When this bus comes, it's going to take me home, and something tells me Dave will be there waiting."

"I…" I feel like my world is crumbling. "I found the cure for you. Now, you're telling me you don't even want it. This whole summer was for nothing?"

"Not nothing, Matt. Heavens no! This cure you've found, it's going to help people. People who need it. People who have their whole lives ahead of them. Even if this cure works, I'm old, Matt. I won't live long. Sooner or later, I'm going to die. And I don't think that's such a bad thing. I wouldn't want to live forever, even if I could."

I sit there for a moment, sifting through my thoughts as if separating sugar and salt. "You're sure about this?"

Judy purses her lips. "I'm sure." She nods her head as if agreeing with herself. "But listen here, Matt. I will be watching you. Instead of lying in that bed, I'll be cheering you on from heaven. I'll be closer to you than I've been in months."

I sit back down on the curb. "So, this is the last time I'll see you?" I say the words, but it doesn't compute. *It can't be true.*

Judy puts her arm around me. "We can talk as long as you'd like. I won't get on that bus until you feel ready." She squeezes my shoulder. "Tell me about the dance. How did things go with Lynn?"

I'm grateful for the distractions "It was nice. We danced. We talked." *I brought back her boyfriend from the dead.*

"And did you kiss her?"

I shake my head. *Only in a dream.*

"Did you *want* to kiss her?" Judy presses.

I shake my head. "I think we're done. Her boyfriend recovered and they're back together."

"If you have feelings for her, you have to tell her. Don't give up so easily. You have to fight for what you want."

I shake my head. "I don't know, Mom. She made her choice. I have to respect that. Besides..." I bite my lip. "The truth is, I have feelings for someone else. There's this other girl, Kendra. I really like her... a lot actually. I kind of chose her. I was hoping my feelings for Rose would disappear, but they haven't. What if I chose the wrong one? What if I ruin my chances with both of them?"

Judy nods her head in understanding. "Matt, love isn't special because it's irreplaceable. That's not how love works. You don't love someone because you'll never find anyone like them. In fact, I guarantee you that you will. The world is full of amazing people. It's the fact that there could be better people out there, and you choose not to look for them. That is what makes love special."

She smiles to herself, "You know, when I first fell in love with Dave, I was sure he was the greatest man on Earth. As I got older, I began to see the flaws. I saw men more handsome than him, and I'm sure he saw women more beautiful than me. Still, we never wavered. Even when I couldn't have children, he never went looking for an upgrade." She smiles. "Whatever girl you choose, don't choose them because you're afraid you won't find better. Choose them because they make you want to be better. Choose them because you don't want anyone else, no matter how many amazing girls are out there." She pauses, thinking for a moment longer. "And choose a girl who feels the same about you. You deserve a girl who will always put you first."

Kendra. Instantly, I think of her. She put me first. She chose me, even when I wavered. *She's too good for me.*

Judy looks down, the pride radiating from her face. "I know you'll make the right decision, Matthew. Whatever decision you make is the right one. Follow your heart and take your time. There's no rush in love."

"Thanks, Mom. I appreciate this. I'm going to miss your advice."

"Oh, hush. Don't go making me cry now." She wraps her arm around me.

"You really think Dave is out there?"

"Heaven and Hell I'm not so sure about, but Dave is out there. I have no doubt." Her eyes wander toward the horizon, wistfully wishing for her husband. "I can't wait for you to meet him. He'll be so excited to take you hunting. Oh, what a good father he would have been."

"I'll try to make him proud," I assure her.

"But you already have!" Judy exclaims. "As you got older, Matthew, I realized you would grow up to be a far better man than he was. A far better person than myself. I'm so excited for what your future holds. Cure cancer, president of the United States, I'm convinced there's nothing you can't do."

"I can't chug a gallon of milk," I laugh. I tried once and puked all over Judy's favorite rug.

"You know what I mean," Judy chuckles. She looks down the road, "You have amazing things ahead of you. Of that I'm sure." She looks longingly down the road as the city bus turns into view. The engine hums as it climbs the hill to the school. "It's time, Matt. Do you think you're ready?"

I'll never be ready, I think, but at the same time, I feel at peace. My soul has only so much room for emotion, and Judy's excitement has displaced my grief. It radiates from her like the noonday sun, thawing my icy heart. I find myself smiling, reflecting her own happiness back at her.

"I'm ready, Mom. I'll miss you more than anything, but I'm ready. Go give Dave a hug for me."

Judy squeezes me one last time before stepping onto the bus. She stops on the first step and turns around.

"Thank you for being my baby, Matt. Thank you for giving me a reason to live. Go bless the world. And know, I've never been happier than when I was your mother."

"I love you, Mom. Thanks for everything."

"Goodbye, my son."

She climbs the final steps, and the hydraulic doors fold shut. I watch her through the glass. She takes the first seat facing me, and waves until the bus moves out of view. I feel her emotions, the comforting aura of excitement, slowly fade as the bus disappears down the road. Finally, the sky turns dark, and the dream dissolves.

When I open my eyes, Judy is already dead. Her chest doesn't move. I don't bother feeling for a pulse.

Goodbye, Mom.

Without Judy's emotions, I feel empty. I expect the sadness to return, but it doesn't. I'm left with an aching, endless void where Judy should be. All this time, I've been trying to save her, and now she's gone.

Who am I without Judy?

I watch her dead body for a long time, letting the pain repossess me. The tears almost feel therapeutic, as if the agony is slowly draining through my eyes. After a minute, I stand and give one last glance. "Goodbye, Mom."

I walk slowly to the kitchen and stop at the threshold. The nurse looks up at me and frowns. "Is everything alright?"

"I... I think she's dead." I know she's dead, but somehow saying it with certainty makes it sound worse.

The nurse sets down the dish scrubber and hurries down the hall. Now is my chance.

I grab a handful of stainless steel utensils from the kitchen. Then, I close my eyes and command the particle to realign, forming new nuclei and electron orbitals.

Transfigure!

When I open my eyes, the spoons and forks gleam solid gold. *I hope it's enough.*

I fish the car keys from the nurse's purse, then I drop the utensils inside as compensation.

On my way out the door, I hit the unlock button on the keys. I climb into her Honda and put it in gear. I'm halfway out of the driveway when the nurse comes sprinting out of the house.

"Stop! That's my car! Stooop!"

"Sorry," I mouth through the window, then I punch the gas to the floor. I don't slow down until I turn onto the service road, following it out of the city and into the mountains.

The ride to the meadow is a bumpy one, but I revel in the familiar scenery. Part of me is devastated, but a deeper part feels free. For years, I carried the stress of her health. I joined the guard to learn healing. Everything I did was to save her. Now, she's moved on. She's happy.

I park at the meadow only long enough to melt the lock on the gate. Then, I proceed, driving up the mountain and through the outer wall. It isn't until I'm cruising past the flats that I start to feel nervous. The palace is my destination, but it's also where I was nearly killed just a few months ago. *This time, Zane won't be here to save me.*

I accelerate up the road, using my momentum to carry me up the cobblestone street. Fresh powder covers the ground, threatening to steal my traction. I'm almost to the inner wall when I hit the brakes.

A set of footprints crosses the road in front of me. The boots are small—a woman's if I had to guess.

Rose!

Next to the first set of prints, are a much larger set of boot-prints. My feet may be big, but these are even bigger—size 12 or 13.

Vyle!

I can't be sure, but something tells me they're his. For whatever reason, Vyle and Rose are wandering through the ring of Hogrum. I put the car in park and push the door open. A gust of wind cuts through my coat, snatching away my warmth.

I trudge down the alley, following the tracks to another full-sized road. The two prints turn and start walking uphill—toward the palace. I trudge along the prints as quickly as I can without breaking a sweat. The last thing I need is a wet coat in the snow.

KERPLUNK!

The noise is a mix of a crash and a splash. Whatever it is, it sounded like it came from just up the road.

Feeders!

I start to run, glancing between the road ahead and the prints at my feet. The prints turn left, cutting through another block of apartments. When they weave right, I slide to a stop in the snow and grab my amulet.

The two footprints lead to the broken ledge of a bridge. Vyle is standing there, looking down at the water, but Rose is nowhere to be seen. Her footsteps lead to the edge of the bridge, then disappear.

No!

I start running. "What happened? Where's Rose?"

Vyle startles, nearly dropping what's in his hand. It's an amulet... a golden seashell spiral.

Rose's amulet!

Vyle looks like he's on the verge of tears. "Matt! It's not what it looks like, I swear."

It's exactly what it looks like.

I feel rage building inside me. It urges me to violence, focusing all of my thoughts on the fiend in front of me. I feel the charge of electrons building, begging to be released, but I hold them back.

"What did you do?" I demand. "Tell me!"

Vyle grabs the hilt of his Adamic blade, glancing toward the broken ledge of the bridge. "I didn't want to do it. It was me or her." He unsheathes the blade. "You have to believe me. She brought it on herself."

But I don't believe him. He harmed Rose, and now he's going to pay.

Lightning!

The current erupts from the tip of my dagger, crackling and sizzling against Vyle's shield. He directs the charge into the bridge, melting the snow at his feet.

I cut the current before it strains my soul, but I'm not finished. I rush Vyle, holding the hilt as Zane taught me. I slash through his shield with my dagger. Then, I press my consciousness against his mind until his intentions are an open book. I let him strike first.

Stab!

Vyle thrusts his dagger at my stomach, but I twist to the side, simultaneously slashing at his wrist. To my surprise, it cuts clean through.

"Aagh!" His hand plops into the snow, his dagger still gripped inside. I want to finish him. I want to drive the dagger through his heart, but I can't bring myself to do it.

Before he can retaliate, I drive my mind into his skull. Submitting myself to the onslaught of his emotions. I feel rage and desperation, but mostly, I sense regret. It already consumes him. Vyle hates what he's done. He wants to undo it, but he fears he's too late.

She's already dead!

The memories are there, ripe for the taking. I see Rose as the bridge comes apart, disappearing into the frothy foam below. I'm looking down at the water, commanding the surface to crystallize, sealing Rose in her icy tomb. I see her hands, pale and weak, scraping against the ice that holds her down.

Rose!

I don't have a moment to spare. Vyle is only slowing the rescue.

Sleep!

I feel his body begin to crumple, but before it hits the ground, I've already reclaimed my own skin. I dash to the edge of the bridge and look down at the ice. The river is frozen from bank to bank, and 20 feet in both directions. I scan the ice for movement, but Rose is nowhere to be seen.

Melt!

The ice directly below me dissolves, slowly melting toward the opposite bank. I don't quite reach it before I feel the strain of dominion. I stop, leaving the outer edges frozen.

It'll have to be enough.

I'm afraid the water will wash away my amulet, so I pull it from my head and coil it around my fingers. Then, I dive headfirst.

The moment my fingertips break the surface, the cold crushes down, filling my clothes and clawing at my skull. Already, my body begs me to return to the surface. Instead, I tighten my grip on my amulet.

Heat!

The cold ebbs momentarily, but as soon as I take the stroke deeper into the water, the warm water is quickly replaced by the liquid ice.

I can't worry about the cold, I have to find Rose.

I can only see a few feet in the water, and Rose is nowhere to be seen. I keep swimming until I feel the algae-covered slime of the canal floor. Then, I move along the bottom of the river, sweeping my hand from side to side.

Rose!

I want to scream. I need to find her. It's hard to say how long she's been in the water. Maybe a minute? Maybe more?

Maybe I can raise the water? I can empty the river! I start playing with the idea, but I know it'll kill me. It'll strain my soul, and when I die, the water will come crashing back down.

The need to breathe becomes increasingly harder to refuse. I clench my core to keep my lungs from expanding and take another stroke.

Another five seconds go by, then five more. Still, there's no sign of Rose.

My lungs demand air, and my brain bypasses my conscious mind. My chest spasms and my mouth opens, freezing fluid pouring inside.

I focus my soul on my lungs, exerting my dominion over them. *Just a few seconds longer.*

I swim downstream, assuming her body has drifted with the current. I scoop the water with my arms and then point my finger flat in front of me as I breaststroke kick.

My arm bumps a rock.

Another stroke.

I feel a twig.

After one last stroke, I plant my feet in preparation for a desperate kick to the surface. That's when I feel the loose silky strands of her hair.

I don't have time to be gentle. I clutch a handful of her hair, yanking her body toward me. I loop my arms under her armpits and kick desperately toward the surface.

"Ptuhhhh!"

I inhale as much air as my lungs can fit, choking on the droplets that I failed to spit from my mouth. Rose doesn't gasp. She's inanimate.

No!

I won't let it happen. Amplifying my muscles. I drag Rose to the channel's edge, whose walls extend another four feet above the water.

Lift!

I command Rose's body into the air, dropping her as softly as I can on the walkway above. I depend completely on my dominion.

Rise.

My own body slowly ascends from the water. As soon as my feet clear the channel's wall, I fall into the snow next to Rose. I'm no doctor, but I've seen enough television to know what to do.

Dry! Heat!

I whisk away the freezing water and surround Rose with a cloud of desert air. I put my quivering hands on her chest and force my soul inside. I can sense the water, flooding the cavities where fresh air should be. With a simple command, I take hold of the water and pull it from her lungs.

Rose doesn't move a muscle as the water bubbles out of her mouth. I feel myself starting to panic, and my thoughts become more hectic.

What do I do? She's dying!

I move my soul until I sense her silent heart. I command it with every ounce of my soul.

Beat!

Bum-bum!

Her heart pumps once but falls still the instant after.

Keep beating!

Bum-bum... Bum-bum... Bum-bum...

Once again, her heart falls silent.

Nooo!

Then, I remember the breath of life. Rose has given me some of her soul. Maybe it's time I give it back.

I urge my soul deep into Rose's skull. I don't sense her soul, so I keep moving deeper and deeper. My body grows ever distant, but I don't stop. I can no longer feel the cold. I can no longer feel anything. And then, on the edge of the void, I sense betrayal... rage... fear.

Rose?

She senses me too, but with each passing second, her emotions grow more dilute in the rising tide of death. I give chase to keep from losing them altogether.

Rose!

Before she floats away, I latch onto her consciousness. Then, I get to work. I focus on my soul and begin to break it away. It hurts. It feels wrong, but I don't stop until some part of me, some part I desperately need, is hanging by a thread. Then, I breathe it into Rose.

I feel it leaving, memories and emotions. Secrets and fears. I breathe until my own soul is on the edge of oblivion.

Live! I need you, Rose. Please! Ever so slowly, her descent to the spirit world comes to a stop. Not only does she sense me, but she's moving toward my voice!

This way, Rose! Follow me! You're going to be fine!

I continue to call to her until I feel the physical world around us. Then, I feel Rose regain her body.

Beat!

Bum-bum... Bum-bum...

She gasps, her reflexes once again animated. Her eyes don't open, but her chest begins the rhythmic cycle of life.

She's alive!

I sit back in the snow, assessing the situation for the first time. My body is still shivering uncontrollably, and in my panic, I neglected to remove the water from my own clothes.

Dry!

Like wringing out a sponge, the water oozes from my uniform and puddles at my feet. Still, the cold is piercing.

I look around. Vyle is still where I left him on the bridge, his stump of an arm lying limp at his side. Now, the sky is covered with clouds, and the snowfall is beginning to collect in my hair. We both need shelter, or everything I just accomplished will be in vain.

I know I'll have to carry her, but before my arms are full. I need to do one thing. I trudge to Vyle's body and pry Rose's amulet from his frozen fingertips. The ice around his wrist looks like a cherry snow cone. The cold has slowed the bleeding, but it hasn't stopped. I reach my soul until I find the severed vessels.

Clot!

I amplify the clotting factor until the blood stops oozing from the stump. It's not healed, but he's no longer losing blood.

If I leave him, he might die. He could be hypothermic within the hour, and dead within the next, but I don't have much of a choice. I can't carry both of them, and even if I take two trips, odds are he'll wake up violent and deranged.

He made his choice!

I don't take his amulet. That way, he has a chance. Leaving him in the snow, I hurry back to Rose. I put her amplifier around her neck, hoping it will help stabilize her. Then, I scoop one arm under her knees and another around her back. Her head hangs limp until it rests on my shoulder.

I don't care about my growing headache; I command more heat into her clothes. I refrain from warming her too quickly, I heat her clothes, not her skin, like a bundle of laundry fresh from the dryer.

I can only hope the snowfall covers our tracks so that Vyle cant hunt us down. I walk a block and then cross a different bridge. As soon as I pass under the inner wall, I find a nice looking apartment and push open the door.

Just as it did months ago, the home looks frozen in time. A frayed blanket is laying in the doorway, and several chairs are knocked over in the kitchen. Opening the door with my foot, I carry Rose into the bedroom and lay her on the straw mattress. For all I know, it's bug-infested, but it'll do.

The room has no windows and no blankets, so I grab the blanket from the hallway and a candle from the dinner table.

Ignite.

I set the candle on the floor and drape the blanket over Rose, tucking the wool under her feet. Then I close the door, sealing off the last of the setting sunlight.

Heat!

I command the energy into the air until the room is verging on sauna-hot. Finally, I sit down against the wall. I'm exhausted. My mind is numb from strain, and my body begs for sleep. Before long, I feel my eyelids closing. *A little nap wouldn't hurt.*

Just when I feel myself nodding off, the wall shudders.

Ka-Crack!

The thunder is distant, but it rattles me awake. I leap to my feet and unsheathe my knife. I glance at Rose who is still deep asleep—or maybe unconscious is a more accurate term.

Opening the door, I slink into the hallway and crack open the front door as quietly as I can. A continuous brigade of snow is accumulating on the ground. If it had been raining, I might assume the lightning was natural, but not during a snowstorm.

Lightning dominion!

It's the only explanation. Was it a signal of some kind? An attack? Is someone in danger?

Ka-Crack!

The thunder rumbles once more, distant and muffled by the snowfall. It came from the direction of the palace, but I have no clue about its context. No inkling as to why...

I peer back in the bedroom, and sure enough, Rose hasn't stirred. I want to stay to protect her. I want to be here when she wakes up, but another part of me is ruminating on the thunder. The more I think about it, the less I like my options. Whoever is out there, they must be in danger. That could be Crasilda, or maybe Vyle.

Or it could be Diego.

I don't want to leave Rose, but I don't know what else I can do for her. She's safe and warm and seemingly stable.

I ask myself the questions.

Will I regret staying? Maybe... if something happens to Diego, I'll regret it every day.

Will I regret going? Probably not. I'll make sure he's alright, and I'll come straight back. Rose will be safe in the meantime.

I take a deep breath and draw my Adamic blade. It's decided. I'm going to the palace.

I'm going to find Diego.

The wind batters me from all sides, blinding me with a flurry of white flakes. I press on, maneuvering my way through the crumbled portion of the palace wall.

Hogrum's castle hunches before me like a crippled old man. It's beaten and aged, looking like it might fall over and die at any minute. Still, it's an impressive structure. The entrance looms before me, the open jaws of an unforgiving monster.

"Diego!"

I know it's stupid, but I yell at the top of my lungs. I can only hope he'll hear me and respond.

"Diego!"

Silence...

As much as I hate it, I know he's in there. I've already checked the plaza and the surrounding rooftops. He'll want something to report, even if it means putting himself in danger.

Light.

I illuminate the hallway and step inside, trying not to think about the last time I was here. Hood, the armored feeder was hiding in this very hallway. He attacked me only a few yards inside the entrance.

I take a deep breath and begin my exploration. With my light dominion, I can see much better than last time, revealing both walls and ceiling. I see a broken vase that I remember from last time. Then, I find a torn canvas.

Right. Left. Right.

I weave my way through the hallways, trying to ignore the eerie silence. Even with my amulet, I feel as unnerved as the last time. I fear at any moment, someone will erupt from the darkness. I can only hope it's Diego and not a feeder.

I continue until I find a massive staircase, the same staircase I descended last time. That's when I see the blood. It's smeared down the center of the steps as if they were mopped with ketchup. The sight of it sends my heart into overdrive. A body was dragged down these steps. A bleeding body.

Everything tells me I should run. I'm in grave danger, but so is Diego. For all I know, that could be his blood. I can't leave until I know he's okay.

I creep down the stairs, careful not to slip in the blood. At the bottom of the last step is a long hallway. I continue down it, my dagger ready to stab at the slightest movement. That's when I reach another staircase, this one spiraling into the ground. The top step has several Adamic symbols.

I take the steps one at a time, no longer trying to be quiet. My light is so bright, someone will see me coming long before I see them. I don't have the element of surprise. I can only hope I won't need it.

Tap. Tap. Tap.

My footsteps echo as I make my way down the staircase. It spirals one full circle before I find a closed wooden door embedded in the side of the wall. The staircase, along with the trail of blood, continues past the door, deeper into the ground.

I follow the blood, passing two more wooden doors before I reach a small landing. Before me, is one final door, the blood trail disappearing underneath. The door itself isn't locked. I lift the latch and pull the door open.

The smell hits me like a wall, and I stumble back. Sewage and death. Whatever resolve I had to find Diego is quickly disappearing. Yet, I can't ignore the blood. It stretches down a new hallway before me.

I tighten my grip on my dagger and move through the doorway. I have no choice but to breathe the toxic air, hoping the putrid smell is harmless.

I only take a few steps when I hear wheezing. It's weak and ragged, like an injured animal. I tilt my head and listen harder. I can hear the harmonic breathing of several bodies, slow and rhythmic. I take a few steps and spot iron bars lining the walls on either side, but that isn't what concerns me. As my light illuminates the cell, several small girls stare back at me. They are filthy and famished, and obviously terrified. They cower at my gaze, shielding their eyes from the light.

It's a prison!

I'm about to say something when something moves behind me, I turn around, finding two men and an old woman in another cell.

"How do I get you out?" I say. "I'm here to help."

Not one of them responds. Either they're too weak to speak, or they think it's a trick.

Heat!

I try melting the bars, but nothing happens. I can see the Adamic symbols on the lock.

441

"Where's the key?" I hiss. "Who has it?"

The old woman lifts her head, her eyes bulging from sunken sockets. "Run," she wheezes. "Save yourself."

But I can't run. I can't leave these people. How did they get here, and why?

I look down at the blood trail. It continues deeper down the hallway. I'm frantic now, running past the cells. Every single one is packed with people.

What is this place? Who's keeping them here?

Eventually, I reach a dead end. The blood leads to the last cell on the right. I look through the bars, immediately recognizing the bundle of red hair.

Crasilda!

The blood is coming from a gash in her leg. Her chest still moves, although barely. I don't have time to help her. Footsteps are approaching from down the hall.

Tap. Tap. Tap.

I hold my knife and face whoever is approaching. They wear a cloak, concealed from head to toe. They stop a safe distance away from me. Then, he speaks.

"Inumkuh Lene Maratagah."

The words reverberate through my skull, and somewhere deep in my soul, I understand.

Be still and unchanging.

I try to move, but my body is rigid. I can't blink. I can't breathe. It's as though time is frozen.

Fire!

I command flames into the air, but nothing happens. The air around me is frozen as well. I'm completely immobilized.

There's only one thing left I can think to do. The physical world may be frozen, but my soul is not. I urge my mind toward the cloaked man. As soon as my mind borders his, he attacks.

His soul seems to move as separate entities, battering my mind from all directions. I try to push back, but it's hopeless. When I retreat into my body, the man follows. Possessing my body and

442

exploring my mind. I can feel him sifting through my memories like a filing cabinet. My date with Rose at the fall festival. My time in Rose's dream. He takes his time, savoring each experience like a slice of cake.

Finally, he stops, hovering on the edge of my consciousness.

Hello, Matt. I've been waiting a long time to meet you.

Who are you? I demand, expecting him to refuse.

I'll give you one guess.

Already, I know. He's a powerful demon. He spoke Adamic. There's only one person I can think of with such power.

Yes, Matt, his mind replies. *I'm the Holy One.*

Chapter 32

Rose

Rose!

Matt's voice calls to me in the void. He's a beacon—a lighthouse on the edge of my sanity, beckoning me toward him. At first, I try to move toward him, but I can't stop myself. I'm in perpetual free fall.

Then, he breathes his soul into me.

I feel his essence mixing with my own, bringing clarity and lucidity. I see images as well, my body—pale and lifeless—lying on the bank of the river. I see Judy, climbing on a bus and riding away. I see Vyle's severed hand lying in the snow.

Live! I need you, Rose. Please!

I want to live, but I don't know how. All I can do is cling to Matt's consciousness, and pray he brings me home.

This way, Rose! Follow me! You're going to be fine!

I let him drag me back to the physical world. Back to the cold and the pain. When I finally find my body, everything goes black.

The first thing I notice is the whistling. I can hear the wind raging in the distance, whistling as it passes through the city streets. I can feel the warmth of a blanket and the straw mattress beneath my back. I'm definitely awake, yet I can't see a thing. For a moment, I worry I'm blind. Then, as I sit up, I spot a tiny crack of light seeping from beneath the door.

I feel for my amulet, and to my surprise, it's resting on the outside of my shirt.

Light!

I'm in what appears to be a bedroom. There are no windows and no lamps. On the floor by the door, a small candle has burned to the base.

How long have I been asleep?

I climb to my feet and stretch. I remember Vyle freezing the river, and suddenly Matt was giving me the breath of life. As for how he got there, I don't have an inkling of a clue.

When I finally open the door, I'm shocked to see the sun spilling into the apartment. Not only is it daytime, it's nearly noon. I've slept through the entire mission.

I hurry down the stairwell and throw open the door to the street. The cobblestone is buried in a foot of fresh powder. Whatever storm raged in the night, it's gone now. The sky is clear and the sun is shining.

I jog through the snow, ignoring the handfuls of ice spilling into my boots. I run until the flats are stretched out before me. There isn't a helicopter in sight, which hopefully means I'm not too late.

I'm still trudging along the trail when I notice a lone figure up ahead. About the same time I notice him, he lifts his head.

Vyle!

He scrambles to his feet, his fear satisfying to see. I clutch my amulet, prepared to kill if necessary.

"No! Rose, I'm sorry! I made a mistake. I don't want to fight you." He takes off his amulet and throws it at me. It lands in the snow between my feet.

Vyle raises his hands—or rather, he raises one hand. The other arm ends at the base of his wrist. He backs away as I continue to advance. "I panicked, Rose. I'm still on your side. We can figure out what to do about the Holy One. I swear, I wasn't trying to kill you. It just hap—"

Commanding the snow around him, I sweep Vyle into a giant heap of slush. Then, I watch as he proceeds to dig his way out with one hand.

The longer I watch, the more enraged I become. I remember what he did to me that morning in my dorm room. The way he suffocated me. The way he drew the air from my lungs and watched me fighting for my life.

He deserves this.

I focus on the pile of snow that surrounds Vyle.

Melt.

As the snow liquifies, it accumulates in a giant ball, clinging to Vyle's torso and slowly crawling toward his neck. His eyes widen as he realizes what I have in mind.

"Rose, don't do this. I'm not your enemy. I'm n—"

A blob of water, like a giant dewdrop, encases Vyle's head. He swats at the water, but his hands pass in and out of the glob without effect. Without his amulet, there's nothing he can do.

He falls to his knees, attempting to scoop air bubbles into the watery sphere. I can see his panic. Now, he knows what it feels like to drown.

After 30 seconds, I know I should stop. Any longer and he'll inhale the water. Still, I don't offer mercy.

Whop-whop-whop-whop-whop!

The chugging of chopper blades echoes over the flats, snapping me from my rage.

Stop!

The water splashes to the ground. Vyle alternates between coughing and vomiting water. Still, I don't feel bad. For the first time in a long time, I feel in control. I don't feel afraid of what he can do.

446

I pick up Vyle's amplifier and place it around my neck. I stuff the amulet into my uniform alongside the other. No matter what happens, he's not getting it back. No matter what he says, I won't believe him.

Vyle is dead to me.

The helicopter hovers for a bit, slowly lowering until it rests on the frozen soil. As Captain Renshu climbs out, his disbelief is even more discouraging.

"Where is everybody?" he calls out.

Before I can respond, Vyle rushes him. "Thank god! The princess is trying to kill me! She stole my amulet. You have to protect me."

"What? You tried to kill me! I was only defending myself."

"How did you get my amulet if I was trying to kill you? I was—"

"HEY!" Captain Renshu waves his arms in frantic circles. "Save it for the council. We need to leave. Where is everyone?"

"I don't know," I admit, but that isn't entirely true. "Vyle says the Holy One is here. If that's true..." *they're likely already dead.*

Then, I remember Matt. "Matt should be coming. He was just with me. He can't be far. He should be coming soon."

Renshu shakes his head. "If the Holy One is here, we need to get help. We can't wait around."

Renshu climbs back in the cockpit as Vyle straps himself in the backseat.

"Please," I beg. "He'll come."

"I'm sorry, princess, but we really must be going. We're sitting ducks here. If you don't board, I'll have no choice but to leave you." He flips a switch and the hum of the rotor overtakes me.

Deep down, I know he's bluffing. He wouldn't dare leave the princess. Regardless, I know he's right. If the Holy One is here, we're all in danger, myself included.

I'm sorry, Matt.

I climb the steps and take my seat, making sure to sit as far away from Vyle as possible.

If something happened to Matt, he'll need real help. He'll need the king.

An armed escort is waiting when we land. They usher us into separate carriages and rush us to the palace. A meeting is already in session.

I've rehearsed the story a hundred times. Vyle might try to lie, but he won't convince the council. Today, he'll finally get justice.

I enter the council room first, then Vyle a few moments after. Quine gasps when he sees Vyle's severed hand.

Antai's eyes are glued to me as I take my position before the council.

He looks me up and down before mouthing, "Are you okay?"

I nod. Then, I notice the soul-anchor around his neck. In my absence, he's been bonded to Quill's soul-anchor.

Antai is a guardian!

Part of me is sad I missed it, but another part is grateful. Now, he'll have a vote, and I'll need all the support I can get.

Grandpa stands, using his cane for support. "Clearly, something terrible has occurred. We need to hear exactly what happened. Don't spare any details. Rose, we will hear from you first. Then, Vyle."

Grandpa sits down as I clasp my hands awkwardly in front of me.

"Council, what I am about to tell you will sound shocking, but I swear on the Creator that it is the truth. When we arrived in Hogrum, most of the champions headed toward the palace. Vyle, however, insisted we search the ring. For the first hour, I accompanied him. Eventually, I decided to go to the palace like the others. That's when Vyle told me the truth. He said that someone had warned him about the Holy One. According to Vyle, he was waiting for us in the palace."

"Preposterous!" Chancellor Bolo cries.

General Kaynes holds up his hand, releasing a quick, condescending laugh. "Hold on now, Bolo. I want to hear about this alleged trap."

I feel my face growing warmer. "Vyle claimed he was trying to protect me, but he failed to warn the other champions. When I threatened to tell the council, he pushed me in the river and froze the surface."

Bolo gives me an incredulous glare. Gwenevere seems curious, but not completely convinced.

"Then, what happened?" General Kaynes asks. "You're here, so that obviously wasn't the end of it."

I nod. "The next thing I knew, Lieutenant MacArthur was giving me the breath of life." I see Antai stiffen, but he says nothing. "He saved me, and I'm assuming he's the one who injured Vyle. I woke up late the following morning in one of the nearby buildings. Matt was gone, and it was nearly noon, so I went to our extraction point. Vyle was there, and that's all I know."

"So," General Kaynes sneers. "You're claiming that you willingly followed Vyle around the ring, a man you already claimed tried to kill you? Already, this seems suspicious. Why would you choose to associate with a man you hate?"

"He..." I have to think for a second. "Over the past few weeks, he convinced me he had changed. I was foolish enough to believe him."

Kaynes rolls his eyes. "And then you make the claim that MacArthur saved you, only to abandon you before you gain consciousness? If he truly thought you were in danger, why would he leave you? Why would he leave my son alive? And most importantly, where is he now? The one person who can corroborate your story is conveniently missing?"

"It's the truth," I growl. "He tried to kill me. I swear!"

"Thank you, Rose." Grandpa soothes. "We take your word with the utmost seriousness. Vyle, you may present to the council."

Vyle steps forward. His face is ashen and his hands are shaking.

"Dear council," he says, "I come before you, injured and lucky to be alive. The story the princess had told is full of half-truths and blatant lies. This is what really happened."

He hugs his stump hand to his chest as he paces. "The princess was right when she said we searched the ring. While the other champions left for the palace, she asked me to assist her in the ring. I viewed it as a chance to prove myself, so I said yes. At the time, I didn't know what she had in store."

Vyle shudders, as if remembering something despicable. "Once everyone was long gone, the princess attacked me from behind. She stripped me of my amulet, and she cut off my hand. Then, she pushed me into the river to die."

"And why would she do that?" Antai demands.

General Kaynes peers at Antai with pity. "I'm sorry, General Elsborne, but that is something you missed during your medical leave. My son admitted to assaulting the princess. He did so with good intentions, but it is not absurd to assume the princess wants revenge."

Vyle nods his head vigorously. "She didn't count on me surviving, but I did. I managed to climb out of the river, and I hid. The next morning, I went to the rendezvous point hoping to find safety in numbers. Instead, I was alone. When the princess found me, she tried again to kill me. She held water around my head until I nearly drowned. Captain Renshu's arrival saved my life. He can affirm what I've told you. He found me soaking wet on the floor. He also found the princess with my amulet. He's willing to testify if need be."

"No!" I cry. "This is all a lie. He's making it up."

Zane, Gwenevere, and Kaynes all begin speaking at the same time. Grandpa stands and slaps the side of his cane onto the table.

"SILENCE!" Grandpa stands, his jagged knuckles bulging. "One at a time, please."

Kaynes raises a hand. "Surely you must all see the absurdity of what the princess has said. She accused my son of colluding with the Holy One. His own brother was slain at the Holy One's command, and you think he'd be foolish enough to join him?"

"I didn't say he joined the Holy One," I clarify. "He said he was warned by someone. The question we should be asking ourselves is who would have the motivation to warn Vyle?"

General Kaynes breaks composure, glaring at me openly. "Princess, are you accusing me of treason?"

Gwenevere laughs. "She makes a good point, General. Who else would warn the boy?"

"Stop!" Grandpa sighs. "With the information we have, we are unlikely to reach any conclusions. Regardless of who is right, the truth lies in Hogrum. If the Holy One is there, we must find out. I am willing to lead an attack in two days' time. If the princess is telling the truth, we will know shortly, and the Holy One will be destroyed. If it was a lie, we will also know, and she will be held accountable."

"Are we sure this is wise," Kaynes says. "It is no secret that you are our greatest defense against the Holy One. If you lead an army, you leave us open to attack. This may be precisely the kind of opportunity the Holy One is waiting for. It reeks of a trap."

"To be very clear," Grandpa announces. "I believe my granddaughter. We cannot waste this opportunity. With time, he'll only grow stronger."

Chancellor Quine chews his lip. "I'm sorry, but I agree with Kaynes. It's too risky to send the king. If we were positive, I would be all for it, but not with this much uncertainty. The champions have failed to give us a clear answer, so I say we send a guardian. Once there's no doubt, then we launch the attack."

"I'll go," Zane volunteers. "I know Hogrum better than anyone. If the Holy One is there, I'll find him."

Grandpa nods. "Very well. We'll await your word, Zane. Prepare to leave immediately."

Once again, I'm in awe. Somehow, Vyle has been acquitted of his crimes. He spun the circumstances against me, convincing half the council.

451

As I leave the council room, one thing is certain.

I should have killed him when I had the chance.

Chapter 33

Matt

Even asleep, I can feel the Holy One exploring my soul. He's lurking in the background of every memory, watching… analyzing. He's learning everything about me, every intimate detail. Then, he disappears.

I'm still half asleep when Diego kicks me.

"Dude, wake up."

He kicks me again and I roll over, squeezing my head between my palms. "What happened?" I don't remember falling asleep. The last thing I recall is seeing the Holy One.

"They got us, dude. We're freaking prisoners."

I sit up. Fighting to stay conscious as the world begins to spin. It's dim, but it's not pitch dark. An Adamic lantern glows from somewhere down the hall. The worst part is the voices. They echo in all directions—quiet whispers from our neighboring cells. Every few seconds, someone moans.

I feel my chest, and sure enough, my amulet is gone. "You have your amulet?" I ask.

"Nope. We're screwed."

I try not to panic, but Diego is right. We're as good as dead.

Across from us, a girl bangs her head against the bar. She stares directly at us lolling her head from side to side.

"New blood! New blood! New blood!" She sings the words over and over like some kind of cynical chorus.

"Shut up!" Diego yells, and the woman falls silent.

That's when I notice the bodies. Two people are curled up at the back of our cell. One is a relatively slender man whose clothes are in tatters. The other is a girl with red wavy hair.

"Crasilda?"

She stares at the wall, unblinking.

I tap her on the shoulder once. "Crasilda, are you okay?"

"Leave the girl," the man wheezes. "She's got the dooms. No point in bother'n her."

"The dooms?"

"The dooms," he says it louder. "It's common for newcomers to hide inside themselves. It's just too much to take in. I call it the dooms."

"Oh… okay." I sit up, focusing my attention on the man. "I'm Matt and this is Diego. What's your name?"

"Chester," the man says. "Nice to meetcha, Matt and Diego. Y'all gotta remember those names. When you forget who ya are in here, those names'll remind ya."

"How long have you been here?" I ask.

"Ohhh, too long. I lost count after my first year. My guess is three. Seen lots come and die. Not all survive as long as me."

He wiggles his back against the wall as if to get comfy. "I'll give ya a quick tour." He points to the opposite corner. "There's no bucket, but there is a hole to go in. It's built right into the floor. It's too small to crawl through if that's what yer think'n. I've seen much smaller than you try. As for the food, they bring it once a day. And that's all you gotta know. Pick a spot of ground and call it yer bed. No one else'll touch it."

"Has anyone ever escaped?" Diego asks.

Chester shakes his head. "Not that I've ever heard of. If you wanna live, it's best not to try. You can last a long time if you don't resist. He only feeds once a week. He's very careful not to kill. In all my time, I've never heard of one dyin' during the feed."

"Who are we talking about?" I ask. "The Holy One?"

Chester shrugs. "I dunno what they call him, but he sure as hell ain't holy."

I stand up and put my hands on the bars. "It's a living blood bank," I breathe. "He only feeds partway; then, he lets them recover. It's a never-ending supply of dominion."

"If ya wanna survive," Chester interjects, "ya have to obey. And pray you don't get chosen for the marks."

"The marks?"

With one arm, Chester lifts up his shirt, revealing a mess of black marks tattooed across his torso. I can tell their Adamic, but they look novice. Half of the symbols are unfinished. It's as if someone was attempting and failing a spell over and over.

They're scratch paper.

Of all the marks on the old man, only one line of symbols resembles something that could pass as a completed spell.

Chester nods when he sees my revulsion. "They cover my back too. I got lucky. Lots of people die getting marked. Their bodies burn up. With as much bare skin as ya got, pray he doesn't use ya next."

"Dude," Diego breathes. "We gotta get out of here."

"Rose is still out there," I remind myself. "She'll get help. The king will come for us."

Still, part of me wonders if it'll be enough.

Then, it hits me.

Soul-travel!

I lie down on the ground, doing my best to slow my breathing.

Diego frowns. "What are you doing?"

"Shhh! I'm trying something. Don't talk to me for a bit."

I lay there for a long time, trying not to move a muscle. Even when my nose itches, I refuse to scratch it. Eventually, after what feels like hours, the whispers stop. The world goes quiet.

I drift from my body and position myself in the center of the cell. I can sense Diego to my right, and Crasilda behind me.

Please, God, let it work!

I push forward, passing directly through the bars. At first, I think I've done it, then, like a rubber band, an unseen force pulls me back into the cell.

No!

I try again, this time urging myself faster. With my momentum, I manage to move a little farther beyond the bars, but then the spell slings me back. It's like I'm trapped in an elastic cube. The walls stretch, but I can't break free.

We're trapped!

Defeated, I urge my soul back into my body, jerking awake. Diego looks over. "You done?"

I nod. "It didn't work. I can't escape."

We sit in silence for a while, staring out of the bars. "I'm sorry." Diego whispers. "I'm sorry I haven't been a good friend lately. I'm sorry for everything I did to you. I know I shouldn't have trusted the Holy One, I just… I just wanted her back so bad."

"Sooo…" I hesitate. "You don't believe his cause anymore?"

Diego sighs. "I don't know. What he promises is tempting, but it comes at a price. If Velma saw how I attacked you… she would think I was a different person… I was a different person. Besides, The Holy One has a dark side. Some of his servants follow willing-ly, but not all. He holds their loved ones hostage, both the living and the dead. Iris told me he'd only bring Velma back if I served him unconditionally. That ended when I lost your sister's trust."

"I'm sorry, dude. I can't imagine. I know this isn't the most private place, but I'm here if you want to talk about it."

Diego sighs, wiping at his eyes. "I'm kind of freaking out inside. Can you distract me? Talk to me about anything."

I smile, unable to hide my amusement. "So... your sister is pretty hot."

Diego socks me on the shoulder. "What the freak, dude. That's weird." A smile slowly creeps onto his face as he sees me laughing.

"What?" I rub the muscle with my opposite hand. "You said distract you."

"I'm gonna tell her you said that!" Diego threatens.

"Please don't!" I beg. I think a moment longer. "Alright. This one's a genuine question. Do you think plants get hungry at night? Like, do you ever think they wish they could get a midnight snack?"

Diego tilts his head. "Shoot, dude. I don't know. And winter, that's like a diet for plants. They eat less and they lose weight."

I nod along to his logic. "And evergreens refuse to follow fad diets." I laugh. "They just eat all year long."

Diego grins, mildly amused.

"Okay, what about this?" I ask. "What if according to tree religion, trees should be buried when they die, but they hate us because we always cremate them?"

Diego shrugs. "Maybe."

I can tell he's no longer listening. He purses his lips as he stared out of the cell bars. When he finally speaks, he doesn't look over at me.

"Remember on graduation day, that guy we followed into the palace, the one I thought killed my mom?"

"Scarface?" I ask.

Diego nods. "Yeah, him. Remember what he said? That my mom served a purpose? That her fate was worse than death? Well... I think she's here. I think she's been here for the last four months. I feel like I'm meant to find her."

Diego still stares at the bars. His knees rock side to side, and I can see his pulse quivering in his neck. Suddenly, he leaps to his feet, grabbing the bars with both hands, and screams at the top of his lungs.

"MOOOOM!!! MOOOM, IT'S ME, DIEGO!"

He turns his head to the side and listens. The entire prison has gone silent. There isn't a single sound, not even the ragged breathing of Chester.

"MOOOM!!!"

Silence. One second goes by. Then a few more. Finally, I hear a distinct noise in the distance.

Creeeeaaak!

No one makes a sound as the footsteps echo down the hall, growing ever closer.

Clop. Clop. Clop.

A man stops in front of our cell. He looks down at us, his skin scarred and inflamed. Sunken in his battlefield of a face are two algae green eyes. I recognize him instantly from Rose's nightmare.

"Jack?"

"Hello, Matt. The Holy One is ready to see you."

Jack leads me up the spiral staircase and back to the main floor. Then, we travel two floors up the Central Tower and across to the Royal Wing. Finally, we stop in front of what appears to be the king's chambers.

The demon opens the door and motions for me to enter. When I don't, he shoves me and shuts the door as soon as I'm through.

Without any other choice, I continue into the room. A man is already waiting for me, lounging on a long sofa. He has short black hair and dark brown skin. His facial hair is trimmed short—a clean beard and mustache. Everything about him looks out of place in Hogrum. He looks modern and charismatic, like he should be running a talk-show.

As I approach, the man sits up and gestures to an armchair on the other side of the rug. "Please, Matt. Take a seat. Make yourself comfortable. There's much to discuss."

I tighten my fists, contemplating my options. I could try to run, or maybe I could fight.

Don't do either. His mind mingles with mine, coating my consciousness with trust. *Take a seat. I'll tell you everything.*

Curious, I take a seat on the chair, forcing myself to appear at ease. I sit back until my shoulders sink into the pillow.

The Holy One smiles, as though he's genuinely pleased. He wants me to be comfortable. Maybe, just maybe, he doesn't want to hurt me.

It's a trick! He's trying to disarm me.

Actually, I'm not. He responds inside my head. *I simply wish to chat.*

I squeeze my eyes shut, trying to wrestle him from my mind. *Liar!*

"Please," The Holy One reaches for a bottle of wine and pours himself a small glass. "Let's keep the conversation in the open. I must admit, I miss the feel of old-fashion communion." He points to a second glass. "Would y—" he stops himself. "Never mind. You don't drink."

When I say nothing, he takes another sip of his glass. "You know, I've waited a long time for this, Matt. I must admit, you're exactly as I remember you."

"Remember me?"

"Adamic is a funny thing," he says. "It's powers are beyond the bounds of space and time."

I furrow my eyebrows, and he laughs.

"I've seen your future, Matt. You will fight alongside me one day. Like it or not, you will join me. It's already set in stone."

"And why would I do that?"

"Because you want to. Because you want what is best for the world. With the book of life, we can change everything. Millions of starving children, saved. Rapists and murderers, condemned. So much suffering, eliminated."

"You can't talk about suffering," I hiss. "You're keeping people prisoner. Torturing them. How can you justify this?"

The Holy One takes another sip of his wine and smacks his lips. "You know, Matt, I thought the very same thing. Some time ago, I was a young demon in Hogrum. There was a man there; Asmodeus was his name. He called himself the Demon King. He was after the Book of Life, and he was willing to do anything to get it. He wasn't like me, Matt. He wanted it for power... for greed. Eventually, I managed to kill him, but I realized something. As long as the library exists, we're all in danger. At some point, someone will find it. The only way to protect the world is if someone righteous finds it first."

"Like you?" I sneer.

"Or you," the Holy One says. "You see, Matt. It's not about what we do to find the Book of Life; it's what we do with it. With the language, we can fix everything. Casualties can be brought back. Sanctuaries can be rebuilt. Families restored. Feeders cleansed from the world."

"And you think that's a righteous solution—just kill all the wicked?"

The Holy One leans back. "Heavens no. I want to cure them. Feeding is a terrible disease, Matt. It's an addiction. Those people suffer. I don't want to kill them. I want to cure them." He sighs. "I want to cure myself."

He looks at me, pupils hidden behind half-closed eyelids. It's an emotion I didn't expect to see on the Holy One.

Shame.

"I know the assumptions you must make of me. The way I feed on these people, it's despicable. But I didn't choose this for myself. When Hogrum fell, my body was ultimately destroyed. In my last moments, I managed to inhabit another man using true possession —permanent possession. When my body died, I remained in his, but he was dying too. I didn't have the energy to heal myself, so I fed."

"You're a mystic?" I gasp.

He smiles, impressed by my knowledge. "I am. I've been possessing this body for 18 years. The point is, I didn't want to become a monster, Matt. So many feeders feel the same. With the language, I can offer them salvation, a fresh start."

Suddenly, the clues start settling into place. A demon in Hogrum —a mystic no less. He fought against Asmodeus. And on top of it

460

all, he's a feeder. Sure, he doesn't look like me, but he's possessing another man's body.

Dad?

The Holy One laughs, nearly spilling his wine. "Oh, heavens no. I'm not your father, Matt. This face you see, it resembles my original. It took a few years of self-dominion, but I've managed to mold it to my liking."

"Oh." I lean forward, both disappointed and relieved.

He takes another sip of his wine, but still, the glass seems almost full. "It wasn't just my face that needed correcting. When my original body was destroyed, so were my tattoos. I stayed anchored in my new body, but I lost my dominion over man. This might surprise you, but I didn't know the spell at the time. I spent the next few years trying to master it.

That's why it took so long.

"You're not wrong," the Holy One says. "It took years to regain my strength and many years more to master the spells required. I've been patient, Matt. I've prepared, and I most certainly will not fail. The only question is, will you join me?"

I grimace, wrestling with reason. "No. I don't care what you say; this is wrong. Adamic is meant to stay hidden."

The Holy One leans closer. "Why? Tell me why, Matt?"

"Because..." I echo what Zane once told me. "Because you can't be trusted with that much power. Because you're not God."

"God!" The Holy One rears back dramatically, tossing his head. "God! You think I want to be God? What good has he done? Abandon the world? Abandon his children to their own self-destruction. No! I want to be better than God. God doesn't do a damn thing! If he exists, let him stop me. But I'll tell you what, Matt. I think... God is no better than you and me."

"I think you're delusional."

"Don't believe me?" The Holy One taunts. "Then, answer me this. What separates man from God? Hmmm?"

I don't have an answer, only guesses. *His perfection?*

The Holy One shakes his head. "God is far from perfect. He kills his people in blind rage. He makes them as imperfect beings. Then, he punishes them for their weakness. God is no more noble than you or me." He stares at me for another moment. "Any other guesses?"

I shake my head.

"For a long while," he explains, "I had a hunch. God cursed Cain. He took away his dominion. That ability, to give or take dominion, I thought it set God apart, and then I discovered he wasn't the only one. Have you ever heard of the twin sanctuaries, Sodom and Gomorrah?"

Sanctuaries?

The Holy One smiles, happy he can enlighten me. "Sodom and Gomorrah were two very powerful sanctuaries. They existed post-flood, in a world ravaged by feeders. Abraham was their king, and he happened to be adalingual—one of the last great prophets. That's where the story gets interesting. The inhabitants of Sodom and Gomorrah were wicked people—Devil worshippers. They marked themselves with the mark of the beast—allowing themselves to possess mankind."

Demons!

The Holy One grins. "Demons indeed, Matt. Abraham warned the people, but when they didn't repent, he cursed them. According to the ancient script, he spoke Adamic, stripping them of their dominion. Not God, but Abraham. A mere man, armed with the Adamic language, can give or take dominion. And that is when I realized: God is merely mortal. Don't you see, Matt? Adamic is the language of the Gods. Adam wasn't created by God. Adam is God. The Adamic language was his language, and we are all his children."

I suck my lips between my teeth and narrow my eyes. I want to argue with him, but it sort of makes sense.

Maybe he's right?

The Holy One nods up and down, energized by my credulity. "It makes sense, doesn't it? Every day, the Adamic people commit heinous crimes, and God doesn't curse them. Yet the moment Adam's son was murdered, God cursed Cain for all eternity. He retaliated because it was personal to God. It was his own child. And now, centuries later, God has abandoned us. Humanity needs a new deity, Matt. It needs a protector."

"Protector?" I spit back. "You're murdering thousands of people. How can you call yourself a protector?"

The Holy One takes another swig from his glass, unfazed by my accusations. "Matt, do you want to know how I managed to destroy the sanctuary walls? The most powerful spell in the world can be obliterated in an instant. Aren't you curious how I do it?"

I don't have to speak. He already knows my answer.

Yes.

The Holy One grins. "Well, I'll tell you. I discovered the answer while studying God. You see, after Abraham cursed Sodom and Gomorrah, the people had no dominion, yet still, they didn't repent. Instead, they began to invite Adamic travelers into their city, only to feed on them. God saw this, and he was distraught. Abraham begged him to have mercy, but in his rage, God sent fire from heaven. It was a powerful spell, easily overpowering the protective spells of the sanctuary. That spell was recorded in ancient scripture, and I've nearly mastered it. You see, Matt? It's God's spell. I'm not doing anything that God hasn't done himself."

I'm speechless. The Holy One has surprised me. He thinks he's the hero. He really thinks he's saving the world.

He's not evil, he's just insane.

"I'm not," The Holy One insists. "I'm not insane. Nor am I the monster they make me out to be. God was a tyrant, but I don't plan on ruling alone. When we find the Book of Life, I will create a council of adalinguals—the Council of the Gods. That way, we can keep each other in check." He raises his glass and dips his head in a toast. "I want you on that council, Matt. You and I will be equals. Power can corrupt, but you will be in a position to prevent that. We will be two gods among men, each striving for perfection."

For a moment, I actually consider the concept. I consider a world without suffering, a world without death. Then, my internal alarms begin to blare.

"How can I trust anything you say? You told my sister that Zane killed our parents. I know that's a lie. I know it is."

The Holy One shifts on the sofa. "Your sister is not like you, Matt. I can't trust her with the truth. She's run by her emotions. You, on the other hand, I'm prepared to tell everything."

Yeah, right.

"Try me." His lips are pursed in a competitive grin.

"Alright, what really happened to my parents? Zane told me they were fighting you. Did you kill them?"

He casually raises a finger. "In part. Your father, I can't speak for, but... I did kill your mother. She had something I desperately wanted. I begged her to join me. I begged her to see the logic, but she refused. I tried to search her mind for it, but she had erased the memories. She was an adalit and a powerful enemy. I couldn't risk leaving her alive, so I did what I had to. It was painless, I assure you."

I ball my fists, once again looking for a weapon. *I'll kill you for that. I'll kill you!*

"No, you won't, because I can bring her back. That's the whole point. I don't do anything that can't be undone. As long as the book exists, no one is truly dead."

"Go to hell!" I spit. "I'd rather die than join you."

The Holy One sighs. "You say that, but I can see inside your mind, Matt. I know that isn't true. Just like I know Judy has passed —my condolences by the way. Your mother was a lovely woman."

"Shut up! Don't pretend like you know her."

"But I do. I know her as well as you do. Don't you see? I've seen your entire life from within your own shoes. I know you as well as you know yourself. Best of all, I know you're going to accept my next offer."

"And what is that?"

"In five days, I am going to invade Cavernum. I will destroy the walls, and I will recover the Book of Life."

"How do you even know it's there?"

"Before killing King Titan, one of my demons was able to search his mind. The memories were damaged, and I don't know the exact location, but I can promise you; The Book of Life is there."

I bite my lip. If he's telling the truth, the Holy One is already one step ahead.

He watches me until he's sure I'm listening. "Once the invasion begins, we'll have no need for our prisoners. I was going to have them killed, but I'll make you an offer, Matt. If you swear your loyalty, I'll have them all spared."

I grit my teeth. I want to say no. I want to be the strong hero that doesn't give in to a threat, but I can't let innocent people die. Refusing his terms is the equivalent of killing Diego.

"I…" *I won't join you.* I can't bring myself to say the words. I can't finalize their demise.

The Holy One smiles. "Why don't you think about it? Run my offer past your friends. I'll give you 24 hours to decide. I know you'll come around."

He's about to stand, and then his mouth opens. "Oh, perhaps I should add, there's a place on my council for Rose. You two would make a strong couple. Complementary even. Two gods, together for all eternity. Think about it, Matt. Think hard."

Then, he closes his eyes. My body goes rigid as he writhes inside. He speaks one simple command.

Sleep!

My first sense to recover is hearing. Whoever is speaking, they sound extremely close, almost directly beside me.

"He's wearing a guard uniform. I think he's a Lieutenant!" The voice is shrill and excited.

"He doesn't look hurt. He wasn't bit, and I can't see any wounds." Another voice, this one soft and motherly.

"Why didn't he feed on him?"

"I don't know."

My eyelids are heavy, but I manage to pry them open. Two women lean over me, one younger and one middle-aged.

"He's awake!" squeals the younger woman—more of a girl now that I look at her. She's about 16, with long Rapunzel blonde hair and optimistic eyes.

There's another man in the cell, but he huddles against the wall, saying nothing.

Slowly, I lift my head. I expect to be sore, but I feel fine. The Holy One hasn't hurt me yet.

As I try to sit up, the middle-aged woman places her hand on my back. Her frail arms don't offer much support, but it's a nice gesture.

"How long have I been here?" I ask.

"Only a few minutes."

That's good. I still have 24 hours to decide.

Rapunzel leans in closer. "You're a guardsman aren't you?"

"Yeah, I am."

"Is Cavernum still standing?" she asks. "Has anything happened?"

"Cavernum is fine," I say. *But only for a few more days.* "King Dralton knows we're here. He should be coming soon to save us."

"You really think so?" Rapunzel shrieks.

"Shhhh," the middle-aged woman hisses. "They're listening. Keep it down."

Rapunzel nods. "Sorry. It's just…" she turns back to me. "Do you really think they're coming?"

"I sure hope so," I say.

I face the opening of the cell, trying to think for just one second, but Rapunzel sits next to me.

"What's your name?" Rapunzel asks. "I'm Nevela by the way. And this is Ana."

"Nevela?" The name rings a bell, but I can't quite put my finger on it. Then, a piece of my soul remembers.

"You knew the princess," I blurt. "You were kidnapped by Jack, the demon with the shape-shifting mask."

Nevela is equally shocked. "H-how do you know that?"

"Rose told me. She's been looking for you ever since she figured it out."

Nevela's eyes widen. "Did they catch the guy? Is she safe?"

I nod. "They caught him... but he escaped." *He's here.*

Nevela nods her head, as if to say she's okay with that. "And how do you know the princess?" She asks.

"We became friends in guard training."

Nevela's lips form an O. Then, she squeals. "I can't believe she joined the guard. I told her she should, and she did it."

I nod. "She finished first in her class. She's a royal guardsman now. Anyway, we went to Fall Ball together. That's where she told me about you."

Nevela's excitement turns sour. She shakes her head. "Fall Ball? No. That can't be right..."

I don't have to read her mind to know what she's thinking. "If you're wondering about Antai, he was in a coma... But he's okay now. They're back together by the way."

Nevela sighs. "Oh, thank God. I was about to have a heart attack."

The other woman watches me with something resembling sorrow. When I meet her gaze, she smiles. "I'm sorry. I have a son your age. He would've been divided this year too."

No way!

I freeze, slowly daring to ask the question. "Ana... Ortega?"

Her eyes double in size. "What did you just say?"

"Is your son named... Diego?"

She lurches away as if struck. "Who are you? You're a demon, aren't you? You're inside my head!"

I hold up my hands. "No. It's okay. We were both refugees. I met him on the ride to Cavernum. He's my friend. For a long time, he thought you were dead. He's a guardsman too." I bite my lip, knowing this next phrase will hurt. "He's actually here. He was captured too."

"My boy is here?" Ana asks, stressing each word in disbelief. "Diego is here?"

I nod.

"My boy is alive. Mary too?"

"Mary too," I echo.

"Tell me everything," she demands.

So I do. It takes an hour, but I tell her everything, from The Dividing to Enrique's death, all the way to the present. Her emotions change like the seasons, from rejoicing to sorrow, and back to joy.

When I finish, she sits back. After a few moments, she clasps her hands together. "Thank you, Lord, for keeping my boy safe. Thank you for sending this angel of a messenger."

After answering more of Nevela's questions, the conversation falls flat. I stare at the iron bars, barely visible in the dungeon darkness. The Holy One's offer plays on repeat in my mind. Join him, or he kills the prisoners. I know he put me in this cell on purpose. He wanted me to meet them. He wants me to know what's at stake.

What would Judy say?

It is better to die than to become a villain, Matthew. Deep down, you know what is right.

But I don't know. I'm confused. He's willing to kill thousands of people to get what he wants, but he doesn't see it as killing. He thinks he can bring them back.

You can't erase pain, Matt. Judy's wisdom would say. *Wounds heal, but the pain lingers. Evil is still evil, even if it can be undone. Killing is still killing, even if they can be brought back.*

I sigh. It's time I ask myself the questions.

Will I regret joining the Holy One? Maybe. Maybe I can betray him later.

Still, I know that won't work. He'll read my mind. He'll know everything I'm about to do, long before I do it.

Will I regret refusing? Who cares. I'll be dead. It won't matter what I think.

"You alright, sweetie?" Ana asks.

"No... I don't know." I exhale and rub my eyes. It's time they know. "The Holy One made me an offer," I explain. "He... he says he's going to destroy Cavernum in five days."

"No!" Nevela squeaks.

"If I pledge myself to him, he'll spare the prisoners here. Otherwise, he'll kill them all. I only have 24 hours to decide."

"You can't join him," Diego's mom insists. "If he wants you on his side, it's because he needs you. You can't help him. Do you hear me?"

I nod. "I know. It's just... I can't let so many people die."

"You can," Ana says. "You can let us die. If he gets his way, we may as well be dead. I will not let him become our God. It's better this way. Promise me, you won't help him."

"I—"

Creaaak!

Once again, the prison falls silent.

Clop. Clop. Clop.

The footsteps grow closer, as does the flickering light of a torch. No one dares speak. Together, Nevela and Ana curl into a ball in the corner. Everyone averts their eyes. All except for me.

By now, I almost expect it. The footsteps stop directly in front of our cell. I squint past the torchlight, trying to make out the figure. He wears a black cloak, hood pulled over his head. What I see of his face is covered in Adamic armor.

"Ezra, do you remember me?" The feeder whispers.

Ezra? I squint, confused at why I'd know a random feeder. "You know my name?"

"How about now?" The feeder throws aside his cloak and lifts a black undershirt. He holds the torch to the side, illuminating his bare stomach and the Adamic armor that blankets his skin. The only thing of note is a two-inch scar that runs above his belly button. It's thick and raised, almost as if he was stabbed.

Hood!

"It was you!" I instinctively reach for the scar on my neck. Then, I stagger back. "You almost killed me!"

"Shhh," Hood hisses. "Not so loud."

Every person in the prison is straining to hear what Hood has to say to us. He crouches down and whispers.

"It's true, I was going to kill you, but that was before I knew who you were. I'm a friend of your father's. When I saw your soul-anchor, I realized you were his son. I was trying to get you away from the Holy One. I was trying to save you."

"But… what?" *He was trying to save me?* It's almost too much to believe. Almost.

Hood nods. "Years ago, I was a spy along with your father. When Hogrum fell, I lost hope, but when I saw you, I knew I had to do something. I'm going to get you out of here. Tomorrow morning, the Holy One will be feeding. We'll do it when he's distracted. Be ready to run for your life."

He turns to leave, but I press my face to the bars. "Wait. I'm not leaving without my friends. They're on the bottom floor, in the last cell on the right. Diego and Crasilda… and Chester." I add.

Hood nods. "First light. Be ready."

I have no way to tell the time. There's no natural light in the prison. It could be noon or it could be midnight. Still, something tells me our escape is approaching. I've slept for what feels like hours. Hood should be returning any minute.

It's a test of my loyalty. It has to be a test. I can already imagine what's going to happen. I'm going to follow Hood out of the prison and directly to the Holy One. He'll kill my friends, and then he'll kill me.

Please don't be a test.

I pace back and forth in the cell. Everyone is ready. Nevela and Diego's mom are on their feet. The other man is ready to go as well. They'll slow us down, but we can't leave them behind.

Still, it's bittersweet. If we go, I know they'll kill the other prisoners. We survive but at their expense.

He would've killed them anyway, I tell myself, but I don't feel any better.

Creeeaaak.

I press myself against the bars as the other prisoners fall silent. Hood marches up to our cell and takes out an Adamic key.

"All of you, come with me. If you resist, I break your legs." I know it's an act. He doesn't want the other prisoners giving us away.

He unlocks the door and swings it wide open. I resist the urge to run for it. *I'm safer with Hood.*

"Alright, this way, and don't make a sound." Hood says it like a threat, as if he's sick of hearing our moaning and groaning.

When we reach the door to the stairwell, Hood holds it open, allowing us to exit first. As soon as I'm through the door, I see them. Diego and Crasilda, are standing on the stairwell. Chester is there too, cowering in the background.

"Mom!" Diego covers his mouth before wrapping his arms around his mother. They hold each other tight as Hood shuffles past them.

"We need to move," he hisses. "Now!"

Diego turns to me. "We can trust this guy?"

"We have no choice," I say, climbing after him.

When we reach the top of the stairs, Hood leads us up another flight of stairs to the ground floor. He didn't bring us amulets. He didn't bring us weapons. If anything happens, we're completely defenseless.

In every hallway, Hood has to stop to allow Chester to catch up. He's slow, and he's putting us all at risk.

Without asking for permission, Diego squats down in front of Chester. The old man climbs on his back, and Diego starts to jog.

With our new pace, we move much faster. Before I know it, I can see daylight down the hall. We're almost out of the palace, and we haven't seen a single fee—

As soon as the thought crosses my mind, a silhouette steps into the center of the hallway. It's a feeder no doubt, It's eyes are sunken and hungry.

"Where are you going with them?" The feeder isn't angry, only annoyed.

"Suffrick!" Hood smiles. "I was looking for you. The Holy One wants these prisoners disposed of. Feel free to have your way with them first."

The feeder looks at us and licks his lips. He steps toward us with murder in his eyes. "It would be my pleas—"

Once he's within range, Hood punches with pointed fingers, driving his hand into the feeder's chest. The Adamic tattoos make his skin like iron, and his hand sinks up to the wrist. When he pulls it out, the feeder collapses on his side, seizing one last time.

"Come on." Hood wipes the blood on his cloak. "There will be more soon."

We hurry out of the palace and across the snow, leaving a clear trail of footprints behind us. We're barely out of palace walls before another feeder gives chase, only this one has Adamic armor.

Hood turns to face him. Both have armor and neither have Adamic blades. I can imagine how this fight will end.

Ka-Crack!

Lightning erupts from the feeder's hand, only to diverge around Hood and into the ground. The snow melts instantly leaving two steaming puddles on either side of him.

Hood closes his eyes, and at first, nothing happens. Then, the other feeder shudders.

Hood is a demon!

The other feeder falls to his knees. His movements are shaky and sporadic, but Hood is making progress. Ever so slowly, the feeder raises both hands to his face. He knows what is about to happen, but there's nothing he can do to stop it. He plunges his fingers into his own eyes, the only flesh that isn't armored.

"Ahhhhh!"

His scream is guttural and raw. In a blind rage, he sends lightning in all directions.

"Run!" Hood yells. He stays for a moment to deflect any lightning headed our way. Then, he takes off after us, leaving the feeder blind and thrashing.

Hood quickly takes the lead once again. "The Holy One will have heard the lightning. We need to get you all out of here." He leads us to the edge of a canal and stops. As he closes his eyes, I hear the distinct crackling of ice. He doesn't just freeze the surface of the water, he shapes it into a big ice bowl.

A boat!

Hood uses dominion to keep the boat from drifting. Then, he motions for us to climb in. "You can ride this to the edge of the flats. If you're lucky, no one will spot you. Get to the forest and get as far away as you can."

Everyone climbs into the boat as if it were the last lifeboat on the Titanic. I'm the last to board. "What about you?" I ask.

He points to our footprints in the snow. "I'm going to erase your tracks and create a new trail. If you're lucky, they'll follow me instead. Now go!" He pushes the boat with dominion, and we quickly drift away from him.

"Thank you," I say, but he's already disappeared over the edge of the canal.

I direct my attention to our boat. The hull and sides are about a foot thick, and with the weight of six people, the water is only a few inches from pouring inside.

"We should lie down," Diego's mom suggests. "We'll be harder to spot that way."

The next few minutes are unbearably tense. We lay flat in our tiny ice boat as we drift closer and closer to the flats. At any minute, I expect our boat will explode apart, and the Holy One will drown us in the river. Yet at the end of every minute, we're still alive.

When we hit the flats, I hold my breath. The canal walls aren't as deep as the ones in Cavernum. We're in plain view as we drift across the fields. Suddenly, Diego tilts his head. "Listen."

At first, I don't hear it, but then my heart leaps.

Whop-whop-whop-whop-whop!

The buffering rhythm of helicopter blades blows across the flats. "It's a helicopter," I gasp. "Look!"

The helicopter must have spotted us, because it heads directly toward us, slowly descending beside the canal.

In a flurry, I pull myself out of the canal. Then, with Diego's help, I assist the others. In less than a minute, all six of us are running toward the helicopter. I'm 30 feet away when the door flies open.

"Matt!"

Zane hops down and runs toward me. "What happened? Who are these people?"

"Prisoners," I say. "The Holy One caught us, but someone helped us escape. We have to go. The Holy One could be here any minute."

"You're certain it was him?" Zane asks.

"I'm sure. He has hundreds of Adamic prisoners. He feeds on them slowly, keeping them alive. It's... it's insane. We have to get the king. They're going to attack in five days."

Zane purses his lips and exhales through his nose. I know he's worried, but he hides it well. "Get in the helicopter. Renshu will take you back. Tell the king everything you told me."

"You're not coming?" I ask.

Zane shakes his head. "The Holy One is here. He's been hiding from the king for decades. I can't let him escape again. Send the king. When he arrives, we'll attack together. I'll see you when the Holy One is dead."

"Matt, let's go," Diego calls. Everyone is on the helicopter except me. They're more than eager to take off.

I turn to climb into the helicopter, but Zane grabs me by the shoulders. "Hey, I'm proud of you. You did good here."

"Thanks."

I grab the handle and heave myself into the helicopter. Once inside, I face Zane. "You sure you'll be okay?"

Zane nods. "I'll be fine. Just remember what I said. I'm proud of you." He slides the door shut and gives it two thuds. As we lift into the air, he waves one last time.

I'm proud of you. Zane has never told me that he loves me, but this is as close as he'll likely get. Something about the way he said it seemed permanent, almost like a goodbye.

Deep down, something tells me Zane won't be okay. Something tells me I'll never see him again.

Chapter 34

Rose

I'm sitting in an extra chair near the window of the High Council Room. The glass behind me is black, reflecting the lamps that rest on the council table. The last of the daylight disappeared hours ago.

I watch as the survivors line up along the wall. Matt, Diego… Nevela! They're all here. They look beaten and battered, but they're alive.

I make eye contact with Nevela, and she gives me a timid smile. We talked for a minute before the meeting. She seemed reserved, cautious, but that's understandable after the trauma she's endured.

Suddenly, Grandpa stands. "Welcome, everyone. We will try to keep this as short as possible. As soon as we finish, you will be returned to the healing loft to rest and recover. If you could each give a brief description of how you came to be in Hogrum and what occurred there. Any information regarding the Holy One is especially critical. We'll begin on this end and move down the line."

A man named Chester tells about being snatched from off the street. Then, a woman named Ana tells a similar story. They outline the Holy One's feeding habits and how the prison operated. Finally, they talk about the marks. At the mention of tattoos, Grandpa perks up. WIthout being asked, Chester lifts up his shirt. Immediately, My eyes gravitate to a long line of Adamic symbols.

Nevela speaks next. I already know her story, but it still pains me to hear.

Matt goes last. He talks about visiting his mother in Kentville, and how he found our footprints in the snow. I can't help but smile as he describes Vyle standing over the frozen water. When Vyle fought back, Matt cut off his hand and dove in to save me. Every word he says supports my previous testimony.

Suddenly, Grandpa holds up his hand. When Matt stops talking, he turns to the guards by the door. "I need Vyle Kaynes brought before the council immediately." He turns back to Matt. "Proceed."

The more Matt explains, the more the missing pieces come together. He carried me to a nearby apartment, only leaving me when he heard lightning. He thought Diego was in trouble, and he was right.

That's where his story diverges from the others. After being captured, he claims he met the Holy One. He describes their entire conversation. Everything from The Holy One's religious views, to Sodom and Gomorrah. Then, he describes their escape. Supposedly, a demon decided to save them. Matt doesn't offer a motive. When he finally finishes, the council is speechless.

Grandpa looks around the council. "Any questions for our witnesses?"

No one speaks.

"Very well," Grandpa motions to the door. "Thank you for your time. You are all excused."

Matt gives me a courteous smile as he leaves. Antai purses his lips, his jealousy on clear display. He's used to keeping me safe.

Once the survivors have exited, General Kaynes shifts in his seat. "Why would The Holy One reveal his plans to MacArthur? Can we really trust this information? And their escape was more than miraculous. Perhaps it's another attempt to lure away the king and weaken the sanctuary?"

"And what if it isn't a trick?" General Katu counters. "Zane is there now, keeping watch. If this is a trick, he'll warn us, but we must act while we can."

Grandpa nods his head in agreement. "I'm ready to lead an attack. As long as the council doesn't object, we'll leave tomorrow at noon."

"Why not earlier?" Chancellor Gwenevere asks.

"Because," Grandpa says. "There's one important matter I must attend to first. It's very possible I should perish in Hogrum. The Holy One is powerful, and should I fail, I need to know Hogrum is in the right hands." Grandpa takes a deep breath and lifts his chin proudly. "I propose that my granddaughter be crowned tomorrow morning. I relinquish all future rights to preside as king."

No! I'm not ready for this, but I don't have much say either. Antai reaches under the table and squeezes my hand.

I'll have Antai. I remember. *He'll help me lead. I can do this.*

"All in favor?" Grandpa asks.

Everyone raises their hand except General Kaynes. After seeing he's alone in his opposition, he raises his hand as well.

"Excellent," Grandpa says. "Tomorrow, Rose is crowned. I'll prepare my forces. The only matter left is that of Vyle." He turns to the guards. "Bring him in."

The guards open the door, and two guards enter. I don't see Vyle anywhere.

"Your majesty," one guard bows. "Vyle is not in his chambers. We are searching for him now. We fear he may have fled."

Grandpa scowls. "So be it. Based on the testimony we've heard today, I declare Vyle to be a fugitive of Cavernum. If he is seen, he is to be arrested immediately. All in favor?"

General Kaynes crosses his arms as the council members raise their hands.

Grandpa takes the time to make eye contact with each diplomat. "We have much to prepare for and dangerous times ahead. Thank you again for your sacrifices. Council adjourned."

I follow Grandpa out of the council room and down the steps. We walk in silence until we reach the Royal Wing.

"So," I say. "You think I'm ready to be queen?"

"I know so," Grandpa says. "I wish it wasn't under such bleak circumstances, but Cavernum is ready for you, Rose. You'll bring much-needed change. I hope you'll correct my failures as a king."

Grandpa turns to his chambers, and I follow at his heels.

"If you trust me to be queen, do you trust me to know who the Holy One is?"

Grandpa stops in his tracks. "I... it's not that simple, Rose."

"Of course it's that simple. How can you trust me with the entire sanctuary, but you can't trust me to know who we're fighting. How does that make any sense?"

Grandpa sighs, leaning on his cane. "I'll tell you what. After you are crowned, I'll tell you everything. I'll make sure you know before I leave for Hogrum. Fair enough?"

I nod.

"Good," Grandpa sighs. He sits down at his desk and pulls out a piece of parchment from the top drawer. Then, he grabs a quill and dips it in ink.

He starts to write a letter, and I find myself dwelling on Matt's conversation with the Holy One. "Grandpa?" I ask. "Do you think the Holy One is right about God? That he was just a man like us?"

Grandpa stops writing. "It might be appealing to some, thinking we're equal to God. If that were the case, no one could judge us. No one could tell us what we do is wrong. Morality would bend to our fleeting desires. I, however, refuse to believe it. I believe the prophets of old. God exists. He is the standard of perfection."

"Then why has he abandoned us, Grandpa? I can't believe that a perfect being could exist and not intervene."

Grandpa's face grows stern. "God hasn't abandoned us, Rose. We've abandoned each other. We are the ones committing atrocities;

humanity is at fault. God must let us choose for ourselves. I have no doubt he suffers to see what we've become, but he cannot stop us. We have dominion over our own destiny, Rose. And no matter how terrible humanity becomes, God will not take that away."

I ponder his words as he resumes his writing. His wisdom resonates, but it does nothing to ease my spiritual turmoil.

"Grandpa?"

"Yes, Rose?"

I bite my lip, afraid of the answer I'll receive. "Do you think you'll kill the Holy One? Do you think you'll win?"

"I hope so, Rose. I hope so."

I'm in a long white dress with full sleeves and gloves. I don't care for the color, but it's symbolic. Essentially, I'm marrying Cavernum. Its needs come before my own. It should be the number one priority in my life.

As I exit the palace gate, the crowd cheers. The commoners are the loudest, but I see some laborers mixed in. Only a few months ago, they were throwing rotten fruit. Now, they're applauding.

Maybe all the protesters were killed in the raid.

I don't like that thought, so I let the crowds distract me. I wave at a little girl and remind myself to smile.

Antai walks a few feet behind me, holding up the train of my dress. When I meet his gaze, he winks.

God, I missed that.

I take my seat on stage, tucking the tufts of extra fabric behind my legs. *This is it, Rose. Today, you become queen. There's no going back.*

The row behind me is filled with my guests. Wendy gives me a thumbs up, and Gideon smiles. Nevela is there too. She offers a half-hearted smile. Poor girl hasn't been the same since she got back. I can't blame her after the hell she's been through.

At the end of the row is an empty seat. I offered it to Matt, but he turned me down. It's probably better this way. A little distance will do us good.

Antai sits next to me and gives my hand a squeeze.

"You ready?"

I stick out my tongue and blow raspberries. "I feel like I'm going to puke."

Antai puts his arm around me. "It's just a little speech. You've got this. The people love you."

I smile, even though he's missing the point. "I know... it's the after part I'm worried about. Grandpa is going to Hogrum, and who knows what'll happen. What if the Holy One kills him? What do we do then? I don't even know how to bond a soul-anchor."

I'm not ready for this!

Antai squeezes my hand again. "He won't, Rose. This is Dralton we're talking about. He'll be fine. Everything is going to be fine. One thing at a time. First, let's get you that crown." He leans in extra close so that he can't be overheard. "I want to be the first to kiss the queen."

The thought makes me blush. And I nudge him with my elbow. "You can be the first to give the queen a neck massage. It can get pretty tight from all of my queenly duties."

"Fine, but you better tip." He gives me another wink before sitting back in his seat.

I repeat Antai's advice in my head. *Stop worrying Rose. One thing at a time.*

I turn as Grandpa takes the stage. He doesn't wait to be introduced. He shuffles directly to the podium, grabbing onto it with both hands.

"People of Cavernum, I come before you with both a heavy heart and great excitement. For 32 years, I've been your king. As such, I've watched my father, Titan, grow old and lose his sanity. I've watched my son become a man, and I watched his body burn when Hogrum was destroyed. Today, the crowning moment of my lifetime, I will watch my granddaughter, Roselyn Malik, be crowned queen. She will usher in a new age for Cavernum, an age of change."

At those words, the crowd cheers, stomping their feet and bouncing up and down. As the people cheer, I notice movement to my right. Ever so discreetly, Gideon draws an arrow and nocks it on his bow. Before I register what's happening, he draws it back, aims at Grandpa's back, and releases.

Nooo!

Thunk.

The arrow whizzes past the king, disappearing into the crowd. At first, I can't see who it struck. Then, I spot him as the victim slumps to the plaza floor. It's a middle-aged man with a black curly beard. An arrow protrudes from his chest, and a revolver is still gripped in his hand.

Another assassin!

I stand up as the royal guard converges on the victim. The man is already dead by the time they take hold of him. As quietly as they can, the guards drag him away.

Grandpa grows solemn. "People of Cavernum, I pray you'll take my next words to heart. Before I relinquish my crown, I'd like to make one last request as your king. Tonight, I will be leaving this sanctuary. I will be traveling to a place we believe the Holy One resides. There, I will kill him. Perhaps I will be successful, perhaps I won't. Regardless, this is my request. Abandon your loyalties to the Holy One. Abandon your hatred and your thirst for revenge. Abandon these notions of assassination. You see the Holy One as your salvation, but only because you do not see his crimes. He is the Demon King, the reaper of souls, destroyer of sanctuaries. Given the chance, he will lead an army of feeders to your door. He will be the end of Cavernum."

Grandpa sighs and looks back at me. "If you are to survive, you must unite under your queen. Unite as a people. Turn to her for change; don't turn to your weapons of war. If we are to survive the days to come, we must do so united. A house divided cannot stand. We must unite!"

Grandpa holds up both hands to the crowd. "Now, with great pleasure, I would like to invite R—"

BANG!

Grandpa shudders, takes a half step back, then grasps the sides of the podium for support. I know he's fine. His Adamic crown protects against bullets. It's myself I'm worried about.

Immediately, the air ripples around me as Antai shields us. I know we should run, but I don't know where.

Grandpa still clutches the podium. Something is wrong. He seems startled... unsteady even. "Rose!" Grandpa gasps the words before collapsing on stage. He clutches at his chest, trying to peel away his robes.

"Grandpa!" I dash to his side. "What's wrong?"

Finally, he manages to pull open his Adamic robes. Blood already soaks his shirt—a deadly amount of blood.

"B-but. I don't understand. I..."

"You must..." Grandpa chokes, "kill him..."

He coughs, and the blood sprays onto my coronation dress. Meanwhile, Antai scans the rooftops, making sure I'm not the next target. When he's confident we're safe, he puts pressure on Grandpa's wound.

"I..." Grandpa squeezes his eyes shut before opening them abnormally wide. "I love you, Rose. No more secrets," he breathes, barely audible above the roar of the crowd.

"It's okay, Grandpa. The healers are here. You'll tell me soon. You're going to be fine."

He clasps my hand in his, squeezing it between his bony fingers.

"No more secrets. You need... to know... the truth..."

"I'm listening, Grandpa. Tell me."

"It's..." Grandpa coughs, and this time he can't expel the blood. It bubbles in his mouth before draining down his throat. He coughs twice more. Before taking another breath. "It's..." his chest grows calmer, and the coughing stops. Then, his chest falls still.

"What is it, Grandpa? You can tell me. I'm listening." I give his head a gentle shake. "Grandpa? I shake him again, this time harder. "GRANDPA! GRAN—"

The sobs overtake me before I can finish his name. Antai squeezes me tight, as if his arms can hold my heart together. I feel it unraveling. I feel everything coming apart. My whole world is broken, and it'll never be the same again.

He's dead. My grandpa is dead.

Chapter 35

Matt

It's far, but I have a clear view of the royal stage. I'm on the opposite side of the plaza, pacing back and forth on the rooftop. My rifle hangs from the strap, one hand resting on the handle.

It feels surreal. One day ago, I thought I was a dead man. Now, I'm defending Rose as she's crowned queen. At noon, the king flies to Hogrum. This whole mess could be over by the end of the week.

Focus. Protect the princess.

I pace back and forth, looking out over the crowd. I can't see much, but I'm afraid to use my scope. Aiming at a crowd just isn't something I'm willing to do.

Eventually, I see Rose. She enters the plaza wearing a gorgeous wedding gown. As she ambles her way to the stage, she waves to the crowd like a Disney princess.

I'm not going to lie to myself; I do feel the slightest bit jealous. Antai follows behind, beaming at her every move. I miss our moments of intimacy. More than anything, I miss our dream adventures, but that is easily overwhelmed by what I feel for Kendra.

After briefing the High Council, we spent the night in my room, cuddling and catching up. When we fell asleep, I slipped into her dream and we continued where we left off.

I made the right choice.

I'm still thinking about Kendra when I notice something odd. A royal guard is walking away from the crowd. Usually, they congregate around the stage, but this one is moving toward the back of the plaza. The coronation will begin any minute, and the guard seems completely unconcerned.

It takes me a second to realize who it is. The closer he gets, the more details I can make out. He's carrying a rifle with him, and he walks with his head down.

Diego?

He walks until he reaches the end of the royal plaza. Then, he stops in front of the apartment next to mine. He hovers his hand above the door handle, unlocking it with dominion. Then, he hurries inside and quietly closes the door behind him.

"What the heck?" I whisper to myself. Confused, I use an access bridge to cross onto the adjacent rooftop. Now, Diego is somewhere below me. I listen, but I can't hear anything. The sound of the crowd is too much. The king has taken the podium and is giving a small speech.

I wait a few more seconds, but Diego doesn't emerge from the house. I try to rationalize what he might be doing. Investigating a reported threat maybe? I try to think of others, but my mind comes up empty-handed.

Maybe he needs backup?

I scan the crowd one last time before moving to the back of the building. There isn't a staircase here, but I don't need one. I swing my legs over the edge; then, I jump.

Thicken!

The air around me pulls on my skin, slowing me gradually to a stop. I release my command, dropping the final three feet and landing in a crouch.

Once on the ground, I move to the front of the building and try the stairwell door. It's unlocked. As I climb the steps, I examine the two doors on either side of each floor. Behind some, I can hear the friendly chatter of family. Others are locked. On the third floor, one of the locks is busted. The door is shut, but the wood is splintered around the frame.

"Diego?"

I ease the door open and cautiously step inside. A window must be open in one of the side rooms, because I can hear the king's amplified voice.

"Now, with great pleasure, I would like to invite R—"

BANG!

A gunshot rips through the apartment, tearing at my eardrums.

I drop to a crouch and grasp my amulet. My eyes dart around the hallway, searching for any intruders. Soon, my eyes settle on the doorway to the first bedroom. I can hear distant screams, as if through an open window. Whatever has happened, it's causing chaos in the plaza.

I'm still creeping toward the doorway when Diego emerges. He startles when he sees me, stumbling back. Then, he just stares, no doubt deciding what to do next.

"Diego? Is everything okay? What happ—"

Diego turns, completely ignoring me. He dashes down the hallway, moving deeper into the apartment. Then, he darts to the side furthest from the plaza. There's a single window that overlooks a small alley. Without a second thought, Diego breaks the glass with his elbow, swings his legs over the edge, and drops 20 feet to the ground below. I watch through the window as he sprints away.

"What the heck?"

I don't follow him. Instead, I move back to the first bedroom, where the sounds of chaos are coming from. It's a small room, with a twin bed and a small table. Sure enough, the window is open and the curtains are blowing in the wind. Most concerning is the gun.

Diego's rifle is lying on its side on the table, aiming toward the open window. Already, I'm filled with dread.

Please, don't be Rose.

I sit in the chair and press my eyes to the scope, scanning the stage. I see Rose hunched over a sprawled figure. It only takes a second to know it's the king.

That's impossible.

I press the magazine release on the side of the gun, and the clip drops into my hand. I remove the first bullet and spin it until the symbols are in plain view.

I'm still holding the bullet when General Katu bursts into the room. "Don't move! Remove your amulet and get on the ground!"

I look at the gun on the table, my heart sinking. "I know how this must look." I raise my hands in the air. "I swear, I found everything like this. I—"

The air ripples in front of my face, and I'm thrown against the wall. Two distinct forces pin my hands to my side as another lifts my amulet off my head. Then, the force disappears on my wrists and reappears behind my back, throwing me flat on my stomach.

I don't resist as Katu handcuffs my arms behind my back.

Finally, he stands, inspecting the bullet on the table.

"Lieutenant MacArthur, you are under arrest for the murder of the king."

Chapter 36

Rose

I don't think I slept at all last night. Mostly I cried. I visited Grand-pa's study and went through his things. Then, I cried some more. Given the choice, I wouldn't leave my chambers, but I can't ignore my duties.

Matt needs me.

When Antai told me who they arrested, I refused to believe it. It has to be a mistake. Matt would never.

As I enter the High Council Room, I hesitate next to Grandpa's empty throne. I don't want to sit. Doing so means accepting that he's gone. Accepting that he's never coming back.

You have to do it, Rose. He'd want you to do it. He thought you were ready.

I look to Antai, who is giving me a painful smile. He nods his head, and I lower myself onto Grandpa's throne. It's not very comfortable, but responsibility rarely is.

For a long while, no one speaks, and then I realize they're waiting for me.

Say something, Rose. You're the leader now.

I clear my throat. "Welcome, everyone." *Stay strong.* "We are here…" I take a deep breath, my eyes beginning to well with tears.

Don't cry, Rose. I command myself, attempting to use self dominion over my emotions. *Don't cry.*

It works. The tears immediately dry up, and I feel a newfound surge of strength.

"We are brought here in the wake of King Dralton's death. Without him, there is much uncertainty for the future of Cavernum. We'll have much to discuss in the coming days, but first, his killer must be put to justice. We must be certain we have the right man." I turn to the guards by the door. "Bring in the suspect."

The doors swing open, and Matt is escorted to the center of the room. His feet and hands are chained, and his eyes are defiant.

Looking at Matt, I know I can't lead this case. "Antai, would you mind directing the trial?"

"Not at all," Antai stands. "General Katu, it was you who made the arrest. Would you please give your report?"

"Of course." Katu looks at Matt as if to jog his memory. "I was looking out over the crowd when the gunshot occurred. Fortunately, I was able to spot the muzzle flash. It came from an open window at the back of the plaza. I ran through the crowd and entered the building as quickly as I could. Upon entering, I saw Lieutenant MacArthur holding a rifle, aiming it at the stage. It appeared as though he was reloading. I could see that the ammunition had Adamic characters. These are the rounds." Katu places two large bullets on the table. The symbols are unmistakable. It's the armor-piercing spell

"It was at that moment that I made the arrest," Katu concludes.

"Caught in the act!" Chancellor Bolo bellows.

Matt opens his mouth, but says nothing, slowly closing it again.

"Lieutenant MacArthur," Antai says. "You may now present your account of what happened."

"Thank you," Matt stands tall. "I did not kill the king. The only thing I'm guilty of is being in the wrong place at the wrong time. I was assigned to patrol the back of the plaza. That is when I saw someone moving away from the stage. They went into the building, and I decided to follow."

"You just randomly decided to follow them?" General Kaynes asks. "How convenient."

"It was a hunch," Matt insists. "They were leaving the moment the king began his speech. It seemed suspicious. Anyway, I followed them into the apartment stairwell, but it took me a while to catch up. I was at the door when I heard the gunshot. I went inside and saw the same man running to the back window. That's when I started investigating. I found the gun, and I was looking at the ammo when General Katu arrived. I was investigating. I didn't shoot the king." He looks directly at me. "I didn't. I swear."

"Council, do you have any questions?" Antai asks.

"In his defense," Katu says. "He did appear surprised during the arrest. He didn't expect it, and he didn't try to run."

"Could be an act," Kaynes says. "This type of shot is his specialty. He's a sniper. He saved Quine's daughter like this, and he stopped the vault thieves like this. It's definitely within his skill set."

"Lots of guardsmen could've made that shot," I defend. "That doesn't mean he's guilty."

Kaynes raises an eyebrow. "Are you saying you believe him, princess?"

I hesitate, then slowly nod my head. "Yes, I believe he didn't do it."

"He was your date to Fall Ball," Kaynes reminds the council. "Must be hard to imagine he would kill your grandfather in cold blood. Perhaps your feelings are clouding your judgment?"

"I didn't do it!" Matt says. "If I had been the one to shoot the king, why would I still be standing there when General Katu arrived? I would have ran. You know it doesn't add up."

Chancellor Quine nods his head. "He has a point. If it were me, I would've run. Maybe there was another shooter."

"Or," Kaynes suggests. "He was reloading because he had another target. And let's not forget about the Adamic bullets. Where did they come from? The Holy One is my guess. MacArthur admitted to conversing with the Holy One. Perhaps he made a deal and supplied MacArthur with the means. Who else could it have been?"

Heads nod around the table.

"No," I stand. "Just this week we discovered that Noyen was in league with the Holy One. The Holy One has influence. He could've supplied those bullets in countless other ways. We cannot be so quick to make assumptions. We have to look at the facts, and the facts alone." I take my seat, and Antai purses his lips. I try to find some support in his countenance, but he's hard to read.

"Another thing," Matt says. "The shooter escaped out of the back window. That's why General Katu didn't see him. If you go back to the apartment, you'll find the window broken."

For a moment, everyone is in thought. Then, the council doors open. A guard steps inside and bows to me. "Your highness, we have a prisoner that claims to have information. He turned himself in a few minutes ago."

The door opens wider, and Vyle shuffles inside. He, too, is chained from head to toe. Unlike Matt, he seems excited to be here. He smiles at the council and then at me. "High council, your highness, I have some very important information to share with you."

I don't even let him begin. "You tried to kill me!" I seethe. "Why should we trust a single word you say?"

"Let's begin there," Vyle agrees. "It's true; when we were in Hogrum, I did try to kill you, but not in the way you think. The princess was correct in her account. I did collapse the bridge on her, and I did freeze the surface. You see, I was suddenly overcome by this terrible, inhumane rage. At the time, I didn't understand it. I was confused as to why I did the things I did. I was ashamed. When brought before the council, I made up a lie. It wasn't until recently that I realized what truly transpired. I believe... I was possessed."

Chancellor Gwenevere responds, her voice soaked in cynicism. "And who was this demon who possessed you?"

"It sounds so ridiculous," Vyle admits, "that I nearly didn't consider it myself. But I believe I was possessed by none other than MacArthur himself."

The High Council peers at Matt, eyes pinched with incredulity. The color drains from his face.

Vyle continues. "You see, he forced me to try to kill the princess. Then, he appeared just in time to play the role of hero. I believe he is trying to manipulate the princess. Killing the king is just another way to gain more control over her."

I look at Antai and find his jaw clenched shut. He's beginning to put it all together. He knew Matt had visited him at the veil, but he hadn't given much thought as to how.

"I'm sorry, but this is ridiculous!" Chancellor Gwenevere exclaims. "This is utter madness."

"I can prove it!" Vyle asserts. "All you have to do is remove his shirt. See if he has the tattoos."

"Guards," General Kaynes commands. "Remove his shirt."

First, the guard turns Matt so that his back is facing the council. Then, he draws a small knife. Because of the chains, he can't remove the shirt without cutting it. They stretch the fabric away from his neck and begin to saw. As the fabric falls away, the council gasps at the symbols.

"I told you!" Vyle celebrates. "He's a demon. He possessed me. He's trying to manipulate the princess."

"No!" I cry, but I realize I'm only playing into Vyle's story. "He isn't with the Holy One. He's not evil. He's on our side. He saved me at the guard graduation party. He rescued the other champions from The Holy One."

"Perhaps it was staged." General Kaynes smiles, basking in his son's redemption. "He pretended to save you to earn your trust. As for the Holy One, it seems probable that he allowed MacArthur to escape. That way, he could assassinate the king. It's the perfect plan. We're only lucky my son came forward, or he might've gotten away with it."

I frantically look to each councilor. "It's just a coincidence! Matt didn't do this. He's innocent!"

"And how can you be so positive, my queen?"

"Because Matt already confessed to being a demon," I say. "He came forward and told me everything. He isn't a killer. You have to believe me. I've seen inside his soul. He isn't lying."

"Oh, you poor thing," Kaynes coos. "He's already infiltrated your mind. Don't you see, your highness? He has persuaded you to keep secrets from the council. Demonhood is a grave sin, and he's convinced you it can be justified. You are already at his mercy, but fear not. We will not let you lead yourself to destruction."

I look at Antai, but he won't make eye contact. *He doesn't believe me!*

"Rose is telling the truth," Matt says calmly, despite the fact that his life is on the line. "Zane knows how I got these tattoos. He knew my parents in Hogrum. When he gets back, he can explain everything. I ask you all to wait until then to decide my fate. If you genuinely value the truth, you'll wait for him to give his account. He taught me how to possess, and he did so with the intention that I would use it for good. You call my spells evil, but they've saved the princess twice now. You'll see. Zane will confirm everything I've said."

General Kaynes looks around the table. "Very well. Zane has been informed of the king's death. He should be returning shortly. In the meantime, I propose that my son be acquitted of his charges against the princess. I also propose that MacArthur be confined to the pit for holding." He looks at me, feigning concern. "And to prevent the princess from acting against her best interest, I propose a guard keep her company at all hours. Hopefully, this mess will quickly sort itself out. When Zane returns, we can discuss the Holy One and our defenses. God help us."

Everyone turns to me, and I realize it's my job to lead the vote. I bite my tongue and clench my fists. "All in favor, please manifest."

Initially, every hand slowly raises around the table, all except for Antai. He looks down, grimaces, and slowly raises his hand as well.

How could he? He believes Kaynes and Vyle over me!

I don't have the emotional stamina to finish the vote. Betrayal clouds my judgment. "Meeting adjourned," I mumble as I run from the room. Antai has voted against me. My grandfather is dead. Matt, my last ally, will be imprisoned in the pit.

In a single day, I've lost everything.

I pace back and forth in my room. Wendy's presence is the only thing keeping me from lashing out.

"He really voted against you?" Wendy asks.

"He didn't even give me the chance to explain!" I cry. "He must think I'm an idiot."

"Maybe he's just paranoid," Wendy suggests. "Your last maid was a demon and nobody saw it coming. He almost died because of it."

Nevela. The thought makes my heart ache. After my crowning ceremony, she asked to be relieved as a maid. Perhaps it's her trauma, or perhaps something else. Regardless, I've given her the space she needs.

"I don't know, Wendy," I sigh. "He says he loves me, but how can he love me if he doesn't trust me? They voted to put me under constant watch."

"Seriously? Like a babysitter?"

I nod. "I left before they could finish the assignment. For all I know, there could be a guard outside the door right now."

She shakes her head in disbelief. "So, if Matt didn't do it," Wendy wonders, "who do you think did?"

"I have no idea. That's why I need to talk to Matt. I think there's something he's not sharing. Whoever did this has to be stopped."

"You should talk to him," Wendy says. "Go before they give you a guard. Maybe then you can convince Antai."

I shouldn't have to convince him, he should trust me. Yet I know Wendy is right. Whatever coup is happening in Cavernum, I need Antai on my side.

"Alright. I'm going to talk to him." I grab a purple cloak and pull the hood over my head. "And Wendy?"

"Yes, princess?"

"Matt said that the Holy One will attack in a few days. I think you should take the day off. Visit your family." *While you still can.*

"I will. Thank you, princess."

I open the door and nearly run into Octavian's backside. He stands directly in my doorway, facing out. At the sound of my gasp, he turns around.

"My queen," he bows. "Antai selected me to keep watch over you."

Of course, he did. Antai knows I'm especially close with Octavian. This is his way of making his betrayal as light as possible.

"Very well," I say, trying not to look disappointed. "I was actually planning to visit my grandfather's study."

"I've been commanded to restrict you to your room…" He looks left and right down the hall. "but, I don't intend to obey such orders."

I blink, utterly baffled. Never in a million years could I imagine Octavian saying such words.

"You see, my queen," Octavian speaks quietly, ensuring he won't be overheard. "When I was possessed by the demon, I felt his caution toward Lieutenant MacArthur, distrust even. He didn't view him as an ally. I have no reason to believe MacArthur has manipulated you in any way. The council is mistaken. I will serve you as you see fit, and I will not impede any actions you decide to take."

Slowly, I feel a smile consuming my face. "Thank you, Octavian. You're a godsend." I wrap him in a brief hug before standing tall.

I look down the hall, a plan already forming. "First, I need to go to my grandfather's study. Then, I need to talk to Matt."

I pray he has the answers.

Chapter 37

Matt

The cell is familiar, almost exactly like the one in Hogrum. I sit against the back wall, racking my brain about the day's events.

Diego killed the king.

It's not unbelievable; Diego has sided with the Holy One before, but why now? His mother has safely returned from Hogrum. He's barely had a day with her, and then he risks his life to kill the king?

Why Diego?

I wish Zane were here. I can't shake the feeling that he's in danger. The Holy One could be torturing him this very moment.

Tip. Tap. Tip. Tap.

The sound of footsteps echoes down the hallway, and my hopes rise.

Rose?

A man steps into view. Stopping in front of the bars. He frowns at me.

"Antai, welcome back to the real world," I hiss. I don't know why I'm angry. His vote wouldn't have saved me.

For a while, Antai says nothing. He studies me, as if my intentions are printed on my forehead.

I roll my eyes. "You know, if you want to marry the princess, I don't think you're on the right track."

"Quiet!" Antai hisses. "I didn't come to be chastised by a demon. Okay? I do trust Rose, but we had already lost the vote. If I had voted in her favor, General Kaynes would want me watched as well. The fact that Rose bought it means Kaynes did too."

I sit up, suddenly more interested. "You're saying you believe me?"

Antai narrows his eyes. "I don't believe you, and I don't disbelieve you. That's why I'm here. I need to be sure before I do anything else." He swallows. "So tell me, why did you bring me back?"

I shrug. "I didn't bring you back, you chose to come back."

"You know what I mean," Antai growls. "You convinced me. You practically begged me. Why?"

"Why does that matter?" I say.

"It's everything. Assuming Vyle's story is true, it's the only thing that doesn't add up. Believe me, I want to believe Rose was fooled. I want to believe she only fell for you because she was forced to, but it doesn't explain why you brought me back. If you wanted to control her, why save me?"

"Because you make her happy!" I wave my arms in the air. "Do I have to spell it out for you? I told you why at the veil. She doesn't love me like she loves you. I'm not trying to control her. You of all people should know that."

"So you really didn't kill the king?" Antai asks.

I roll my eyes. "I risked my life to bring back her boyfriend, and you think I'd go killing her grandpa? How does that make any sense?"

"And you're not with the Holy One?"

"No. And I never have been." *He killed my mother.*

Antai nods; he assumed as much. "Alright, take this." He tosses me an amplifier through the bars

498

"But…" I frown. "Won't they know you—"

"It was a gift from the king," Antai interrupts. "He gave it to me years ago so that I could practice dominion off-duty. It's off the record if that's what you're worried about."

I nod, looping it over my head.

"Now…" He reaches into his pocket and pulls out a thick skeleton key, engraved with rusted Adamic symbols.

"You have a key?" I gasp.

Antai nods. "Every guardian does. Now listen. Even with Zane's vote, the council may not accept the notion of a demon. You'll be burned at the stake. Now, I'm going to unlock the bars, but don't try to leave yet. Wait until nightfall, and try to escape. This is your best chance."

He turns the key, and I hear the deadbolt slide. The key is still in the lock when I hear footsteps. Antai's head snaps up, and his jaw falls open.

"Rose? What are you doing here?"

Rose steps into the torchlight and notices the key in the lock. "What am I doing? What are *you* doing?"

"I'm trying to save him. I believed what you said, but I knew the council never would. I had to convince them that I wasn't a liability. You're supposed to be in your room. Octavian was supposed to be your alibi so the council can't blame you."

"Oh.." Rose says, suddenly rethinking everything. "Well… you could have at least warned me."

"I didn't have time," Antai says.

Rose looks at Antai, a smile slowly forming on her face. "Lucky for you, I have another plan. I went to Grandpa's study and I—"

"Hey, guys," I interrupt. "Before we make any plans, there's something you should know… Diego is the one who shot the king."

"Diego?" Rose gasps. "But… you're sure it was him?"

"95 percent sure," I say. "He was fleeing right as I entered the house."

"Why didn't you tell that to the council?" Antai asks.

"Because," I say. "I'm not sure it was him. The entire flight home, he hardly spoke to his mom. They said a few words, but… it didn't seem like him. I'm worried he might be possessed—true possession, like Octavian was. Tonight, when I sneak out of here, I'll go read his mind. I should be able to tell if he's possessed or not."

"You don't have to wait until tonight," Rose smiles. She reaches up to her face and digs her fingernails under her chin. At first, it looks like she's peeling off the skin, but as it comes away, the skin transforms into a sleek metal mask. The complete mask lifts off her face, revealing her normal face underneath.

"Wow, that was weird."

"It's a morph mask," Rose explains. "It'll change your appearance. You can be anyone you can think of. You can walk right out of here right now." She hands me the mask through the bars. "Put it on."

I press the inside of the mask to my face. The inside feels sticky and wet, like fresh honey. It adheres easily to my skin.

"Pick someone," Rose says.

Mr. Wixom. He was my middle school gym teacher. Mostly bald, medium build, face of a grump. As soon as I picture his face, I feel my skin tremble, a wave of vibration rolls from my face, descending down my body. When it finally stops, I pat the top of my head.

"I'm bald!"

Rose grins. "That'll do." She pulls the cell door open. "Now, act natural and follow our lead. Let's go find Diego."

"Sooo?" Antai asks as we walk. "What do we do if we discover he actually killed the king?"

"I… don't know," Rose admits. I can tell the thought makes her uneasy.

"And what if he is possessed?" Antai asks. "What do we do then?"

Both of them glance at me.

"I don't know," I sigh. "I honestly have no idea."

We approach Diego's door slowly, stopping in the hallway outside.

"You guys wait here," I say, my voice husky and coarse, like a long-time smoker. "I'll try to talk to him alone. I'll call you if I need any help."

Antai looks at Rose, and she nods.

I could use the mask to be anyone. I could walk in looking like the Holy One and see how Diego reacts, but I decide against it. If this really is Diego, I want to be there for him.

Myself!

A wave of vibration passes over my body, returning me to my proper form. Once I'm sure I look normal, I knock once. "Diego?" I push on the door open and it swings open. I take a look inside. "Diego?"

Diego is sitting on his bed. He's in his white royal guard uniform. The silver chain of an amulet is visible above his collar. When he hears my voice, he looks up. "Dude?" His relief looks genuine. "I thought they were going to lock you up?"

"No, I convinced them I didn't do it," I lie, standing awkwardly by the door.

"Did you tell them it was me?" Diego asks

I shake my head. "Nah, I told them I didn't see your face."

Diego looks down and nods to himself. "Thanks, dude. I... I guess I owe you one. I didn't mean for you to take the fall."

"It's okay," I say. "But I have to ask... Why did you do it? I thought you were done with the Holy One."

Diego looks down. "I thought so too, but he didn't really give me a choice. A few hours before we were rescued, he brought me into his room. He said he wouldn't bring Velma back if I didn't do it. When I refused, he said he'd kill my mother first, then the rest of my family. He would mark them all with death. He said that when he got the Book of Life, he'd make me live forever, so I'd never see them in the afterlife."

Oh my gosh!

"I'm so sorry, man. I can't imagine..." I reach my mind toward Diego and let it settle on the outskirts of his consciousness. If I go too deep, and Diego is possessed, the demon will sense me too.

I didn't want to do it. The thought is little more than an idea. It doesn't have a voice or tone, nothing to prove it came from Diego. Although I have to admit, it does sound like him.

"You don't get it, Matt!" Diego cries. "We can't beat him. He's attacking in three days. If you join him now, he might forgive you. Please, you have to trust me on this." *It's better this way.*

"Diego! He only wins if we let him. We have to fight back."

I push my soul a little deeper, getting the tiniest sample of his emotions. Desperation. Fear. Dread. I don't go deep enough to see his memories or feel the essence of his soul, but at the very least, the emotions feel authentic.

It is Diego! I realize. *He killed the king.*

Diego turns his back on me, looking toward the back wall. "I'm sorry, dude. I know you wanted this to end differently, but I've made up my mind. This is the best way to protect my family."

I'm about to retract my soul when I sense one last thought fleeting phrase.

Don't trust him! Hel—

The second I sense it, the thought is suppressed, shoved deeper into the abyss that is Diego's body.

No! My blood runs cold. This entire time, I was wrong. The emotions that I thought were Diego's were someone else's. Someone equally desperate and afraid. Someone else who has been forced into a position they can't escape.

He's still facing away. I have the perfect opportunity to strike first. Maybe I can expel the demon with my soul. I can save Diego.

I take a deep breath and catapult my soul at Diego's body. Immediately, I collide with the demon's consciousness. I can feel Diego's body around me, but already my hold is slipping. I can't control his limbs. I can't control anything.

The demon's soul seems to expand, slowly forcing me from Diego's body. I try to push back, but I can't get any traction. I can't find a way to anchor myself.

Next thing I know, I'm opening my eyes back in my body. Diego glares at me, reaching for his amulet. I'm just the tiniest bit faster.

Force!

The air ripples, and Diego is thrown from the edge of his bed. I immediately form a force dome above his head, the same way Quill had done to Iris. I press down, sandwiching Diego against the floor.

Slowly, his face darkens as the metal spreads across his skin. Then, flames erupt at my feet, instantly engulfing me.

Extinguish!

I beat the flames back, but to do so, I release my hold on Diego's restraint. A moment later, he comes barreling through the flames.

He swings at my face, and I don't have time to form an energy shield. I dive back, landing on my butt. Before I can even raise my hands, Diego is swinging down.

I squeeze my eyes shut, and the air reverberates over my head. I open my eyes just in time to see Diego crashing into his dresser, wood splintering under his weight.

Antai and Rose burst into the room. Antai forms a shield around them both. Then, he forms a shield around Diego.

At first, I can't tell what Rose is doing. Then, I see Diego gasping. He makes no sound, but his mouth is open wide, and he's struggling for air.

A vacuum!

Diego kicks and thrashes, but eventually, he succumbs. First, his metal skin slowly fades to brown flesh. Finally, his head slumps. As soon as he's unconscious, Rose drops her hands and releases the vacuum.

"So? I'll take that to mean he's possessed," Antai assumes, still maintaining a barrier around Diego.

I nod. "I tried to expel the demon, but he was too strong."

"I bet that means Nevela is possessed as well," Rose thinks aloud. "She seemed off, even considering everything she's been through. It can't be a coincidence. They must've been possessed before you escaped from Hogrum. It's a way to weaken our defenses before the final attack.

"What now?" I ask.

"Maybe we could torture him out," Antai suggests. "If we cause enough pain, maybe the demon will leave by choice."

"I don't know if that'll work," I admit. "Diego knows how to turn off pain, which means the demon probably knows too."

"Ugh! I wish Grandpa were here," Rose groans. "He'd know what to do."

"What does it take to do an exorcism?" Antai asks. "A master demon?"

"That's it!" I exclaim. "I know someone who can help us. Rose, you bring Diego to the pit. Nevela too. I'll meet you guys there in a few hours. I have someone I need to find.

"Who?" Rose asks.

"My sister."

The walk to Bob's Brew is brutal. The wind whips through the streets, and grey clouds gather on the horizon. A storm is fast approaching.

I hesitate outside the door, peering over a puddle to ensure I'm in character. Diego's face blinks back at me. When I'm satisfied, I push the door open.

Bob is behind the counter. He smiles when he sees me approaching.

"Diego, my friend. I was wondering when I'd see you again."

"Just the regular for me," I say. I peer around the room. I see a few cadets, a lieutenant, and a captain. Without the morph mask, any one of them could recognize me.

Bob begins filling a mug as I extend my soul into his head.

Bob, listen very carefully.

He shudders, nearly dropping the mug.

It's me, Ezra, Iris's brother. I need to speak with her immediately. We're all in danger. Where can I find her?

He doesn't offer the information, but the moment he thinks it, it's there for the taking.

Upstairs in her bed.

"Thank you."

I slap a few bars on the counter and accept the mug from Bob. He looks nervous, but he doesn't try to stop me.

I move toward the back of the bar. Next to the cloth-covered piano is a small door. I open it and climb a skinny stairwell into the apartment above. The stairway opens up into a modest apartment.

"Dad," Iris calls from one of the rooms up ahead. "Can you bring me some painkillers, please?"

Myself!

My skin vibrates, and I feel my spine stretching. Then, I open the door.

Iris bolts upright, wincing as she reaches for her dagger on the nightstand. She's not wearing a shirt, only a bra and the bandages that cover her bloodied ribs.

"It's okay!" I raise my hands. "I'm here as an ally."

Iris relaxes. Then, she groans as she swings her legs off the edge of the bed to face me.

"How are your wounds?" I ask.

"They're healing. I don't think they're infected." To my surprise, she smiles. "And what about you? Are the rumors true? Should I call you king-slayer?"

I shake my head. "Another demon did the job."

"Pity," Iris says. "Still, you've proven yourself. You made quick work of Quill. At the very least, you've killed a guardian. That's why you're here, isn't it? You've finally made up your mind?"

I feel my lips turning down. "Not exactly. I have something I need to tell you," I admit. "I'm not sure how you're going to take it."

"What is it?" She demands, her own walls rising once more.

"I went to Hogrum on a scouting mission, and I met the Holy One. He told me some things. He... he said he killed our mother."

"No!" Iris's eyes narrow into slits. "You're lying!"

"I'm not! He said she had a relic he wanted, but he couldn't find it. She erased her memories of it. When he knew he couldn't find it, he killed her. He told me himself. He's not the perfect savior you thought he was. He's a liar, Iris. If he lied about that, who knows what else he's lied about. He can't be trusted."

I feel her soul probing around my mind. I don't resist. I let her find the memories. I let her find her truth. The more she learns, the heavier her anguish becomes. Everything she worked for was in vain. The people she killed may never rise again. Jazon is never coming back. Just when I think I'll drown in her despair, she looks away.

"I need your help," I say. "My friends are possessed. I need to do an exorcism. Can you teach me how?"

Iris shakes her head. "I'm injured, Ezra. I—"

"What if I heal you?" I interject. I don't wait for an answer. I kneel down next to the bed and look at her bloodied bandage. Kendra's advice echoes in my memory.

It's only awkward if you hesitate. Be confident.

I place my hands over the bandage and move my soul into the wound underneath. I feel the torn muscle, and veins. Even worse, I sense a laceration to her liver. I work as quickly as I can, concentrating her biological resources to the site of the wound. To the best of my ability, I maximize cell reproduction.

Iris groans from discomfort, but she lets me work. After several minutes, I stand, covered in sweat. Already, I feel a slight headache coming on.

Iris hesitantly presses on the outside of the wound. Then, a little harder. "Where'd you learn that?"

I take a step back, ignoring her question. "I couldn't heal it completely, but it shouldn't reopen."

"This was nice of you, Ezra, but I'm a wanted criminal. Without my invisibility ring, I can't go anywhere. I'm not risking my life for some stupid strangers."

"Iris, the Holy One is going to destroy Hogrum. Your dad, your mom, they're all going to die. What if you can save them?"

"If they die, the Holy One will revive them," Iris tells herself.

"And what if he doesn't? What if he decided it's too much work to revive millions of dead? What if you never see them again. He's already proven he's a liar."

I can see her considering it. Her loyalties have been severed, but she's hesitant to align herself with the queen.

"What if I can make it worth your sacrifice?" I say.

Iris rolls her eyes. "How?"

"What if I can get you back your soul-anchor."

Iris considers this before climbing shakily to her feet. "Fine, but I want my soul-anchor first."

"No. Only if it works," I say. "You have my word."

Iris frowns. "Fine... deal."

"Okay! So, what do we have to do? How does an exorcism work?"

Iris smiles. "First we need a pig."

Chapter 38

Rose

I watch Nevela sitting on the floor of the cell. Two days ago, she escaped from one cell, now she's locked in another.

Capturing her was easy. Unlike Diego, she didn't have an amulet. I suctioned the air from her lungs until she passed out. It was the only way to ensure her safety.

What if she isn't possessed?

Doubt poisons my demeanor, but I refuse to believe it. *I didn't suffocate her for nothing. I'm helping her.*

Antai paces back and forth behind me. "Are you sure he didn't ditch us? Maybe he took the mask and ran?"

"He'll be back," I say.

Another moment passes when I hear footsteps down the hallway —the loud clacking of a wooden heel.

Matt?

My heart sinks as General Kaynes appears in the torchlight. He's keeping a tight hold on a girl behind him. She's fair with ear length blonde hair. Her hands are handcuffed behind her.

The demon!

I'm about to scramble for an excuse when I see something else. In General Kaynes' other hand is a long rope. Attached to the end of the rope, trailing a few yards behind them, are two hogs from the slaughterhouse. They happily explore the pit, shoving their snouts against the bars of each cell.

Antai stiffens, and I squint. "Matt?"

General Kaynes laughs. "Don't worry, guys. It's just me." Suddenly, his face transforms back into his normal playful grin. "Everyone, meet my sister Iris. Iris, this is Rose and Antai."

I don't wave. "You were the angel of destruction. You killed those people."

Iris nods. "I'm not ashamed of it. I made Cavernum a better place. And now, I'm going to save your friends. If you have a problem with that, then leave."

I look at her, and then slowly back to Matt. They look similar, but Matt is respectful, and Iris is so... not.

If he trusts her, I guess I can as well. At this point, I don't really have much of a choice. I step aside and motion toward the cell with Nevela. "After you."

"First things first. Ezra promised me my soul-anchor. How do I know you actually have it?"

Ezra?

I look at Matt, and he gives me a subtle smile. "Our amulets are in the king's study. Rose has a key. When we finish, you'll get your soul-anchor."

Soul-anchor?

"Are you sure about this, Matt? With a soul-anchor, she could—"

"We can trust her," Matt insists. "At least for this, we can trust her."

Iris doesn't wait for permission. She takes one of the swine from Matt and leads it into Nevela's cell. Then she focuses on Nevela. "The demon is using true possession. Which means if we kill her, the demon dies too."

"You're not killing her!" I interrupt.

Iris rolls her eyes. "No duh! The point is, no matter how much we eject the demon from her body, it will keep coming back. True dominion only has one weakness: the host. Animal or human, if the host dies, so does the demon."

Suddenly it clicks. "You're going to force the demon into the pig, and kill it?"

Iris points at me with her index finger. "Bingo."

"But how do we force him out?" Matt frowns. "I've tried that, and I'm the one who got ejected."

Iris looks over at Matt. "Alright, Baby Bro. It's time I give you a lesson on possession. The strength of a possession comes from your investment. It can be difficult at first, but you have to learn to leave your body behind. Abandon your senses. Abandon your individuality. The more committed you are to the new host, the more powerful your hold becomes. Does that make sense?"

Matt nods.

"Good." Iris points at Nevela who is watching us with wide eyes. "She's possessed by true possession, which gives an unparalleled hold over the host. That's why it's called true possession. It's the only possession in which the demon's body is completely left behind. The demon is fully invested in the host."

Matt frowns. "If it's so powerful, how are we going to force him out?"

Iris shrugs. "Alone, we probably couldn't, but together, we might stand a chance."

Iris narrows her eyes at Nevela's. "Unlock the cell."

"Wait," I say. "Can you make sure she's possessed? I'm not certain that sh—"

"She's possessed," Iris insists, still staring at Nevela. "I'm sure of it. Open the cell."

Antai unlocks the door and slides it open.

Nevela scrambles until her back is against the wall. "Please, Rose, don't listen to her. It's really me. If you do this, it'll kill me. I don't want to die. Please."

Iris takes one of the pigs and guides it into the cell. She turns to Antai. "You, can you keep them still? I want the pig directly behind the girl."

The air ripples, and the girl's arms are pinned to her side. The hog snorts and kicks its legs as it is dragged behind Nevela. Once they're aligned, the air ripples around them both, pressing Nevelas back against the pig's side.

"How's that?" Antai asks.

Iris gives a thumbs up. "Perfect. Now, Rose, you take this." She hands me her Adamic blade. "As soon as the demon enters the pig, kill it. If you hesitate, it might have a chance to escape."

"Got it."

Finally, Iris turns to Matt. "Alright, Baby Bro. It's you and me. We have to move together to flush him out. Remember, leave your body behind. Invest yourself in the new host. You have to commit."

Nevela is looking around frantically. "Princess, please! Don't do this. It's really me. I don't want to die."

It's not her, I tell myself. *It can't be her.* I clench the Adamic blade and position myself beside the pig.

Iris and Matt stand shoulder to shoulder directly in front of Nevela. "Alright, Matt. We move together. On three. One... Two..."

She never says the word 'three.' Instead, her eyes roll into the back of her head and her head rolls to the side. Despite everything, she somehow remains standing.

Matt is no better. His eyes are glazed and his chin dips to his chest.

"Please, Rose! Don't kill me." She thrashes against the force field, disturbing the air with every swing of her head. "She'll kill me. Don't trust her. She's—"

Suddenly, Nevela shudders, her hands curling into a gnarled fist. Her back arches and she screams.

"AAAHHHHH—"

Nevela falls silent, her screams instantly replaced by the incessant squealing of the pig.

For a moment, I hesitate. I imagine my innocent servant trapped in the body of a swine.

"Rose, now!" Antai's voice dispels all doubt.

I swing the blade into the top of the pig's neck. Then, I stab again and again.

Shlink! Shlink! Shlink!

I don't stop until the squealing has gone silent. The pig is dead, held on its feet by Antai's force field. I watch as the blood drips on the stone floor and trickles toward the middle of the cell.

Iris comes to first and Matt a few moments later. Antai's force field finally disappears.

I drop the knife and fall to Nevela's side, ignoring the pig blood that wets my knees. "Nevela, can you hear me?"

"Hmm?" Her eyes flutter open. "Princess! You saved me!" Her eyes glance over my uniform, and she smiles weakly. "Matt was right. You are a guardsman." Slowly, her eyelids close.

"Nevela?" I give her a gentle shake. "Nevela."

"She'll be alright," Iris says matter-of-factly. "Resisting possession can put strain on the soul. She'll need some sleep. Come, let's finish this."

I stand and retrieve the Adamic blade. I know it's only for a moment, but it feels wrong to leave her. She's unconscious in a cell next to a dead pig. *She deserves better.*

"It's okay," Antai soothes. "We'll take her to her room as soon as we save the other."

We walk several cells down to where Diego is being held. No doubt, he has been listening to the entire exorcism. He knows what we have in mind. When we reach his cell, he's sitting in the center, his hands still cuffed behind his back.

"I won't fight you. I know when I'm outmatched," Diego says.

His words set me on edge. *He's trying to get our guard down.*

512

Iris leads the second pig into the cell and behind Diego. Antai holds them in place with dominion. Just like Nevela, Diego's back is positioned against the hog's side.

I tighten my grip on my knife and stand over the pig's head. It snorts and looks up at me innocently, wagging its curly tail.

I'm sorry.

"Ready?" Iris asks me. She and Matt are shoulder to shoulder in front of Diego. Everyone is in position.

"Ready."

"You're wasting your time," Diego hisses. "You can't defeat him. Even if you kill me, he'll raise another demon in my stead. His resources are endless. His power is endless. You're only delaying the inevitable."

Once again, Iris and Matt fall into a deep trance.

Diego looks straight ahead, talking to no one in particular. "If you want to save the ones you love, you must join him. He will still show you mercy. It is the only w—"

His body convulses and his head is thrown back. Finally, Diego screams, perhaps out of pain, perhaps out of desperation. Then, as the demon is torn from his body, Diego goes limp.

"Wreee! Wreee wreeee—"

This time, I don't hesitate. I silence the pig with a single stab to the skull.

It's over.

Matt is uncuffing Diego when he suddenly startles awake. Before Matt can finish. He pushes himself shakily to his feet, the pit of handcuffs dangling from his left wrist. "We don't have time. I know what they're planning. It's today! The Holy One is attacking today!"

Today!

The thought is nearly enough to stop my heart.

"They marked us," Diego rambles. "We're the weapons. We're supposed to destroy the walls. The feeders are already waiting in the forest." Diego pulls up his shirt, revealing a patchwork of symbols intersecting his stomach.

"Fire from heaven," Mat gasps. "It destroys sanctuaries. He turned you into a living bomb... an Adamic bomb."

Diego nods. "At noon, I was going to cut into this symbol." He points at the first. "That symbol prevents the spell from taking effect. Once I destroyed it, I would've been blown sky-high, taking the palace wall with me. And there are others." Diego can barely keep up with his thoughts. "Every Hogrum prisoner has one, two for each wall. Nevela and I were going to target the palace. My mom has a bomb for the ring. Crasilda for the core. And the other two survivors as well. Matt was the only exception. He's a demon, so they didn't even try."

"He wanted us to escape," Matt shakes his head in frustration. "We brought his weapons right into the sanctuary. We did exactly what he wanted."

"Do we have time?" I ask. "We've already stopped two. We just need four more. We'll get the guardians on our side." I point at Diego's stomach. "They can't argue with this."

"It's almost noon," Matt says. "First we have to find them, and then we'd need all of us for the exorcism. We don't have time."

"What if we split up?" Diego suggests. "If we destroy the last few symbols first, we basically deactivate the bomb. Without the spell, the demons might just leave. This way, we can split up. I'll find my mom. Matt can find Crasilda. Rose and Iris can look for the other two."

"I'll go to the core with Matt," Iris volunteers. "Give me my soul-anchor, and I'll look for the other survivor. Matt can share the memory of what they look like."

"I'll talk to the council," Antai says. "You guys go. Stop the demons. I'll try to send help as soon as I can." He takes off toward the exit, sprinting up the steps.

"Antai's right. Let's go!" I say. "We don't have a second to waste." I reach into my pocket and remove the key to Grandpa's study, tossing it to Matt. "Go get your soul-anchors. You know where they are, right?"

Matt nods. "Be careful, okay?"

"I will."

He and Iris take off up the steps. I take one last look at Nevela, making sure her cell door is left open. As much as I want to carry her to her chambers, I don't have time. Too many lives are at stake.

I hurry up the steps, finding Octavian waiting at the pit entrance. "Everything alright, your highness?"

"Octavian, I need your help. The Holy One is attacking today. We only have a few minutes." I reach into my pocket and remove a second key—the key to the amulet vault. "Take this. I need you to get the amplifiers from the vault and distribute them in the core and ring. The more people armed, the better. If the feeders break through, they need a fighting chance."

Octavian hesitates. "If you do this, your highness, you can't undo it."

He's right. If we succeed in saving the walls, the equalists will become more powerful than ever. Still, it's worth the risk.

"Do it," I command. "Disperse them all."

The storm is picking up as I ride toward the outer wall. I'm riding a brown mare, pushing the horse to her limits. My quiver bounces against my back, and small snowflakes pelt my face, melting on impact.

We rocket down the road, and I fear she'll slip at any moment on the ice-covered cobblestone. The snow is already beginning to accumulate in an undisturbed blanket. Fortunately, there isn't any traffic to slow us down. All but a few of the laborers are taking shelter from the storm.

When I reach the flats, I begin to lose hope. The storm has cut my visibility in half. I can see the outer wall, but only barely.

"*Forward!*" I command the mare and we take off toward the wall. As we approach the archway, I direct the horse to the left, and we circle the inside of the wall.

Faster! The mare gallops at full speed, and like a spring, my legs absorb the shock of each gallop. Soon, my quads begin to burn, but I don't let the mare slow down.

I've circled a quarter of the sanctuary when I see him. A man is walking along the road, approaching the western archway of the outer wall. He has a thick coat pulled over his head, and his arms are huddled at his side.

That's must be him!

He turns as I gallop alongside him. I don't let him explain. I focus on the snow around his feet.

Melt!

Rather than absorbing into the ground, I capture the water with my mind and command it to accumulate around his feet.

Freeze!

The water crackles as several inches of ice encase his ankles

"Hey! What's going on!" the man gasps. "I haven't done anything."

I dismount, bow in hand, and approach the man. To my relief, I don't see an amulet on him.

"Lift up your shirt!" I command. "I need to see your stomach."

"My stomach?"

I focus on the cloth of his coat and command it to rise.

Lift!

"Hey!" The man pulls his shirt back down, but I've already gotten a glimpse of his hairy belly. There were no symbols. *It isn't him.*

Melt.

I leave the man and move toward my horse. Something catches my eye at the archway. The air ripples and molds as a figure steps through the threshold. I almost can't believe what I'm seeing.

"Zane? You're back!"

Zane strides over to me, the end of his lips curling down.

"Princess? What are you doing out here?"

"We don't have much time," I gasp. "The demons are already here. They're suicide bombers. They have these spells. If we don't find them—"

KA-BOOM!!!

I don't see the explosion, but I feel it rumbling through the Earth. When I turn around, I see the flames. They billow on the horizon, expanding above the city skyline. The blaze is enough to turn the surrounding clouds red. The longer I watch, the wider the smoke billows.

No! No! This can be happening.

KA-BOOM!!!

Another explosion shakes the earth. First, the ground rumbles at my feet. Then, the shockwave hits me, compressing my chest and roaring in my ears. This time, the blast is in plain view, flames consuming the inner wall. In less than ten seconds, two walls have been destroyed.

Zane steps beside me. "And so it begins. Come. We have to act fast. Get the survivors and get out." His voice is somber, already accepting his own demise.

"Wait! We saved the palace. We can hide there. We can!"

Zane winces. "You're sure the palace is secure?"

"For now it is. I'm sure."

Zane nods. "Very well."

We move on foot, running through the flats. The blast scared off my mare, and we don't have time to chase her down.

As I look out over the fields, I see the faint silhouette of feeders dashing across the flats. The snow flurries blur their movements and limit my view.

We're almost to the outskirts of the ring when the feeders overtake us. They charge recklessly, not quite realizing who we are.

Ka-Krack!

A bolt of white light surges from Zane's hand, striking the first feeder square in the chest. It goes limp, tumbling to a stop in the snow. Zane swings his hand, and the air ripples. I wince as another

517

feeder divides in two, his upper body landing several feet from his legs.

At this point, the feeders grow cautious. Most scatter, no doubt in search of easier prey. Two feeders however come forward. Their faces are covered with Adamic armor.

I draw an Adamic arrow, but Zane is faster. Before I can nock the arrow, he takes a step forward. As the armored feeders charge, a pale yellow mist swirls in front of us. The feeders charge through the mist, growing slower with every step. Then, they clasp at their throats and cough.

Poison gas!

Their skin may be armored, but their insides aren't. The feeders squeeze their eyes shut and groan in pain. One starts coughing hysterically. The other claws at its eyes.

Zane doesn't wait for them to die. He draws his sword and finished them both with two quick sweeps of the blade.

I look back to the fields, but I don't see any feeders. The initial wave has passed us, tearing into the homes of the ring. I can hear the desperate screams of mothers.

"Oh good! You found her!" The voice belongs to General Kaynes, but I don't see him. I find only a set of footsteps growing ever nearer in the snow. Suddenly, General Kaynes materializes, standing at the end of his footprint trail. His hand is fiddling with a ring on his finger.

"Come," Zane growls, marching past General Kaynes. "Help me get the princess back to the palace."

"I can handle it from here," General Kaynes insists. He takes a step closer, standing possessively in front of me. "You go find, MacArthur. I'll get her back safely."

Zane frowns. "Since when do you give a damn about the crown?"

"Since she's the last adalit," Kaynes sneers. "Now go! I'll make sure no harm comes to her."

"I'm not leaving her," Zane refuses. "Why don't you worry about your own family? You wouldn't want to end up like me."

"So be it," Kaynes turns away, drawing his Adamic blade. After a few steps, he turns invisible. I wait to see his footprints appear in the snow, but he doesn't move.

"Rose! Lookout!" Zane tries to warn me, but he's too late.

Clank!

Something metal collides with my crown, sending it flying into the snow. Already, I know it must've been Kaynes' dagger.

As soon as my crown has left my head, I raise my bow, an arrow already knocked, but I don't have a target to shoot at.

Where are you?

Out of nowhere, a wave of snowmelt lifts me off the ground. The water soaks through my clothes and climbs all the way to my collarbone. At the peak of the wave, the water solidifies around me, trapping me several feet off the ground. I can move my head, but everything below my chin is encased in ice. My bow is still nocked, frozen in my fist.

Melt!

Nothing happens. My connection to my soul-anchor has been severed. A layer of ice separates the metal from my chest. I'm powerless.

Desperate, I look around, spotting my crown a few feet away in the snow.

No!

A deep gash cuts clean through the outer layer of the crown, deforming the symbols inside. It's ruined. My most powerful defense has been destroyed by the single swing of a dagger.

Finally, I avert my attention to Zane. He stands with his sword drawn, spinning in circles. Kaynes speaks to him, his voice projecting from all directions, no doubt manipulated by dominion.

"It's not too late for you, Zane. You can join me on the winning side. He wants her alive. If you help, I'm sure he'll find a place for you on his council. We can be gods."

"Shut up!" Zane shoots a bolt of lightning, dragging it in a long sweep of his arm. He's attacking blind, trying to cover as much area as possible across the snowy field.

519

That's when I notice it. A tiny tendril of warmth, no bigger than a candle's flame, begins to heat ice above my chest. I can feel it melting the ice between my skin and my amulet. A thin stream of water trickles down my stomach. I crane my head to look down. I can see my amulet hovering in the cloudy ice. As the ice melts, my amulet sinks closer to my skin.

Zane!

He appears engrossed in the battle. He surrounds himself in a swirling sphere of fire, expanding it in all directions like a super-nova. 20 feet directly above Zane, the flames are deflected. Zane notices it too and immediately shoots a beam of lightning in that direction!

Ka-Crack!

If Kaynes was there a moment ago, he's gone now, moving unseen through the air. "Don't tell me you haven't considered it," he asks, projecting his voice from all directions. "Wouldn't you like to see your little girls again? The Holy One can make it happen."

"And what if I do?" Zane growls. "Say I do want to join the Holy One. How do I know you won't betray me the moment I join you?"

"I haven't attacked you once," General Kaynes laughs, still invisible. "But you've made it clear that you're willing to kill. That's said, I'll make you a deal. If you throw down your soul-anchor, I'll endorse you to the Holy One. He should be here any minute."

The heat grows more intense against my chest, and the ice melts faster. If Zane wanted to, I know he could free me in an instant. Instead, he's choosing to empower me covertly.

Finally, my amulet shifts, resting against my skin. With my soul-anchor, I can free myself. I can melt the ice and attack right now, but I don't. As soon as I become a threat, Kaynes will treat me as such.

I'm the secret weapon.

Zane slowly lowers the tip of his sword. "If I do this, can you promise me he won't hurt the princess? And MacArthur? He's part of the deal too."

"You can ask him yourself." Kaynes' voice seems to blow with the wind, moving without origin.

Zane reaches up and loops the amulet from his head. Then, he tosses it onto the road. "There. I surrender. Show yourself."

Suddenly, Kaynes materializes, hovering above the ground 10 feet in front of Zane. He doesn't move, he just floats there looking at Zane.

Melt!

The ice falls away, and in one smooth motion, I draw back the bow and fire. The arrow whizzes through the air, passing harmlessly through Kaynes, and buries itself in the snow.

It was an illusion!

Shlink!

As the apparition fades, Zane arches his back and gasps. He tries to swing his sword, but it falls from his hand. I look wildly around the flats, but I don't see anyone. Then, the blood begins to soak through his Adamic shirt.

The real Kaynes materializes behind Zane, thrusting the Adamic dagger deeper into his back. "Say hi to your daughters for me."

I fumble to nock another arrow, but Kaynes turns his attention to me.

Fire!

The flames rush from my hand only to splash against his shield. He raises his hand, and an unseen pressure squeezes my throat. I focus on my pressure, trying to fight against his command.

Stop! Release! Weaken!

I command with my whole soul, but there's nothing I can do. His dominion is too strong. His commands are unbreakable.

Kaynes paces closer, grinning from ear to ear. With a hold on my throat, a second force appears in my shirt. It lifts my amulet off my chest and pulls it out of my collar.

"It's a pity the Holy One wants you alive." Kaynes looks down at me with disdain, his dominion squeezing tighter on my throat. "You've been nothing but a nuisance to my son. I would love to do what he couldn't and kill you."

The pressure increases, and I'm sure my throat will crumple at any moment. It feels like a grown man has both boots over my neck.

Kaynes grins as my vision begins to fade. "Let's see how long you last."

I kick and grasp at the gravel road. At this very moment, feeders are ravaging my city. Zane is bleeding out. My friends will likely die. It's over. The Holy One has won.

Shlink!

I look up in time to see Zane's blade erupt from the front of General Kaynes' chest. As he chokes on his own blood, the pressure on my throat dissolves, and I suck in a gasp.

I'm about to thank Zane when I see who saved me. The man is holding Zane's sword, still hilt deep in General Kaynes. Only, it isn't Zane. He's blonde with curly hair and icy blue eyes. His beard is fair and unkempt, hiding what might have been a handsome face.

Before I can say a word, the man bites down on General Kaynes' neck. He only feeds for a few seconds before releasing his jaws. He wipes the blood on his cloak and removes the sword from Kaynes' back. As soon as it's free, Kaynes slumps into the snow, this time dead.

"Well good riddance to that guy!" The blonde man doesn't acknowledge me but immediately turns to Zane. "Thanks for the sword, buddy." He spins the blade once in his hand as he inspects the craftsmanship; then his eyes widen. "I know this sword!" He turns to Zane and peers down at him, his jaw dropping open. "Demons!" He squints, then leans in closer. "Zane? Is that you? My god! It is you!"

Slowly, Zane's eyes flutter open. "Kildron?"

Chapter 39

Matt

I race on top of the inner wall. To any bystanders, I look like a 40-year-old gym teacher in a lieutenant's uniform. The growing layer of slush slows my pace, but at least the streets are empty. I only have to scan a few faces at a time.

My body may be unfamiliar, but the weight of my soul-anchor is nostalgic. It offers unlimited dominion, but it also prevents me from possessing. That's why I keep it on the outside of my uniform. Inside my shirt, I have an amplifier as well. With a quick reach to my soul-anchor, I can switch between the two—unlimited dominion or dominion over man.

In the king's study, I found my Adamic blade as well—the one my parents gave me. It jostles on my hip as I dash across the wall.

Please, God, let this work.

At this very moment, Iris, Diego, and Rose are all doing the same as me. Four bombs remain. Four opportunities for failure.

Finally, I spot her. Her red hair is the only color in the white backdrop. I can't see an amulet at this distance, but she's wearing a black guard uniform. I can only assume she's armed as well.

Crasilda paces parallel to the wall, pausing every few steps to kill time. At any moment, she could turn herself into a weapon of mass destruction.

I'm about 40 feet above her, and with the raging wind, I'm sure she won't hear me coming. Unless she looks straight up, she won't see me coming either.

I jog so that I'm a few feet ahead of her. Then, I climb onto the parapet. I lean over the edge, and when she's only a few feet away, I jump.

Thicken.

I condense the air to slow my fall, but I don't let it stop me completely. I plummet at half pace, extending my hand as I approach impact.

I land almost directly on top of Crasilda, sending her flat on her back.

Electricity!

She shudders as the current courses through her. While she's still convulsing, I grab onto the chain around her neck and pull until it snaps. Then, with her amulet in hand, I immobilize her.

Liquify!

The stone beneath her grows soft, and her hips begin to sink into the stone. She tries to sit up, but it only makes her legs sink faster. Without any other options, she uses her hand to prop herself up. The moment she pushes against the ground, they sink up to her elbows in liquid stone.

Solidify!

The stone hardens around her, stapling her in a seated position. Her upper body is mostly free, but she's half leaning back, her arms rooted in the ground behind her.

Crasilda lets out a string of curses, and I assume it's the demon talking. Then, as I lean over her, she spits in my face.

I'm sorry, I think as I lift the base of her shirt, revealing six spells tattooed across her abdominals. I unsheathe my blade.

Not the first one. Don't cut the first one.

As I bring the blade down, Crasilda thrashes, trying to impale herself on the first symbol. "No! This is my destiny. Let me ascend. On the flames, I will rise!" Her hair falls in her face, sticking to her lips.

Thicken!

I condense the air around her torso to restrict her thrashing. Then, I make a quick slash across the last four spells, being certain not to cut too deep. When I'm sure the spell is severed, I lower her shirt and take a step back. My work is done.

Liquify.

I only liquify the stone directly around her limbs. Once she's managed to pull herself from the ground, I allow it to solidify once more.

Finally, I turn and run. I don't give the demon time to think more about it. I'm afraid if they do, they'll use Crasilda's body as a hostage, threatening her with harm. I've deactivated the bomb. All I can do now is hope they leave her alone.

One down, three to go.

I run toward the flats. The outer wall has the most surface area and thus will be the hardest to defend. I can only hope Diego has already found his mom by now. The fact that I haven't heard any explosions can only be a good sign.

Maybe I was the last one. Maybe we already succeeded.

I'm only a few streets from the flats now. I can see the opening in the road up ahead.

Ka-Boom!!!

The earth jolts beneath me, nearly knocking me off my feet. I slide to a stop in the icy slush, looking for a smoke cloud. I can't see anything, so I assume it was the outer wall, most likely on the far side of the sanctuary.

Ka-Boom!!!

The second blast is closer. It sends a wave of hot air rocketing down the roadway. Plumes of red flame overtake the sky behind me.

Already, I'm beginning to panic. When this happened to Hogrum, I lost my parents. Who will I lose today? Kendra? Rose? Diego?

Will they lose me?

The storm is almost a blizzard now. I can't see much of the outer wall, but as the feeders get closer, I can see them sprinting across the flats. They look tiny from this distance, but there are dozens of them. No, hundreds of them. I only have a few minutes before they reach the ring.

I double-check my amulets as I wander into the open flats. Finally, I stop, ready to face the imminent onslaught. Every feeder I kill is one less that can kill my friends.

I clutch my soul-anchor in my left hand as the first feeder emerges from the snowfall. He slows to a stop before me, confused by my courage.

"Come to offer yourself as first blood?" the feeder hisses, slowly advancing. "How considerate."

SCREECH!

I direct the sound waves at the feeder, amplifying the frequency as much as possible. Immediately, the feeder falls to the floor and covers his ears, unleashing a wail of his own. I close the ground between us and plunge the tip of my dagger into his heart.

I turn as another feeder races past me. It doesn't try to fight, but sprints for the easy pickings of the ring. Already, he's too far to attack directly.

I focus on the snow, commanding it to form a needle-sharp icicle. Then, I pick my target.

Propel!

The icicle whizzes through the air. I gave the feeder a mild lead. To my relief, it runs directly into the path of the icy projectile. The icicle strikes the feeder in the thigh, sending it face-first into the snow. It isn't dead, but it'll be much easier to outrun.

Now, the feeders are all around me. Most run past, but two slow to a stop. Their skin is a sickly yellow, and their eyes sunken. I can tell they're ancient and therefore experienced.

"A guardian?" One of the feeders smiles. He's missing several fingers and nearly all of his teeth. "I've only tasted one in my lifetime. His dominion was exquisite."

"Why don't we take him together?" the other feeder says. "We can split the spoils."

Their lack of fear makes me nervous. Suddenly, I have an idea.

"How disappointing." I try to mimic an amused tone. "You don't recognize your master?"

I imagine the Holy One, his dark skin and trimmed beard. His careless smile.

The Holy One.

My skin trembles, and I watch as my skin darkens. When I see the fear in their faces, I know I've succeeded.

"Master!" The toothless feeder falls to his knees. "Forgive us. You were in disguise." The other feeder falls to its knees as well. Now, they're side by side. Their throats are equal height, only a few feet apart.

"I will forgive you." I approach slowly, keeping my blade in hand. I stop when I'm an arms-length away. "But first I have an assignment for you both. I need—"

I swing the blade, slicing one neck immediately after the other. I turn away as they bleed out. I don't think I can stomach it.

Once I've distanced myself from the dying feeders, I survey my surroundings. I can't find any more feeders in the flats. They've all moved into the city. I can hear screams as the helpless fall victim.

Ka-Crack!

A flash of lightning catches my eyes to my left. The snow makes it hard to see, but I can see people in the distance, several of them.

Ka-Crack!

I can't see the intended target, but another bolt of lightning flashes across the fields. Whoever it is, they're in trouble.

I take off toward the lightning, sprinting as fast as I can without slipping in the snow. I watch the ground to keep from tripping, occasionally glancing up at the figures. As they grow closer, I can make out four figures. Two are on the ground, and two are standing. I watch as one of the figures—a feeder—bites the other in the neck. I'm close enough now to recognize the feeder. It's the archangel. The victim is General Kaynes. Now, the archangel approaches another man. He's lying on the floor, a bloodied hand clutching his chest. The archangel squats down in front of him. That's when I see his face.

Zane!

The archangel is holding his sword. He stabbed him.

He's going to kill Zane!

"Noooo!!!"

I know he's powerful, but I don't care. I charge, my soul-anchor in hand. I let my anger strengthen my soul. I let it focus my mind.

The archangel stands, leaving the sword in Zane's hand. "I didn't—"

Fire!

I let my rage stoke the flames. They coil around the archangel's shield. The snow beneath him immediately begins to boil. Steam billows around us, burning my lungs, but I don't relent. I can feel his shield slipping. His dominion grows weaker by the second.

"Matt!" I hear my name, but I don't turn around. I won't stop until he's dead.

He killed Zane!

His shield grows weaker. I can see him squirming under the heat. Any minute now, his shield will give.

I don't have the patience to wait. As the flames billow around him, I step steadily closer. Finally, I'm close enough. I slash my blade across his shield, allowing the flames to spill inside.

The archangel cries out, falling on his back in the snow. Another shield ripples around him, this one weaker than the last. I raise my knife.

Before I can swing, a hand catches my wrist from behind. "Matt, stop!" Rose's voice scolds. "He didn't stab Zane. General Kaynes did. He saved my life."

I lower my dagger and look down at the archangel. His eyes bulge, not from fear, but something else. He's staring at my amulet. "That's my soul-anchor," he breathes. "W-where did you get that?"

"This?" I hold up my soul-anchor. "It's mine. My mom made it for me."

"Your mom?" The archangel shakes his head. "No... no..."

"What?" I ask. My curiosity ebbing my anger.

The archangel looks at my hair first, then his eyes meet mine. "Ezra?"

A shiver runs down my spine. "How do you know my name?"

"Because... I gave it to you." The archangel throws his cloak to the side and lifts up his sleeve, revealing an identical bonding spell on his shoulder.

"You're my son."

My son?

My mind goes blank. I can't think. All I can do is stare at him. Finally, I find my voice. "You're Kildron?"

He nods.

If this were a movie, I would hug him. We would embrace and hold each other, our broken hearts finally mended. Instead, I can only think of one thing.

"But... I thought you were dead."

Kildron laughs. "I thought the same about you." Suddenly, his face lights up. "Jenevrah, your mother...is she somehow...?"

I shake my head. "The Holy One killed her."

"Oh," His shoulders sag. He looks me over once more, and slowly, his smile returns. "I can't believe you're alive."

Zane!

Suddenly, I remember. I turn away from Kildron and dash to Zane's side. He's still breathing. There's still hope.

"Zane! Zane, talk to me." His eyes drift open as I press my hand to his chest. The knife missed his heart, but the damage is extensive. His lung is punctured, and he's bleeding worse than I thought.

Clot! I command, but the blood keeps oozing.

"Matt," Zane groans. "You're okay. You're dad... he's alive."

"I know. I just met him. He's right here. We're going to get you to the palace. Okay, Zane. You're going to be fine."

Zane closes his eyes. "Too many feeders. Leave me. You go."

"No. I'm not leaving you."

Zane pushes his sword toward me, barely moving it an inch. "Take it. It's yours." He coughs, but it's more of a gargle. "I'm proud of you, Matt. I couldn't have asked... for a better son. I'll see you on the other..." His voice trails off.

I push my soul into his head.

Wake up!

His eyes flutter open, only to fall flat once more. His chest deflates, and he falls still.

"Zane?" I reach out with my soul, but this time, there's nothing there.

He's gone.

I sit there, staring at his body. I want to heal him. I want to bring him back. Anything. It isn't supposed to end like this. Zane survived Hogrum's collapse. He's not supposed to die now.

"Matt, we have to go." Rose's words echo meaninglessly in my head. "If we stay here, we'll die."

"You go," Kildron suggests. "I'll stay with Ezra."

Rose hesitates a moment, then I hear the snow crunch as she jogs away.

Kildron kneels next to me in the snow. He waits a while before putting his hand on my shoulder. "The princess was right. We have to go."

I say nothing. I can't leave him here. He needs a funeral. He deserved better.

"I don't know you, Ezra. I don't know anything about you, but I know what you're feeling right now. I've lost people too."

530

"Shut up! You don't know anything!"

"I lost everyone!" Kildron shouts. "I know what it's like. You think this hurts? This is just one? How many more can you bear to lose? The princess? Others? Every second you sit here, their lives are at stake."

I want to lash out. I want to destroy something. Kill something. I have so much anger inside me. Then, I think of Kendra. I think of what a feeder could be doing to her this very second.

I need to find her.

"Goodbye, Zane," I whisper to myself. *I'll come back for you.*

I climb to my feet, pick up his sword, and start running. I don't wait for my father, but I know he'll be close behind. The storm rages around us, and the screams grow louder with every step.

Kendra can't die! I won't let her die!

Chapter 40

Rose

I fiddle with the relic on my thumb. It was the only finger big enough to fit the ring. I've yet to use it since snatching it from General Kaynes' corpse. I twist the metal until the symbols align.

When I look down, I see my legs. They're as normal looking as ever—far from invisible.

It didn't work.

Then, I sense it. When I extend my soul to the photons around me, I can feel the ring's effect. It doesn't make the light pass through me. Instead, it rotates the photons 180 degrees around me. Then, it releases the light in its normal trajectory. The light bends around me as if I was never there at all.

Incredible!

I move through the ring with confidence, my footprints the only indication of my presence. Soon, the bodies begin to appear. They're staggered in the snow, staring blankly at the heavens.

I hear a woman screaming somewhere nearby. I move down an alley, following the sound of the scream. I only take a few steps when the screams go silent.

I'm too late.

I turn back down the alley and continue toward the 8th District. I keep an arrow nocked at all times, ready to kill on sight. I only have 10 arrows, so I have to use them sparingly.

"Noooo!" A woman's voice echoes through the alleys, originating somewhere to my right. In the end, I ignore it. *I don't have time to save them.*

I'm a few blocks away when a feeder emerges from the roadside apartment, its mouth smeared with blood. Totally oblivious to my presence, it moves in my direction.

Twang!

I let the arrow fly, catching the feeder in the shoulder.

9 arrows left.

It lets out a cry and looks wildly around the street. The air ripples around it as the feeder forms an energy shield. When it doesn't see anyone, it reaches up for the arrow.

Twang!

This time the arrow hits home, thudding into the center of its chest. It takes two steps before falling face-first into the snow.

8 arrows left.

I run over the feeder's corpse and roll it onto his back. One of the shafts has snapped against the street, but the other is still viable. I pull it from the feeder and renock it on my bowstring.

9 left.

Then, I run. I'm only a few streets away now, I turn right and find a dead guard in the snow, a large gash in his neck. Another guard is lying against the apartment wall, equally dead. I keep running. I'm only a few streets away.

Please, don't be too late.

I stop in front of Wendy's apartment, but the door to the stairwell has been pulled off its hinges. My heart is pounding as I step inside.

Immediately. I see signs of a battle. The walls are scorched, and a section of the stone wall has crumbled into the adjacent building.

On the second floor, I spot the blood. It trails up the steps— several drops at a time—leading directly beneath Wendy's front door. I'm afraid to open it. I'm afraid to know the truth.

I take a deep breath and push the door open. The blood trail stops at a body in the hallway. I tiptoe closer and breathe a sigh of relief. It's a feeder, bleeding from a gash in its head.

But who killed it?

"Hello?" Diego peers down the hallway at me, his body encased in metal. He doesn't see me, only the opened door.

I twist the ring and step into the open. "It's just me."

Diego motions for me to enter, closing the door behind me. "I'm glad you're here. We're preparing for a final push to the palace. We could really use your help."

I move into the living room and find a mass of people huddled together. Wendy's family is here, along with Diego's. I spot Abuela in the corner, Jorge and Javier, Maria and Isabela. Then, I see a woman I don't recognize.

His mother.

Diego follows my gaze. "Don't worry, the demon left. I destroyed the spell."

Suddenly, a scream erupts from across the street.

"The sooner we move, the better," I warn. "The feeders are working their way toward the palace. If we can get ahead of them, we'll have less of a battle."

"You heard the queen," Diego's voice reverberates like brass. "Let's move. I'll be in front, the queen will guard the back. Jorge and Javier, carry Abuela if you have to. We need to move fast, and we don't stop for anything. Got it? We're leaving now." He moves down the hallway slowly, gaining speed as his family follows suit. As Wendy waddles past, she takes my hand. "Thank you. Thank you for being here."

Once we're in the street, we make a dash for the palace. Diego moves fast but stops every so often to let the others catch up. For the first minute, we don't see many feeders, then the screams get louder. I hear the hiss of fire and several gunshots.

I'm scanning the windows when I see movement up above me. A feeder peers over the rooftop ledge, then another head appears alongside it.

The moment I aim my bow in their direction, they retract their heads out of view. At first, I think they've fled. Then, I hear the pitter-patter of feet racing toward the edge.

Together, the two feeders leap off the rooftop, falling directly over Abuela's head.

Shield!

The air ripples a few feet above Diego's family, forming a shield parallel to the ground. Each feeder lands effortlessly on the shield, eliciting shrieks from both Jorge and Maria.

The feeders look down, eyeing their prey through the translucent shield. One feeder takes several steps to the side, but I extend the shield to each alley wall. Then, I aim my arrow at the center of its chest.

Twang!

The arrow flies, catching the nearest feeder in the gut. It screams and quickly snaps the protruding end of the arrow before falling to its knees.

8 left.

The second feeder aims its hands down, sending flames cascading across my shield. The flames roll above the family caravan, no more than a few feet overhead.

Diego closes his eyes, and the second-floor window breaks apart, sending glass shrapnel into both feeders. The flames diminish, and the feeder collapses onto my shield. They're both dead.

The family caravan continues forward as I tilt my shield to the side, dumping the feeder bodies on the side of the road.

We don't make it another block before a feeder emerges from a side alley. It stands in the middle of the road, blocking our path.

It's a woman, and she looks like a walking corpse. She's gaunt and hairless, and her fingernails are unnaturally long. Most disturbing of all, there's an empty socket where her right eye should be.

"Leave the weak ones, and I'll let you pass in peace," the feeder croaks.

Diego doesn't bother responding, he grips his Adamic blade and charges. The feeder doesn't run. In fact, she doesn't do anything.

When Diego is a few feet away, he suddenly stops. His metal muscles grow taut. Then, they relax. "I warned you," his metallic voice sneers.

No!

Diego lunges at María, swinging the knife down.

I'm at the back of the caravan, but I'm close enough to counter

Force!

The air ripples, tossing Diego back. He rolls twice in the snow, before scrambling back to his feet. Immediately, he's scanning for his attacker.

"What's going on?" Jorge demands.

He's possessed! I don't say it aloud. I don't want to give away my position.

The one-eyed demon is in a trance, staring mindlessly ahead. All I have to do is hit her with an arrow, and Diego will be freed. I nock an arrow and aim for her chest.

I'm about to release when Diego dives in front of the feeder. He stands tall, covering her entire body with his titanium frame.

"I know you're out there," Diego says. "Show yourself, or I kill your friend." Diego raises his dagger and aligns the point with his own heart.

No! Not again!

The last time this happened, Tick killed himself. I won't let Diego do the same.

"Alright," Diego smiles. "Your choice."

The knife dips effortlessly into his metal skin, slowly sinking deeper.

"Wait!" I rush past the families and twist the ring.

536

"There you are!" Diego grins victoriously.

Before I can make a shield, a wave of snow sweeps me against the wall. My skull cracks against the stone, and my bow falls from my hand. Then, the wave recedes, and I fall flat on the street.

Shield!

I blindly throw up a force field as I climb to my feet. When I look up, Diego is already cutting through it with his dagger. He lifts his hand, and the flames roar toward us.

Ice!

I condense the snow into a small wall of ice, no taller than my head. As the flames roar against it, I try to hold it together, but it's melting with every second. The ice becomes dangerously thin. Suddenly, the flames stop, and an energy wave shatters my ice shield to pieces.

Before I can retaliate, Diego looks up at the apartment to my right.

I follow his gaze just in time to see two large cracks run up the apartment face. To my horror, the entire front wall begins to tip toward the street, falling directly over the families.

Shield!

Several tons of stone crash down, reverberating against my shield. The wall breaks into pieces, and the air vibrates. I clench my jaw as I struggle to hold the rubble in the air. Thanks to my soul-anchor, the effort isn't straining, but it demands every ounce of focus to maintain.

I look over just in time to see Diego raise his hand. I can either defend myself or save the family. I can't do both.

Twang!

An arrow flies, striking the demon in the ribs. It isn't lethal, but it's just enough to break the possession. As soon as he's free, Diego turns and throws his dagger, embedding it directly alongside the arrow. The feeder topples over, lying still in the snow.

How?

I look around and find Wendy standing on the side of the road. She's holding my bow in her hand, watching the dead feeder in disbelief.

"Everyone, move!" I gasp. As soon as they've rushed out of the impact zone, I dissolve my shield. The street rumbles as the rubble crashes against the cobblestone.

"Thank you," I wheeze as I retrieve my bow from Wendy. I want to say more, but it's all I have time for. I snatch up six arrows from the snow and toss them back in my quiver. Then, I twist my ring until the symbols align.

"We need to move!" Diego shouts. "C'mon!"

This time, I take the front and Diego covers the rear. We see a few more feeders, but I quickly fill them with arrows, collecting them again from the corpses. Nearly every arrow is now smothered in blood.

As we move into the Royal Plaza, the palace comes into view, utterly untouched by the feeders. We're not alone as we run to the gate. Several other citizens make the very same dash, collapsing in the snow as they pass through the wall and into safety. On the walls, guards aim rifles in our direction, ready to shoot at any feeders who wander close enough.

We're going to make it!

I keep my bow nocked as we run the last 100 feet. I stand watch as the two families file past. I can see through the archway. Refugees loiter on the palace grounds, huddling in their families. The snow falls down around them, making the scene that much more dreary.

With a twist of my ring. I make myself visible. I'm about to follow them in when someone grabs me from behind.

"Thank God, you're okay!" Antai squeezes me against his chest, nearly impaling himself on my arrow. "Hurry inside. Our lookouts say the feeders are almost here."

I follow Antai through the gate, slinging my bow across my shoulder. "Has Matt made it back yet?"

"If he has, I haven't seen him," Antai says.

538

"And what about Octavian? Is he back?"

Antai shakes his head. "General Kaynes went out to look for you. He also hasn't returned."

"He's dead," I say matter-of-factly. I don't bother explaining how.

"Dad!" Kendra's voice calls out from behind me. She's dashing through the crowd, head on a swivel. "Mom!" She gives the exhausted refugees one last scan as she moves toward the gate.

"Kendra?" A man limps through the gate, and Kendra runs to him, throwing her arms around his neck.

"What happened? Where's mom and Deklin?" Kendra gasps.

"I thought they were here. I came from the university. The blast collapsed the roof there."

"I'll go find her," Kendra promises.

"I'll come too." Her dad hobbles after her, but she quickly leaves him behind. "You're hurt. Wait here. I'll be back." Then she dashes into the plaza.

"Kendra!" I call out. I want to warn her about the feeders, but she doesn't turn around. I keep watching as she races across the plaza and disappears into one of the bordering apartments.

From on top of the wall, a guard calls down to Antai. "Feeders approaching, general."

I look out through the archway, and sure enough, the feeders begin to emerge. They enter from the different streets, converging on the Royal Plaza from all sides of the sanctuary.

I count a dozen feeders, and more join with every second. The longer I look, the deeper my heart sinks. These aren't just feeders. Some are armored. Others carry Adamic blades. These are the strongest among them. While the weak ravage the ring, the feeder elite have come to storm the palace.

Suddenly, an armored feeder steps forward and aims directly at the archway where I'm standing.

KA-CRACK!!!

A deafening bolt of lightning strikes the air in front of me, activating the defensive spell. The air ripples, and the lighting crackles along the surface of the invisible barrier. The survivors behind me shriek.

After a moment, the lightning stops, and the archway returns to being translucent. When they see that we're unharmed, the feeders snarl and pace restlessly on the far side of the plaza. They expected the walls to be destroyed already. They expected the palace to be the crowning feast, and they're more than disappointed. Still, they keep their distance.

As the seconds tick by, more and more feeders accumulate in the plaza. With each passing second, Matt's odds grow slimmer. He's cut off from the palace by no less than an army.

Matt isn't going to make it.

To my horror, some of the feeders begin to spread out along the far side of the plaza, moving into the apartments in search of more prey.

Not that door. No!

An armored feeder opens the door that Kendra entered, and creeps inside. One moment later, another feeder follows at his heels.

If her family is still alive, they won't be for long.

Chapter 41

Matt

Diego's front door is already open as I descend the steps. I hold Zane's sword in front of me, then I step inside. Everything is silent, which is either a good sign or a very bad one.

I open the door to the first bedroom and peer inside. No feeders. No bodies. No blood. The next room is the same. When I reach the kitchen, I let out a sigh of relief. Our detour was a waste of time, but I don't regret stopping by. I had to be sure.

"They're already gone," I say. "Hopefully, they made it to the palace. Let's go."

As we move back into the street, I imagine Hood, the feeder that first bit me. I imagine the tattoos that covered his face and his shaved head.

Hood!

My skin trembles, and a wave of Adamic tattoos descend down my arms. The spells don't actually work, but they look like they do. Any feeder would be foolish to mess with me.

I take off toward the Royal Plaza, and my dad follows close behind.

"So, your sister is in Cavernum too, right? Have you met her?"

"Yeah, I've met her. She's... cool I guess."

Kildron points at Zane's sword. "Do you know how to wield a gladius?"

"A gladius?"

Kildron smiles. "It's the type of sword. Roman design."

"I don't," I admit. "Do you want to use it? I'm better with my dagger."

Kildron shrugs. "Sure." He accepts the sword and I unsheathe my dagger, sad to give it up, but grateful to be rid of the extra weight.

As we jog up the main road, a feeder steps out of an alley, instantly spotting us. Perhaps it's my disguise, or maybe it's my father, but the feeder doesn't bat an eye. It turns away and scurries down the next alley.

I don't chase it. I need to get to the plaza. *Kendra first, feeders later.*

As we approach the inner wall, Kildron hesitates. He slows to a stop and slowly extends his hands. As they pass through the archway, he frowns.

"C'mon," I say, trudging ahead through the snow. I don't say it aloud, but I know he's thinking it. When we get to the palace, Kildron won't be able to enter. We'll have to part ways.

As we pass through the core, the feeders become more plentiful. I see one crawling out of a window to my right. Another is feeding in the middle of the road. I look at Kildron and he nods.

He charges the feeder in the road, thrusting Zane's sword into his back. I focus on the feeder in the window. She's standing now. Her hair is grey and soaked with snow. She smiles at the sight of us, revealing two rows of needle-sharp teeth.

Finally, I have a target for my rage. As she emerges from the doorway, I command the air in front of her face.

Combust!

Ka-Boom!

The resulting explosion launches the feeder against the stone building. She slumps to the sidewalk and doesn't get up.

For once, I don't feel remorse. In fact, I feel better.

That was for Zane.

We continue, attacking any feeder that crosses our paths. If they run, we don't pursue.

I'm beginning to feel hopeful until we reach the plaza. The feeders are everywhere, dozens of them. Instead of facing them, we turn one street early, jogging down a side alley.

"What's the plan?" Kildron asks.

"I'm going to check on my friend's family. They live along the plaza. They might already be in the palace, but I have to be sure. Then, we'll make a break for the gate."

Kildron nods. "We need to blend in as much as we can. Don't fight if we don't have to."

Still disguised as Hood, I dash out of the alley and toward the Royal Plaza. I don't scan for enemies. I hunch my shoulder and act as feederly as possible, eyeing the apartments as if searching for my next meal.

As crazy as it sounds, it works. The feeders ignore us. They don't attack. We might as well be invisible.

I creep the last few yards and open the door to Kendra's stairwell. I climb the steps slowly, listening for any sign of feeders. Everything is quiet.

Please be in the palace!

I listen for a second outside Kendra's door.

Silence.

I try the handle. It's locked. I reach my mind through the wood and find the deadbolt.

Slide!

The metal clicks, and I push the door open. As soon as I step inside, flames erupt around me. Blinding me with bright oranges and yellows.

Extinguish.

The flames recede as Kendra charges. She swings a kitchen knife at my face, and I barely deflect it in time with my dagger.

"Kendra, What are y—"

Then, I remember my disguise.

Myself!

A wave of vibration returns me to my normal form. As soon as Kendra sees my face, she drops the knife and dives into my arms, burying her chin against my chest. "Thank God! You nearly gave me a heart attack."

I squeeze her back. "And you almost stabbed me in the face. Good job by the way."

Kendra looks around me and spots Kildron. "Who's that?"

"That's my dad," I say. "I met him today. I'll explain later."

Kendra's eyebrows rise, and she steps back. She turns toward the kitchen and half whispers, half shouts. "Mom, you can come out. They're friends."

Mrs. Esecks and Deklin emerge from the kitchen pantry. When Deklin sees Zane's blade, his eyes bulge. "Mom, look at his sword!"

"Shhh," she hisses.

"I have bad news," I start. "I don't know if you've looked at the plaza, but there are feeders everywhere. It's going to be a battle to get to the palace. We have to move fast and stick together." *We might not make it.*

Kendra turns to her mom. "You guys ready?"

She puts her hand on Deklin's head. "We're ready."

I move toward the door. "Okay. I'll lead. Kildron will take the rear. Stay between us. As soon as we're close enough, make a run for it."

Everyone nods.

"Okay, follow me." I lead us down the steps to the ground floor. I'm about to open the door to the plaza when I hear the snow crunching outside. The door flies open, and a feeder takes a step inside.

Fire!

He's not expecting an attack, and he doesn't raise any defenses. I douse him in a stream of fire. Then, while his flesh is still burning, I lunge forward and thrust my dagger into his chest.

"Wow!" Deklin breathes behind me.

"Come on!" I step over the body and through the doorway, moving into the open plaza. Already, the dread weighs me down. Feeders are gathered in the center of the plaza, dozens of them. They pace back and forth, like hungry dogs. Ever so slowly, their heads turn in our direction.

I take a deep breath and advance.

Shield!

I surround us with a massive energy dome. Now that we're in the open, an attack could come from any direction.

A feeder charges at us, and I let it draw close. When it's 20 feet away, I command the air around its head.

Combust!

Ka-Boom!

The feeder's body goes limp, propelled by the explosion. Two armored feeders charge next, and I change tactics.

"Protect them!" I call to Kildron as I sprint ahead.

Darkness!

I surround myself in a massive black cloud. I don't stop there. I let go of my soul anchor, using my amplifier to probe the darkness around me. I sense a feeder to my right, and I slash with my dagger, cutting into his arm.

The feeder cries out, and I finish him with another slash to the throat.

Ka-Boom!

I can't see it, but an explosion erupts somewhere in the space to my left, knocking me off my feet. My cloud of darkness disappears.

I spot the feeder as I scramble to my feet. He raises his hand.

Ka-Crack!

Before he can attack, an arc of blinding light strikes the feeder in the back. The lightning crackles over his armored skin, but it has no effect. Fortunately, Kildron doesn't stop there. The plaza floor erupts around the feeder. Four slabs of stone squeeze the feeder from all sides, pinning him. With a few quick strides, Kildron closes the gap between them and plunges his sword into the feeder's chest.

I'm barely on my feet before a volley of needle-sharp icicles rains down on me.

Melt!

The ice shards dissolve, and the remaining water pelts my face.

Crunch, crunch, crunch.

I hear the hurried footsteps in the snow behind me. I turn and raise my dagger as another feeder swings a knife.

I parry his blade and stumble back as a second feeder charges from my left.

Lightning!

Electricity courses from my hand, crackling against the second feeder's energy shield.

Then, I exert my mind into the knife-wielding feeder, leaving my body behind.

I have to commit!

I let myself free fall into his mind, embracing the visions of bloodshed and murder. When I open my eyes, I see myself staring blankly ahead. The second feeder extends his hand and flames erupt toward my abandoned body.

Shield!

I deflect the flames from my body and lunge, thrusting my host's knife into the second feeder's shoulder. Then, I focus on his throat.

Slice!

A thin ripple of air cuts cleanly through his neck.

Finally, I take the blade and plunge it into my host's heart.

"Gah!" I gasp in my body as the pain recedes from my mind. I spin around, expecting to be instantly overwhelmed by dozens of feeders. Instead, the feeders are facing the palace. I see a flash of lightning as allied forces advance against the feeders.

They're helping!

That's when I remember Kendra.

I turn around and find her huddled with her family a dozen yards away. Kildron is standing beside them, four dead feeders at his feet.

As I look back, I see more feeders moving into the plaza. Soon, we'll be sandwiched between two armies.

"We have to move!" I call out as I rush over. Once again, I form a shield around them. Kildron nods, dragging his feet in the snow. He looks like he might collapse at any moment.

"You okay?"

"I'm running low on juice," Kildron admits. "I need to feed but we don't have time."

"Here, take my amplifier." I pull it off my head and toss it to him. He quickly loops it over his head and tucks it into his cloak.

We approach the center of the plaza, where the highest concentration of feeders is focused. Once again, I lead. At least 20 feeders stand between us and the palace. Now that we're closer, I can make out our allies on the other side. Diego's metal body flashes as he charges through a blast of fire. I see another man—an archer. He's flinging arrows left and right.

We might make it!

I charge an armored feeder, forming a shield around me. His flames glance off, and I continue to advance. I ram the feeder, wielding my force field like a riot shield. The feeder stumbles back, and I land on top of him, pinning him to the floor with my shield. Finally, I drive my dagger through them both.

I'm standing when I see another feeder. It's charging a guardsman, cutting through his shield with an Adamic blade exactly the way I just had.

I build up the electrical charge in my hand until it's begging to be released.

Lightning!

The bolt is fleeting, but it strikes the feeder square in the back. It seizes once before collapsing in the snow. The guardsman is quick to respond. He scrambles on his hands and knees to grab the feeder's dagger. Then, he thrusts it with one hand into the feeder's heart.

When the guardsman stands, I notice something odd. He doesn't have a right hand.

"What are you doing here?" I demand.

Vyle stands. He holds the dagger in his left hand, raised and ready to kill. "Same as you," he sneers, nodding toward the palace. "Trying to survive."

"No!" I shake my head. "You don't get to hide in the palace. Not after what you did. Leave, before I kill you myself!"

Vyle takes a step forward. "You can't keep me out."

The anger builds on me, and all I can think of is Zane's dying breath. "You're on their side," I scream. "Your dad killed Zane! You tried to kill the princess! You're one of them!"

"I'm not my father!" Vyle shouts back. "I'm not!" His own face begins to fill with blood. "But I know one thing. You're no hero either. You're a demon. You killed the king. You deserve to die with the rest of them."

As Vyle raises his arm, I do the same.

Ka-Crack!

Our lightning bolts surge in unison, but they don't collide. They repel each other, both arcing off target and into the snow.

Without an amplifier, I can't predict his attacks. I form a precautionary shield just in case. Vyle mimics my shield; then he charges.

When our shields collide, Vyle slashes through them, nearly cutting my uniform. He may only have one hand, but he wields the knife effortlessly.

He swings again, and I catch his blade with my own. The blades slide until our cross guards lock.

Before I can withdraw my blade, Vyle swings the stump of his hand, catching me in the jaw. I stumble back, forming a shield between us.

Vyle doesn't attack directly but commands the snow around me. In a single wave, it washes around my boots, liquifying before freezing my feet in place.

I don't dissolve my shield. Instead, I split my mind, focusing on two places at once. With the soul-anchor, my mind can finally withstand the strain. As I maintain my shield, I command the ice around my ankles.

Melt.

The ice falls away, soaking my boots and puddling at my feet.

Vyle's charges, using the ice distraction to eliminate the distance between us. He's cutting through my shield when I retaliate.

Fire!

A vortex of flames surges between us. They hiss against his shield and eat away at his defenses. The ice beneath the flames instantly melts, and soon Vyle is shrouded in steam.

Just when I think I've won, Vyle dives from behind his shield. I move the flames to follow him, but I'm too slow. As he raises his hand, I reform my shield.

I realize my mistake too late. Vyle doesn't aim at me, he aims at the snow—or rather, the melted snow. I'm standing in a massive puddle of water that stretches nearly all the way to Vyle.

Ka-Crack!

This isn't just a taser; it's an electrocution. The energy rips through me. Singeing my clothes and turning the world black.

When I open my eyes, Vyle's blade is already in motion.

Shlink!

The blade slices into my stomach, igniting an unparalleled pain. I want to scream, but instead, I emit a hideous wheeze. My muscles spasm, and my body involuntarily curls around the blade. A second later, Vyle rips the dagger free.

Before I can recover my thoughts, Vyle grabs hold of my soul-anchor and tears it from my neck. I watch as it melts in his hand, dripping gold into the snow. What took me months to recover only took Vyle two seconds to destroy.

I'm powerless.

"Matt!" Kendra comes running, but with a wave of his hand, Vyle sends an energy wave in her direction. It hits her hard and sends her tumbling across the snow.

Vyle sneers at me, tightening his grip on the dagger. I know it's foolish, but I have no choice. If I don't do something, I'll die. He's only a foot away. I might just survive.

In one last effort, I extend my soul toward Vyle. I only need to possess him for a second. However, the instant I sense his emotions, a splitting pain pierces my skull.

"Ahh!" I grit my teeth and abandon the possession. The colors swim before my eyes, and my muscles go limp. When my vision clears, Vyle is smiling.

"Now, you can see your precious Zane again."

He lifts the dagger and swings it down.

Chapter 42

Rose

Every scream makes me cringe. I can hear them drifting over the core. Each cry is a plea for help, a supplication for salvation. As their queen, it's my job to deliver them, yet I do nothing.

I'm sorry.

I turn away from the wall, focusing instead on the survivors. Most of them are commoners, and most are unharmed. They scatter across the grounds, huddling amongst themselves for warmth. The majority watch the gate, hoping their loved ones will wander in. Others meander their way toward the Central Tower.

I don't even want to think about the long term. Who knows how long the palace walls will stand. The Holy One could create another bomb at any time. He could already have one now. We could be blown to bits any minute.

Focus, Rose! One thing at a time.

I call out to a Royal Guard as he moves past. "Excuse me? Are the refugees being allowed into the palace?"

"Yes, they're being sent to the ballroom, your highness. Chancellor Gwenevere commanded it. Would you like them sent somewhere else?"

"No, that's good. Have any available healers report there as well."

"Of course, your highness."

I hurry back to the gate, standing beside Antai. His face is grim... defeated. "It's not over yet, Rose. We still have the palace."

"I guess," I sigh. *It sure feels over.*

Cavernum as I know it is gone. Thousands dead. So much death, my mind can't comprehend it. All I can do is stand there, watching the snowflakes descend. No one has crossed the gate since we arrived. The feeders still have hold of the plaza, and they're not leaving anytime soon. By morning, the city will be nothing but a graveyard.

Ka-Boom!

Instantly, my heart takes off, pounding in my ears. At first, I fear it may be an Adamic bomb, but the explosion didn't come from the palace, it came from the far side of the plaza.

Ka-Crack!

Lightning flashes on the opposite side of the plaza. Now, I see it. Across the plaza, a battle is underway. A small group of survivors is taking on the full force of the feeders.

"They don't stand a chance," Antai breathes.

I strain my eyes, trying to make out the figures. *Could it be?*

Suddenly, the battle is absorbed in a mist of darkness. It slowly moves forward, eliminating all light.

It is!

Ka-Boom!

In the blink of an eye, the cloud disappears, and another flash of lightning rocks the plaza. I watch in horror as more and more feeders flock towards the conflict.

"That's Matt! We have to help them."

Footsteps crunch behind me as Diego jogs over. "Did you say Matt?"

I point.

Ka-Crack!

Another flash of lightning. I only catch glimpses through the horde of feeders, but I have no doubt now.

I unsling my bow from my shoulder. "We have to help. I'm going out there!"

Diego's body glistens silver. Without a word, he takes off into the plaza.

Out of nowhere, Gideon steps up beside me, his bow in hand. "I overheard, and I'm prepared to assist."

"Yes, please. Thank you, Gideon."

Without another word, he takes off after Diego.

I take a step through the gate, but Antai grabs my hand. "No! It's too dangerous, Rose. The Holy One could be out there as we speak."

"I don't care."

"You better care," Antai growls. "You're the only adalit left. You're our only hope. I can't let you risk your life like this." He lets go of my wrist, but he stands in my path.

"Fine." I pull my arm away and back up. Then I reach down to my hand and twist the ring. I don't feel anything, but I know it's worked. Antai's eyes widen.

Before he can stop me, I sidestep Antai and sprint past him into the plaza.

"Rose!"

I hear his footsteps behind me, but I don't slow. The feeders are 75 yards away, much too far to attack. Diego and Gideon are almost to them now. Two armored feeders turn to face them. Gideon draws back his bow and releases.

The feeder shudders as the arrow rips into his chest. It staggers for a moment before collapsing.

The second feeder lifts a slab of the stone floor to form a shield against arrows. Diego charges with his knife raised. With a running start, he launches himself over the slab, slashing down with his knife. The feeder's cry tells me he hit his mark.

He doesn't land gracefully. He crashes into the snow and slides to a stop, but he's unharmed. He leaps to his feet and barrels toward the nearest feeder.

Finally, I catch up. I have the ultimate advantage. I'm invisible, and I'm armed with six Adamic arrows. I pull back the bowstring and align my arrow with the nearest feeder's torso.

Twang!

The arrow drops slightly, striking the feeder in the thigh. It looks around wildly, but I know it won't find me.

5 left.

I nock the next arrow, this time pulling back even further. I aim at a different feeder. They're everywhere. Even if I miss one, I'll likely hit another.

Twang!

The arrow hits the feeder in the ribs. From my peripheral, I see a second feeder drop, Gideon's arrow protruding from its head.

4 left.

Antai has joined the fight now. He sends a rolling force wave crashing into the feeders. As I scan the scene. I can see Matt's group 20 yards away. Unfortunately, there's a long row of feeders between us.

To my left, Diego is thrown back. A feeder charges, wielding a massive Adamic sword, at least 4 feet long. It sweeps the blade as Diego scrambles back. I nock an arrow and release.

Twang.

The arrow whistles past the feeders head, disappearing into the snow. Diego launches a slab of stone, but it disintegrates before striking the feeder.

I nock another arrow as the feeder swings its sword. At any second, Diego could be sliced in two. I aim and release as quickly as I can.

Twang!

The arrow strays right, whizzing past his shoulder!

No!

Thunk!

Gideon's arrow hits home, embedding itself above the feeder's ear. It's sword plops in the snow, which Diego immediately grabs and starts swinging.

I don't have time to thank Gideon, the horde of feeders are now advancing in our direction. At least five are swarming Gideon, who must be nearly out of arrows.

I reach up and grab another arrow from my quiver.

2 left.

I'm nocking it when a feeder stumbles toward me. It's looking at my feet, squinting at the snow. Suddenly, it raises its hand, and a wave of fire billows toward me.

Shield.

I sidestep as the flames swirl around me and manage to move out of their path. As I sidestep, the snow crunches beneath me. The feeder smiles, redirecting the fire in my direction.

Twang!

I send an arrow through the flames, striking the feeder in the stomach. It stumbles back as I raise my hand!

Fire!

The flames engulf him, and the feeder screams before falling to the snow.

At the sight of my flames, more feeders look in my direction. The element of surprise is spent.

They know I'm here.

I nock another arrow and scan the feeders. We've diminished their numbers, but it doesn't look like it'll be enough. We're still badly outnumbered. Gideon is backing up now, his bow is slung over his shoulder.

He's out.

"Matt!" The cry carries across the battle. It's Kendra's voice. I find her as she's thrown across the snow by an energy wave. Then, I see Matt.

No!

He's on his back in the snow. Vyle leans over him, holding a bloodied blade in his hand. As quick as I can, I nock an arrow. He's far—at least 20 yards—but I have to try.

God, let this hit!

As Vyle raises the dagger, I let out one last breath. Then, I let it fly.

Chapter 43

Matt

Vyle lifts the dagger over my chest.

Time seems to slow. I wait for a feeder to flank him. I wait for anything to save me, but I know it's over. This is where I die.

I'm sorry, Kendra.

I close my eyes as Vyle swings down.

Thunk!

I open my eyes as the knife falls from his hand. An arrowhead protrudes from the side of Vyle's neck, the fletching coming out the other. He shudders, then reaches for the shaft, breaking off the tip. He tries to pull it out as he falls in the snow next to me.

I'd like to think I'm saved, but it's only earned me moments. I'm bleeding from my gut, and my soul is severely strained. I look around and find Kendra lying in snow 20 feet away. She's on her stomach, and her hair covers her face. She doesn't move, but she's alive. As I look around, my stomach drops. I see Kildron huddling next to Kendra's family. He's holding an energy shield while two feeders bombard him with attacks. In the distance, I see Diego. He's swinging a long sword, but he's retreating toward the palace, several feeders in pursuit. Antai is beside him, running as well.

No!

There's no one to save us.

I sit up, biting through the pain. Kendra begins to stir. As she does, a feeder notices her, its eyes narrowing. Immediately, the feeder charges.

"Nooo!"

The feeder dives at Kendra as she forms an energy shield. I know it won't last long. I have seconds at most to save her.

In a frenzy, I crawl to Vyle's side. He's still breathing, but I can't tell if he's conscious. He doesn't resist as I reach into his shirt and grab his amplifier.

I look toward the feeder and command with all my might!

Lightning!

Sparks crackle on my fingertips, and I clutch my head as the pain sears into my cerebrum. I can't use dominion. I've strained myself to capacity.

Ka-Boom!

An explosion obliterated Kendra's shield, tossing her back in the snow. I only have seconds.

I have no choice! It's the only way!

I take one last look at Vyle as I pull the arrow from his neck. Then, I place my mouth over the wound, gagging as his blood hits my tongue.

Instantly, I can feel his soul rushing through his bloodstream. With every beat, I feel the power flowing past. Knowledge and memories... dominion.

Rather than projecting my soul onto his, I pull his soul into my own. I inhale his dominion, drawing it out of his wound. For a moment, he kicks, moaning beneath my mouth, but I can't stop now. The entirety of Vyle's dominion is inside me. I feel the power. It expands my mind. Expands my senses. The pain in my side begins to subside. My hold over the elements is amplified.

Kendra!

I turn as the feeder bites down. Her scream cuts me to the core.

Force!

The air ripples, throwing the feeder off of Kendra. He rolls twice, before landing on all fours. Once he's a safe distance, I don't hold back.

Lightning!

The bolt blasts the feeder back. It lands in the snow, steam rising from its flesh. It doesn't get up.

Another feeder rushes me from the side, but I'm ready.

Combust!

The feeder is blown back, I don't watch to see if it survived.

I stumble to my feet, suppressing the pain with self-dominion. I wipe the blood from my mouth as I race to Kendra and fall at her side.

"Kendra! Are you—"

"I'm okay." She says, pressing a hand to the wound on her neck. "What about you? You were stabbed!"

"I'm fine," I lie as I direct my soul to the site of the wound.

Clot!

I help her to her feet and look out over the plaza. We're on the brink of destruction. I may have Vyle's dominion, but already the strain is returning. I can't fight them all.

Kendra knows we've lost. "Should we run? Maybe we can hide somewhere?"

Suddenly, I hear a torrent of footsteps behind me. I turn, prepared to fight for my life. Instead, I see Iris. She's running alongside Octavian. A mass of men and women stampede behind her, each with an amulet in their hands. I can't count how many, but there are at least 30 of them. As they rush past, I spot Bob waddling at the back.

"The equalists," I whisper. *They're on our side!*

With a war cry, they fall upon the feeders. They may be novices, but at least they're not outnumbered.

"C'mon!" Kendra grabs her mother by the hand. "Mom, C'mon!"

We follow behind the equalists, rushing into the slaughter. I hold a shield around us, but I don't take the offensive. All that matters is getting Kendra to the palace.

Bodies are falling all around us—most of them equalists. Lightning courses across my shield, but my defense holds. Finally, we burst through the combat, rushing into the open on the other side.

Up ahead, I see Rose and Diego retreating as well. The feeders give chase as we dash for the gate. 50 yards away. 25 yards. As we approach, the soldiers on the wall fire at the feeder. Gradually, the feeders pull back, keeping their distance from the wall.

We made it!

I watch as Rose stumbles through the archway. Diego and Antai follow immediately after. I stop a few feet from the threshold, watching as everyone passes through.

Slowly, I reach out my hand. As soon as it reaches the front of the archway, the air ripples. I can feel the spell putting pressure on my hand. The harder I push, the harder it resists.

I see Kendra looking around. Then, she looks back. "Matt? Come on!"

I don't know how to tell her, so I say nothing. My lips compress, and I slowly shake my head. "I can't... I'm sorry."

She frowns, still not understanding. "Hurry. I need to heal you. You're bleeding."

She steps through the archway and grabs my hand, tugging me toward the palace. I pull away. I feel my throat constricting, and I have to speak before I lose my composure.

"Kendra... I fed. I can't come in. I can't enter the palace ever again. I'm sorry. It was the only way to save us."

Kendra looks at me a moment. Then, she notices the dried blood on my chin. "No," She shakes her head, her hand lifting to mouth."No..." She looks down, then suddenly her face brightens. "It's okay. The wall will know you're on our side. It'll let you through. It has to."

She takes my hand and pulls until it hits the barrier. She keeps tugging, hopelessly trying to force me through. She shakes her head once more. "This doesn't change anything. I'll come out there with you. We can escape!"

"No." I take both her hands in mine. "Please, Kendra! Don't make this harder than it has to be. You need to stay here. Promise me you won't come looking for me. Do it for your family. Take care of them." I bite my lip. "I'll find you when I can. I promise, I'll find you. This isn't the end."

She wraps her arms around me and squeezes. I don't stop her. For a while, we just hold each other. I try to take in as much of her as I can, like one last breath before being dragged to the bottom of the ocean.

"Ezra, we have to go!" Kildron is waiting a few feet behind me. To my surprise, Iris is at his side. Immediately, I see what concerns him. At the far end of the plaza, the feeders are regrouping, gaining numbers by the second. "I'm sorry. It's time," he sighs.

"Wait!" Kendra calls. She pulls off her amplifier and fits it in my hands. "You'll need this."

I kiss her hard, but my lips are numb from the cold. It's not the final goodbye I imagined. "I'll find a way," I promise one last time. "I'll do whatever it takes. This isn't the end. Don't lose hope."

She nods, and her expression gives me strength.

She won't give up on me. She'll wait.

Then, I'm running. I don't have time to say goodbye to anyone else. I don't have time to explain.

We take off parallel to the palace wall, moving away from the plaza. Iris immediately takes the lead.

"Where are we going?" Kildron asks.

"The tunnels," Iris replies. "I know them better than the feeders will. At the very least, we'll survive."

I barely hear what they're saying. I can't stop thinking about Vyle. I killed him. No, I consumed him.

I'm a feeder. Just like the Holy One, I did it to survive. I did it to save the ones I love.

Maybe we aren't so different after all.

561

Chapter 44

Rose

I gaze out at the plaza. I don't know what I'm looking for. Hope perhaps. Something to believe in.

It's been hours since the equalists arrived. They were the last survivors to enter the palace. Now, the city is almost quiet. The screams are less frequent. The war is all but over.

We lost.

I hear footsteps coming up behind me, but I don't bother to turn around. I already know it's Antai. This is the third time he's checked on me.

"You should come in, Rose. You need to eat."

"I'm not hungry," I reply.

He stands next to me and takes my hand. "Rose, your hands are freezing. At least come in and warm up."

"I'm fine," I lie. The storm has nearly passed, but the air is still bitter cold.

"Please, Rose. There's nothing left we can do. We need to think about the survivors. We need to rest… recover."

"Just leave me alone," I snap. Then, when I see the worry on his face, my heart softens. "I'm sorry. Just… give me a few more minutes. I'll be in soon."

"Alright," Antai sighs. "I'll see you inside."

I look out at the plaza as his footsteps fade behind me. Still, the feeders haven't abandoned their siege. They pace in the center of the plaza, growing ever impatient. They don't feed. They simply wait.

I ignore the feeders, focusing instead on the gentle snowfall. I try not to think of anything else; it's all too overwhelming. My first day as queen, the sanctuary was destroyed. Our future holds nothing but disappointment. Without the fields, we can't survive. The palace only has so much food. Our reserves will be gone in weeks, maybe days.

We're all going to die.

I'm about to give in to despair when I see movement across the plaza. Someone emerges from one of the streets, strutting confidently into the plaza. The remaining feeders don't attack him. They kneel, pressing their heads into the snow.

The Holy One.

He walks closer and closer. The other guards must see him, but they don't shoot. They sense his power. They know any attack is futile.

Finally, the Holy One stops. He's only 50 feet away, looking right at me. His gaze chills my blood, and goosebumps erupt on my arms.

Still, the Holy One does nothing. He only stares. His skin is slightly darker than mine, as is his hair. It's combed back, not a strand out of place. His beard, little more than scruff, is trimmed close to the skin. His eyes are dark and commanding. His shoulders, broad and robust.

Something about him is familiar. Very, very familiar.

Strangest of all is his expression. He doesn't look bitter or indignant. He doesn't seem disappointed to see the palace standing, and he doesn't look vengeful. In fact, he almost looks relieved. The faintest hint of a smile tugs on his lips.

He stares at me a moment longer; then he turns and walks away. He's only taken a few steps when it hits me.

The painting.

I've seen the Holy One thousands of times. His painting hangs in the Central Tower, right next to mine.

The Holy One is my father.

Dear Reader,

long sigh Here we are, gathered again at the back of a book. I don't really have much to say except thank you. Thank you so much for coming back for book 2. If you could leave a review (or even just a quick rating), it would make me a very happy little author. I can't emphasize enough how important those reviews are. Also, I read every one, so rest assured that your words are meaningful. As for book 3, I plan on having *The Reviving* released by September 2021.

Hopelessly seeking your approval,
Devin

Devin Downing grew up in Temecula, California, spending his childhood reading books on the beach and bashing bones at the skatepark. Today, Devin lives in Provo, Utah with his drop-dead gorgeous wife, Melissa. Apart from crafting complex stories, he enjoys hiking, ice-hockey, and writing about himself in the third person (yep, it's me! Hi, guys!). Devin is currently studying neuroscience at Brigham Young University because he wants his friends to think he's smart.

Learn more about Devin at **devindowning.com**

Made in the USA
Monee, IL
26 January 2021